"My employers have a task for you," Gumley says.

In his lap is a book. He must have retrieved it from the satchel, but Lark has no memory of that. The ghost of Another Lark is still here, smashing a glass, taking it to Gumley's face, flying down the hall and out the front door of the stone house.

He snaps his focus into place. His clothes feel looser, like there's a pocket of air trapped between skin and fabric. The gleaming onyx falcon leers from its perch.

Gumley holds out the book, clamped at its corner between thumb and fingertip, as if he were retrieving something he accidentally threw in the garbage. Or carefully handling a small creature prone to biting. Disgust. Reverence. Both.

"Take it," Gumley says, "please."

Lark takes the book. *Organic*, he thinks upon touching its binding. His sculptor's hands practiced in tactile assessment, his overstressed brain crackling with responses. *Animal. Tanned hide. Old.*

Praise for Andy Marino and

The Seven Visitations of Sydney Burgess

"Marino offers horrors both existential and visceral. From a stunning opening, the sense of dread just builds and builds."

—M. R. Carey, author of *The Girl With All the Gifts*

"Odd and dark and fascinating. Not quite like anything I've ever read before. A strange, compelling, late-night page-turner. It kept me reading way past my bedtime."

—T. Kingfisher, author of *The Hollow Places*

"Andy Marino's *The Seven Visitations of Sydney Burgess* is a gripping portrait of addiction and an innovative take on demonic possession, delivering a shocking ending and powerful themes of how love heals but can also be corrupted."

—Craig DiLouie, author of *The Children of Red Peak*

"Equal parts surreal and hyperreal, darkly hypnotic. Marino puts his main character's throbbing heart on full display, and we are swept along on the dark journey into waters both mystical and terrifying. With every new revelation, the dread just mounts and mounts to the mind-shattering conclusion."

—David Wellington, author of *The Last Astronaut*

By Andy Marino

The Seven Visitations of Sydney Burgess
It Rides a Pale Horse

IT
RIDES A
PALE HORSE

ANDY MAR|NO

REDHOOK

Copyright © 2022 by Andy Marino
Excerpt from *The Seven Visitations of Sydney Burgess* copyright © 2021 by Andy Marino

Cover design by Lisa Marie Pompilio
Cover photographs by Shutterstock
Cover copyright © 2022 by Hachette Book Group, Inc.
Author photograph by Stan Horaczek

Redhook Books/Orbit
Hachette Book Group
1290 Avenue of the Americas
New York, NY 10104
hachettebookgroup.com

First Edition: October 2022

Redhook is an imprint of Orbit, a division of Hachette Book Group.
The Redhook name and logo are trademarks of Hachette Book Group, Inc.

The publisher is not responsible for websites (or their content) that are not owned by the publisher.

The Hachette Speakers Bureau provides a wide range of authors for speaking events. To find out more, go to www.hachettespeakersbureau.com or call (866) 376-6591.

Library of Congress Cataloging-in-Publication Data
Names: Marino, Andy, 1980– author.
Title: It rides a pale horse / Andy Marino.
Description: First edition. | New York, NY : Redhook, 2022.
Identifiers: LCCN 2022006901 | ISBN 9780316629522 (trade paperback) |
    ISBN 9780316629546 (ebook)
Subjects: LCGFT: Novels.
Classification: LCC PS3613.A7485 I82 2022 | DDC 813/.6—dc23/eng/20220224
LC record available at https://lccn.loc.gov/2022006901

ISBNs: 9780316629522 (trade paperback), 9780316629546 (ebook)

Printed in the United States of America

LSC-C

Printing 1, 2022

For Cameron

PART ONE

THE PSALTER

1

Peter Larkin moves through a snow-blown trench. His boots stamp prints into the sidewalk's ugly slush. Start with the solstice, he thinks, skip twelve weeks, and here we are. The dregs of a Northeast winter hang on. Out in the street a bundled kid on a bike goes by, rock salt winking in the tires. A runner follows in mittens layered to boxing-glove size.

"Morning, Lark," the runner calls out.

"Sure is, Jamie-Lynn," Lark says.

She lifts her knees high to dance through a mound of plowed snow on the shoulder of the road. "You seen Wrecker today?"

"Just brought him half the breakfast menu from Roberta's."

"The Saturday Special."

"He ate with great relish. Takes four sugars in his coffee now too."

Jamie-Lynn plants a leg calf-deep in a drift and hops delicately up to the sidewalk. "Working on his next heart attack."

"Never let it be said the man lacks ambition."

"Maybe I'll see him later." She scampers around the corner, a puff of frozen breath hanging in her wake, and vanishes up Market Street in the direction of the Wofford Falls Memorial Ambulance Service: three garages, picnic table, grill. LED sign reminding you to get your flu shot.

"Jamie-Lynn switch to mornings?" A voice comes from the door-way of Clementine's Yarn & Tea. Lark turns to behold a hulking figure, half shadowed by the shop's faux-rustic eaves. A meaty tattoo-sleeved forearm moves through a patch of light. Fragrant smoke billows and drifts. Lark sniffs the air.

"Mango?"

"Coconut." The man steps out of the shadows. Linebacker-size, meticulously bearded. A tabby cat twines around his ankles, a slinky blur of peanut butter swirl.

"Clementine," Lark says to the cat, "you little sneak." He lifts his eyes to meet the man's, half a foot above his own. "When'd you embrace the vapor, Ian?"

"Last night. Literally overwhelmed by guilt." He nods his head toward the storefront next door—Hudson Valley Vape HQ—and lowers his voice to a conspiratorial whisper. "Guy just stares at me with those big sad eyes every time I smoke a butt. Kills whatever enjoyment I have left."

Ian reaches into the pocket of his ripped black jeans and retrieves a crushed Camel soft pack. "I bequeath what remains to the Peter Larkin nicotine deficit."

Lark takes the smokes. "I'll pay it forward. From what I hear, Jamie-Lynn's on mornings when Terry's got the girls."

Ian takes a dainty puff on a device the size of a kazoo. He reaches behind his back to crack the door. Clementine darts inside. "What's that little prize you got there?"

Lark slides out the baking-sheet-size object he's got tucked under his armpit and brandishes it like a shield for Ian to inspect. "Tin. Original purpose unknown."

Ian leans in. "Shaped kinda like a manta ray."

Lark stuffs the smokes into the pocket of his old Canada Goose. "Might've been a drugstore ceiling." He tucks the tin scrap back under his arm. "Peace be with you, brother."

Coconut smoke curls up into the eaves. "And also with you."

Lark moves on down the sidewalk, past the vacant storefront where the bagel place opened and closed in a six-month span. *Mob front* went the chatter down at the Gold Shade. *Shitty bagels* is what Lark would counter with, if it was worth tossing his two cents at the calcified regulars camped out by the video poker. Regardless, the glass still says FREDDIE B'S BEST BAGELS in the style of a nineteenth-century newspaper's masthead. Inside the darkened interior a lone table saw rests atop a workbench. Lark pauses to catch a reflection just so—the murmurous EKG line of the Catskills, hazed in gray permafrost, crowned by a poppy seed bagel painted on the window.

The overhead lights flicker in the empty shop. There's a muffled entreaty for them to *just fucking turn on*. Then the lights come up and stay. A man as elongated as a Giacometti sculpture, twig limbs sticking out of a sleeveless Danzig shirt, turns away from the switch on the wall. Lark waits. The man pretends not to see him, comes to the window, presses his forehead against the glass. Lark raps a knuckle against the B in FREDDIE B and the man doesn't flinch. Then Lark pulls the Camels from his pocket and slaps the pack against the center of the painted bagel.

The gaunt face retreats from the glass. A moment later the former bagel shop door opens with a chime and out comes the man, hands cupping the tough knots of his biceps for warmth.

"Krupp," Lark says, "you wretched creature. Put on a coat."

Krupp snatches the Camels from Lark's outstretched hand. "Filthy enabler." He peers into the pack. "What have I done to deserve this bounty of"—he closes one eye and pokes carefully inside—"six whole cigarettes and one broken one."

"Courtesy of Ian J. Friedrich."

"He quit again?"

"Switched to vaping."

"Another one bites the dust." Krupp sucks air through his teeth, squeezes his upper body tighter, rocks on his heels. "Cold today."

"Colder tomorrow. Vaping's not the worst idea. It might help you cut back."

"Says the guy who just gave me *gratis* smokes."

"You're now officially the only asshole I know who still smokes actual cigarettes. But seriously, stop smoking. It's bad for you. They've done studies."

Krupp raises the pack to his mouth and pulls forth a smoke with his lips. Then he pats the pockets of his paint-spattered jeans, frowns, and gazes off toward the mountains, lost in thought.

While Wayne Krupp works out the last known location of his lighter, Lark's eyes drift to the awning of the neighboring shop: KRUPP & SONS HARDWARE. His oldest friend, Wayne, representing the full & SONS portion as the sole Krupp who stuck around.

"How goes the expansion?" Lark says.

The unlit Camel bounces. Krupp scrunches his face as if he's just zeroed in on a vital clue somewhere in the mountains. As if he could pinpoint anything at all from Main Street in Wofford Falls, twenty miles away and down in the valley. The tin scrap slips down the side of Lark's coat and he traps it with his elbow and slides it back up.

When Krupp finally opens his mouth, the Camel tumbles out and lands in his upturned palm. "Supposed to be demolition day today but I don't have it in me." Krupp turns, nods at the shop's interior. A sledgehammer leans against the subway-tiled back wall, next to the deep farmhouse sink.

"I have to make a delivery this afternoon," Lark says, laying a hand on Krupp's bare shoulder, "but if you wait till tomorrow, I'll come by and trade you one dozen of Roberta's finest mozzarella sticks for the privilege of smashing the living hell out of that wall."

Krupp shakes his head. "It's not the labor of it that's getting to me, it's something else. All the things the place has been—there's remnants. You know what I found behind the counter?" He moves closer to the window, taps the glass. Lark lets his arm fall away. "One of those jars the Red Vines used to be curled up in."

"From the candy store?"

"Every day after school, you and me, sliding dimes across the counter. When's the last time you had a Red Vine?"

"The Clinton administration. You were wearing that same shirt."

Krupp goes to the door. "Come in and smell the jar."

Lark gestures vaguely in the direction of his house. "I gotta get going."

"I sat there with it in my lap and I cried, Lark. Uncontrollable tears. You believe that shit? It was the candy store, then the leather repair place, then the hat lady, then Freddie B's. And the jar's still there. Do you want it? You can have it. We could trade off, you keep it for a week, then I keep it for a week."

"Yeah, we could do that." Lark studies Krupp's expectant face, crow's feet branching from those hollow eyes. "Listen, I'll see you later at the Gold Shade."

Krupp nods at the tin scrap. "You been out to Wrecker's?"

"Bought him like five breakfasts."

"The Saturday Special. Hey, I think Jamie-Lynn's on mornings now."

"Saw her too. Anyway."

Krupp lifts the unlit smoke back to his lips. "See you at the Shade."

The door chimes and closes behind him.

Lark turns a corner and heads south on Market, the ambulance service at his back. Roots of a venerable elm disrupt the sidewalk. The commercial strip thins out, its end punctuated by a ramshackle dwelling of boarded windows but for one hung with a Tibetan flag. Past this squat rises a low stone cemetery wall frosted with a thin drizzle of snow. On the other side of the wall an old woman bends to lean a wreath against a weather-beaten headstone.

"He would've been eighty-seven today," she calls out.

Lark tugs at his wool hat. "Happy birthday, Harry."

Past the rust-pocked gate, perpetually ajar, the sidewalk meanders into dense evergreens. Here it becomes, abruptly, a gravel path. A new kind of quiet descends. Lark's boots squelch in the soggy earth beneath the gravel.

The first figure looms darkly, bent overhead like a carrion bird, a half tunnel draped in scorched chrome to mark the sudden clearing: a flat half acre carved out of the forest. The modest house rises up from the clearing's center, rendering its yard a grassy moat.

Lark carries his prize across the yard past the second figure, a ten-foot amalgam of wire and wood, petrified and braided, punctured and sewn.

Beyond this he comes to an anvil sheltered by a small wooden hut. He lays the tin scrap on the cast-iron surface. Salvage beyond salvage, he decides: junked once long ago, recovered, junked again. Cut with strange precision—yes, vaguely manta-shaped—its purpose unknown. From the hut's single shelf he selects a metal-setting tool, more shark-like than your average hammer, fitting to pound down what could be the tin's dorsal. He lowers blow after blow and the anvil clanks, absorbs, directs the force into the tin.

By the time Lark makes his way to the backyard studio, the hammered tin has shed all evocations of manta. There's the working of material. Then there's the joining. Between the two states he blanks his mind, sheds associations, so the material can become what it needs to be: part to a whole that has yet to become anything at all.

He lifts the tin to the edge of a bulbous plastic amoeba composed of half-melted hubcaps. Considering. From the open garage door of the studio's industrial-heated indoor half spills low, dissonant classical strains: Shostakovich.

He thinks of the legendary Russian composer eating boiled leather during the siege of Leningrad in 1943. Germans at the gates, citizens carving up dead horses for meat, the genius in three dressing gowns and an overcoat breathing steam at his frozen piano. Is that how it happened? He moves his toes inside thick, dry socks.

Lark slides the tin up the melted gray lava of the hubcaps and closes one eye.

There are winters in this world that make the Hudson Valley seem like the Florida Keys.

Dead horses. Boiled leather.

One thing the tin will never be is a face. He heads inside to find a railroad tie.

2

Lark leaves his wet boots on the rubber mat and pads in socks down the stairs to the basement. A long hallway is lit by miniature spotlights dangling from tracks—gallery lighting for rows of framed paintings. Earthy odors of solvent, deep peanutty fixative, and sterile oils curl through the corridor. Two doors open to clean, empty rooms. More spotlit paintings, more track lighting. The only missing elements are the taciturn museum guard in the corner, the climate sensors on the wall, giggling kids on field trips.

The third door is closed. Lark regards his face in a small square mirror. A thirty-six-year-old bird of prey, but one with kind eyes, he'd like to think—a raptor gone vegetarian.

He contemplates himself for a full minute—the agreed-upon price of admission. It's not necessary to come to any conclusion. All his sister asks is a little buffer, a moment of stillness to blunt any manic surge that might derail her day's work.

From behind the door comes a rhythmic, steady *thwack thwack thwack*. His sister's Spaldeen bouncing against the hardwood, her painter's version of his mind-blanking journey from workshop to studio. He imagines the fluid toss, her fingers splaying with invertebrate quickness while her body squares itself up to contemplate the new piece.

He knocks. "Betsy!" he calls into the mirror, noting the shape of his sister's name in his mouth, the way the *sy* drops his lower lip oddly. "I have to go out again, you good?"

The Spaldeen *thwacks* once more and is silenced. Lark imagines one last epic bounce, a chalky pink dot stuck up in the firmament.

Bare feet on hardwood, mousy footfalls. The door swings open and here's Betsy Larkin, all rat's-nest hair and magnified eyes behind glasses with lenses thick as checkers. Vintage hip-hop thumps from the wireless speaker mounted to the upper corner of the wall by the small window, upon which she's painted a thin, quavering spiral. She holds out a gift-wrapped, shoebox-size package. The wrapping paper is decorated with grinning elves, a holiday leftover. Betsy has Sharpied the elves' eyes bright red. White ribbons dangle and curl from the package.

"Happy birthday," she says, her voice coated in the husk of an all-nighter.

"Jesus." Lark studies the hollows of her eyes, the flecks of dry skin at the corners of her chapped lips. "You look like shit, Bets."

"After I sleep I'll look better. You'll still be you."

"Churchill?"

"Paraphrased."

Lark takes the gift. "We agreed, this year. No presents." He hefts the box despite himself: light as cotton balls. No sound from inside. "If this is an empty box I'm supposed to learn some kind of lesson about consumerism from, I'll be pissed I wasted the energy opening it."

A crooked smile breaks out on his sister's face. "Some people say *thank you* when they receive a gift."

He tilts his head to glance over her shoulder. "How's that Edward Hopper coming?"

Betsy steps aside to give him an unobstructed view of the painting. Neither Larkin sibling is precious with the other about works in progress. Price of admission paid, Lark is free to roam his sister's studio. First, he stands in the doorway, peering at the large canvas clamped to the studio's central easel.

"Nighthawks at the diner," Lark says—an unlikely pick for his sister, who prefers the obscure margins of an artist's oeuvre, paintings less likely to be reprinted on dorm room shower curtains.

"It's just called *Nighthawks*," Betsy says.

Indeed, straight ahead is that most uncanny Hopper, four noirish figures in the big window of a dream-diner. There's something awful and airless about the empty street outside. A stage set, a movie backlot. It strikes Lark now that it's like looking at an exhibit through glass: a diorama of midcentury humanity in some alien museum. A struggle to understand these creatures, to place them in an appropriate setting. So one is approximated (diner, window, city street), the mannequins propped, the scene complete but inhuman.

There's the counterman in his immaculate whites, the three patrons (fedora, fedora, red dress). Betsy's forgery impeccable down to the brushstrokes. So much more to her art than simply reproducing an image: There's the matter of getting the oils Hopper would have used in the '40s, the mimicry of his style, his process. (It would occur to him later, the contrast of 1942—Hopper painting *Nighthawks* comfortably in his Washington Square studio and Shostakovich composing at his piano while German snipers cut down his starving countrymen in the streets.) And if Lark knows his sister she'll be altering her diet to eat like Hopper did while he worked.

He shudders at the memory of her Method-acted Jackson Pollock phase, the endless drinking, the rage he endured as she splattered and staggered and dripped.

Lark steps inside the studio, searching the canvas for the plot twist. All around him lie the vestiges of his sister's process, the stacks of books on Hopper, the trial-and-error palettes of colors that didn't quite make the cut. Weeks spent only mixing: She's always been the patient one. Her studio's the opposite of his airy workspace. His sculptures are born outside—weathering nor'easters and downpours and gusts straight out of arctic fishing. In here, sheltered and hermetic, everything's coated in a single-minded obsessiveness.

He has to get right up next to the canvas before he sees the twist, the out-of-joint turning that only Betsy can pull off. He estimates that the world holds a handful of forgers as skilled as his sister. One or two generational talents, passing off even the hoariest of old masters as genuine. A freakish control of Renaissance-era technique and material, fooling scholars dedicated to the study of a single artist's output. Yet still this is a lesser, more pedestrian skill than whatever it is Betsy Larkin possesses.

Which is what?

Lark doesn't know, not really. He can only sense it, the way you might look at a sea anemone for the first time as a child and know like you might know a face in a dream that it will sting you.

Shit, Betsy, he tries to say, but only weak exhalations come out. The quality of light in the painting takes him by the throat and squeezes. The world inside the canvas is coated in a nacreous wash. The haze of the lint-colored dawns that have been breaking over Wofford Falls for months. He feels, all at once, like he just woke up. But the worst of it is localized in what the woman in the red dress holds. She studies an object propped in her slender fingers. A book of matches, perhaps, in the original. Her pallor is ghostly. What she holds is Betsy's turning: not a book of matches at all but a sickly compulsion. An out-of-focus thing as focal point. The paralysis of an unknown object that doesn't look like anything at all. Figures in the painting (in the *diner*) either involved in it or studiously ignoring its existence.

What is that? he tries again, leaning forward to press his face nearly against the canvas. The words catch in his throat. He has the impression that the woman in the red dress picked the object up off the ground before entering the diner. The one piece of litter marring an immaculate sidewalk that sports not so much as a scuff or a blot of old gum. It's organic in nature, he decides. Yes: There's a fibrous stalk sprouting from a tiny crack in its shell.

Shell?

The longer he looks, the more is revealed. Remarkable, in such a tiny section of the painting, that his sister has hidden so many layers. The figures frozen in the last moment before they comment on what the woman is holding in her hand. Or, Lark thinks, perhaps they won't say anything at all, and the object will evolve, unremarked on, and the business of the diner will go on into the long night, humdrum and quiet, while the woman's arm, idly propped on an elbow, drips with a foul corner of reality. Because this thing she holds is not right, not the way Betsy has rendered it.

There are teeth hidden inside of it, he's never been so sure of anything in his life. Little Chiclets of baby teeth. The man next to the woman in the red dress stares straight ahead. Nobody looks at anybody else.

Lark flashes once again to boiled leather, horses rotting in the snow.

Bile rises in his throat. His stomach revolts. Up in the corner of the room, a hi-hat clicks tinnily. Sweat beads his upper lip, drips from his lower back to soak his waistband. The canvas tilts.

He turns away from the painting, covering his mouth, clutching the gift box to his damp chest.

"It's not finished yet," Betsy says.

Lark finds himself out in the basement hallway again, waiting for the nausea to subside. Like the figures in the diner, he turns away from everything, fixes his gaze on the blank wall. Ignorance. Bliss.

"What is it?" he manages to get out, after a while.

Betsy leans against the side of the doorframe, arms folded, and yawns.

Lark pads away down the hall, toward the stairs. "There's lunch stuff in the fridge," he calls back—the message he came down to deliver in the first place. "Cold cuts and pickles. Make sure you eat something."

"I'm not hungry," she says.

He pauses at the bottom of the stairs. What the woman in the red dress holds still reaches for him. The stalk a dendrite joined with thin tributaries to each little tooth inside its unformed, sickening veneer.

He turns. Betsy, at the other end of the hall, a wraith in an unzipped, paint-spattered windbreaker that's far too big. His sister's never worn a smock. She favors oversized clothes, cardigans the size of lab coats, an ancient duster now composed entirely of crusted pigment. She shifts her weight and the gallery lights flash off her glasses. He considers the potency of this new turning, the heat wave of some bad affliction radiating out from her *Nighthawks*.

"You have to eat," he insists.

She shrugs.

"You look like you have some kind of Victorian-era wasting disease. Like you're haunting a grim estate."

She cracks another smile. "Shrouded in fog. Mastiffs and limestone and old Mrs. Poole who keeps the family secrets."

"Listen, Bets." The words lead a half-formed thought on a tether. "You know what I really want for my birthday?"

"You have your present." She edges back inside the studio. There's a practiced elision to her weird, sleepy grace that he's seen develop over the years. Not meekness but an acknowledgment that she can't resist what's pulling her back to her canvas—a beck and call they both understand but which has shaped in Betsy's very figure a lightweight, wispy acquiescence. "I have to get back to work."

"I want to take you to lunch," he says.

Silence falls between them. Lark can scarcely believe that he was able to successfully utter the sentence. How unpracticed that little string of words is in this house. How alien the phrasing.

Betsy halts. She slides a finger up under a lens and scratches at the raccoon bruise beneath her eye. Then she steps out into the hall and pats down a matted clump of tangled hair like she's dabbing at a carpet stain. "I can't go."

"You don't have a choice. My birthday, my rules."

"I have to work."

"It'll be here when you get back."

"You have a delivery to make."

"So I'll be a little late. It's not like they're going to un-buy the piece."

It strikes Lark as funny, how they could run through a litany of the small excuses a normal person might use to get out of a normal invitation. As if this is some weekly tradition of theirs instead of wholly unprecedented. As if he's poking his head into her office and she's buried in paperwork.

A queasy blast slinks out of her studio door and washes over him and is gone. He can see his sister's weary mind click through excuses.

The smudges of her glasses and the strands of her hair are sticky and clipped together with Hopper's transitory hues. For a moment he swears he can *see* the woman in the red dress reaching for Betsy herself, drawing her creator home.

The idea that for Betsy Larkin, *home* is inside the world of the canvas strikes him, at that moment, as immeasurably sad. Not so much tragic as the kind of gray depression sparked by a thick graphic novel, a study in miniature of a lonely anonymous character in a big city. An artist spending panel after panel on quotidian minutiae to convey with a sledgehammer this mood of quiet desperation. A sense of failure descends. He has not been doing what he set out to do, all those years ago, when Betsy needed help and he stepped in. He has been caught in a mire of his own, of routine and various paths of least resistance.

What is it about lunchtime that gives him the self-reflexive heebie-jeebies? He never wallows in failure over breakfast. Maybe he's just hungry.

"Me and you," he says. "Roberta's. Counter seats. Free tiny muffins."

"No," Betsy says.

Lark sighs. But then Betsy comes toward him, windbreaker sleeves swishing. He stands there, motionless, holding his breath, waiting for one of those brain-clicks to stop her in her tracks, send her about-facing back to the safety of her studio to finish her work on that little slice of *Nighthawks* seemingly wrenched into this world from elsewhere. But his sister keeps coming.

"Not Roberta's," she says, nearly upon him. "The Gold Shade."

"You want to *eat* at the Shade?"

The Shade is nominally a bar and grill, but Lark doesn't know a single local who'd risk the grill part. Eaters at the Shade tend to skew tourist.

"I do," Betsy says, and brushes past him up the stairs.

"Why?" he asks after her. But he already knows the answer.

3

The Gold Shade's peculiar reek is accentuated by noonday emptiness. It's as if the odor has taken on the dimensions of a sound, a cavernous echo of deep-fried batter and urinal cakes and surfaces sticky with sloshed beer. At least when Lark and Krupp take their places at the bar every Saturday at dusk, the crush of drinkers blowing off the week's steam lends some variation.

Just inside the front door, Lark unzips his Canada Goose. Behind the bar, Beth Two glances up from her phone. She's been the Shade's Saturday bartender for as long as Lark can remember, with Beth One lost to the mists of local legend. Only a true Wofford Falls archivist like Wayne Krupp Jr. could attest to her current whereabouts.

It was Beth Two who served Lark his first drink with his fake ID, senior year of high school, then told him to get his ass outta there.

"You're five hours early," she says to him across the empty barroom. "And minus a sidekick."

He stamps his boots on the floor, *one two*, shaking off slush. The jukebox is low, Beth Two letting it run on random play for the three regulars who might as well be bolted down to the stools.

"The prodigal son!" ratlike Angelo calls out, hoisting a Bloody Mary.

"Christ, Ange," says Jerry Baker, who was once literally a baker. "Lark wasn't prodigal fifteen years ago and he ain't prodigal now. Less so if anything."

"It's an expression."

"Which you been misusing as long as I've known you."

"Constance," Lark says, pointedly ignoring the two men, "how come you let these degenerates sit with you?"

The old woman stirs her white-wine-with-ice concoction. "They're buying," Constance says.

"That's one way to put it, what they're doing." Beth Two makes a noise approximating clipped laughter. "You wanna see their bar tab?"

"Unfurl the scroll," Angelo says.

The bar's poised on that relaxed edge of ritual, all of them sticking to an approved script as facile and cozy as cheap nostalgia. The recycled comfort of the familiar, simple and free of cost. Then Betsy comes into the bar at his back, and the air in the room sucks up into itself and becomes a moonscape of astonishment. It's that old-west moment when the outlaw steps in through the swinging doors and the whole joint hits pause—poker cards unflopped, whiskeys halted mid-pour, the rollicking piano grinding to a halt.

Even Beth Two's practiced grace, that selective and studied lack of observance, fails her. Everyone gawks. Beth Two clutches a rolled-up bar rag in her fists like she's ready to garrote somebody or towel-whip them locker-room-style. Angelo hacks up a lung into the crook of an elbow. Jerry closes one eye and peels the label from his Labatt Blue.

"Hey," Lark says, as Betsy heads over to the corner booth, the only one with a window, where he knew she'd want to sit. He watches her slide the age-yellowed curtain aside. The ancient fabric is emblazoned with NFL team logos, including the long-defunct Houston Oilers, who haven't existed since Lark was a little kid.

"Um," Lark continues, looking helplessly at Beth Two. This whole birthday lunch thing was his idea, and he's come unglued fast.

Beth Two lends a hand. "Menus?"

"That'd be great." Lark offers up a goofy smile. "Thanks."

"*Menus?* You lose a bet?" Angelo inquires.

Jerry musters up the will to swivel his head. "Hot tip," he says, addressing Betsy without exactly looking in her direction, "the food here's been on a steady decline since the Summer of Love."

"Same as you, Jerry," Angelo says, then coughs wetly into a bar napkin.

Constance glances over to the booth—the only regular, Lark notes, to look directly at his sister. "Don't listen to 'em, Betsy. The french fries are perfectly safe and adequate. Each plate made from a single russet, I'm told."

"By who," Angelo says, "the executive chef?"

Instead of heading for the booth and risking an interaction with Betsy, Beth Two holds out the menus for Lark to come grab. He takes the menus, absorbs the regulars' gaze, and slides into the seat across from his sister.

"Bets," he says, keeping his voice low, which is silly—it's not like there's anyone here who hasn't already clocked Betsy Larkin, out and about in Wofford Falls. He imagines, cartoonishly, the local stringers dashing off to file their stories for the late edition. Teletypes crackling down the wire. Wofford Falls's own Howard Hughes, the recluse loosed once again on the unsuspecting town.

Betsy can't seem to tear her gaze away from the window. Lark slides his half of the curtain back. The glass is speckled with sticky amber droplets. Across the street is the row of historically preserved buildings that mark the site of the original Dutch settlement. There's the Hudson Valley's oldest brewery, the courthouse, the printer's office—and, directly across from the Gold Shade, the empty lot where the narrow wooden church once stood.

Stood strong, in fact, for more than three hundred years, even as the British burned Kingston and fanned out into the surrounding valley towns on a mission of destruction and pillaging. Survived until Lark headed for the city to make a name for himself and left his sister to her own mad devices.

"Bets," Lark says again.

"It's been a long time since I've seen it," she says.

He makes a point of opening his menu theatrically. "Am I in a sandwich mood? I don't know. Roberta's has all-day breakfast too, is the thing."

And Roberta's is at the other end of town, far from the view of this forsaken lot.

"It's still just dirt," Betsy says. "Like nothing was ever there."

She runs a finger down the dirty glass. Eddie the Can Man pushes his old grocery cart past the bar, catches Betsy's eye in the window, stops, blinks, then clatters onward, shaking his head. The street is empty in Eddie's wake and Lark flashes to *Nighthawks* and a prickly sensation draws itself over him like a hood going up slowly. They are the subjects of the museum piece now, Lark and Betsy, sitting here exposed and frozen in the exhibit. Is this how the diner patrons in *Nighthawks* felt, enduring Hopper's scrutiny as he filled in their faces and bodies?

"Nobody's too keen on rebuilding," Lark reminds her.

At last, Betsy turns away from the window. She meets his eyes and Lark reads a fresh rush of emotion in her face, amplified, he believes, by sleeplessness. It's as if the fog is lifting when she speaks.

"I'm not going to do it again," she says. There's a hitch to her voice, a kind of plea for understanding, that breaks his heart. As if convincing Lark, her brother, the one person in this town who doesn't need convincing, will change anything at all. Get her invited to the 4-H club meetings. Compel Beth Two out from behind the bar to visit their booth and get within six feet of Betsy Larkin.

"You and I know that," he says, "but these people don't." He swirls a finger in the air to indicate *these people.* Beth Two, the regulars, all the patrons of the Shade, all the citizens of the town. "People have long memories here, especially for something like that, something so..." He trails off, unable to conjure up the proper word. *Unprecedented? Fucked up? Insane?*

"It was so long ago now," she says. "I was a different person when you were gone."

"I've heard people talk about it like it was *yesterday*, Bets. It's not fair, I know, but it's the way it is."

She takes one more look out the dirty window. The lot sits empty behind a wooden fence, built in the simple style of a seventeenth-century

homestead. Bare earth, dirt so black it looks perpetually wet. Errant
snowdrifts hugging the fence line.

"They didn't even plant grass."

"You know the deal with these historical sites, there's all kinds of
red tape. I guess people just got lazy and let it go."

What he's never had the heart to tell her, and what he'll keep
from her forever: The Wofford Falls Garden Club *did* try to plant
grass, along with rows of cheery perennials. But they never took root.
The sod just sat there, untethered to the earth—a body rejecting its
donated organ—while the hydrangeas wilted and died. The upside to
her hermetic life is that she'll never learn this by accident from some
loudmouth in town.

He reaches across the table and opens her menu for her. "Order
anything you want," he says. "Live large. I hear the fries are adequate."

He glances over toward the bar, and the sudden uptick in pointless movement—Jerry swirling the dregs of his Labatt, Constance
checking her lipstick in a gold-plated compact, Angelo shredding a
napkin—tells Lark that everyone's been staring. When he turns his
attention back to Betsy, he finds her once again gazing out the window
at the empty lot where the church used to be.

He clears his throat. "So *Nighthawks* is almost done, then?"

"Hopper never liked to talk about his work," she says without turning her head.

"My fault for bringing it up. I don't really want to talk about work
right now either."

"I barely remember it."

"What, *Nighthawks*?"

Betsy taps a ragged fingernail against the glass. "That. What I did.
The act of it, I mean."

"Like you said. Long time ago. If you don't pick something to eat
I'm defaulting to fries for you."

"I'm sorry." She breaks away from the view of the empty lot. Then
she pulls up the hood of her baggy windbreaker and pulls the drawstring tight.

"Since when does that have a hood?"

"It rolls up into the collar."

"You need it up right now, this minute?"

She shrugs.

Lark takes a deep breath and lets it out. The phone rings and Beth Two picks up the portable stowed by the register. A moment later she hangs up and shakes her head.

"Telemarketer," Jerry says.

"Robots," Angelo says. "Every goddamn time."

Lark slides out of the booth. "Fries it is." He takes the menus over to the bar. Beth Two's busy mixing Constance another white wine concoction.

"I'm gonna go with the Shade Burger," he says, "and Betsy'll have the fries."

Beth screws the cap back onto the Chardonnay and reaches for the bitters. "Drinks?"

"Two waters. From the good tap."

"I don't go to your house and tell you how to make sculptures."

"Just saying."

She adds a dash of inky crimson to the drink and swaps it for Constance's empty glass. Then she goes to the register to ring up Lark's order.

"Psst!" Jerry says. "You got a runner." He points. Lark turns.

The booth is empty.

"Shit," he mutters, and heads for the door.

Outside it strikes him that he's violating the sanctity of Hopper's street-in-a-vacuum, that airless world that fails to gather dust only because someone unseen dusts it after hours. This end of town is easy to overlay with Hopper's desolate weirdness—it's hard to imagine it as its own organic place when it doubles as a seventeenth-century museum preserved by the state. The other end of town, *his* end of town, by the cemetery and the shops and Krupp's hardware store, is the place where people actually live. This end, where Main drifts westward until it meets Route 78, is patrolled by college kids in colonial garb interning as tour guides for the brewery and the printer. But nobody's out here now—the tours don't start running till April.

"Bets!" he calls out as he crosses the street. She's crouching down by the fence that surrounds the empty lot, the former churchyard. He comes up behind her and sees that she's reaching through the slats. She grabs a clump of dirt and opens her palm to examine it.

"Hey." He reaches down and gently nudges her up to her feet. "You're in the slush."

She lifts the dirt to her nose and takes a sniff. Then she lowers her arm and lets it fall away.

He glances up and down the sidewalk. There's only Eddie the Can Man, steering his cart around the corner. "Fries are on their way," he says. "Let's go back in."

"I can smell the paint," she says. "It's in the dirt."

The wind kicks up and blows the thin hood up and off her forehead. Her eyes are wet.

"Shit, Betsy," Lark says. He wraps her up in a hug.

"I remember now," she says, "how good it felt."

He holds her tight. Then, keeping his hands pressed against her shoulders, he backs away so she can see his face.

"Listen to me. You couldn't help it, okay? It was my fault for not being here."

She begins to sob.

"Hey. Hey! No crying at birthday lunch. This is ancient history."

She wipes her eyes on the sleeve of her windbreaker, smearing the damp across her face. "I'm so tired."

Lark registers the rattling cans in some recess of his mind before he can react.

"Hey, Betsy!" Eddie calls out. "I thought that was you! Before, in the window!" He breaks into a trot. The loose cans in the cart are a symphony of bouncing aluminum. "Then I said to myself, Eddie, you're looney tunes. But holy shit, it is you! Betsy fuckin' Larkin! I'll be goddamned!"

Lark lifts a hand in a halfhearted wave. "Okay, Eddie, we're heading back in now, have a good one."

Eddie picks up the pace, then stops about ten feet up the sidewalk, coming to a quick halt that sends a Molson can flipping out of the cart. "Hey! I was one of the kids, you remember?"

"Come on," Lark says, ushering Betsy across the street.

"I pissed myself right here!" Eddie yells after them. "Watching you work!"

Betsy ducks her head like she's on a perp walk and tightens her drawstring.

"*Pssssss!*" Eddie the Can Man says, drawing out the phonetic piss-noise with a cold grin. "Right down my fuckin' leg, you witch!"

4

The sculpture stands like a shrouded man in the bed of the black F-150. Tall as an NBA center, tented in a blue tarp and bungeed to metal clasps. Wrapped, fastened, battened down—still the sculpture can't help but bounce as the truck heads west out of Wofford Falls.

The sky cloaks itself with the threat of snow that won't hit the valley till night, but in the foothills the flurries are spitting.

Six miles out of town and Lark leaves Route 212, picks up a numberless road that winds up into the mountains. The road threads a low creek, crossing back and forth as it rises, steeply in parts, so that the truck is angled up toward the flinty sky that comes in patches through bare trees.

The string quartet on the truck's stereo moves from sad, draggy largo to an allegro molto that really fucking rips. Lark turns it up to chase away vestiges of his sad Shade birthday lunch: scorched burger patty, lukewarm in the center, soggy fries that went untouched by Betsy. Eddie the Can Man posting up across the street and laughing to himself, pointing at the empty air where the church used to be, stopping passersby to insist they take a look inside the window of the Gold Shade for a bona fide no bullshit Betsy Larkin Sighting.

Eventually, Lark closed the curtain and held it shut with one hand while he ate with the other so Betsy couldn't slide it open again.

Now, as he tries to put it behind him, Betsy's painting rises up in its wake. What the woman in the red dress holds has rooted itself in the back of his mind and taken on a new form. His sister has painted it slightly out of focus, leaving room for it to grow, implant itself, clarify its vagueness in its own time, away from the painting. It's part of her gift: Her turnings transcend proximity. All it takes is one look to plant the seed, and it will live inside you forever.

He slows down for an old railroad crossing, flicks his eyes to the shrouded figure in the mirror as he jounces over the tracks. The sculpture bobs, tilts, rights itself. The tires grip smooth pavement, the quartet dashes into the next movement, the road winds ever upward.

In the back of his mind, the airless atmosphere of a diner that never existed holds a sprouting thing. The heat's cranked in the truck but Lark is seized by a shudder. His sister's Spaldeen echoes in his mind. He turns up the volume. The creek is long gone, the view out the passenger side a craggy wall of granite. To his left, beyond a guardrail, the world drops away to a huge bowl of nested evergreens.

The quartet cuts out to make way for his ringing phone. Lark eyes the display on the dash—Asha Benedict—and thumbs the button on the steering wheel to answer the call.

"This is why we have people for this." The voice of his agent and dealer, a hint of her Staten Island youth running like a solo violin through her SoHo symphony of manners. Different strains of toughness—one hardscrabble, one honeyed. "This is why you pay me a commission."

"I don't mind," Lark says, "the guy's half an hour from me."

"People who are professionals in the field of art handling. Who have all sorts of special vehicles and padding and insurance. Who have dedicated their lives to preserving the integrity of works priced like luxury items, purchased by collectors accustomed to white-glove service."

"I got gloves I can wear."

"Don't banter. Your career isn't something that simply *is*, Lark. It's something I manage. Carefully. And part of that involves optics—you think Gerhard Richter is out driving around, delivering his work? You think he bubble-wraps it himself, sticks it in an Amazon box, drives it over to the Koch Brothers in his truck?"

"Gerhard Richter is a hundred years old. He shouldn't be driving in the first place."

"What if you damage the piece?"

"I got it up into the truck by myself. It's not a solid hunk of steel, it's found objects. It weighs like fifty pounds."

A detachment settles over him. He's wending through a mountain pass older than man while his agent spins in her Eames chair. A chilly synth wash enters the truck, the gallery soundtrack leaking in through Asha's phone. Up here, patches of roadside ice glint dully. A deer could plant itself in the path of Lark's truck at any moment. He tightens his grip on the steering wheel, anticipating an abrupt swerve. Relishing it, a little. The deer fails to manifest.

"The point is," Asha says, "my logistics team is never late. You, however, are——as we speak."

"I had to take my sister to lunch."

"Funny."

"Listen, Asha, this guy's filthy rich, lives in East Bumblefuck by choice, and it's *Saturday*. You think he's got other obligations? He's stocking his doomsday bunker, reading some Ayn Rand, getting all worked up about turning off the engine of the world or whatever." Asha makes a breathy, noncommittal noise. Lark glances at Betsy's gift box, still wrapped, on the passenger seat. He'd tossed it into the truck without really thinking. The elves' markered eyes strike him as more stoned than malevolent. "Anyway, how'd you know I was running late?"

"Because I know *you*, Lark. I've known you since you were scrounging junkyards for rusty old Chevy bumpers. Developing a natural immunity to tetanus."

"I still source all my own material personally, Asha. You think I got myself a team of interns up here?"

His agent sighs. A colleague in the gallery greets someone with exclamatory glee. Lark imagines air kisses near-missing fine cheekbones.

"You don't have to prickle at the notion that success has softened you for *my* benefit, Lark. I assure you, your scrappy blue-collar cred is intact. You're my upstate Rauschenberg in Carhartt and you always will be."

"Save it for *Art Forum*." Lark's eye catches a homemade sign—varnished wood, letters etched and burned: PRIVATE DRIVE. He hangs a hard left down a gravel road studded with rocks. The shrouded sculpture tests the limits of its bungees. "Listen, Asha, I gotta go. I'm here."

"The buyer's not. That's why I'm calling."

Lark catches a glimpse of a stone-and-mortar manor house through the thick pines—pre-revolutionary, or at least a dead ringer for the style. "What?"

"Your man with no obligations apparently tore himself away from his Objectivist gratifications for the weekend. His assistant's here to inspect the work, take possession, complete the payment. He'll be waiting where the horseshoe drive meets the garages. His name is Brandt Gumley."

"Really? That's a stupid name."

"We can't all be called *Lark*."

"Maybe he goes by *Gum*."

"I'll text you when I see that the transfer's gone through on our end. Don't leave before you hear from me."

"Not my first greasy little art-fuck, Asha."

"Be professional."

The trees part as the gravel gives way to blacktop with a smoothness that feels newly paved. Lark follows the horseshoe's gentle curve as the house swings fully into view.

"I'll tuck in my shirt," he says, taking in the dwelling's odd magnificence. Asha ends the call and the string quartet comes gallivanting back. Lark swings the truck around the long, lazy drive. The garages—four of them, each with a bright, soccer-jersey-blue door—are built in the same style as the adjacent main house: stones of all sizes, oblong, joined by thick mortar-work. None of it looks marred by weather—this place was built in the last decade or so. One more plot of secluded Catskills acreage snatched up by a cashed-out tech exec.

Lark stops at the apex of the horseshoe, between garages two and three, and kills the engine. No sign of Brandt Gumley. His eyes drift across the house. The stone portion is expected, unremarkable—large, yes, but the kind of stately facade that wouldn't look out of place in a manicured cul-de-sac, a single candle in each of twelve identical windows, ivy winding up the portico's somber columns. A postcard of comfortable living, not an advertisement for rarefied eccentricity.

It's the back half that accomplishes that. Behind the house the mountainside rises, lifting dense woods along with it, a cascade of greenery dulled eucalyptus blue by the late-winter sky. Poking out, here and there: windows, strange abutments, the entryways of Hobbit-houses reimagined by some Scandinavian modernist. No logic to their placement—just the tip of an architectural iceberg visible, rising up the slope as far as he can see. Lark has the impression that the quaint, pre-revolutionary stone is the model house, the living room that's solely for entertaining guests. The real dwelling is what he imagines to be the vast hollow crammed into the mountainside. What he said to Asha about the doomsday bunker turned out to be true—he simply wasn't thinking big enough.

The bifurcated design of the place takes him back to a summer job, the year he turned seventeen. Some rich old guy who hired Lark and Krupp to tame a hopelessly overgrown yard. The kind of neglect that hints at an interior of hoarded knickknacks and thirty-seven cats. There'd been an outbuilding in the backyard, bigger than a garden shed but smaller than a caretaker's house. The old guy whose name escapes Lark now claimed there was a tunnel from the main house to the outbuilding. Every day, he'd bring out a pitcher of sickly sweet lemonade and ask if Lark and Krupp wanted to see the tunnel.

No thanks, guy. Just gonna finish up here and go home.

They'd power-washed that old bastard's siding too, Lark recalls now. Dirt sloughing off in great wet swaths. Sedimentary remnants of a thousand storms.

"Brandt Gumley, where are you," he says out loud. "Mr. Gumley. *Brandt.*"

He figures he might as well get the sculpture down off the bed of the truck while he waits. As he shifts in his seat to unbuckle he spies Betsy's gift.

"Fuck it," he mutters, and rips off the stoned-elf wrapping paper to reveal a cardboard box. He turns it over, scans all sides. Uniformly blank. Still, he inspects it like a jeweler. He's careful with things like this now. Once, years ago, Betsy gave him what appeared to be nothing, and it was only after he'd discarded a box very much like this one that she'd let slip that the gift had been secreted between the corrugated sections of cardboard. He'd had to rescue the box from the trash and peel its stained halves apart to find what she'd hidden there for him. After he discovered it, the gift had consumed itself along with the memory of whatever it was, so now he could recall only the act of retrieving the box, damp and stinking, from the plastic bin at the end of the driveway.

He slides the teeth of a key along the single piece of packing tape and opens the box. An inkling of bad air escapes, a hint of impending nausea.

There's a small object inside. No cotton or Styrofoam or packing peanuts. Just this thing. Somehow it failed to rattle when he shook the box earlier. He shakes the box again now, staring directly at it, to find that it doesn't move at all.

"Fuck, Betsy," he says. Sour heat settles in his stomach like he's just eaten bad shellfish. He can't get a good look at the object. It's about the size of a book of matches but thwarts his attempts to parse it directly. He thinks it might be painted onto the cardboard, which would explain the total absence of weight or any indication of mass at all. His head goes light. The object's doing something prismatic with the air, with the space that surrounds it. He tilts the box, half expecting a staggered trail of afterimage, a holographic stutter. Instead, perception catches up with sight and he understands that he's looking at the real-life model for what the woman in the red dress holds. The stale air of a backlot diner turns the truck's interior plastic, a soundless air lock. He takes a deep breath, gathers resolve. He's going to touch it, he decides. Not wrap a hand around it, just lay a finger. He has to know what it feels like, this object either sprung from Betsy's painting or the inspiration for it. Earthy, tensile, filigreed yet hard. Hand-stitched? Quivering? He places a flat downturned palm over the top of the box like a magician readying an illusion. His skin's proximity to the object twists his guts into a cramped wet rag. One moment it's the shape of an old-time pocket watch, the next a wet book of matches, bloated with moisture.

"You're a piece of work, Bets," he mutters thickly. He swipes the back of his hand across his forehead and it comes away wet. He grits his teeth and lowers his palm. His vision swims. The truck hazes. Out of the corner of his eye he catches sight of a midcentury man in a suit and fedora, smart and lonely. The counterman all dressed in crisp whites.

Outside the diner's window, a street forever empty. An urban vacuum, a silent void.

His guts turn over, rebellious and heaving. The smell of oils and fixative, oppressive. He tosses the box to the floor of the passenger seat and at the same time opens the driver's-side door. He leans out over the smooth, immaculate pavement of the horseshoe driveway and vomits.

"Mr. Larkin?"

Lark glances up. A thick-necked man stuffed into a button-down and khakis is coming toward the truck. Lark paws at the glove compartment, finds a stash of napkins to wipe his mouth, a few mints to crunch.

"Are you all right?" The man pauses just outside the blast radius of the spatter on the pavement.

"Somebody puked on your driveway," Lark says, exiting the truck, crunching mints. The mountain air is bracing. He shuts the door behind him and feels better instantly. He extends a hand. "Brandt Gumley, I presume."

The man meets his eyes, unblinking, and executes a firm handshake. His demeanor and build ooze tactical training. Former military, now private sector, Lark guesses.

"Thank you for coming," Gumley says, dropping Lark's hand. "My employers send their regrets—they were looking forward to meeting you in person. They've been admirers of your work for some time."

Employers, Lark notes. *Plural.* Gumley's face pixelates, indistinct and fuzzy. Then it snaps back to its hard-edged self. The object in the truck, Betsy's gift, lingers in his mind. Asha's voice cuts in: *Be professional.*

Lark clears his throat. "That's nice to hear. Really sorry about the, uh..." He gestures vaguely at the pool of vomit.

"Think nothing of it." Gumley glances over Lark's shoulder and nods his head in a gesture that might be some kind of signal. Lark turns as one of the garage doors comes up. Three men emerge, Gumley acolytes: khakis, button-downs, high-and-tight haircuts. One bears a bucket and mop and goes directly to work on the vomit. Another wheels a dolly toward the rear of the truck, the third man at his back. Gumley places a hand on Lark's shoulder and guides him toward the front door of the stone house. "I'm authorized to transfer the rest of your payment. Join me for a drink?"

"Uh..." Lark looks back to watch the two men climb up into the bed of the truck and undo the clasps on the bungee cords holding the sculpture in place. Their efficiency evokes sailors freeing a boat from the dock before shoving off. The pair lift the shrouded figure with ease, shuffle in tandem to the edge of the flatbed, and set the sculpture down to rest on the feet of the dolly. The other man attacks the puddle on the driveway like he's swabbing the deck.

"Your work is in good hands," Gumley says.

"Once more into the breach, dear friends," Lark says.

Gumley opens the front door of the stone house and ushers him inside.

5

The study, Lark thinks, is a room from the game of Clue come to life. Clubby and refined if not exactly lived-in—all leather furniture and shelves lined with lawyerly volumes that have never been touched. Vintage ashtrays. An onyx sculpture of a falcon resting on an oak desk. Gumley flicks a switch on the wall and the fireplace instantly crackles with warmth and light. There's something just-for-show about it all—the smoking lounge of a nonsmoker, the library of a person who seldom bothers to read.

"Please," Gumley says, gesturing to a high-backed armchair. Lark sits. There's no give to the leather. At a brass bar cart, Gumley lifts a decanter full of amber liquid, bourbon or scotch. He pours a splash into a crystal glass, then pauses before pouring a second.

"I've also got ginger ale," he says, "if your stomach is still unsettled."

"Whatever you've got there is fine," Lark says.

"Ice?"

"Neat."

Gumley matches the first pour, brings a glass to Lark, then sits down in an identical armchair across from him. Between them is a round table, cherrywood with curious etchings.

Gumley raises his glass. Lark expects a toast but Gumley says nothing. Lark clinks the man's glass and they both sip. Scotch: peaty, with thick fumes almost gasoline-like in their intensity.

"Thanks," Lark says, "this is outrageous."

"I can have a case sent to you."

"Oh, that's really not necessary."

Gumley smiles without showing teeth. "My employers own the distillery on Islay, off the Scottish coast."

"Wow," Lark says. "So, they're in the liquor business, then?"

"I believe they consider it more of a hobby."

"Beats stamp collecting."

"Indeed." Gumley sips his drink. Lark's mind spins forward a few hours, bellying up to the bar at the Gold Shade, splitting a pitcher with Krupp, regaling his friend with the tale of his afternoon.

I kept expecting it to be one of those human-hunting things. Like any second I'd have to choose a crossbow from the wall and chase a homeless guy through the woods.

"One moment," Gumley says, reaching down into a satchel propped up against his chair. He produces an iPad and begins swiping at the screen. "I believe you'll find that your payment is complete."

At nearly the same time, Lark's phone vibrates against his thigh. He slides it out of his pocket to find a text from Asha Benedict.

$$$ received. BEHAVE YOURSELF.

Lark puts his phone away. "Thanks, I appreciate it." He drains his drink. "I hope they enjoy the piece."

"As I said, they've been following your career with great interest for some time. Now. There is one more matter to attend to—would you like another drink?"

"No, thank you. Gotta drive." Lark suppresses a private smile. *Here come the crossbows.*

"Before I get to the heart of it, my employers wish for me to give you a small disclaimer. It may be confusing to hear this, but in a moment your instinct will likely be to call the police. I urge you to refrain from doing so. Police will overcomplicate things, and it will be better for everyone if we keep this between us."

Lark laughs—the absurdity of this actually unfolding is too much for him.

For the first time, Gumley appears nonplussed. "I assure you, Mr. Larkin, this is not a joke."

Lark shakes his head. "What the hell, I mean—did Krupp put you up to this?"

The notion that Wayne Krupp of Krupp & Sons Hardware in Wofford Falls could have any connection to Brandt Gumley and his distillery-owning employers is even more absurd—but Lark's mind is churning.

Gumley narrows his eyes. "Please bear in mind what I just said about the police."

Lark puts up his hands. "Ah. Right. My birthday. I get it." He glances around the study, half expecting his shitkicking, degenerate friends to emerge from behind the thick velvet curtains.

"*This* is happening as we speak, Mr. Larkin."

Gumley flips the iPad around so Lark can see the screen. A video is playing. There's the entrance to the basement of his house, framed in the center of the shot.

Lark blinks, disbelief and confusion muddling his thoughts. The video shakes a bit, keeping the doorway in frame. Handheld. A phone camera.

Someone's standing in my kitchen, Lark's mind tells him. *Someone's in my house, filming.*

"What the hell?" he says.

"Wait a moment," Gumley says. He turns up the sound on the iPad. Lark can hear a faint rhythmic thump coming from the basement. Betsy's studio speaker. Then he hears footsteps coming up the stairs. An odd shuffling sound. A man dressed in the plain khakis-and-button-down uniform of Gumley's team comes sideways through the door, turning his big body to pull someone else through.

Betsy.

His sister's head lolls on her chest as she's brought up into the kitchen, propped across the broad shoulders of the two men who carry her between them as if she were made of straw. They take Betsy across the kitchen. She is limp and utterly insensible. Nobody speaks. Her toes drag on the linoleum. They move out of frame.

Lark leaps from his chair. "What the fuck is this? What did you do to her?"

Gumley pauses the video and slides the iPad back into the satchel.

"Rest assured, she's merely been sedated." He folds his hands in his lap. "She'll come to in a little while and be perfectly fine."

Lark's eyes dart to the study door as his mind replays the journey through the stone house to this room, then plays it in rapid reverse: left out the door, down the hall past the living room, another left, into the foyer, out the front...

And those silent men who took the sculpture from the truck, are they lurking in the corridor, waiting for him to come tearing out of the study?

"I know what you're thinking," Gumley says. "But by the time you get home, your sister will be long gone. The best thing you can do for her—the *only* thing you can do—is sit back down and listen to what I have to say."

"Fuck that," Lark says. The study walls press in on him. The gleaming black falcon looms. Gumley stares placidly up at him from the leather chair.

"My employers do regret the imposition. They'd like me to under-score that they wish there were another way, but time is growing short."

"Jesus Christ," Lark says, voice edging higher into hysteria. "What do they want from *me*?" He gestures at the walls of the sumptuous room. "I don't have this kind of money. Not even close. They have to know that."

"This has nothing to do with money."

Lark takes a deep breath, tries to quell the flight instinct urging him in no uncertain terms to *run*.

"If you take a seat," Gumley says, "I'll tell you what you have to do to ensure your sister's safe return. It's simple. Transactional." He pauses. "It's really the only way, Mr. Larkin. Please."

In another reality, Lark sees the ghost of himself, a blur, sprinting out of the study, breaking free of the men lying in wait, calling the cops despite Gumley's warning, fighting, *fighting*...

In this reality, he sits down in the leather chair. Scotch fumes drift from his empty glass. There's a potency to everything now, a dialed-in sharpness. Emerging from a fever into a bright new day.

Lark leans forward and meets Gumley's eyes. He digs deep to level
a credible threat, calling upon the man he was during the nervy fog of
his Lost Year. It's a skill he's let rust, to the benefit of his humanity.

"Don't you fucking hurt her."

He gets about halfway to credible, voice cracking on *her*.

Gumley receives the threat impassively, lets it lie there for a beat.
Lark has the impression he does this as a *favor*, letting Lark have his
impotent say, ticking out three blank seconds in his cleanly buzzed
head before delivering his reply.

"Betsy's continued well-being is entirely in your hands."

A stray bit of advice surfaces unbidden, a tip from one of those true-
crime shows he binged with Krupp back in the day, enthralled by the
trippy quality of the cheap reenactments. Kidnapping statistics. Guidance
that most people will never make use of. Survival rates hinging on *when you
take action*. Pure, incorruptible math versus that split second that changes
your life forever. You have a window of time from the moment the kid-
napper accosts you to the moment he puts you in the car, takes you to the
basement, orders you deeper into the woods. A shadow zone where your
free and captive selves overlap. Here the math dictates you should do everything you can to get away, or else it's much more likely that you never will.

So don't freeze up.

"Transactional," Gumley repeats. Lark, gripped by Lost Year rage,
calculates the angle to jab a shard of broken glass into Gumley's eye.
"Straightforward."

Lark wonders what Betsy's statistical window was like. The well-
manicured hands of the Gumley acolytes. Betsy's sleep-deprived haze.
What must she have thought was happening?

The placid figures on the *Nighthawks* canvas looking pointedly away
as those big hands swallowed her up.

"My employers have a task for you," Gumley says. In his lap is a
book. He must have retrieved it from the satchel, but Lark has no
memory of that. The ghost of Another Lark is still here, smashing a
glass, taking it to Gumley's face, flying down the hall and out the front
door of the stone house.

He snaps his focus into place. His clothes feel looser, like there's a pocket of air trapped between skin and fabric. The gleaming onyx falcon leers from its perch.

Gumley holds out the book, clamped at its corner between thumb and fingertip, as if he were retrieving something he accidentally threw in the garbage. Or carefully handling a small creature prone to biting. Disgust. Reverence. Both.

"Take it," Gumley says, "please."

Lark takes the book. *Organic*, he thinks upon touching its binding. His sculptor's hands practiced in tactile assessment, his overstressed brain crackling with responses. *Animal. Tanned hide. Old.*

"Skin," he says.

Gumley drains the ice-melt from his glass.

The book is unlabeled. No title or author, no cover art or embossed symbols. The binding material has the dusky reddish tint Lark associates with the Southwest. It's a thin book in an odd size—almost, but not quite, a square, though Lark can't really tell which sides are longer.

Unable to help himself, he moves a fingertip down the binding. There's a hint of fur. Peach fuzz. A shiver builds inside him. Restless legs and an elevator-drop stomach.

"Open it," Gumley says.

The first page, yellowed and brittle, strikes Lark as a placard of some sort. The type is set in a variety of fonts and sizes. The boldest letters form an unwieldy title.

A Panoply of ſilent Hymns for the New World
or
A Non-Liturgical Pſalter
relating to the ſculpting of paeans to geographical dislocation and the
relief of burdenſome obſtacles to reſurrection

Stretched-out lowercase *f* characters in place of *s* are sprinkled throughout—lettering that evokes for Lark the seventeenth century, the textual companion to the region's stone-and-mortar architecture.

Dutch settlers. Fucked-up headwear. Mouths set in grim bloodless
lines.

"I don't understand," Lark says.

"Turn the page." Gumley's patience appears boundless. All the time
in the world. His sister's life in his hands, Lark turns the page with
great care, as if to flick off a brittle corner would be to lop off an ear,
sever a toe. The title of the first "silent hymn" appears:

The Insomniack

Beneath this title is an intricate diagram, remarkably clean in its
rendering—confident lines, protracted curves. A confluence of cold
geometry and cartoonish figures troubling the margins like sea mon-
sters at the edges of ancient maps. *Here be dragons.* An adolescent boy
with curly locks dangles at the crux of some elegant pulley system.
A hollow cutaway in his side, an unseamed cavity, displays his intact
bowels. It's medical in its precision, an anatomical display. His legs are
skeletal and riddled with tiny notations that match the strange geometries that orbit his body. The boy's teeth are bared. His eyes are closed.

"Non-Euclidean," Lark says, his knowledge of such things limited
to terms he's picked up from his sister's various obsessions. A vibra-
tion courses through him—non-Euclidean geometry, non-liturgical
hymns. A psalter outside the boundaries of known science or religion,
especially of that era when the two fed off each other.

"I still don't know what I'm supposed to do," Lark says.

"Skip to the end," Gumley says.

Lark thumbs carefully through the thin volume, noting the com-
plexity of the diagrams. He spots two more titles in massive type as the
pages flip.

The Worm & the Dogsbody
The God of the Noose

There is grandiosity in the final product, the symphony of silent hymns. Instead of expressing this in unhinged scrawling or massive typesetting, the author has gotten nearly pointillist in his attentions. Lark narrows his eyes. Words jump out at him.

Aether
Lateral depths
Hollow earth
Metaphysickal reckonings
Harbingers

And one word, bold and underlined in his mind: *fculpture*. He pauses. There's one page left to turn.

"Look at it," Gumley suggests. He tents his hands in his lap. The falcon seems to lean forward, curious. The smell of excellent single malt—diesel and peat bogs and chrome and oil—washes queasily over him.

Lark turns the page.

The sculpture—the true silent hymn—reveals itself in a diagram that seems to leap from the page like a children's pop-up book. Overwhelming in its intricacy. Precise lines laid in centuries ago on a page as thin and flaky as an onion skin. The atmosphere of the room becomes the grease that smears the margins of a lens. He's looking at this final page, this grand symphony, down the barrel of a spinning tunnel, like the opening credits of an old James Bond film.

The culmination of silent hymns is a magnificent sculpture, impossible in its geometries. All three hymns are represented here, fused into contortions of material that defy physical laws.

The Insomniack is a head-spinning calculation, an abacus of tragedy—the sum total of townspeople whose lives have come and gone and amounted to nothing at all. Sharp thin protrusions (fish bones?) radiate, spoke-like, to support the sculpture's un-geometric craftsmanship. It's more than non-Euclidean, Lark understands at once. It's an inversion of the whole field of study, not simply favoring one axiom. *The Worm & the Dogsbody* rings Freemason alarm bells with its pyramidal—and disgusting—assemblage of rot. There are encouragements in the tiny diagrams. Suggested materials. Lark holds the book close to his face. An odor wreaths his head, some trapped Enlightenment-era stench, and for a moment he flashes to the creator's hand, bejeweled and long-nailed. What the diagram suggests for *The God of the Noose* makes him sick. How prescriptive is this non-liturgical psalter? Must he adhere to these principles? Because now he knows what Betsy's captors, Gumley's employers, require of him. Perhaps seeing this understanding dawn on him, Gumley confirms it.

"My employers wish for you to sculpt what the book proposes."

Proposes. So it's never been done.

Of course it hasn't.

Lark slams the book shut. He feels like he's just run a race. He takes a moment to catch his breath.

"This is impossible," he says.

Gumley's body hints at a shrug. "Complete this sculpture, and your sister will be set free."

"This isn't a sculpture," Lark says. "You can't ask me to do this. Nobody can do this." He holds up the book, now fully grasping Gumley's distaste in his earlier handling. What's inside these covers is wrong. The fibers of its binding seem to wriggle like cilia against Lark's palm. At the same time he notices another quirk of the book—the binding wraps around the spine, as you'd expect, but fails to cover the back of the last page. It's as if the book's been severed, split in half. Meaning that there are, perhaps, more of these silent hymns out there, and he's been given only what he needs to know.

"My employers believe that you can. As I said, they've been admirers of your work for quite some time. You and your sister have been carefully vetted."

You and your sister . . .

"What's Betsy got to do with this? She's a painter. Just let her go."

Gumley stares back placidly.

"Fuck you," Lark says. "Fuck your employers." He swivels his head to every corner of the room, eyes darting to imaginary cameras. "You see me?" He holds up the book. His voice goes ragged. "This is bull-shit. This is *insane*. Let her go." He is pleading now, any veneer of threat leached out of him. Deflated, he focuses on the vein in Gumley's fore-head. "You can have me. Let her go. Please."

"What's done is done, Mr. Larkin. The only way out is through." He checks the matte-black face of his silver watch. "Now I really must insist that you begin."

(Another Lark takes a shard of glass to Gumley's jugular. Arterial spray speckles his face as he drives it in deep.)

Lark says, "Begin how?"

At this, Gumley sighs. He picks up his phone, taps the screen, then holds it to his ear.

"What are you doing?" Lark says.

A muffled voice comes through the speaker, answering the call.

"Cut her," Gumley says.

"No!" Lark shouts.

Gumley raises an eyebrow.

"Okay," Lark says, clutching the book to his chest. "Okay. I'll do it. You don't have to hurt her. Please."

"Cancel that," Gumley says into the phone, then ends the call. "You're free to go," he tells Lark. "My employers will be monitoring your progress."

Lark swallows. "My truck?"

"Where you left it, in the driveway."

Dazed, Lark moves toward the door of the study. The falcon looks on, a hundred pounds of impassivity.

"Oh, Mr. Larkin?"

Lark stops moving but doesn't turn around. He's afraid that if he catches one more glimpse of Brandt Gumley, he and Another Lark will merge and he will give in to Lost Year rage and by doing so sacrifice Betsy's life.

"Keep an eye out for that case of single malt."

"I don't want it."

"It's already been sent."

6

Lark is aware that he drove from the house in the mountains down to Wofford Falls but recalls nothing of the journey. One moment he's emerging from between the stately columns, the next he's practically crashing through the door of the house he's shared with Betsy for thirteen years.

He tosses the psalter on the kitchen table along with the box that holds Betsy's birthday gift. He sheds his coat on the stairs on his way down to the basement. The lights have been left on. So has Betsy's music. Her studio door is ajar. He catches a glimpse of himself in the square mirror, and the reminder of their little workday ritual breaks his heart.

Somewhere in the back of his mind, he registers what he's just moved past in the corridor: Each one of those framed paintings—Betsy's most successful forgeries—has been altered, made lesser.

He enters his sister's studio and this becomes a certainty. The *Nighthawks* canvas rests upon its spattered easel. It was only a few hours ago that Lark came down to this room to remind his sister to eat and brush her teeth. Betsy Larkin at work, all unruly hair and bloodshot eyes. For a moment he's paralyzed by a sweet hurt: *Take me back.* Rewind the day. Unspool it differently. Lark approaches the canvas. It gives off no sickly heat, no swampy persuasions. It does not make him want to retch. There's a hole cut in the canvas, sliced with the precision of the diagrams in the psalter. What the woman in the red dress holds—replicated in his birthday present, all that bad energy trapped inside a swollen pod—is missing. They have taken it, along with his sister. So there's a synthesis to this abduction: Betsy and her uncanny turnings.

He kills the volume on the speaker and goes back out into the hallway. He moves down the two rows of framed Betsy originals, forgeries of the utmost skill. Each painting is a treasury of recall, like a song whisking him back to long-gone summers in the mountains with Krupp, tucking into a twelve-pack by a crackling campfire. They have all been desecrated in the same manner as *Nighthawks*.

Here's Betsy's take on René Magritte's *The Lovers II*, that kissing couple with shrouded faces. Lark remembers Betsy telling him of young Magritte, all of thirteen years old, finding his river-drowned mother with her sodden dress pulled up over her face. This fact, he knew, would be oblique in Betsy's consideration, not translated into a literal wish for a parent to be dead and shrouded. There would instead be angles of resonance.

He remembers, with a sharp ache, the green apples she ate by the bushel during her Magritte period. Visits to the orchards near Albany. A season of cobblers and cider and pie.

And now here are *The Lovers* with a neat hole cut in the canvas where the knot in the man's black tie should have been. Lark places his fingers in the absence and lets this particular turning come back to him: a knot rendered knotless, a flat clip-on effect. A careful intermingling of the tiniest threads. He remembers leaning in close to figure this one out, seeing the necktie and white collared shirt resolve into fine braids to form a gray cross-stitch patchwork. It was beautiful, painstaking work, and also completely at odds with the way she'd captured the soft, buttery textures of Magritte's shrouded couple. Her turning featured brushwork more suited to Dalí, a photorealistic segment that had no business in a Magritte.

Lark traces the edges of the cutaway. Removed, he thinks, with a very sharp tool. There are no stray fibers. It's as if the turning has been medically lanced by the kind of laser that vaporized his unfortunate plantar wart of two summers ago. He tells himself he's looking for clues, examining the scene of Betsy's abduction, but that's just pretense and he knows it. He's down here immersing himself in her art, her sole vocation, as if it might be a way to conjure her up, to reverse the afternoon's events. Perhaps he simply wants to find a way to be close to her before he undertakes his cruel task.

He pulls his fingers from the hole in the Magritte, moves to the next painting, and enters the airspace of a Mary Cassatt. *Young Mother Sewing*, imposing in its domesticity, formally ambitious yet soft as an afternoon with nothing to do. Despite this, there's no languor in Cassatt's (and by extension Betsy's) work. None of the rich-folks'-idyll that permeates her male impressionist counterparts. The cherubic kid leaning on her mother's knee and staring out at the viewer is there because the subject of the painting, the Young Mother herself, is multitasking. Minding a child while simultaneously making her a new dress. Lark knows why Betsy chose this particular scene to replicate down to the brushstrokes: That fucking kid is looking right at you. It's like a photograph, the way the kid is caught. Except you know that the time it took Cassatt to capture this moment stretched out into weeks—so at what point was the child glancing at her?

Mother and daughter are foregrounded. Behind them, a Delft vase holds a bouquet of autumnal flowers that evoke the dusky orange of the flared base of a candy corn. Behind the vase, a triptych of windows overlooks the suggestion of a field bordered by dark trees. Here, in the upper left corner of the field's farthest reaches, is the neat hole where the turning used to be. Lark reaches in, seeking a hint of that birthday-gift friction—blurred vision, a throat full of bile—but no, he remembers the Cassatt turning now. A rarity for Betsy, this one. A departure. In the Cassatt she didn't twist an existing element to her purpose—she added a new one. A presence beneath a tree: looming, feminine, smeared. Slenderwoman, Lark had joked at the time. He could only see it out of the corner of his eye. To look at it directly had been like a magnet repelling another magnet. Pressure on his eyeballs. But now there's nothing because Slenderwoman has been taken.

"Jesus, Bets," he says. Despair coats his voice.

He takes his fingers from the painting, wondering if anything down here could be considered a clue. It is, after all, a crime scene. The notion of *police* drifts through his mind. How much could Gumley really know of his movements from one second to the next? His eyes stray to the track lighting. He imagines the abduction team prying open a fixture to install a tiny camera. Gumley, in his subterranean command post embedded in the mountainside, sipping his employers' fine whiskey and surveying a bank of monitors.

His phone vibrates in his pocket, startling him. The phone is a link to a world he departed when Gumley played for him the video. He looks at the screen. Krupp's calling, no doubt from their designated spot at the Gold Shade, opposite the fossils, where the bar curves toward the server station. Wondering where the fuck he is, Lark having not missed a Saturday at the Shade in months.

He stares at Krupp's name on the screen. His best friend, calling from a world that's just been knocked loose from its moorings.

Lark imagines Gumley's attention turning to a smaller screen, a remote viewing of Lark's phone, Gumley waiting patiently for him to answer the call. Leaning back, resting a loafer on the steel console, observing.

Lark sends Krupp to voicemail. He'll just have to sit tight, at least until Lark can get a burner from Wrecker.

He pockets the phone and walks down the hall to survey the desecrated paintings. Each absence is keenly felt.

Lonely Giorgio de Chirico towers casting long shadows, out of which a hole has been clipped. Missing: an unlikely fluctuation in the shadow thrown by an unseen object that always struck Lark as envious.

A floral O'Keeffe, that peculiar flat-plane affect that hints at folk art and Weimar expressionism's unholy offspring, a vaginal Metropolis with a petal carefully cut away. Missing: a clitoral in-joke, a reference to the obvious O'Keeffe 101 interpretation that so often sells her work short, a few perplexing brushstrokes that Lark remembers filtering his vision through a not-unpleasant gray mist.

A stunning Frida Kahlo, *The Wounded Deer*, self-portrait as hybrid animal, a Kahlo-faced doe whose body is riddled with arrows, Sebastian-like, in a forest clearing. Lark slips a finger through the hole sliced neatly around the tip of an antler. He recalls the period of this forgery, three or four years ago now. He traces the edges of the cutaway, the coarse canvas weave. It had been a miniature sprouting thing, not unlike the Hopper turning, but more tree-like in nature. The tip of an antler branching into nine mini-points—mirroring the nine arrows piercing the hybrid deer itself—that made Lark feel, upon approach, a sharp nostalgia for a singular childhood event: Betsy and Lark, hiding from their father in the closet of the spare room, sharing a Cadbury egg stolen from the corner store. Lark tries to conjure up this vivid recollection, but without the sprouting antlers—the power of Betsy's turning—the sweetness of the egg's cream and the companionship of the shared moment is lost, as lost as Betsy is unless he opens that awful book and completes the impossible. He knows the second he goes upstairs, he'll be confronted with the sheer un-reality of his task. So he keeps moving down the row of altered works, soaking up his sister's presence.

Here's the Max Ernst he's never been able to approach before. Now, with its Betsy-ness removed, it has never felt so pedestrian. He stops, hesitating, almost recoiling at an energy that's no longer present. *The Triumph of Surrealism*, his favorite Ernst—selected by Betsy as a gift of sorts. He steps forward, gingerly, leaning in so close he can practically taste her brushstrokes. He remembers the marvel of it taking shape in the months after his frantic return from the city. The massive, rampaging, birdlike creature emerging, its vicious beak and tattered patchwork of a baggy hobo's outfit—Eddie the Can Man transfigured by snatches of laundry snatched from disparate lines and integrated with seamless, ever-flowing precision that's also somehow ragged and in constant motion. Lark had come home to find his sister's prodigious talent blossoming—no, *exploding*, out of control, a garden watered and fed by some alien fertilizer and fast-forwarded into hypergrowth. Together they'd come up with a way for her to paint within boundaries, to keep the nature of her ability tame—and to keep Betsy from pushing the citizens of Wofford Falls completely over the edge with another public incident. No more running wild and trance-like wherever the muse dragged her.

So the forgeries began with this brilliant copy of a Max Ernst masterpiece. Constrained by another artist's work, hemmed in by the process of learning style and new ways of composition. She threw herself into the project. Just as Lark was beginning to relax, to tell himself that they could manage this together, in this house of their own, with space to work for each of them, her first turning emerged. The first wrinkle in the grand plan to put guardrails in place for the rabid energy of her art. The creature formed of windblown tatters, its limbs culminating in pointy leonine digits—claws pulled from some full-body costume of jester's motley—except for one bright honking anomaly that reached out and grabbed him as soon as he ducked into her studio for his daily visit. A human hand, photorealistic and painstakingly rendered, its style instantly clashing with Ernst's soft and malleable forcefulness.

He nearly breaks down now, in the presence of her very first forgery, remembering that moment when she looked at him, helpless and beguiled, as both of them realized how this new containment would proceed. There would be a release valve in every painting, a turning that bled through their forged attempts at containing Betsy's potent ability.

That perfectly rendered human hand, like all the other turnings, has been cut out of the canvas and taken.

It wasn't enough for Gumley and his employers to abduct his sister. They had to strip away her life's work at the same time. He nearly chokes on the injustice of it all.

How long have they been watching?

Lark casts an eye once again at the spotlights that run the length of the ceiling. Paranoia surges. Is each one a camera? Gumley's maddening voice comes and goes: *Cut her.* Lark's vision swims. He leans against the wall, wonders if he should eat something, then wonders if this notion is a betrayal of his sister. Why should he get to indulge in normal things like food while his sister is gone?

Not gone, he reminds himself. Not as long as he completes his task. He thinks of the book's baffling pages, which felt like they could so easily crumble in his hands.

Upstairs, *The Insomniack* awaits.

Lark's phone buzzes for a second time. He checks the screen, expecting Krupp. Instead it's a single text message from an unknown number. He opens it and a photo appears.

There's a vast, high-ceilinged, windowless room. Large enough to contain an Olympic swimming pool, though its floor is nothing but an unbroken flat expanse of concrete or clay. The walls and ceiling seem to exist in permanent middle distance. It could be a hangar, he supposes. But the dimensions don't make sense. He chalks it up to the photograph's poor quality—taken in haste, perhaps. Blurred.

A lump sits in the center of the space, the only interruption of that blank, airless chamber. Lark zooms in.

It's Betsy, of course. Kneeling, palms resting on her paint-spattered jeans. Eyes closed, head bent slightly as if hearing grace said over the dinner table. He sucks in a breath.

With trembling fingers he types, *prove she's alive.*

He anticipates some kind of retort: *You don't call the shots here.*

Instead, he receives a four-second video. He hits PLAY.

It begins from the same vantage point as the still photo: the hazy margins of that vast room. Then it rockets forward—not a zooming lens but a physical approach. The camera *swoops in* on Lark's sister. There's no sound, but some kind of noise seems to rouse Betsy. She lifts her head. Despite moving at great speed, the camera somehow freezes, perfectly still, to frame her face. He takes in a breath and holds it. She appears unmarred by any rough treatment. A deep sense of relief fills him and he exhales. Back against the wall, he slides down to the floor.

A second video arrives. He plays it.

Betsy opens her eyes.

Museum Interlude

The painter wakes. Hi, lady! Welcome to hell.

I won't know your name till they say it out loud, so for now you're "lady" to me. I figure you're a painter because that's the streak they've been on for eighteen months, after their love affair with installation art. You know, the kind of exhibit where your parents from Iowa, visiting your big-city museum, can't hide their disgust. It goes like this: Your mom's trying to be accommodating and makes fake interested *hmmm* noises, but your dad, irked and hungry for lunch, tells a total stranger he can't believe they make you pay to see this shit.

A dark room with a mummified burrito on a windowsill and a TV from 1987 playing a VHS porno on silent.

A tunnel that leads to a giant ice cube slowly melting.

Stupid-ass shapes, furry balloons, walls made out of diapers.

If you think normal artists are weird and obnoxious, you should meet the installation people. Also, it turns out that the farther you get out on the let's-fuck-plants-and-call-it-art limb, the longer the manifestos get. The justifications that go on and on. The WHY behind the work. Like, why make this in the first place? Believe me, Diaper Wall Guy, we all wish you hadn't.

I used to think music wasn't like that. In my defense, my little pop-country corner of the industry really wasn't. Was it cringey and eye-rolly and self-important in other ways? I mean, yeah. Just not in the *check out my manifesto* type way. HOWEVER, I once worked with a soundcloud-famous producer. I know what you're thinking. His name wasn't rx75!!dirtfuckcer! or whatever. It was *Gary*, the only twenty-one-year-old named Gary I ever met. Anyway, Gary told me about this other cat he was working with. (Gary called people *cats*.) So this cat went by the stage name of Braahl, and Braahl had a one-man band. Did you know those still existed? Indeed they do—especially in the world of black metal, which I was totally unfamiliar with before Gary's story about this Braahl cat. There's not a whole lot of black metal exposure in the Christian pop-country youth group *hey y'all* scene, but Gary gave me a crash course. It started a while back with those Norwegian kids who painted their faces and wore spiky gauntlets and burned churches and eventually started murdering each other. ANYWAY, it spread way beyond Scandinavia to places like French Lick, Indiana, which is where Spectral Pall is from. That's Braahl's one-man band. Spectral Pall. For whatever reason, black metal is full of one-man bands. Probably because so many of the band members murdered each other back in the day, people figured it's safer just to do it all by yourself. Braahl played guitar, bass, keyboards, a little cello for the slow pretty parts, and also "sang," aka shrieked like a person burning alive. The problem was, he couldn't get the drum parts right, and decided to program them with a digital drum machine, but he couldn't get that right either.

Enter Gary. And what Gary told me, over hard seltzers in the studio, is that the first day of their collab, he's expecting to get some unfinished tracks, riffs, song ideas, demos, et cetera. But what he gets instead from Braahl is a padded mailer. Inside the mailer is fifty pages, *typed and printed*, of Spectral Pall's statement of intent. So Gary's like, what is this, the cat's grad school application? It turns out to be this whole manifesto about how Braahl, with his Spectral Pall project, is transcending a whole bunch of earthly shit and making some kind of grand cosmic overture toward whatever. Keep in mind this is a guy who just needs some drum programming assistance. He thought it was, like, essential for Gary to understand Spectral Pall on the deepest possible level before he got around to sending him some drum parts to put under the unintelligible screaming Braahl was doing.

The point is, nothing's exempt. Every pursuit's got its Diaper Wall Guy. There are probably insurance salesman with boring-ass philosophical frameworks for bundling your home, life, and auto.

Anyway, lady—this is gonna sound sick, because I'm definitely not *glad* you're here, but it's always nice to see a painter after that last series of fuckheads. Respect. I wish they'd pull that thing away from your face and let it slither back into the shadows where it belongs. It must be unpleasant, with that whole *situation* frozen there, an inch from your eyeballs. Proof of life video, I'm guessing they're making, the way it's pointing the camera at you like that. And that room they've got you in, that's crazy deep in the warren. I've never even seen it before. I sure as hell wasn't aware of it before they stuck you in it. Sometimes this place is like the map in a video game for me, a Zelda kind of thing. Like, I can sense the outer reaches, but I can't really see them until something changes. A floor plan revealed over time.

I used to play Zelda in the studio while the engineer was cleaning up tracks and I had nothing to do. I'd give anything to go back and do that again. Do *anything* again. Even the shit that's so annoying at the time, you can't wait to get it over with. The dentist, bathroom lines, traffic. Just to sit in a car with a playlist while assholes honk at me. What a dream.

I'll give you this, lady: You're stoic as hell, kneeling there like a monk with that thing all up in your face. Did they give you something?

Ah, shit.

Here they come. The khaki pants mafia (KPM). Four of 'em, hot off the douchebag presses. I couldn't see the entrance to the room you're in until now, and I gotta say, that's one weird door, even for *them*. The KPM's fanning out. Dear sweet Lord, it takes forever to cross this room. Does it even qualify as a "room"? It's more like an indoor soccer stadium. The kind of midsize arena I thought I'd be packing on my third tour, after the clubs got too cramped to hold my rabid fans.

What a joke. Man plans, God laughs, my grandmother used to say. True, except I'm not a man and there is no god. But the concept is relatable.

What the hell is the KPM doing? It looks like they're scattering little round things the size of coasters around the room. Coasters with pictures on them. There's an antler-y looking one, and a long-limbed alien lady, and the knot of a necktie, maybe—that one's hard to make out. This one's definitely a human hand.

While I wait for them to finish doing whatever it is they're doing with the picture-coasters—really only the ninth or tenth weirdest thing I've seen in the years I've been stuck in this place—allow me to properly introduce myself. I mean, where are my manners? My mother would be appalled.

My name is Rayanne Lane Boyd. I went by Rayanne—no Lane, no Boyd. You might remember me from such regional almost-hits as "Boyfriend Jeans" and "Canary in the Coal Mine," if you were a regular listener of KRDM in the Greater Des Moines metro area, or caught me on one of the Rising-type playlists on your streaming service of choice. If it was the latter, I received $0.005 per play, so thanks for the sweet cash.

There I am on the cover of my first and only album, which, statistically, you did not own. I'm cavorting in a hedge maze, shot from above by a semi-famous photographer perched on a crane. (Note: I had never seen *The Shining* at that point in my life, so for me a hedge maze evoked what I thought of as British sophistication, mixed with a sort of easy-to-grasp emotional metaphor for the teens who would be my primary audience if all went according to plan and stupid nonexistent god didn't laugh as hard as he did. The metaphor being along the lines of, adolescent emotions are like a maze, and as an artist I can totally relate, but I can also find the center of the maze through my music, which will, in turn, help lead you through the maze. Crucially, I'm not actually at the center of the maze on the album cover, but I'm pretty close. See, I don't have it all figured out, either. We're in this together, you and me, and in the meantime I'll be wearing a cute aspirational outfit you can't afford. We'll get through it with the power of pop-country backed by slick one-take session players bankrolled by *them*, and some trendy laid-back beatmaking and melancholy acoustic guitar. The idea being that I'm tipping my hand toward shedding my Youth Group roots, priming the audience for a sheen of indie-lite accessibility as they move through their College Years and take me with them—and then strap in, because the sky's the limit for Rayanne's brand equity.)

Looks like the KPM is finished arranging the picture-coasters. Is it totally random, or according to some pattern? If I know *them*—and I do, quite well, after all this time—it's the latter. Method, always, to the madness. And you, lady—I'm guessing there's still some pretty serious sedation happening. I know the feeling.

Now that I know where the entrance to this arena-room is, lemme just follow the KPM on out of here so I can fill in the map.

This door is seriously ostentatious. It's pointy in all the wrong places, like one of those medieval torture coffins you'd get shoved into to get either poked or suffocated to death. I'm sure they had it shipped here from some Eastern European dungeon where it was never meant to be for sale. See, for *them*, everything's for sale. I stayed in a hotel like that once, in London, when I was meeting with this A&R creep. Everything had a price tag, from the pillows to the bidet, if you looked at the room through this special augmented reality app you had to download, which I did—

Oh.

I see now.

They stuck you in the back of their private collection. I have to work my way out through this forsaken wing if I want the map to be correct. Don't know if I have the stomach for that right now. I mean, I know I don't literally have a stomach, or a liver, or any other organs. I mean it in the *figurative* sense, if I remember my shitty homeschooling correctly.

The installation wing. All eye-rolling at Diaper Wall Guy aside, what happened to him would give me nightmares if I ever slept. He might have been a toolbag, but he didn't deserve what they did to him. No one deserves that. Since then, I've watched this become a savage, untamed place. It's like a forever-wild nature preserve now, left to its own strange devices. *They* rarely even come here anymore—on to the next one, easily bored, buzzing from one obsession to the next. The KPM move through in tactical formation, guns drawn, laser sights weaving in and out. A low tone, a note you can never hear directly, hangs in the air and always reminds me of a dead guy in the distance slumped over on his car horn. I do value every chance to see the KPM freaked out, so I'll chill here for a second and soak in their fear. It's not as satisfying as it could be—they're well trained. A private little mercenary army led by King Douche himself, Mr. Brandt Gumley. What a stupid fucking name. I can still smell the Tic Tacs on his breath from the day he came for me.

One of the laser sights sweeps across something throbbing there in the dark. I used to wonder why they didn't turn on a light in the installation wing of the warren, but now I get it: Some things are better left in darkness. You can't unsee them. On the other hand, the mind is pretty good at filling in the blanks. It's kind of like the way I map the warrens—I can sense the edges of them, dug into the far reaches of the mountains, and I can imagine what lurks there.

The KPM's moving right along now, a well-oiled machine, communicating with each other in the dark through movement alone. I'd be impressed if I didn't hate their guts. Some people can separate the art from the artist, but I'm not one of them.

It's times like these when I'm reminded for the millionth time what a raw deal I got. There's the way it all ended, of course—but beyond that, I can't even properly haunt this place. I should be able to scare the living shit out of the KPM, but I can't even rattle a stray plate. I used to try to shriek at the top of my lungs. I figured, maybe that's one way to break through whatever barrier keeps me from doing ghost shit. I'd holler and holler and wait for Gumley or the KPM or even one of *them* to hold up a finger for silence, narrow their eyes, strain to hear that distant sound...

But, nope. Nothing. All I can do is watch.

And listen.

I hate that there's still pleasure for me in listening to *her*. I've had nothing but time to examine it from every angle—I'm my own therapist now—and I've come full circle, back to the simplest answer. I just like the way her voice sounds. Despite everything, there's something in her timbre, the twang of her vocal cords, that just does it for me. There's this part of vocal training called registance, which is a register and resonance mixed together. When a sound "tugs on your heartstrings," it's this registance effect that's literally doing the tugging. The theory is, we're each of us special snowflakes, born with some innate, fixed tunnel into our ears, straight to the emotional core of our beings. We learn to appreciate music, we grow up and shed the stuff our parents listened to, we get into stuff that speaks to us for a whole mess of reasons—but there's always this special tunnel, waiting to be filled by this combo of register—the shape and pitch of the note itself—and resonance—the lyrical or even more buried and inexplicable thing that makes us *feel*. It's kind of like when you talk to someone you've never met on the phone and you think they "sound hot." For some people that registance is a minor-key chromatic melody like the *Star Wars* theme. For other people it's whatever the fuck Braahl is doing. For a handful of people it might have been the way I sang the word "love." Maybe one or two of them got goose bumps.

I have my own theory, developed over a long night with Gary's weed gummies, that my corner of the industry is actually being deprived of the registance to hook listeners long-term, thanks to too much auto-tune and vocal sweetening. People are looking for a short-term quick fix to make artists sound instantly "better" (or at least more polished) but what they're sacrificing, mused gummie-fied me, is a chance to fill those listeners' special ear-tunnels. Then again, there's always the chance it's a wash, because who's to say that auto-tuned and digitally sweetened sound isn't registance for a certain percentage of listeners?

ANYWAY, I'm telling you this because my own ear-tunnels are being filled. My non-body is shivering. I can hear *her* voice, way out beyond the installation wing, so I'll leave the KPM and their laser-sighted crawl through this dark place. From here, I know the map. I'm part of the layout. I might not be able to break through to make my presence known to the KPM, or Gumley, or *them*—but the museum itself, the labyrinth of warrens dug into the mountains, is a different story. The well-worn territory on the map, the rooms and passages I've been haunting for eight years now—there's a give-and-take between us. The museum and me, we've got a relationship. You should know that I only call it a museum for lack of a better word. I mean, "mountainside compound" seems like a mouthful. Over the years I've considered "Upstate Area 51," capital-L "Labyrinth" like the Bowie movie, and a million more I've forgotten by now. Titles were never my strong suit. I crowdsourced my album name to my cousins. Thanks, Sheena & Allie.

Getting out of the installation wing is like a sigh of relief, a big old exhale, even for me (or what's left of me). *Her* voice is louder now. I'm much closer to the residential wing. I just have to zip through the sculpture garden and—hold up.

There's a new piece here, something I've never seen before. Disclaimer: I don't "get" sculpture. I mean, obviously the ones you learn about in school, the ancient ones, those at least make sense. Muscular dudes with tiny dicks and angels and biblical scenes. A guy with a funny old Italian hat chipping away at a block of marble with his chisel, spending five weeks carving out a breast. It's the more modern ones that drive me up the wall. For whatever reason, they got really into the whole found-object thing. For me, whenever there's a bunch of old tin cans stuck together with shellacked candy wrappers or whatever, I feel like I'm being given the most obvious lecture of all time about pollution or Modern Life or the industrial revolution or something. Then there are the ones that look like the weird playthings I made out of Legos and doll parts when I was six. And last but not least, the Vaguely Steampunk. (I remember the woman who made those—she wore a top hat.)

But this new one's something different, outside the usual categories. I'm not at all sure what it's made of. I'm hovering over it now, and also kind of curling around it, checking out all the angles. The first thing that comes to mind is frozen smoke. Something's been melted or poured or disintegrated and then made to settle in place in its new state. Solid, liquid, gas: Who can say? One state becoming another, a snapshot of frozen time. It's the size of a pretty tall dude. It's mostly the *shape* of a tall dude too, but that's where it stops being in any way human. This is not an attempt at a classical-type sculpture. No abs, no face, no tiny dick. No dick at all as far as I can tell, and if I tried to find one, that would probably say more about me than the sculpture. It seems more aimless than the tin-can-and-candy-wrapper bullshit I've seen come and go over the years. Less purposeful, but *created* more than *made*, if that makes sense. Almost like some monster birthed it. Probably why it appeals to *them*, whose tastes have changed so much. If most of the other found-object sculptures seem like they were made by kids, this one seems like it was sculpted by an alien creature with OCD. I think the melted and re-formed bits at the back are supposed to be the stumps of wings.

Her voice, louder now, interrupts my scrutiny of the new piece. "You're humming. You're humming again. You're *always* humming and you don't realize it. No, you know what, it's not even *humming*. Humming would be pleasant. It's like this noise from inside your throat, like a garbage disposal for melody, where other men have Adam's apples."

I tear myself away from the sculpture and head for the residence. The garden is behind me now, the drippy echo of its grottoes and diverted stream fading away.

"I have an Adam's apple." *His* voice, booming and perfectly enunciated, the better to be heard across the deck of a superyacht.

"In addition to a garbage disposal." That timbre, that twang, that low hint of tobacco that costs more than a car. "What's that even supposed to be? Bach?"

"I'll give you a hint."

"I don't want a hint, I want you to be more self-aware."

"Twentieth century. Postwar."

She laughs. I tremble. "You've got to be kidding me. It sounded positively Baroque coming from you."

"The problem isn't my throat, it's your ears." He hums again, slowly, like an overbearing piano teacher frustrated at the student's inability to play a scale. *His* voice, as I move through the twisty confines of the outer residence, with its seldom-used sitting rooms and studies, irks me in ways I can't explain. It's like the netherworld version of registance. Flooding my ear canals with cringe-inducing confidence born of four or five lifetimes of privilege.

"We need to hash out these timelines," she says. Whiplash subject change sends me spinning through their personal spa, with its temperature-regulated chambers, doors like massive kilns.

"That first minimalist expo, the show at the Beak Lounge in New York." His exasperation is hilarious to me. "Philip Glass debuted *Chimes*. Peter Sellers spilled a vodka tonic on your dress and did an impersonation of a stuttering uptight Brit as he tried to mop it up with his sleeve."

"It sounds like Vivaldi. Bach. Whichever one we saw in Vienna."

"Neither. We came too late. You're thinking of Haydn."

"They all run together for me."

"Father of the string quartet."

"I haven't willingly listened to a string quartet since the advent of recorded music."

"Philistine."

"Focus. Did Brandt stress the urgency to Larkin?"

"No, he told him to take his time. *Yes*, dear sister, Brandt has it in hand. Not his first rodeo. Three hundred years and delegating anything still makes you insufferably anxious. Go have a drink."

All at once their main living room is upon me and they swing, magnificently, into view.

Helena and Griffin Belmont.

I'll start with her, goddess-voiced Helena, Queen Bitch of Upstate Area 51. Imagine the word *imperious* (a word, incidentally, I learned from watching her, like lots of what I've learned over the past eight years). If you're anything like me, you're picturing an Old Hollywood type, imposing and beautiful and magnetic and glamorous and all that. Smoking a cigarette in a long black holder like Audrey Hepburn in *Breakfast at Tiffany's* (a movie I watched them watch). Chic, glowing, erudite, quick with a cutting remark but never sour enough to upstage her innate charm. And yeah, she *is* all those things, but they're little shards of her personality. Her imperiousness isn't haughty. She's hyper-conscious, in public, of radiating that one-percenter stuffiness, that golden mothball effect. (I know because I've heard her confess this to Griffin, late at night, all hopped up on certain ketamine-based drugs not available or even really known about outside of rarefied circles.) It's in the way she moves: like the coolest girls I knew back at Westville High. Not necessarily the richest, the prettiest, or the most popular. It's a way of moving that has more in common with a fuck-the-world outcast type, but mainstreamed with the rougher, more disaffected edges sanded off for the widest possible avenues of respect and admiration. It's an authenticity that's studied so hard the cracks never show.

Look at her now as she crosses a carpet so deep you have to wade through it. (Brought back from Dubai. I actually learned a lot about carpets from eavesdropping in the aftermath of that trip—did you know that carpets are similar to high fashion? See, there's the weird runway carpets that are the fullest realization of carpet and rug concepts in the most artistic way possible, then that trickles down to the actual wall-to-wall that this hotel in Dubai outfits its rooms with. Nobody buys the runway versions except people like the Belmonts. And there aren't that many people like them.) Anyway, here's Helena, with that cool-girl saunter, heading for the Prohibition-era bar cart they got from a museum devoted to speakeasies (a museum they now own). Helena Griffin, patron of artists and musicians, producer of indie films with serious cachet under the banner of her production company, Lacuna Salad, whose logo, rendered in flickering artsy-grindhouse style, elicits hushed murmurs of anticipation from audiences for every trailer it precedes.

She pours a chartreuse liquid into a precious-metal-encrusted shaker, which fetched $23.8 million at auction and generates a non-fungible token via an embedded chip each time it's used to mix a drink. (The things you learn in eight years of silent observation.) "Cocktail, brother?"

Goose bumps on my nonexistent skin. She throws her brother a look over her shoulder. Griffin, paging idly through an illuminated manuscript, gives Helena one in reply that says *What do you think?* in a way that acknowledges the shared joke. Like, *When have I ever said no?* Their sibling bond is sly, their connection often unspoken.

What can I say about Griffin? He's got the huge bound manuscript perched on the thigh of one leg crossed over the other, flipping through it with half-assed attention like it's a coffee-table book of famous Irish pubs instead of some priceless artifact from the thirteenth century, painstakingly crafted by a dozen silent monks in a windswept abbey. They've actually got a bunch of these fanned out on one of their coffee tables. That's a pretty good summary of Who They Are: medieval manuscripts worth millions, kicking around like some kid's Where's Waldo collection.

Griffin Belmont is tall and well-built and favors artfully ripped denim and black shirts. I want to make it clear that he's not swanning around in linen suits like some of the idle-rich cheeseballs in his cohort. But he definitely doesn't wear his studied normal-person coolness as authentically as Helena. There is nothing cool about Griffin. If not for their true pursuit—if they were simply normal filthy rich people with odd hobbies—Helena would come across as someone who genuinely loves the arts, while Griffin values the cool points that being close to up-and-coming artists earns you. He also loves the gamble, betting on artists at the tipping point of their career and tilting that make-or-break scale toward make (which was their deal with me). But they're far from normal rich people, so that's neither here nor there.

Griffin's got an angular face with some Zoolander cheekbones. (I watched that movie with them in a double feature in their screening room with—wait for it—*Cruel Intentions*. The rich-people-toying-with-lesser-mortals parallels were not lost on them, and they found it hilarious, more hilarious than the actual jokes in *Zoolander*.) He's had a little work done but nothing super plasticky and off-putting. He shrugs often, with the air of someone for whom a shrug applies to most things in life. It's neither here nor there, how things play out. The winds of fate blow right past Griffin Belmont—except when it comes to the pursuit that's consumed three centuries of his life. There's nothing shrug-worthy about that. It's the only thing that lights that fire in his supremely well-fed belly.

Helena comes to him now, highball in hand, green faerie-liquid giving off a hint of dark smoke, like a blown-out candle. It took me a while to figure this one out: The Belmonts mix a lot of "cocktails," but none of them contain any booze. The Belmonts do not, as far as I know, consume any alcohol, although they own vineyards and distilleries around the world.

Griffin accepts the drink and sets his illuminated manuscript aside. I wonder: Is there a monk trapped in those pages, silent as he was in life, looking out and wondering *What the fuck?*

At one time I would have chalked that thought up to an overactive imagination. But I don't rule out anything anymore—not with what I've seen. And what I've become.

They clink glasses. "To Father," Helena says. I shiver—this time, not entirely because of her voice.

Any mention of their father can be a bit triggering.

They sip their smoky beverages. These drinks are microbe stews, organic stimulants unavailable to most people outside of those with access to a certain experimental drug lab in Jakarta.

"Oh!" Griffin says, sparked by the drink. "Guess what I found."

"Astonish me."

"One guess. Live a little."

"It's never just one guess with you. There's rigmarole. Mischief. A series of annoying twinkles in your eye. The fact that you play games like a child is so deeply bizarre to me, considering the time that's passed since you've actually been one."

"The fact that so many things I do get on your nerves is getting on my nerves. It's an ouroboros of irritation."

"I don't think that's right."

He gets up and wades through that impossibly plush rug until he gets to one of those rolltop desks—you know, the ones where fancy people in period pieces sit to compose their letters while the narration runs neck and neck with the loopy cursive scrawl of the lady of the house. This desk, if I remember correctly, comes from the courthouse at Appomattox, where, if my homeschooling is to be believed (bless you, Mama), the War of Northern Aggression came to an undignified end. He rummages through a drawer till he comes up with a rolled piece of parchment.

Back at the sofa, he unfurls it for Helena to see. It's a sketch, a bare-bones study over some grid lines, tiny measurements and plans, like an artist might do as prep work for a much larger painting to come. A portrait of a man with shaggy hair and a deeply creased forehead—a man of burdens and heavy worries. A man who's seen some shit. As these kinds of studies often do, it has just a head and a neck that fades into oblivion below the collar—but I can tell, even with the vague linework in the lower third of the drawing, that the garment he's wearing hasn't been in style for a few centuries now.

"Oh." Helena inhales with some force. "It's a wonderful like-ness," she says, running the very tip of her finger along the side of the drawing—in search of the barest tactile sensation without daring to smudge the lines. There's some calligraphy-type lettering above the man's head: MARIUS VAN LEEMAN, 1749.

"Do you remember who did it?" Griffin asks.

Helena sets her drink on the long, skinny end table that runs the length of the sofa and rises to the top of the cushions. It's home to some lamps they made from Giacometti sculptures, a stack of brass coasters from the *Titanic*'s sister ship, and the pearl-handled knife with the curved blade Helena used to cut off my face.

Slowly.

She stands close to her brother and leans in to peer closely at the parchment. Places a finger against it once again and closes her eyes.

"A man sitting on a rock. His sketching is light and free. Joyful. He's happy to be there, a new arrival at Father's colony. I remember his wife would take us to pick apples."

"I can't remember," Griffin says softly. "It's all just trees to me. A forest in a dream. The people there are shadows."

Helena opens her eyes. "Even Father?"

Griffin thinks for a moment. "Even him," he says softly. He gazes at the parchment. "I can never see this face in my memories. Looking at it now, I know it's him, but that knowing is academic. It doesn't stir up any feeling to see this. I was excited to find it, but like I'd be excited to find any number of likenesses of people we used to know back then. Members of the colony, just before it all came to an end. It's all the same for me. I can't connect this face to anything paternal."

He lets the portrait roll loosely back on itself, sets it on the end table, and lifts his drink to his mouth.

"You put too much stock in imagery," Helena says. "Close your eyes."

He drains his glass and does what his sister asks. She takes his hand in hers.

"We're walking with him down the path to the well."

"I don't know if I can do this right now."

"Shut up. Concentrate. All three of us hold buckets. It's noisy—the forests were all noisier back then. We hadn't yet built the roads and industry that would drown out the madness of the underbrush. There were animals there, in those days, that I never saw again, anywhere."

"Yes," Griffin says. His mouth begins to reluctantly stretch into a wistful smile—the not-quite-all-there smile of somebody in the grips of hypnosis. Except this past-life regression from 270 years ago is his *actual* life.

"Father points them out to us. There were strange species of rabbits, lithe and skinny like coneys, bad to eat."

"Mountain hares, he called them," Griffin says, his voice hovering somewhere between hushed awe and childlike wonder.

"What do you smell?"

"A cooking fire from the colony." He pauses. "Fire is different today. Wood is different. I can't explain it."

"What do you feel?"

"Father's hand in mine. Callused. Warm."

"What do you hear?"

A longer pause. Then, eventually: "His voice. We're almost to the well."

"What's he saying?"

"I don't know."

"What does his voice sound like?"

"Gravity. Pipe smoke. The wind. Home." This little exercise has taken Griffin by storm. He's fully bought in. "I remember..." He trails off and I expect him to open his eyes, blink his way out of this tender little trance, but instead he doubles down, seems to retreat more fully inside his memories. "I remember how he would leave little drawings on scraps of paper by our bedside, so we'd wake up to little...I suppose now you'd call them cartoons. Little caricatures of the other artists in the colony. I can't remember what any of them looked like, but—"

"You have a sense of it. What they meant to us. I have it too. I remember being excited to wake up, to see what he'd drawn while we were sleeping. I remember thinking how wonderful it must be to be a grown-up, and be able to sit up late by the fire, sketching and talking with the others."

"The way the morning light hit the bedside table."

"The dust motes. There was so much more dust back then."

"I remember little errands, like the trip to the well. Not specific tasks, but the routines. Like grooves in a record worn into my mind."

"Father, always talking. I have a sense that he knew so much about the world, though I can't remember anything he taught me."

Now Griffin opens his eyes. He squeezes his sister's hand and lets it drop. "Thank you, Helena."

Moments like this, my emotions get complicated. I have a father too, of course. And, courtesy of Helena and Griffin, he has no idea what happened to me. I just disappeared without a trace. I hope he's still alive. There's no way for me to find out.

One thing nobody tells you about being dead is that anxiety, depression, lust, joy, boredom—all of it gets twisted up in ways you can't anticipate. When you're alive, things feel, more or less, like you're moving in a straight line. You've got career goals, relationship goals, something you want to do for fun later, whatever. Even the distractions from those goals—the long nights at clubs you'll never remember, weekends away with some forgettable asshole, the hard seltzers in the studio with Gary, the dumb spending spree with your meager first-album advance that you didn't realize you were essentially paying back with every show for the rest of your life—are still their own little journeys. The detours, and the detours' detours nested like Russian dolls, are still attached to the straight line you're moving in. Even if you romanticize the Web of Feelings you're caught in from roughly ages fourteen to twenty-three, you realize after you're dead that it wasn't a web at all. Because now that you're everywhere and nowhere, existing both above and beside Griffin and Helena, you've got no more lines to travel in.

I used to set goals in this place. Every time they brought home somebody new, for years, I'd think—now's my time to shine. This is the one. This time I'm going to figure out how to save them before the Belmonts suck them dry. But I never could. I can't even rattle that plate, remember? I'm nothing but a watcher now. Goals belong to linear time and I'm beyond that, which sounds cool and philosophical but really just fucking sucks.

Griffin turns and begins to cross the sumptuous chamber.

"Where are you off to?" Helena asks.

"I want to see him," Griffin says without looking back.

Helena tenses up. It's almost imperceptible. But I've seen it so many times, over the past eight years, that I can recognize it right away. It's like she pauses just long enough to imprint an outline of herself in the air with shoulders slightly hunched, then does her best to erase it.

She finishes her drink, takes a breath, and follows her brother. "Now?"

"Now."

She follows him past the backlit wall of aquariums, a sort of meta-Bond-villain display of hybrid fish that are dead but preserved and animated by nanotechnology (aka tiny robot bugs). Bits of their scales and fishy skins flake off and float up to a recycler, which sucks them into some aquatic netherworld behind the display and incorporates them into fresh grafts for the hybrids. It is as insane as it sounds and was here before my time, but I've used context clues to glean that the artist who designed it was a polymath MIT scientist type whom Helena took a particularly vicious interest in. I follow them both and try not to be too distracted by the lionfish floating with the rictus grin of decaying catfish for its face. The fish-thing moves as the Belmonts pass by, bobbing up and down in some kind of unholy, half-conscious recognition. Then it drifts down to the bottom and a fin detaches and floats up and that's about all I can take of that whole scene.

Past the crown jewels of a twelfth-century Saxon king festooned between a gathering of vintage Chuck E. Cheese animatronic mice arranged like Stonehenge, and we come to an ordinary wooden door. Griffin leans forward and traces symbols on the door with the tip of his tongue. I recognize the glyphs—a word I learned from Helena during her thing with that celebrity calligrapher—from one of Griffin's old manuscripts.

Oh, by the way, Aleister Crowley was a British intelligence plant. MI6. A literal and figurative spook. Just thought I'd throw that out there. I have no dog in this fight—I didn't even know who Crowley was before Griffin pounded a microbe brew and prattled on about it to Helena. Story for another time, but his ritualistic licking reminded me.

Anyway, the door pops open and I realize I've been stuck in this sort of puppy-doggish segment of time where I'm just following the Belmonts around, like they've absorbed me into their business. I don't even mean to do it, then they start bickering or bantering or doing some weird tender shit and I'm part of the aura and suddenly it's twenty minutes later.

I really don't want to go into this room. I've been inside once, several years ago, and that was enough.

Helena's not too keen on it either.

"Griffin." She tugs at his sleeve. "This isn't going to do what you think it's going to do. You know that."

"You don't have to come with me," he says.

"I don't think you're in the right headspace."

I can see the petulant anger come and go behind the skin of his face, like a burrowing horror worm pushing against the backside of his flesh. But he keeps it tamped down. He takes a breath and turns to Helena and gives her an elbow-squeeze. Sometimes his gestures of affection are hilariously halting and stiff. You know that feeling when you mean to say something but it gets mixed up with another thing because your brain is firing too quickly? That's what his arm just did, like it couldn't decide which part of Helena to perform a reassuring movement on. You'd think after nearly three hundred years he would have mastered this aspect of, like, being a person. Although maybe it was once natural and has begun to rust?

"I appreciate what you did just now," he says. "But seriously, I need to do this. I won't linger. Why don't you have another drink."

Helena glances inside the doorway. "I'll go with you."

Griffin smiles. "All right, then. Family time."

I should go check on you, lady. See if you're more awake and alert, and what the hell the KPM have planned for you.

But, like I said, it's been years. And curiosity, that cat-killer, has its claws in me now.

I follow them through the door, your humble floating-eye narrator, taking one for the team, here.

What's so jarring about this space is that it's small—maybe the only room in the entirety of Upstate Area 51 that you could call normal-size. No bigger than my bedroom back in Hart Springs. The Belmonts are immediately on edge. The walls and ceiling act upon them. They're not used to being in non-vast chambers. All those galleries and sumptuous drawing rooms have given them this kind of relative claustrophobia in normal-size spaces.

The walls are paneled in rough-hewn wood. It's a very handmade look, rugged and proficient but with the appearance of something constructed before modern tools were in play. There's a low table carved from a stump, upon which rest several lumps of charcoal and a few sheets of parchment. A long shelf against one wall is cluttered with tins of paint. A desk in the corner is piled with more supplies: brushes and jars of murky liquid and leather-bound books.

The modern world falls away, except for the light coming in from a faux-window installed in the wall. A thin shade is drawn but the warm afternoon-ish light from an embedded sun-mimicking lamp seeps in. Still, it does a pretty good job of simulating a pre-electrical scene. It's like one of those exhibits where the bedroom of some old luminary is preserved and you can belly right up to the velvet rope and giggle at the concept of a chamber pot and marvel at their weirdly small bed.

This room has one of those beds. It's the centerpiece—a pile of blankets, a lumpy mattress stuffed with goose feathers. A headboard carved with more of those glyphs, angular designs marching across the wood. A black hat with a wide brim hangs from a bedpost.

Helena and Griffin stand at the foot of the bed. I can hear Helena's breathing quicken. Griffin swallows drily.

Underneath the blankets, the outline of a figure is as hazy as the petering-out of the sketch below the collar. The mere suggestion of form. Impossibly thin limbs, splayed in a way that looks arranged. It's all very still. Dust, disturbed by the Belmonts' intrusion, catches some minor updraft through a beam of false light. The blankets are pulled up to the figure's neck, above which protrudes a head. My first instinct is to call it a skull, but that would be painting the wrong picture.

The head is decayed, but not in a cheap-gore effect way. There's no wound, no squirming maggots, just an overall sense of something so long dead as to be inorganic. Skin sags in dry, papery flaps, almost like the wings of some flightless bird, dormant against a thin pillow. Excess flesh waiting to be stretched like canvas across a frame.

The word here might be *desiccated*.

Lidless eyes in the sockets are the color of old milk. There's no slickness to them, no moisture. But they slide, ever so slightly upward, to regard Helena and Griffin. Pearly, desiccated grapes. A noise like a faint sandpaper-scratching.

"Father," Griffin says.

Marius Van Leeman, the man in the sketch, opens his mouth. No breath escapes. More dust floats up.

Helena places a hand on the bed frame. "Griffin came across a drawing of you that someone from the colony made." Her voice is too loud. "In 1749." She smiles broadly. "It was so nice to see your face."

She turns to Griffin, smile plastered, and urges him with her eyes to take over.

He clears his throat. "We've enlisted a very capable sculptor. And he has a sister. A painter."

"She's much more than a painter," Helena says. "She's just what we need."

"Yes." Griffin reaches out, slowly, and places a hand on the bony suggestion of a leg. "It won't be long now..."

PART TWO

THE INSOMNIACK

7

The Gold Shade, hot and crowded, incubates its Saturday-evening drinkers in a miasma of off-shift bodies.

Lark slides past a table of out-of-towners, a pair of couples whose ruddy, peeling faces tell of a frigid hike or wind-whipped ziplining. They glance around with tight smiles, hoping to flag down a server. There are no servers. There's only Beth Two. What little charm the place offers non-locals has already been leached away by the atmosphere, which is somehow both raucous and downbeat.

The jukebox, as fossilized as the old-timers who crowd the corner of the bar, plays some pop-country tune about boyfriend jeans that Lark's heard in here roughly seven million times. The selections are a time capsule of a decade earlier, when Beth Two got ambitious and made a bunch of mix CDs, hand-lettered in the jukebox window, and then never updated them.

Lark runs the gauntlet of friends and neighbors, enduring nods, backslaps, winks, hollers of drunken welcome. He feels cold inside—an icy, nervous depression threatening to blossom into paralysis. It's similar to what Betsy calls his artist's block—days of numbness and inactivity, forever on the cusp of some breakthrough that will require enormous effort. At least tonight there's a clear path forward—the book clutched inside his jacket. What he must do. What he's already late in starting.

Betsy's eyes are etched in his mind, floating above the long bar mirror like old T. J. Eckleburg's over the ash-heap in *Gatsby*—a reference he's able to deploy at will because the paperback edition he stole from Wofford Falls High School features cartoon eyes on its cover.

"The prodigal son!" Krupp shouts a wide-eyed welcome at him.

"Ha!" Across the bar, Angelo slams down a palm while Jerry scowls.

"Bethany the Second!" Krupp gestures. "Your finest pairing of malt and hops for the artist in permanent residence, *por favor!*"

Lark lets his hip hit the bar and plants an elbow to anchor himself. "I need to talk to you."

"Look what I got." Krupp spreads his legs and folds his wastrel's body down into the dim, stale space in front of his barstool. He rummages. Lark catches Beth Two at the taps out of the corner of his eye.

"I'm good, Beth," he says, waving her off.

She plunks down a half-full pint. "I already got it started."

"You got any coffee back there?"

Beth Two grows suspicious. Her short gray helmet of hair slips down her forehead as she narrows her eyes. "You quit," she informs him.

"The devilish bean!" Krupp says, popping upright, bearing a glass jar. "We'll address your tragic caffeine relapse momentarily, but first look at this."

Beth Two glares from Krupp to Lark and back again. Her hoop earrings swing. "I'll put on a fresh pot when I get a second."

"Trick him with decaf!" Krupp tells her back. Then he shoots Lark a wet grin. The pitcher in front of him is drained, dried foam sticking to the sides like an old man's patchy beard. "Here it is," he says, gesturing like a tour guide at the jar. The glass is cloudy with age and neglect. A long-dead fly speckles the base.

Lark stares dumbly. His grip on the book inside his jacket is tight and white-knuckled.

"The Red Vines jar from the candy store," Krupp says finally, an unspoken *dipshit* tacked onto the end. "Happiest of birthdays to you."

"I really need to talk to you, okay?" He lowers his voice to blend into the din of the crowd. Somebody says *Buy me a scratch-off, a two-dollar one.* Lark is conscious of the phone in his pocket. Can Gumley hear him through it? He'd have trashed it by now, except it's his only link to Betsy. What if he misses another video, or new instructions? It's this feeling of need and also repulsion that cast him headlong into the artist's block zone.

"I called you sixteen times," Krupp says. "There was ample opportunity to talk. But! Water under the Kingston-Rhinecliff Bridge. You're here, you've got some catching up to do, but nothing you can't accomplish if you set your mind and liver to it." He gestures to the empty stool next to him. "Your chariot awaits."

Lark imagines opening the psalter on the bar, yelling over this goddamn song, trying to explain to a three-sheets Krupp what's going on. An errant elbow spilling a drink, eighteenth-century onionskin pages ruined forever. Reporting that to Gumley, *My dog ate my homework . . .*

One more time, Lark reviews his decision to enlist Krupp's help. Gumley's mandate was *no police,* but he didn't say anything about friends. So Lark figures he's operating in a semi-permissible gray area. At least that's what he hopes, because he can't do this alone.

"Lark." Krupp slaps a palm down on the stool. "You're looming. Freaking everybody out. Look, the taxpaying citizens are hightailing it for the door in droves. Beth Two's calling Johnny Law. Assface Hank's gonna burst in, six-guns blazing."

With a two-handed grab, Krupp drains the dregs of the pitcher and slams it down on the bar. He leans forward, waving at Beth Two, who's indisposed with the fossils, mixing old-man drinks in Bloody Mary mugs.

Lark glances around. "Can we get a booth?"

"Said the casting agent for *My American Cousin* in 1864."

Lark stares.

"John Wilkes," Krupp says. "Read a book. Jesus, what's with you today? Hey, I found my lighter. You know where it was?"

"Up your ass?" Ian, proprietor of Clementine's Yarn & Tea, squeezing past on the way to the dartboard in a cloud of mango vapor.

"Yes!" Krupp says. He looks at Lark with baleful honesty. "It was up my ass."

Lark points to a vacant booth strewn with empties. "That one." Just above the table, a framed Stroh's ad hangs askew.

Krupp swivels and frowns at the booth. "Will you just tell me what's going on?" He shudders, clutching his bare arms. "You're making me feel weird. You haven't acknowledged the jar. I brought it for you."

"I'll tell you over there."

"Why there? We're already *here*, in our spot."

Beth Two swings by with a steaming mug. "On the house."

"*Here* is where shit happens," Krupp continues, almost pleading. "Nothing happens over there. Over there's Siberia."

Lark takes the mug and heads for the booth. Krupp lets out a long growl of annoyance, but follows. Lark shoves aside an abandoned sweatshirt and slides into the seat. Krupp plunks down the jar that once held coiled Red Vines and takes the rickety bench across the table.

He shifts in his seat, a parody of discomfort. "Were people smaller when this place was built?"

Lark glances out into the crowd. The tourists, getting the hint, have dispatched one of the guys to the bar. Ian hurls a dart, roars, points at the chalkboard where score is kept and draws an X in the air with a finger. There's a blur of khakis, a tucked-in button-down—Lark's heart hammers—but it's only the divorce lawyer whose shingle's hung on Main for as long as Lark can remember.

"You're radiating some weird energy, my man," Krupp says.

Lark turns his full attention to his friend. "They took Betsy," he says. It's practically drowned out by the intro to some awful mall-ska tune from the mix Beth Two's kid curated.

Krupp blinks. Unsure of what to do with his hands, he folds them on the table, then whisks them away to hide in his lap.

Lark imagines Gumley in his secure monitor-lined bunker, some acolyte tech filtering out the noise from the Gold Shade.

Isolate that voice.

Enhance.

"Um," Krupp says, "what?"

Lark swallows, finds his voice, plows ahead. "I needed to talk to somebody. I was just sitting there, alone in the house, thinking, and I couldn't do it anymore. So I came here."

"Okay, okay," Krupp says, voice laced with concern. "I got you. Just back up. *What's* going on with Betsy?"

Lark breathes deep. Then he leans in and lays out the fragments of his afternoon, in more or less the order that they happened: the dwelling in the mountains, Brandt Gumley, the video on the iPad, his limp and senseless sister, Gumley's employers' impossible task—and that strange psalter, the hide-bound manual.

Krupp's gaze is fixed on Lark's face. A hand goes to his mouth, fingers pinch and knead his lower lip. Wordlessly, Lark pulls *A Panoply of silent Hymns for the New World* from his jacket, swipes empties aside, and slides the book across the table.

"No way," Krupp says.

Lark blows steam across his mug's rim, then sips hot coffee. The bitter drip stuff he always favored. Strong black sludge.

"You're fucking with me."

Lark shakes his head. "They've got her, Krupp. I saw these assholes drag her out of the house. And they sent me this."

He shows Krupp the two video clips on his phone. Betsy kneeling almost peacefully in a murky, cavernous space. That sweeping, inhuman approach. Betsy's eyes opening.

"Jesus." Krupp's hand comes up from beneath the table, fidgeting with a Zippo lighter. "This can't be real."

"But it is."

"You know I'm normally the last person to ever suggest this, but you gotta call the cops."

Lark shakes his head. "Gumley said no cops. He was pretty specific on that point."

"I'm not talking about Assface Hank and the local smokies. I'm talking about state police. FBI. Justice Department. ATF. These people you're dealing with here seem like, I don't know, Branch Davidians or something."

"The only thing I can do to get her back is this."

Lark taps the book. When his fingertip makes contact with that microfiber fur, that peach-fuzz hide, his mind reels.

Despite all the trust Krupp's placed in Lark over the years, and the physical evidence of this book, he moves like a man convinced a joke is being played on him. Slowly, he opens to the title page.

With a low caffeine tolerance, half a cup of black coffee has sent Lark's mind into overdrive. He watches someone in Ian's crew erase the chalkboard while Ian mock-throws a dart at the back of his head. Jamie-Lynn comes in wearing a Fire & Rescue fleece the color of tomato soup. Beth Two stink-eyes a couple of construction workers as they take Lark and Krupp's tacitly reserved barstools.

"What the fuck is *filent*?" Krupp says at last.

"*Silent*," Lark says. "Those weird *f* letters are actually *s*'s. It's an eighteenth-century thing. I remember from Betsy's William Blake phase."

"Geographical dislocation?"

Lark shrugs. The jukebox kicks back in with something from Beth Two's short-lived Dire Straits obsession. Everything is phases, he thinks, sipping coffee.

"Holy shit," Krupp says, lingering over the title page. Lark watches as Krupp's finger goes to the bottom third of the page, tracing detailed, abstract linework that Lark had taken to be a meaningless pattern, some kind of labyrinthine design he'd barely registered.

"You buried the lede," Krupp says. He taps the center of the design, where the lines coalesce into letters that Lark hadn't noticed until now. "Marius Van Leeman." Krupp's voice goes down to a reverent, astonished hush. He glances up to meet Lark's eyes. "Marius Fucking Van Leeman wrote this." He shakes his head. "Marius Van Fucking Leeman. That doesn't sound right either, it's hard to put 'fucking' in a 'van' name. Anyway. Marius Van Leeman."

"I have no idea who that is."

Krupp frowns. "Buddy. Come on."

Lark shrugs. "Help me out here, Krupp."

Krupp plays up his exasperation. "Who founded Wofford Falls?"

"I can't remember exactly."

"Which *people*?"

"Oh. The Dutch, I guess."

"Oh my God, Lark, you did *better* than me in Ms. Renner's class, when we did the New York State history unit? I remember you got an eighty-four on the final."

"Would you just tell me who Marius Van Leeman is?"

"It wasn't just *the Dutch*. There's lots of kinds of Dutch back then, right? And it's all about religious persecution, the whole deal with them coming to the new world to steal Native land in the first place. Whatever weird shit you're into, establish a church, slap the name *reformed* on it, and watch your little settlement grow like Sim City. Some dig baptism, some don't. Procedural differences, whatever. Live and let live. And Wofford Falls is no different, you got your Anabaptists, some Calvinists, various Catholics kicking around. But they were all still varying degrees of Christian, any way you slice it. Grim, judgy motherfuckers. It wasn't like religious freedom led to some Dutch satanists rocking out and being totally accepted in the town meetings. Tolerance always has its limits, right? So enter Marius Van Leeman. The guy's a hotshot artist from the old country. Pretty respected around town at first. Gets some commissions." He pauses. "Do you really not know this?"

"It's starting to ring a bell."

A haze, in the recesses of Lark's mind, speaking of an entire artistic movement: massive canvases, turgid roiling weather, landscapes dwarfed by sky, tiny humans dwarfed by landscapes. Van Leeman's work?

"One day," Krupp continues, "his wife's mucking the stables when the horse kicks her in the head and she dies. Boom, everything changes. His artwork gets weirder and weirder. He can't fulfill his commissions anymore. Like *that*"—Krupp snaps his fingers—"he's the town freak. Until one day, he's just gone. Him and his two kids. Vanished. The good Christians of Wofford Falls are more or less relieved, until word comes down from some trappers that he's holed up in the mountains west of here. Well, no harm, no foul. Everything's status quo for a few years until word comes down *again* that there's a new community growing up there. A few dozen people, a colony of fellow artists. It's like a mirror of the Dutch settlements, escaping religious persecution, coming to the new world—except Van Leeman's new world, his artists' colony, is right up there in the mountains, not across the Atlantic. A little too close for comfort for the God-fearing squares down in the valley. Rumors sweep the town—satanic panic type stuff. Van Leeman's sacrificing goats and maybe a newborn or two for his art. He mixes virgin blood in with his paints. Pagan altars, orgies with satyrs, that sort of bullshit. So, naturally, the townspeople couldn't abide occult shit fucking up their chances at a sweet afterlife."

Lark eyes the book. "I think I know how this ends."

"I think you do too, there's no last-minute twist or anything—a good Christian posse invades the colony under cover of darkness, drags Van Leeman out to the cliffs at the edge of town by the waterfall, strings him up from the gallows, says a bunch of prayers, and hangs his ass. Not taking any chances."

Lark takes this in. "What waterfall? There are no falls in Wofford Falls, that's the whole joke."

"Legend has it that the falls dried up at the exact moment Van Leeman's neck snapped in the drop."

"That's bullshit."

"Don't shoot the messenger. That's the legend. Anyway."

Krupp turns the page. At the same time, Lark self-corrects—those wide-open skies and unspoiled landscapes, those humans-as-tiny-interlopers at the bottoms of giant canvases—that's the Hudson River School. This neck of the woods' claim to their very own artistic movement. And Van Leeman was most certainly not a part of that one, or Lark would have known the name right away. So what was this colony of artists in the Catskills, and why were they lost to history?

He wonders how much of this story is rural hogwash, as real and true as the waterfall magically drying up when Van Leeman's body dropped. He recalls other manifestations of Krupp's folkloric bent.

His refusal to dip a toe into Colgate Lake, for one, because it's the alleged home of the Colgate Mangler, a truly wacky-looking aquatic cryptid.

"*The Insomniack,*" Krupp reads aloud, flipping through the diagrams. After a while, he looks up. "*This* is the thing you're supposed to make?"

"It's the first part of it. Keep going."

Krupp thumbs through *The Worm & the Dogsbody,* then turns to the third and final section.

"*The God of the Noose,*" he reads aloud. Lark watches shades of disbelief cross his friend's gaunt face. He looks up, hollow eyes boring into Lark's. "We can't do this."

Lark's acutely grateful for Krupp's matter-of-fact *we.* His oldest friend, always down, even for something that feels like a bad dream. His eyes go to the jar that sits beneath the Stroh's ad. Is that little smear a remnant of a Red Vine? The chime of the candy shop's door, a silver bell on a string. A sound forever linked to a sugar rush in his brain. Krupp and Lark, borne back recklessly into the past by a dirty glass jar.

"We have to," Lark says.

"There's gotta be another way."

"It's transactional," Lark says. "I do this, Betsy comes home."

Krupp shuts the book, leans back as best he can in the straight-backed booth. "Even just getting the stuff we need will get us noticed pretty fast. And by *noticed* I mean *arrested.* Or *shot in the face.*"

"We start at the beginning," Lark says. He drains his mug and the artist's block feeling begins to dissolve. Pins and needles prickle up and down his back. He flexes fingers, clenches and unclenches fists. The working of materials—discovery and juxtaposition. The triage of composition—first this, then that. The click when it sits right from every angle.

"Here," he says, taking the book and flipping back to *The Insomniack.* "Look." He slides a finger across the base of the first diagram.

Krupp leans in to study the fine lines and the tiny script. "Whale-bone corset?"

"I think we're just going to have to approximate some of this stuff."

"What the fuck is *tallow*?" Krupp pauses. "You know where we gotta hit first."

"Wrecker's."

Krupp rubs his eyes. "I'm getting overwhelmed here."

"Don't do it, Krupp. Now's not the time."

"I need to rest. Just give me five minutes."

"It's never just five—Krupp?"

Krupp folds his arms on the scarred tabletop and rests the side of his head gently on his forearms, like a kid at a classroom desk playing 7-Up. Then he closes his eyes.

"Goddammit," Lark says. Krupp's coping mechanism has taken on many names over the years: Shutting down. Processing. Rebooting. Given that Krupp's first episode came over him in the computer lab at James A. Garfield Elementary, the terminology makes sense. Lark recalls the two of them at nine years old, sitting at a boxy computer screen, in thrall to the Oregon Trail. Krupp stricken with option paralysis on the banks of the Snake River, so stressed out it's as if his family's lives and futures are *actually* at stake. Subsequent generations of Krupps thriving in the Willamette Valley or being snuffed out, right there, coming down to one decision.

Caulk the wagon and float it across? Attempt to ford? Take a ferry? Wait to see if conditions improve?

Krupp frozen with his hands poised over the keys, a weird rictus grin on his face. Lark, waving a hand in front of his best friend's eyes, *Earth to Krupp.*

Lark remembers his astonishment as he watched Krupp's eyelids droop, his hands sink languidly to the Cheeto-dusted keys. *Dude, are you falling asleep?*

The pixelated river, forever uncrossed.

Lately, Krupp's dubbed his narcoleptic episodes "reformatting my drive." Lark has learned to let reformatting take its course, but right now there's no time. He nudges Krupp's shoulder. Interrupting can have unpredictable consequences. Lark braces himself. Krupp doesn't stir. Lark slides the book out from where it's wedged beneath Krupp's forearms. At the moment a piggish half snore comes from Krupp's open mouth, the jukebox cuts off. The Shade crowd grows oddly hushed. He turns his head in time to catch Beth Two climbing up onto the bar, nimble and quick. She looks knowingly around the barroom, then lifts her arms like a conductor. Everyone begins to sing in a sloppy chorus.

"Happy birthday to yoooouuuuuuuu!"

"Shit," Lark says as Beth Two stares him down and a dozen heads swivel to pin him with drunken gazes to the booth. Jamie-Lynn raises her beer glass in his direction, gives it a sloshy tilt.

"Happy birthday TO yoooouuuuu!"

"Krupp," he says, shaking his friend without mercy. "Come on, man, wake up."

"Happy BIRTHday dearPeterLarkin...Happy birthday to yoooouuuuuuuu." Ian bellowing the last line with operatic flourish and capping it off with a deep bow.

The divorce lawyer launches into "How old are you now?!" and Lark puts on what he hopes is a sheepish grin and lifts a palm in a halfhearted wave. The tacked-on coda grows in volume while Beth Two remains on the bar, conducting.

"Krupp!" Lark shouts over what he thinks is the end of the singalong—except the divorce lawyer shouts *"One more time!"* and the whole Shade crowd launches into it again with drunken glee. Lark feels the eyes of his neighbors. A prickly heat begins at the top of his chest, his collarbone, and rises up his neck. His face flushes. He's being standoffish, acting uppity, *above* these people—a constant fear. The famous artist who deigns to live among the huddled masses. Or, worse, who uses them for *inspiration*.

What did Asha call him? Her upstate Rauschenberg in Carhartt. He flashes a weak smile as he shakes Krupp's shoulder with great vigor. Applause and cheers ripple through the crowd.

"Speech!" Ian hollers from over by the dartboard.

"Krupp!" Lark hammers a fist into his friend's bony shoulder.

Krupp bolts upright and stares at him with a blank look. Then he pulls the crushed Camel soft pack and Zippo from his pocket, shoves a bent smoke between his lips, flicks open the lighter, and holds the flame to the end of the cigarette.

The crowd takes up the chant. *"Speech! Speech! Speech!"*

"You can't smoke in here," Lark says. Krupp stares back dumbly. The tip of the cigarette begins to burn down.

Lark plucks the Camel from Krupp's lips and crushes it out on the lid of the glass jar. Krupp blinks his senses back, at least partially.

"Speech! Speech! Speech!"

"We gotta get going," Lark says.

Krupp lays a hand on the book's awful binding. "Everything's different now," he says softly.

Lark's gaze sweeps across the gathered crowd, all of them waiting for a few words from the hometown boy who came back to live among them, and whose dreams, wildly achieved before their eyes, represent something different for everyone here.

Lark stands up, cradling the book and the jar. The cries die down. An expectant hush sweeps across the room. Beth Two folds her arms.

"I gotta go," Lark says, "sorry."

Silence. Lark exits the booth and the crowd parts, clearing a reluctant lane to the door. Lark hears Krupp shuffle along behind him. He meets Jamie-Lynn's eyes, then turns away.

"Asshole," someone says. Lark opens the door and steps out into the cold night as the jukebox kicks back on, drowning out the replies—a few of which, he knows, will be in agreement.

8

Take me home," Krupp says.

"We're going to Wrecker's."

"I can't think straight. I only reformatted halfway. Maybe one-third. I'll be better tomorrow."

"It's gotta be tonight."

"A few hours. Reconvene. Strike at first light."

Lark, at the wheel of his truck, takes a deep breath and lets it out. "Time's a factor here, Krupp. Betsy's alone, in that *place*."

He turns off Market Street onto Prospect—a suburban through-line from mixed residential to the baseball fields, ice rink, high school, and eventually the countryside that's still technically Wofford Falls but feels like the middle of nowhere.

Behind living room windows, TVs throw muted shades of blue against curtains. Just ahead, the truck's headlights pick up a looming figure in the darkness. Braided copper salvage, tall and human-oid, armored in titanium patches like skin grafts, evoking a video game hero, a helmeted first-person-shooter protagonist. The Make-A-Wish boy for whom Lark sculpted it has been gone for six years now. He'd be nineteen today. The sculpture passes into darkness in the truck's wake.

"Right," Krupp says, as if he'd forgotten the impetus behind their task and is just now recalling those videos of Betsy in captivity. "I just think we should pull over and hash out a plan."

"No time," Lark says. "It's called *The Insomniack* because it has to be done in one night."

"Brandt Gumley tell you that?"

"The book told me that."

He hangs a left onto Post Road North, the kind of desolate stretch where the jogger in the opening scene of the crime show finds the dumped bodies of the missing women. A small animal stirs the underbrush. He clicks on his brights, scans the road, and grips the wheel tight.

"Make a list of the things we need on your phone," Lark says.

"Okay, but here's problem number one."

Lark doesn't answer, just eases his foot down on the gas pedal.

"You want to hear problem number one?"

"No."

"Wrecker's gonna be passed out by now. Sweet slumber of the satiated."

"I'm counting on it," Lark says.

"So we're just gonna steal." Krupp pauses. "From *Wrecker*. Do you understand what a colossally shitty idea that is? Do you remember when Turkey Tom and Lou the Chaplain huffed paint and broke into Wrecker's yard and—"

Lark hits the brakes. The truck's wheels lock and skid. The stink of scorched rubber fills the cab. "You want out?" He tries not to yell—he knows it's not fair, Krupp's on his side, always—but nervy irritation has him operating at a harsh forward lean. "I'll take you home. I realize how fucked up this is, Krupp. I do. I won't hold it against you."

"I said I was with you!" Krupp yells back. "I said *we* from the start of this, like I always do, okay? So don't stop the truck in the middle of the road to yell at me like you're Wayne Krupp Senior."

"Then quit fucking around and make that list!"

Krupp slams a palm into the overhead light so he can see the book. Lark hits the gas. The reflected glow turns the world outside to half-lit confusion.

"What's this?" Krupp says.

Lark glances over as Krupp retrieves Betsy's gift from the floor. He sets the box in his lap.

"Don't open that," Lark says.

Krupp opens it. "A giant pocket watch?"

Instantly, the air in the truck turns thick with a milky sourness, like heavy cream about to go bad. Lark keeps his eyes on the Post Road, a straight shot to nowhere, and tries not to breathe too deep.

"Why is it so sad?" Krupp asks after a while. Lark doesn't remember Post Road being this long and wonders if he missed his turn. But he hasn't even hit the adopt-a-highway sign yet. The Libertarian Party of Wofford Falls, all three members cleaning up the roadside to prove that The State doesn't have to do shit in an ideal society. Krupp's voice seems to reach him through a prismatic ether. His words, scrambled and out of order, are slow to come together into a linear phrase.

Why is it so sad?

He grips the wheel to make sure it's still firmly in his grasp and formulates a reply.

"Close the box, man."

His words hit the air and scatter into refraction. There's *box* floating out through the windshield, getting snagged on a wiper. *Close* drifting over the dashboard, flitting about the fuel gauge. *Man* identifying its subject, teasing Krupp's eyebrow...

The phrase snaps together and vocalizes itself. The adopt-a-highway sign comes and goes. Krupp makes no move to close the box. Lark understands—once you see Betsy's turning come to life, how can you deprive yourself of its ever-shifting corporeality? He thinks of what the woman in the red dress holds, and at that moment Krupp's words truly sink in. *So sad, so sad.* Nobody deserves to be abducted, but Betsy even less so, somehow—he feels this as objective fact, despite Betsy being the person in this world he's closest to, besides the man currently sitting in his passenger seat. Betsy with her unique talent they both work to nurture and preserve. Betsy with her low-risk lifestyle, one devoted to craft, solitude, study, and work. The specific tenor of the sadness Krupp expressed washes over him now—the sadness of a dry waterfall, an arid cliffside carved by a deluge long exhausted.

The snap of a taut rope…

"Jesus," Krupp says, the two syllables spiking distinct sound waves in the atmosphere of the truck.

Then Krupp cries out, swatting at himself, flailing in the front seat as if he's just dropped a wasp's nest in his lap. Out of the corner of his eye, Lark catches an impossible sight. The object Betsy painted on the cardboard jets up from the box, latches onto the front of Krupp's shirt, gathers the folds in its teeth, and uses its tiny jaw to leapfrog up to the ceiling of the cab. There it clutches and hangs, a heaving blemish.

Lark's head swivels forward to see the sharp turn down the dirt road to Wrecker's compound coming up fast. He hits the brakes.

Krupp's screams ribbon through Lark's head from different directions. The object gripping the ceiling throbs in reverse, as if each outbreath makes its lung cavity expand. Lark can't believe how it's grown since this afternoon—once the size of a matchbook, now a soda can.

It lowers itself like a dangling spider. The strand of its web, in this case, is a thin rope of glistening spittle, firm and tensile as fishing line. Krupp sinks low in his seat as it comes toward him. A sound escapes it—through its *pores*, Lark thinks, because if anyone could render perfect, microscopic pores, it's Betsy. A sound like a sibilant rush of air behind a pane of thick glass. The sound implants a word in his mind, lit up like a title on an old-time marquee: *HISS*.

Lark stares dumbly at the object descending toward his horrified friend.

He's pretty sure it just hissed phonetically at him.

"Help me!" Krupp cries out, and Lark reaches into Krupp's lap, takes the lid off the jar, and traps the object from below. Then he slams the lid down, severing the thin filigree. The strand drips slowly down the side of the jar, a trickle of sparkling ooze.

Inside the jar, Betsy's gift scuttles about for a moment, then lies still. Lark sets it carefully on the console.

The air's sour thickness dissipates. Krupp, breathing hard, shrinks away from the jar, cowering fetally at the very edge of his seat, pressed against the door.

"Holy shit," he says after a while.

"I told you not to open that," Lark says.

"Holy *shit*. Can this day just end?"

"Betsy made that for my birthday."

"That explains, like, ten percent of what just happened."

"It's changed a lot since earlier."

Krupp hesitates, then taps the jar with a fingertip. The thing inside seems to have reverted to its bloated matchbook shape, closer to what the woman in the red dress holds, though much larger now. Lark, with a pang, thinks of all the neat holes cut out of Betsy's work, all of her turnings stolen by Gumley's acolytes. This particular turning does not stir.

Krupp rolls down the window of the truck and with trembling hands lights a Camel. Cold air rushes in. Krupp exhales smoke that's snatched by the wind as Lark turns down the narrow road to Wrecker's place. Branches rake the sides of the truck as it jounces along.

"Betsy and birthdays," Krupp says. "Remember that mouse from your thirtieth?"

A flash of a gray felt abdomen, a painted head, a tail that turned inside out and revealed the delicate skeletal remains of itself. Lark shudders. "Let's not speak of it."

At the same time, the thought of his sister applying her talent to giving him what no one else ever could, even if it's grotesque, makes him light-headed with loss.

A moment later, he's gripped by rage.

The truck hurtles down the path carved into the ten thousand acres of wilderness that hug Wofford Falls.

"I feel like nothing's ever going to be the same," Krupp says.

"You say that every weekend."

"Yeah, but this time it's true."

Lark slows the truck to negotiate a winding stretch of hidden road. So his day began with Wrecker, so now it will end. Earlier, strolling down Main to Wrecker's little shop in the town proper, the charmingly cluttered, tourist-facing outpost of the remote hoarded stockpile they're heading for now. Carrying eight pounds of Roberta's breakfast menu to trade for a choice new material. The man himself, sitting on his double-wide chair behind the Plexiglas enclosure, keeping his hooded eyes on the store from his panopticon. Star linebacker before Lark's time at Wofford Falls High, DI recruitment squandered for reasons still murky. Gold Shade rumor mill: 'roid rage exacerbating latent psychosis.

Lark's theory: Guy's as pure a misanthrope as they come. Some kind of nihilistic embodiment of cosmic futility in the form of an antiques dealer. And also an anything-else dealer.

"Okay, then." Krupp opens the psalter and takes out his phone. "Item one: fcabbards."

"Scabbards."

"Right. Item two. This thing is hard to read ... *secal* residue?"

"I think that *f* is probably just an *f*."

"So we have to find some *actual shit*?"

"Just the residue. Wrecker's got cats."

Krupp sighs. "I forgot about those cats."

Lark cranks the wheel and the trees part. A razor-wire fence comes into view, the lighted tower at its corner a bright incision in the night.

"Hey, Krupp?" Lark says.

Book balanced on his skinny thighs, Krupp jabs at the notes app on his phone. "Hey, Lark."

"Thanks."

"Don't mention it, buddy. I got nothing else to do."

9

The edge of Wrecker's compound smells like raw meat. The truck's backed up to the darkest section of the fence, where the forest creeps into the clearing. Lark lowers the truck's liftgate carefully. There's only three feet of empty space between the chain link and the edge of the flatbed. A quarter mile to the east, the pair of back-to-back concert-stage spotlights atop the tower throw one long beam across the compound and another out beyond the perimeter. The tower itself is a marvel of homespun ingenuity, informed primarily by the jungle guard posts in '80s action movies. Lark knows this because Wrecker once told him he loved the parts in *First Blood Part II* and *Rambo III* where men go flying out of their towers in a hail of sparks and high explosives. This is because, Wrecker continued, it got him hard to think about being a sitting duck in a tower, knowing there's no escape. Lark has come to realize that Wrecker doesn't care for the main plotlines of movies but devotes hours of consideration to the meaningless deaths of extras.

Krupp and Lark crouch at the edge of the fence. Lark pulls a pair of industrial bolt cutters from a black duffel. He fits the sharp steel jaw around a corroded link in the fence and rides out a surge of nervy joy at the cheap thrill. He's nineteen again, scrounging in random scrap heaps in the margins of Alphabet City under cover of darkness. He wonders what Asha would think of her upstate Rauschenberg now.

"What's the first thing we need?" he asks before he snaps the pliers shut.

"The book said something about *where the unclean go*, which seemed super metaphorical and up for interpretation. So, I think we should go for a bathtub."

"That works." Lark snips the link. The tips of the severed wire curl back sharply. "I know where the kitchen and bath stuff is."

He snips another, and another. The wind kicks up, and he wishes he wore a hat. Krupp, coatless as ever, shifts his weight back and forth. Lark thinks of Turkey Tom and Lou the Chaplain's legendary glue-brained misadventure in this place. Gold Shade scuttlebutt: They were fed, piece by tiny piece, to the feral cats. Either way, after boasting they were gonna be set for life after a raid on Wrecker's, they never resurfaced. *Set for life* was some glue-brained thinking to begin with: Wrecker's got a ton of rare finds, but snagging armfuls of used lamps and fireplace grates and old bathroom fixtures and dubious taxidermy isn't exactly a get-rich-quick scheme. Lark's theory: Turkey Tom and Lou the Chaplain grabbed something they *thought*, in their addled mania, was of great value, and split Wofford Falls forever to live off their ill-gotten riches, which they blew on dirty biker drugs in a day or two and then kept moving.

"What's up?" Krupp lays a gentle hand on his shoulder. Lark realizes he's paused with the cutters' teeth around a wire.

"Just thinking about Tom and Lou."

"You're back on the coffee. You're in avoidance mode. Your mind's jumping all over the place. Remember what you told me, for you it's like the anti-focus, different from how everybody else uses caffeine."

"I know what I told you. I'm fine." Lark snips, moves the cutters, snips again. "Let's do this."

"Also Tom and Lou are morons," Krupp assures him. "Morons from the moment of birth onward. Christened that way by the church." But there is also some equivalency in his voice: *We, too, are morons.* Lark sinks into a methodical rhythm. The bolt cutters, like all his tools, have been

kept oiled and honed. He wonders if Gumley is somehow watching
this unfold. Drone cameras. Wrecker's home security, hacked. Some
other more esoteric method: remote viewing, perhaps. *My employers fund
a transcendental agency contracted to the CIA...*

Krupp, beside him, blows warm breath onto his palms. Ten minutes
later, Lark and Krupp slide their hands carefully between links and
pull down the newly snipped fence-flap. There's a satisfying give to the
chain link as they peel it down to the earth and step on it to bend it
flat.

"Straight down the center aisle," Lark whispers, "about a hundred
feet. Then left to kitchen and bath stuff. Watch out for cats."

They step through the hole in the fence. Inside, the ground is a
patchwork of dirt, gravel, and untended grass. Just ahead, a pair of
structures loom, as makeshift as the unmanned guard tower. Nighttime is deceptive out here in the sticks—midnight, two in the morning,
four—all those hours that can be ticked off more clearly in Wofford
Falls proper, where the Shade might not empty out for a while yet, blur
together at Wrecker's. And Wrecker himself? Sprawled in his king bed
in the exact center of his dwelling, itself located in the exact center of
the compound—yet another panopticon.

Together, Lark and Krupp creep toward the narrow lane between
the two structures. The soft earth turns to smooth pavement as they
enter a city of junk and scrap, sprung up from the wilderness, as
planned and logical as Midtown Manhattan. The eastern structure
is a hybrid of half-built parking garage and circus tent. A system of
interlocking girders and I-beams, three stories high, cloaked in thick
canvas the color of maple syrup. Tent flaps whip in the wind. Inside,
Lark knows, the girders form shelves, superstructure pulling double
duty as interior organization. This is tent one: old engines, air conditioners, car doors, miscellaneous scrap metal, and a few dentist chairs.
The likely source of the manta-shaped tin he traded Wrecker several
breakfasts for earlier. Tent two, on the other side of the aisle, stands
like a tattered skeleton on some ancient battlefield, uniform of fabric
and tarp mostly rotted away, long ribbons blowing in the wind like a

forlorn battle flag. Wrecker's not exactly on the ball in terms of patching up in the aftermath of a vicious upstate winter.

Up ahead, a shadow slinks low across the path and darts behind tent one and vanishes. Lark puts a warning hand on Krupp's ice-cold forearm.

"Cat," he whispers. Krupp nods. They move slowly. Tent two, guts exposed, reveals its contents, all deep shadows of arcane geometries, bent by the spotlight and the angles of the girders. Massive commercial signs, faded molded plastics as big as his truck, leer at him from the darkness. There's a Dunkin' Donuts sign that must have once emblazoned a proud local franchise. It's been there as long as Lark can remember, tempting him, but he has an aversion to using any kind of brand reference in his sculptures. The sight of the familiar hits people with an instant postmodern wink, giving them permission to feel smug about understanding a shallow reference best exorcised in the earliest days of one's career.

A red-headed Wendy from Wendy's leers at him, eyeless and desecrated.

"I'm starving," Krupp says, and Lark shares the visions of Dollar Menu Jr. Bacon Cheeseburgers dancing in his friend's head.

Past the two tents, the spotlight shines down the lane. Lark and Krupp stay low and dart through the beam until they're safely between tents three and four—mirrors and strollers, respectively. Lark once spent hours in tent four, on the cusp of some artistic breakthrough, but couldn't get past the *Rosemary's Baby* evocations.

Strange to be here now as an illicit prowler after a decade of cultivating a transactional relationship with Wrecker. Not a friendship, of course—the big man doesn't have friends—but something akin to trust, however tenuous, has sprouted between them.

"Here," Lark whispers, turning left into a district of hovels and lean-tos, themselves sprung up from scavenged goods. Lark's heard tales of squatters in this place—sightings by dubious Shade characters of entire families picking through junk-heaps and never leaving, like hardy Dust Bowl types transplanted to the North Country. Steinbeck on ice. Which means some of these dark, barnlike huts might actually be occupied. Lark doesn't really believe that Wrecker is the type to allow people to linger inside the fences, but the man is often inscrutable.

Krupp stops short, gripping Lark's arm. A cat squirts across the lane, a puddle of shadow, there and gone. They take a few steps before it's Lark's turn to stop them. He pulls Krupp into a pitch-dark Quonset hut and uses his phone as a flashlight. He sweeps the beam across a mess of porcelain toilets and bathroom sinks. Startled roaches scatter. The air in the hut smells of mildew. Lark holds the beam steady on a clawfoot tub, its inner sides caked in grime.

"Where the unclean go," Krupp says, grabbing hold of the end of the tub. Lark positions himself directly across. On a whispered three-count, both of them lift the tub—or try to, at least. Lark fares better than Krupp, who can't get his end off the ground.

"Jesus," he says, breathing hard.

"Come on," Lark says, straining to keep his side from touching the earth, knowing it's unlikely he'll be able to pick it back up.

Lark senses the strain radiating off his friend's sinewy frame. "I got this," Krupp says in a weird strangled voice.

Lark sets his end of the tub back down. "How about a sink?"

A cat's mournful cry—the late-night yearning of the unspayed and feral—floats across the grounds.

"A sink works," Krupp said. "Still somewhere the unclean go. For their hands, anyway. The book probably means, like, a *church* or something, but I'm sure a sink is fine."

Lark moves his flashlight beam across the piles of discarded sinks. Some, torn carelessly from cheap motel walls, are attached to ragged bits of plaster. A second cat answers the first and their howls mingle in dissonance. Lark shudders. It's astonishing how *loud* cats can be. A bunch of little hollow vessels flinging a hive-mind cat voice back and forth.

"Cats are fucking weird," Krupp says.

Another cat voice joins the hive.

"Like Tuvan monks," Lark says, with a pang of loss that accompanies every stray thought of his sister. "The throat singers Betsy got into for a while."

He trains his flashlight on a classic sink with silver fixtures attached to a U-shaped pipe.

"Beautiful," Krupp says.

To the rising accompaniment of Wrecker's strays, they haul it away.

10

By three A.M. the bed of the truck holds *The Insomniack*'s raw materials, the elements of the first silent hymn: For the unclean, a sink. For the lonely, a pile of half-burned candles (wax being the closest they could get to tallow). For the sleepless, a bed frame. For the fever-stricken, a carpenter's vise (the diagram in the book here depicting some kind of medieval-looking clamp). For the dispossessed, the bricks of a foundation. For the starving, a cast-iron pan. For the plague-stricken, a tarp (close enough to a shroud). For the idle, a lathe. For the mute, a typewriter. For the freezing, a radiator. For the burning, a fire extinguisher. For the dead, a coffin.

Through the small hours of the morning, an organizing principle takes shape in Lark's mind. The obscurities of the psalter's text begin to unravel, sort themselves into a kind of lizard-brained framework. He thinks back to Betsy's Vermeer period, when people apparently lived in dark clouds of perpetual melancholy, and like the chiaroscuro margins of the Dutch masters, the shadows of understanding gather. *The Insomniack* is the foundation of the ur-sculpture, the base composed of found objects, combined in precise array over the course of a sleepless night. Framed as remedies for every malady that might afflict a populace. The counterbalance. A certain cause and effect that defies the artistic principles he's learned to live by, namely that there is no one-to-one relationship between his materials and what they evoke. Each object isn't intended to fulfill a *purpose*—it's precisely that brand of didactic intentionality that renders most other sculptures he sees so bland. And yet within this defiance comes the sort of breathless experimentation couched in quasi-religious dogma he associates with Aleister Crowley and his ilk. Occultists, as brand-savvy as social media influencers and just as cynical.

He leans against the liftgate, wishing he brought a bottle of water. Krupp, coated in sweat, Danzig shirt plastered to his body despite the chill, lights a Camel. Lark lets a dull sort of satisfaction wash over him. How impossible this all seemed, sitting in that study with Gumley, scrutinized by the onyx falcon. And now, here they are, twelve hours later, with the raw materials gathered for the first leg of this absurd journey.

He sets the book down on the edge of the gate and illuminates it with his phone. A single cat receives the hive-mind voice and flings it skyward. Krupp blows smoke silently into the night air.

Lark flips to the end of the *Insomniack* chapter. The assembly instructions are vague enough to allow for artistic license. The personal stamp of the creator. Otherwise, he supposes, Gumley's employers could have contracted just about anyone to put it together.

He turns the page. "Shit."

"Problemo?"

"Not really, just something I didn't notice before. Did you see this little map?"

Krupp joins him, leans over to peer at the book. "Wait, is that…?"

"Looks like the Backbone to me."

"*That's* where we're supposed to put this thing together?"

"Guess so."

As little kids, Lark and Betsy heard whispers of the Backbone—a place for sloppy teenage keggers that the cops mostly left alone as a release valve for the town itself. A tacit understanding forged with Assface Hank: Keep it localized to that desolate place, don't kill each other, don't anybody fall into the gorge, and your right to party will be respected.

When it gets too cold to party outside, the Backbone fulfills its secondary role as the Teen Makeout Spot. What the town elders called a Lover's Lane, what kids today probably call Fuck Alley. The site of at least one obligatory 1970s slaying. Steamed-up car windows, furtive unbucklings, a tinny car radio drifting across the gorge to bounce off the dry falls.

Lark can feel Krupp's eyes boring into him in the dark. An edgy, unblinking quality to his stare. Like he's waiting for Lark to catch on to God knows what.

Eventually Krupp boils over. "Well, that makes total sense. That's where they hanged Marius Van Leeman."

"I'm glad it makes sense to one of us."

"It's like..." He snaps his fingers. "Poetic justice."

"Yeah, but he would've written this book before he got hanged."

"Oh yeah."

"So maybe hanging him there was poetic justice in reverse."

"Poetic justice *for* the good Christian citizens, instead of *against* them."

"I don't know."

Wearily, Lark recalibrates his plans for the rest of the early-morning hours. He had anticipated heading back home, unloading the truck, integrating the material into his studio. A dose of comfort, a place where he might lose himself in the work—after all, Betsy's life depends on him doing a credible job. But according to the book, there's a different location in mind for the sculpture.

"I'm gonna need some more coffee," Lark says, killing the light and closing the book. The chorus of feral strays hits a jarring swell, allegro molto. He watches the bright dot of the Camel's cherry ascend to Krupp's weary face.

"One last box to check and we can get the fuck outta Dodge," Krupp says, blowing smoke. He checks his notes app. "For the despondent, release. I'm thinking a suicide thing. The book had a picture of a Japanese sword. Maybe a seppuku-type deal."

"I'll tell you one thing: Wrecker's got no shortage of swords. It's actually pretty crazy. Tent fourteen."

Krupp tosses the butt, stamps it out. "Let's hit it."

The second they cross the compound's threshold and head down the path between tents one and two, something feels off. He chalks it up to the need for a fresh coffee infusion. They hang a right. Through an inner ring of low-slung tents, Lark glimpses Wrecker's gabled dwelling, an early twentieth-century farmhouse gone to seed and reinforced with scrap metal to give it the vibe of a Mad Max vehicle put out to pasture, its gas-town-raiding days long behind it, a contemplative twilight for a once fierce desert rover.

"Fucking cats," Krupp says.

Now it clicks for Lark: The cats' symphony, ebbing and flowing throughout the night, has reached a new phase. He feels their screeching deep in his bones. Wrecker's dwelling vanishes behind a tall structure that was never a tent at all—more like a three-story plywood cube, accessed via tunnel. Lark's been inside exactly once, back when Wrecker went through a gregarious winter thanks to methamphetamine. Three months when Wrecker was predisposed to share aspects of his life with his nominal, tenuous-at-best friends. Inside the cube is a climate-controlled space free of humidity or cold or moisture. In the center of the cube—its own lonely panopticon, Lark realizes now—is a glass case that contains the skeleton of Wrecker's first and long-dead cat, Piglet.

This town has a long and storied tradition of weirdos inviting him to see the most hermetic spaces of their odd little lives.

"Hey, Krupp, what was the name of that old guy whose vinyl siding we—"

"Priest!"

"*Shhh.* I don't think that was it."

"We called him priest, dipshit. Because he was so obviously a molester. Remember he always tried to get us to go see his—"

"Tunnel."

"*Shhh!*" Krupp stops short, a hand on Lark's arm. Together, they listen. Somewhere, one cat attacks another and the droning cries slide upward into cold, dispassionate encouragement.

"Just cats," Lark says.

"I heard something else."

"Come on." Lark takes a hard left toward tent twelve. "Last thing, then we're gone."

Tent fourteen once belonged to a horse show, and the ad banners still hang from the interior. Lark's phone light plays across them. RICHARDSON'S HAY, THE BEST HAY SINCE 1924.

"We can't forget the fecal residue, either." He pauses. "But I guess we can get that anywhere."

"Can we?" Krupp walks over to a set of wooden shelves twice his height. Lark lights them up. There are rapiers, daggers, dirks. Broadswords forged for reenactments or Renaissance fair costumes. Epees and foils and sabers for fencing. A battle-ax that may or may not have been a movie prop.

"There's gotta be a samurai sword here somewhere," Krupp says.

"Just pick one."

"I feel like the more accurate we can get with the sword might make up for us being off the mark with some of the other stuff."

"Come on, Krupp, I still have put all this together on the—"

Now Lark hears the *something else* Krupp pointed out a moment ago. The creak of a door, opening and closing. The cats fall silent.

Lark kills his phone light. Tent fourteen is dark except for a sliver of light from the guard tower, leaking in through the open flap.

A moment later, a hulking presence interrupts the light, throwing the tent into full darkness. Lark catches a whiff of bacon and fried potatoes—the aftermath of a long day spent grazing on a Roberta's feast. A single cat scampers across the opening, deploying a quick triumphant *mrrroww*. Labored breathing drifts into the tent.

"What are you doing."

The soft voice is a marvel, every time. Rolling, mellifluous vowels, gorgeous consonants. The voice of an NPR host or award-winning podcaster.

"Wrecker," Lark says, going straight for an introduction before they get shotgunned sight unseen. "It's Lark and Wayne Krupp."

"Junior," Krupp specifies.

"Lark," Wrecker says. "Wayne." There's no indication that this is any kind of surprise. "My babies woke me up."

"Those cats are *super* loud," Krupp says with a rushed, hollow note of sympathy.

"You made a hole in my fence," Wrecker says.

Lark swallows. Even in the darkness, he can sense Krupp looking at him insistently. There's no plan for this.

"Wrecker," Lark says, "I know this is out of line. I know that, and I'm sorry. I'm going to take a second, right now, to tell you exactly what's going on. Will you listen to what I have to say and keep an open mind? We're in a bit of a jam, here."

"My babies woke me up and I watched you on my screens."

A deep stillness in the compound takes over, until Wrecker shifts his bulk and the light transfers from one side of the open flap to the other.

"You know my sister, Betsy," Lark says.

"Betsy." Wrecker sounds sad. "The last time she came into my store she was in heat," Wrecker informs him. "I could smell her sex."

Lark swallows a surge of Lost Year rage. He takes a deep breath and reminds himself that Wrecker has the upper hand.

"That must have been a long time ago," Lark says, taking a moment to compose himself. How many times had he bruised his knuckles on some asshole's facial bones on Betsy's behalf, back in the day? "Well, she's in a lot of trouble, and—"

"Have you seen the movie *Cannibal Holocaust*?"

"I have," Krupp says. "Back in my *Faces of Death* phase." He sounds relieved to be connecting with Wrecker on any level. "VHS shit from Laser Video, every time."

"Did you like it."

More stillness. Krupp, clearly, has no idea how to answer.

"Yes?" Lark offers.

"They kill a large turtle with a machete," Wrecker says. "It's not a special effect. I watched it five times today. It made me sick."

Lark's silently screaming at Krupp not to blurt out the obvious and just move on.

"It made you sick but you watched it five times?" Krupp blurts out.

"I hadn't showered," Wrecker says. "My legs were sweaty. My crotch smelled like bread dough while they killed the turtle. I rubbed my finger down there and then held it to my nose and it became the smell of the dead turtle."

"Huh," Krupp says, as if the bread-dough crotch revelation was thought-provoking in some way. Lark knows exactly what Krupp would say about it if this situation weren't dire, and they were settling into their seats at the Shade: *It really is like listening to some fucked-up, alternate-universe NPR.*

"I wept," Wrecker says.

"That does sound sad," Lark says. "Hey, you remember earlier, when I brought you breakfast at the store, and picked up that tin scrap?"

"Yes," Wrecker says. "But I didn't invite you into my parlour."

More stillness. Lark, with his weary, wired mind, struggles to latch onto what Wrecker is trying to say.

"You call this place your parlor?" Krupp says. "Like, this whole compound, or just this specific tent, or…"

"Parlour spelled with a *u*," Wrecker specifies. "British English." He advances into the tent. For a moment, his physique fills the opening, dousing the light completely. Lark strains to see if he's carrying a weapon, but it's too dark. In the expanse behind him, the cats rejoin their chorus. The scent of far too many breakfasts for one man wafts pestilentially through the tent.

"It's always two men who come in the night." Wrecker advances farther and the light reappears at his back. Now he's a mountainous silhouette, a creature out of some Catskills folktale come knocking at your cabin door.

Lark senses Krupp making slow, deliberate motions in the darkness. Edging closer to the shelves full of blades. Wrecker calls forth a great glob of phlegm from deep within and spits into the dirt. Lark sends a silent plea to Krupp to quit moving—he has the sudden and dreadful impression that Wrecker can see in the dark.

"Wrecker," Lark says carefully. "You've known me for a long time. You know how much I value our relationship. I would never do anything to jeopardize it."

Wrecker sighs. His bulk seems to sag a bit. "I watched you come and go on the screens. My babies saw everything."

"Do you have cameras attached to the cats?" Krupp asks.

"What I was saying about Betsy being in trouble," Lark says, "she's been kidnapped, and the only way to save her life is to make a sculpture."

"That sounds like a lie," Wrecker says mildly.

"I realize that," Lark says, trying to keep the nervous edge out of his voice. "But I swear to you on Betsy's life, and on my life, that it's true. Do you know me to be a liar?"

"I don't know you at all."

"Wrecker," Lark says. "There's a ticking clock on this, and we *really* don't have time to explain it all right now. Also, you do know me, we've interacted literally hundreds of times in your store. I'm by far your best customer."

"You stole from me," Wrecker says.

"There wasn't time to get you out of bed and bargain for every little thing, okay? I promise, when this is all over, I will *more than* compensate you for—"

"You made me into the turtle," Wrecker says. "You violated my life for my babies to see." He takes another step forward. Lark estimates he could reach them in three seconds if he rushed at them like the linebacker he used to be. He doesn't know how to get the man to stand aside. He suspects there's a magic phrase out there, some potent keyword, an angle of conversation to unlock some reasonable pathway of resolution, but at the moment nothing scans. He's not sure if Wrecker's even listening.

"You're dreaming," Lark blurts out. Off to his left, in the darkness, he can sense Krupp's sharp intake of breath at this sudden change in tactics.

Wrecker's silence emboldens Lark to continue. "You're dreaming this, safe in your bed. Your babies are sleeping too."

Silence.

Then Wrecker begins to laugh. Lark's struck dumb: He's never heard the man so much as chuckle before.

"It worked," Wrecker says, astonishment gilding his voice. Lark remains speechless. The sudden animation of Wrecker's personality is so hard to wrap his head around that Lark wonders if *he* might actually be the dreamer.

That would explain a lot.

"*What* worked?" Krupp asks.

"I'm in control of this world," Wrecker says.

Shit, Lark thinks. "It's not that kind of dream."

"I'm fully lucid," Wrecker says. Lark hears massive knuckles crack like a backfiring truck. The cats howl. "Like in that movie *The Cell*, and I'm Vincent Innofrio."

"*DI*-nofrio," Krupp says.

"I can wind your guts around a spit and spin them out of you slowly." Wrecker laughs again with the glee of a child set free in an amusement park, *What will I ride first?*

"Oh, fuck this," Krupp says. A moment later, there's a metallic clattering as he rummages in the dark for a weapon. Wrecker laughs, coughs, doubles over to catch his breath. Lark backs up toward his friend. His eyes have adjusted but it's still difficult to see. He thinks he should reach for a weapon—but what if he wraps his hand around a razor-sharp blade?

He's always been fearful that some freak accident could snatch away not merely the life he's built for himself but his very ability to rebuild it after a collapse.

"You're a good man, Wrecker," Lark says. "You're an important part of this community. I have a lot of respect for your place here."

Wrecker straightens up. His composure is eerie and immediate. "This community is whatever I want it to be."

What kind of life must a man lead to disassociate so easily, Lark wonders. Guilt presses down on him, grows oppressive inside the tent. The final word of the Gold Shade crowd echoes inside his head: *asshole.*

Everyone finds Wrecker so distasteful, and the distaste compounds as the years pry his sensibilities farther from acceptable standards of being. And so in its distance the whole town cultivates his unpleasantness, allows it to flourish. Lark tries to remember the last time he wasn't either bartering with Wrecker, or nodding and smiling his way through some rant about the finer points of vintage pornography, waiting to rush away at such speed that he'd leave a lingering cartoon cloud in the place he'd just been. When Lark invokes *community,* is it not partially his responsibility to help steer lost causes like Wrecker onto tracks that might allow them to find their footing? When Wrecker tosses out dreadful provocations, is that not partially down to everyone turning a blind eye to his serious needs for so long that—

Lights come up in tent fourteen, silencing Lark's inner voice. Wrecker stands before them holding two strands of holiday lights, joining them between his closed fists. The soft white globes hang from the struts of the tent.

Wrecker is completely naked and hairless as a grub. The crown of his bald head nearly reaches the underside of the tent. His erect penis juts from the shadowed folds of his crotch. His sunken eyes slide from Lark to Krupp, who's brandishing a long, dull, useless fencing sword.

Wrecker grins. "Let there be light."

In his headlong, jangling rush of fear, Lark wonders how the man could possibly be this far gone. Just this morning Wrecker was his usual unpleasant self behind the scuffed Plexiglas of his booth, capable of acting normal enough to sell rustic tchotchkes to tourists.

Lark glances over as Krupp mimics a Hollywood fighting stance, fencing sword en garde. Wrecker ought to appreciate that, at least. Behind Krupp are racks and shelves crammed with all manner of blades, most of them rusty and dull. There are even some of the infamous knives he recognizes from his short-lived direct-sales stint in high school.

Wrecker drops the strands of lights. He raises his arms, elbows bent and palms up, and basks in some form of glory only he can see. He closes his eyes. His erection persists.

"Lark," Krupp hisses, counting on Wrecker being in another world, "can we crawl underneath?" He indicates the place where the tent canvas meets the earth.

Lark eyes the swords. "Or we could just cut a new hole."

Wrecker opens his eyes. "The walls of this place are steel."

"Um," Krupp says. "Okay." He tosses away the fencing sword and selects a machete. Then he heads for the side of the tent, moving between racks of charred bits of metal that look scavenged from a bad car accident.

He plunges the machete through the canvas. It pierces the side of the tent with no resistance. Krupp begins to slice a vertical seam.

Wrecker looks puzzled for a moment. Then, without a word, he lowers his shoulders and slips into the skin of the Division One linebacker prospect of two decades ago. Before Lark can react, Wrecker barrels straight at Krupp. His bare feet kick up clumps of earth.

In that moment, Lark is struck by the memory of Wrecker's given name, his pre-Wrecker identity.

"Benjamin!" Lark screams. "Enough!"

Why did he think this would be some kind of magic word that could stop the juggernaut in his tracks? It has no effect. Benjamin doesn't exist. Wrecker moves shockingly fast.

Krupp, having never stabbed a living thing before, reflexively tosses the machete away—even facing down Wrecker, the instinctive urge to *not be a killer* outweighs self-preservation.

Lark has taken no more than two steps when Wrecker collides with Krupp. It's remarkably fluid—both of them off their feet, frozen at their midair peak before Wrecker's momentum carries them both even farther. His massive shoulder, as big as Lark's head, is buried in Krupp's belly. Krupp's skinny limbs are flung out straight, zombie-like, as he's slammed into the dirt. Metal clatters. Holiday lights blink.

Lark is upon them a moment later, though he has no idea what to do. Wrecker's obscenely smooth and muscular ass is oddly square. Krupp's screams are muted by all that flesh he's buried under.

"Let him go!" Lark says. He has a brief vision of driving a sword straight down through Wrecker's lower back, pinning both of them to the earth like a speared triangle of club sandwich.

Pressure builds in his head. Without thinking, Lark grabs the hilt of a long straight knife encrusted with inlays of chipped and soiled bone. "I'm dead serious, Wrecker. Get up now."

With surprising elegance, Wrecker drives a fist into the dirt and heaves himself to his feet. At the same time, he drags Krupp upright by the neck, then lifts him off the ground. Krupp's feet scissor-kick in the air, a blur of dirty white Converse. Krupp claws at the meaty fingers wrapped like constrictors around his throat. His face is the color of a plum, his eyes bulge.

The cats mewl and howl and cry.

Lark brandishes the knife, its grip slick in his palm, and moves so that the blade is a foot from Wrecker's neck, held out straight. If he were to lean forward, it would plunge into his jugular. He remembers that old hard-boiled maxim, *Don't point a gun at someone unless you're prepared to shoot*, and wonders if it applies to knives, because he is decidedly not ready.

"I am not joking, Wrecker, put him down now or I will fucking cut you."

There's a moment when everyone pauses—even Krupp's legs quit their frantic kicking—and Lark wonders what Wrecker will do, and what he will do in return. What the cause and effect of this moment will be, and how that will ripple out to Betsy's ordeal.

The *Choose Your Own Adventure* version of this results in death, as all choices do, eventually.

To Lark's immense relief, Wrecker opens his hand. Krupp falls to the ground and crumples up fetally, gasping for air. Lark tosses the knife aside and goes to his friend. Down on his knees, he puts his hands on Krupp's bony body, unsure of what to do, or how to help him take in more air.

"I'm not dreaming," Wrecker says.

Lark is vaguely aware of Wrecker sitting down on a workbench, his penis gone flaccid. "I'm not dreaming," he says again.

"I'm good, I'm good," Krupp rasps out. He runs a tender hand along the underside of his jaw, the bone that rested upon Wrecker's hand and propped up all 145 pounds of him in midair. "That feels bad," he croaks.

Lark takes a look. "How bad?"

"I don't think anything's broken." Krupp sits up, sucks in a few breaths. "I'll live." He winces, places a hand just below his heart, by the Danzig devil skull logo's horn. Lark, riding a delayed adrenaline surge, can't stop his eyes from darting around. There's the bone-encrusted blade, the bruise already blooming on Krupp's twiggy neck, Wrecker sagging on the workbench, thousand-yard-staring out beyond the tent, the fence, the town itself, into some world known only to his haywire neurons.

"You were right," Lark says. "Nothing's ever going to be the same."

He helps Krupp to his feet and picks up the bone-encrusted blade, figuring it's as good as anything else for *The Insomniack*. He keeps an eye on Wrecker stewing in his disbelief, radiating sour heat. He wonders what he would have done, had Wrecker maintained his death grip on Krupp's neck. Run him through with the blade?

Talk about no going back. The tent spattered with arterial spray. Forever a killer. The weight of that. It's so easy to suspend your disbelief for characters in movies. The everyman pushed to the edge. A ninety-minute arc of vengeance and impulse. But what happens afterward? How does somebody go about their business after killing? How could you sit and listen to music, or watch a movie, or run to the gas station for an Almond Joy and a Dr Pepper, ever again?

Lark and Krupp, supporting each other, head for the edge of the tent, just as a cat slinks in.

Behind them, Wrecker mutters something.

"What's that?" Lark turns.

Wrecker makes no move to meet his eyes. "I don't ever want to see you again."

"Yeah, well. It's a small town."

11

The Backbone in the hour before dawn is a hub of peculiar memories. Lark and Krupp at sixteen, orbiting their first midsummer kegger with juniors and seniors and townie lifers in their twenties. Plunging headlong into the firelit chaos, where Krupp lost a flip-flop and Lark, shirtless and grinning, shotgunned his first beer.

Lark at seventeen on a late-March night like this one, parked high up in the pines with Kara McGee, who'd go on to co-found a dating app, get pushed out by the board, create another one, cash out, and retire at thirty-four to an estate in Napa where one of Lark's wire-and-wood figures now looms over her back gate—a sculpture he called, cheekily, *The Kiss*, which she never acknowledged as an inside joke but paid handsomely for.

Now, two decades later, Lark and Krupp drag the last item out of the truck's flatbed, down the dirt trail made by years of teenage feet, and out onto a clearing at the cliff's edge. The stars in the night sky are muted by a dawn they can't yet see.

"Can I ask you something?" Krupp strains to keep hold of his end of the sink, pastel drywall still clinging to the porcelain, as they emerge from the last of the evergreens. It's going to be a clear dawn, Lark thinks. They set down the sink at the edge of their pile of stolen scrap.

"You don't have to ask if you can ask me," Lark says. "You can just ask me." He wipes his palms on his Canada Goose.

"Would you have really stabbed Wrecker?" Krupp's voice is hoarse. Lark wishes he'd quit talking—every word's obviously painful coming from his damaged throat. He wonders about his friend's rib cage, too—Krupp hit the ground with at least three hundred pounds crashing down on him.

Lark gazes out at the sheer cliffs across the dry gorge.

He thinks of Van Leeman's last moments, and that timeless local joke: There are no falls in Wofford Falls.

"I wasn't going to stand there and let him choke you," Lark says, and in the silence that follows they both know that's not quite an answer.

"I'm glad you didn't have to," Krupp says.

"Me too." There's movement atop the cliffs across the chasm, some forest critter scrambling along the edge of the tree line.

"His dick was weird, huh," Krupp says.

"I guess all dicks are weird in situations like that."

"Can I ask you something else?" The light from Krupp's phone illuminates the open psalter cradled in his left hand.

"Again, just fire away."

"This next part of the sculpture—"

"—*The Worm & the Dogsbody*—"

"—how the hell are we going to do that? I mean, stabbing Wrecker would have been small potatoes compared with what we'll have to do for that one."

Lark eyes the scattered material spread along the rocks and patches of scrub grass. Something like despair wells up—a tidal wave far out to sea, gathering strength from the epic undertow. He feels it now between his feet, humming in the ancient igneous core beneath Wofford Falls. He raises his eyes to the night sky and considers saying a prayer but does not. Who would listen?

"I don't know," he admits. "Let's just get this part done."

"I think this is all you now," Krupp says, gesturing like a museum guide. "The artist is present."

They make one more quick trip to the truck for the best portable studio Lark could throw together in a hurry: flame-resistant gloves, leather apron, portable welding kit with eleven-amp heat gun, Sterno to heat the "tallow," safety glasses, various clamps and tongs, hammers and nails, pliers and snippers and rasps and chisels and bankers and grinders.

Halligan bar and torque wrench, because fuck you.

Back in the clearing, Lark feels like a marathoner going through his pre-race prep. What's second nature in his home studio now has to be applied to a new place. It's like trying to sleep in a strange bed in some-one's guest room—you have to relearn the basics before it takes hold. Quietly, he goes to work. Krupp trails Lark with the flashlight, antici-pating his movements. In unspoken agreement they select a mostly flat spot at the edge of an outcrop, a bald spot on the Backbone between the jagged vertebrae of its rockiest points. Lark sets up the Sterno and the camp stove. Krupp places the first canister of pilfered wax atop the metal grate. About twenty feet separate the materials from this outdoor "studio"—just enough distance for Lark to experience a sim-ulacrum of his process, honed over many years, of minimizing each object's personality and former function as he carries it to the assembly point.

He sets a portable Bluetooth speaker upon a flat-topped rock and cranks up Shostakovich. What is it about Russian dissonance that gets his juices flowing? The strains of the opening largo seem to spike out from the speaker, nimbly casting themselves like doomed lemmings over the side of the Backbone, toward the dry creekbed far below, to splinter into a million violin skronks.

With the aid of Krupp's light, Lark consults the psalter for one last look at *The Insomniack* before he frees himself from the book to create on his own terms. This, surely, is why he's been selected for the task. If the silent hymns were meant to be prescriptive blueprints for any old pair of hands, then Gumley himself could have thrown it together. But therein lies the difference between construction and creation. Lark would rather sever his own limbs than publicly discuss what makes him an artist—it took him a solid decade to even self-apply the term without feeling like his face was on fire—but it would be self-effacing

to the point of obnoxiousness to deny that he is one. Gumley's employers didn't abduct Betsy to coerce him into sculpting because they
wanted a builder. Gumley's final edict was *Make it your own.*

Lark closes the book. The framework for the awful things to come
is a series of afflictions and cures. He imagines plague doctors in the
old country descending upon Van Leeman's Flemish smear of a town,
smoke curling from pyres where the infected corpses burn. Birdlike
masks stuffed with herbs to keep the stench at bay. A trio of robed
doctors crossing a lonely moor beneath an ashen sky, approaching yet
another town, another weary trudge through a sea of the dead and
hopeless. The strains of Shostakovich drive him to lay the bricks, one
by one, dripping "tallow" as a binding agent. He blanks his mind as
best he can, relegating the psalter's diagrams to a free-floating, non-
bothersome presence—a framework that hovers over the proceedings
without guiding his work with too heavy an eighteenth-century hand.

What does creep in is guilt. The fear that, deep down, it reflects
poorly on his character that he's actually able to get into a rhythm
here. The enjoyment he derives from the patterns only he can see. Even
working under duress to save his sister's life, he can't help but surrender
to the pressure that always seems to gather between his eyes, as if the
impulse to create is massing in his frontal lobe and pushing through
the flesh of his forehead. A giddiness he associates with riding the mall
escalator as a child, watching the crawling stairs eat themselves.

The wax hardens in great undignified globs, oozing from between
bricks placed in defiance of the notion of a wall. Lark automatically
begins to inhabit the growing sense of deconstruction frozen in time
he will use to put his stamp on *The Insomniack.* This motif grabs him by
the lapels and drags him forward, solidifying itself like so much cooled
wax. He's using Van Leeman's conceptual backbone for a springboard
here: this notion of cause and effect, affliction and remedy, turned
inside out. It's molecular gastronomy—the reverse-soup where the
broth is disintegrated noodles and the chicken stock given density.
With Krupp's help he sets the radiator on the brick foundation to look
like it might have sprouted that way organically.

Next they take sledgehammers and bash the child's coffin to smith-
ereens. He fires up his welding gun and scars the lacquered wood,
scorches the interior cushion. Without consulting the book, he tries to
remember Van Leeman's careful description of his process—is there
any kind of thematic progression in the order of materials used? Lark
wonders if he's in for a cruel reckoning, having perhaps paid attention
to the wrong elements of Van Leeman's breathless descriptions. He has
to assume that if there was to be a more one-to-one relationship with
the psalter, Gumley would have warned him not to stray too far. Either
way, there's no going back now. With practiced sloppiness he drives
eight-inch casing nails through the cushion and sides of the coffin.
Thus spiked and remade, his reverse coffin-parts are scattered about
the radiator like gifts beneath a Christmas tree.

A parabola of light spreads across the sky from the east like a fridge
door cracked open in the dark. Lark answers with his welding gun,
that sliver of deadly blue heat that's just now joining the bed frame to
the disassembled lathe—old, rounded, and cantilevered bits of steel
machinery that soften under the attack of the arc-flare. The trees that
run the ridges of the Backbone are alive with blue jays and robins and
chickadees, sharp little chirps contrapuntal to the grinding lows of
the symphony. A hint of what's to come troubles his thoughts—the
squishy, writhing matter he'll have to weld to this unwieldy frame—
and he pushes it aside. There is too much still to accomplish. He's a
sweaty mess beneath his leather apron. Krupp visits the edge of the
outcrop and looks down for a long time. When he rejoins Lark at the
half-finished *Insomniack*, he seems pensive and sad, idly rubbing his
throat, where it's now light enough to see the imprint of Wrecker's
massive hand.

Lark releases the trigger and the flame vanishes. He lifts up his safety
goggles and takes stock of what he's done. In accordance with the mood
of the psalter and Van Leeman's mad pronouncements, it is very much
taking the shape of something that feels both inevitable and insane.

Krupp thumbs through the psalter, reading by the light of the
morning. " 'Be not fearful of putting forth the ignominious for all to

see. This silent hymn cannot fulfill its purpose with timidity.' " Krupp regards the sculpture in progress. "I definitely wouldn't call this timid."

Lark finds that he cannot speak. All shame cast aside, he's in thrall to the process. He takes the torque wrench to the typewriter and soon the keys are scattered at his feet. Krupp melts down more candles and Lark sticks the keys in wax poured into the sink. He joins sink to radiator to bed frame with tough strips of leather he brought from home. He twists wire around the vise, making of it a thorny crown. While he contemplates the pan and the fire extinguisher, a new hum fills the sky. Lark and Krupp turn in time to see a sleek little drone rise above the tree line. Its four turreted rotors are a blur in the dawn as it swoops down and then pauses in midair to regard the sculpture.

Lark thinks of the watchers at the other end of the drone's camera, examining his progress. There is pure intention in the way the drone hovers like a floating eye, taking him in dispassionately. An extension of Gumley's maddening, businesslike calm to remind him that he's playing a part in a *transaction*.

He's never once worked with anyone looking over his shoulder. Even Betsy, who pops in and out of his studio, does so in a way that makes it feel like she's just in there looking for a misplaced palette knife.

He picks up the fire extinguisher and considers heaving it at the drone, but gives the floating camera the finger instead. Krupp, to his satisfaction, follows his lead. They stand like this for a moment, a good ten-second *fuck you*, and then Lark turns back to *The Insomniack*. There's a moment of reentry when he struggles to regain the flow state. Interruptions have happened before, of course. And every time, he fears there will be a seam—an obvious line of demarcation in the work, a slipping of technique that will drag the whole piece down into mediocrity. This fear persists despite hundreds of finished pieces offering no indication of a point where the pizza guy came, or Lark simply quit, sick of staring at his work.

It's something only Betsy would understand. He quells a surge of anger. Then he flips down his safety goggles and begins joining fire extinguisher to radiator with a simple edge joint so that it protrudes like a cannon. *The Insomniack* has taken on a vaguely martial air, a war-like quality that he finds fitting, somehow. His tired mind links it with Shostakovich and the brutality of the eastern front. There's a new string quartet playing now, some late-period opus filled with dirge-like drips of sad viola. The morning light sharpens the edges of the sculpture. His agency in the shaping of the piece feels amplified. He has nearly forgotten the diagrams in the psalter. The book itself seems to him now like the figment of some half-forgotten dream.

He is stunned to find that he's *already* incorporated the cast-iron pan, though he managed to alter its properties somehow.

"Krupp, do you remember this?" He indicates the handle of the pan, poking out from between fragments of the child's coffin. It's encased in hardened wax from a red votive. When Krupp doesn't answer, Lark turns—and finds him sleeping in the lee of the outcrop, where it curls inward like a half-pipe. He's hugging his knees to his sunken chest, mouth slack, a strand of drool connecting his face with his jeans.

Lark takes off his leather apron and drapes it over Krupp's body. Krupp stirs, mutters a word or two. The drool strand breaks and falls away. Then Lark retreats to the empty expanse where they'd gathered material. There's only one item left: the bone-encrusted knife he'd held to Wrecker's throat. He pulls off his heat-resistant gloves and picks it up. With a glance at the hovering drone and a quick, absurd calculation—what are the chances he could hit it with the blade from here?—he paces around *The Insomniack*, taking in what he's wrought in the full light of day. He reminds himself that it's unfinished—there's an unwelcome, queasy jolt as he remembers *The Worm & the Dogsbody* and all that comes later—but there's still the tentative sense of accomplishment.

It's not satisfaction, exactly. Even now, on this quick survey, his inner critic picks out flaws. He's willing to concede this much: There's a welcome attitude to the piece. If he were to adopt the tone of the *Art Forum* editorial board, he'd begin to describe it in terms of its energy. Punkish, or at least post-. Compositional rigor bursting through slapdash atmosphere. Immersive world-building, dream logic, intrinsic language.

He shakes his head. Whatever. It looks pretty fucking righteous, especially perched on this forlorn outcrop. There's a teetering-on-the-edge feeling, a jazz fusion group playing in 7/4 about to fall to pieces before the drummer pulls it back together. Maybe, he thinks, Van Leeman was onto something. Maybe the whole thing isn't so crazy after all. Cheers, you old Flemish fuck. Around and around the sculpture he stalks, playing the part of the careful warrior, building feints and jabs into an architecture of disguise to mask the moment when he moves in for the kill. He eyes the drone. He wants Gumley to see this. There! Where the bed frame meets the radiator at a scrap of child's coffin. He rams the blade down into the depths of the sculpture. There's a shriek of metal on metal, an ache that numbs his wrist, and he releases the grip. The blade's hilt glints in the morning light. The sword, driven home, quivers, then stops.

The Insomniack is finished.

The drone swoops down from the tree line and glides over the sculpture. He expects it to bob and weave and inspect his work, but instead it keeps on going. Lark turns to follow its path as it soars out over the cliff's edge and buzzes across the chasm, heading for the sheer granite rock walls. The newly risen sun hits his eyes. Just before he turns away, something bright glints with kaleidoscopic pixels at the top of the eroded channel. He shields his eyes, nearly losing the sudden sparkle all in that brightness.

"Krupp!" he says. "Wake up!"

But Krupp doesn't stir, and Lark is left staring with burning eyes into the dawning of a new day as *The Insomniack* settles in behind him. The light eats the drone, and Lark wonders if his mind is playing tricks, or if there's really—

Museum Interlude

—"Water," Helena says as she taps a gorgeously manicured nail against a curved screen the size of the damn wall. Then she says it again, really putting her tongue into it, rolling the word around in her mouth, savoring it like I've seen her do with the choicest Wagyu from the Belmonts' free-range cattle ranch and luxury spa retreat on three hundred pristine Wyoming acres: "*Water.*"

Griffin leans back in his chair and puts his hands behind his head. His pits are sweaty, knees weak, Mom's spaghetti, et cetera. He tried to have his glands rerouted last year but the procedure was only a partial success. From what I gather he's always been a sweaty guy.

"Water indeed," he says. There's a hushed kind of theatrical awe in his voice.

This isn't the screening room where I watched them watch *Cruel Intentions* with icky giddiness, along with a thousand other movies. That room, to be perfectly frank, kicks ass. Credit where credit's due. It's got that TV-set coziness of a sunken living room from the *Mad Men* era, where you'd listen to records with your hip downtown pals and coo at your mistress. But instead of a bunch of fine old midcentury relics, they've got these convertible beds set up, like bigger versions of what regular rich people get to lounge in on international first-class, which I got to fly exactly once, to London, to meet an A&R guy who had that affliction common to forty-something married dudes, where his eyes are magnetically repelled by your eyes and so—for medical reasons no doubt!—can only see as high as breast level. Poor *Antony*. It must be so difficult to watch movies that way. If only he had access to the Belmonts' screening boudoir, he could prop himself on a bedlike thing and rest his eyes.

The room we're in now—the Belmonts literally *in*, me in my own existence-adjacent way—is more bunker-ish and makes me want to use words like *protocol* and *tactical* and *defcon*. Like I'm on a CBS drama about a Team of Experts, and I'm the girl who tells the socially awkward computer hottie to *enhance*. This room is shoved down in the deepest part of the compound. The walls are some kind of *polymer* (I made that up, I don't know what they are, but they look like they serve a purpose, insulation or noise-canceling or signal-blocking). The Belmonts have had, over the years, a total of three elevators to this hockey-puck-shaped war room. The first one went absolutely fucking bonkers a few years after I got stuck here. Those were the initial Leif Days, when every week was a different kind of chaos. Leif was almost poetic justice for Griffin and Helena. It would've made a good CBS drama, actually—*What happens when the person you abduct is just as psychotic as you are?* Hijinks ensue! Hijinks that the khaki pants mafia is still picking up the pieces of, all these years later. Every now and then one of those buttoned-up turds will be doing maintenance on the old residence warren where they stuck Leif for a while, and the turd in question will emerge like six months later with nubs instead of fingers and a mouth that chomps involuntarily on his bloody lips 24/7. Gumley shot the last guy in the head like he was a sick dog in a tragic kid's story from 1892. He cried when he got down on his knees, then he laughed and laughed, and spoke words that didn't make sense, then he died facedown and his legs did a little fishy flop before he was still.

Speaking of Gumley, aka King Douche, he's here now too. He was hovering at the back of the room, except now he's moving up closer to the screen, sharing in Griffin's awe. He's even making a bug-eyed face. The giant curved monitor is broken up into a grid around the outer edges that frames one big display in the middle. The little boxes in the grid keep tabs on different parts of the compound—some J-horror ghost hitchy movement in the dim installation wing, nothing much going on in the industrial kitchen, and there *you* are, lady, busy as a bee in your underground hangar—and the big square display in the middle is what I take to be a drone's-eye view.

Helena sips from a skinny glass and takes a step back so she can see the whole screen at once. She's in head-to-toe Fendi loungewear. I say *toe* because each one has a little toe-condom, a comfy little shoe of its own, a thousand-dollar lounge thimble.

I'm a little late to this party, but I got here in time to see the pretty scenery. Looks like a nice morning out there. I was always a morning person, not because of the light or the quiet, but because my anxiety liked to yank me up out of sleep with a racing mind. It's a great way to start the day, your dumb brain screaming at you that you're a piece of shit, that other singers are working twice as hard, that you could have hit the gym by now, that you could write one song per day if you were more dedicated, that you're just wasting time all the time. Some crippling recrimination with your morning latte, THANKS BRAIN, now fuck off. Except it never does fuck off, not really.

Not even when you're dead.

"It's giving me goose bumps," Helena says.

"Mm," Griffin says. "It's a *start*, H. There's still a long way to go."

She lays a hand on his shoulder. "Lemme just…take it in."

Helena's blissed out on one of her more chill cocktails, and the mild downer effect gives her voice an even squishier timbre. I take it in right along with her. The drone hovers just above the edge of a cliff, recording a wide shot of the rock face across the way. There's a grand vertical canyon cut deep into the cliffside. At the top of it, like somebody stuck a faucet there and turned it on, is a trickle of water. If I still got thirsty it would make me thirsty, the way it sparkles in the morning light. It's beer commercial water, *Tap the Rockies, cold-filtered.*

"Get us closer," Griffin says. I notice that Gumley's holding what looks like a video game controller. He pushes forward on an analog stick. The drone jets across the chasm, and the effect is perfectly high-def and fluid. I assume it's a very nice drone.

Now it's like we're hovering six inches from the source of the water. I'd expected to see a river that hits the edge of the cliff and takes a flying leap off into wave-crashing ecstasy and a steep foamy drop. But there is no river, not as far as I can tell. It's like the stream is pouring right out of the cliffside itself, like there was a million gallons in a tank just behind the rock face, and somebody punched a hole in it like a giant Capri Sun. Ah, what I wouldn't give to hold that little foil breast-implant pouch in my hand and struggle to pop in the straw. It's the little things, lady, trust me. I hate to be one of those Bed Bath & Beyond wall hangings, LIVE LAUGH LOVE and all that, so I won't hit you with platitudes about appreciating what you've got, but you should appreciate what you've got. Not presently, of course, since what you've got is a giant underground hangar they stuck you in, but I mean afterward, when I get you back to your life, which I'm working on, or at least thinking about, anxiously.

Getting zapped with nostalgia for the act of inserting a straw into a Capri Sun and at the same time feeling regret that I didn't Appreciate It More is just another way my brain likes to be a total dick. If I could somehow access Younger Alive Me at the precise moment she's struggling to get the straw in without spraying herself in the face with sugar-juice, and implore her like the ghost of Christmas Future to CHERISH THIS PRECIOUS MOMENT, Younger Alive Me would be like, *Fuck off you hag, I'm trying to get this straw into this thing, why do they make it SO HARD.*

Griffin rises slowly out of his chair, now fully in the grips of awe. He places a palm against the curved screen. Reverent, loving. "The return of the falls," he says. "The first harbinger."

"It's beautiful," Helena says dreamily, "isn't it?"

I gravitate closer, so I can press my non-face right up against the glass. Griffin, mesmerized, hums tunelessly to himself, and blissed-out Helena forgets to be annoyed with him. Gumley stands at attention with his eyes on the screen and a totally unreadable expression on his face.

"So strange, to work toward something for several lifetimes, and then to see it actually start to happen." I swear his eyes are getting misty. "I confess, there were times when I lost faith."

"Kind of casts a new light on last year's *Art Forum* piece about Peter Larkin, if you ask me." Helena speaks in a lilt that I would die for if I wasn't already, you know.

"That was a somewhat tepid appraisal of his recent work, if I remember correctly."

"It was Morgandorff's byline. Tepid is his default, and only, setting."

"Not strictly true, at times he ascends to slight moralistic scolding. It's like they found a Puritan to be an art critic as a joke, and when nobody got the joke, he became an actual critic."

"You rehearsed that." Helena sips her drink and licks her lips.

I can confirm that Griffin does, in fact, rehearse lines he's going to use in conversation with his sister. I've also seen him practice various smiles in front of the million-pound mirror they had shipped over from Versailles. And new ways of holding his hands at his sides when he walks. Again, you would think abnormally long lifetimes would severely iron out the self-conscious tics we all have, but I suppose it can work the other way too, make you get deeper inside your head about the way you carry yourself.

"You know what?" Griffin says, tapping two fingers against the glass in an off-kilter rhythm then pulling his hand away from the screen. "I think I'm going to buy *Art Forum*, fire the editorial staff, and turn the print edition into one big advertorial." He pauses. "*Quarterly.*"

"Morgandorff reminds me of the vicious scolds who came after Father," Helena says, her soft eyes lost in the past. The glow from the high-def screen flickers across her face.

"I'll deal with him separately," Griffin says.

"What if he were compelled to write longform critical pieces analyzing his own slow and methodical dismantling." Helena's voice is like a woodwind in a magical forest clearing, some musical interlude in a modern version of *A Midsummer's Night's Dream*.

"Eh," Griffin says. "Been done."

"There are no wrong answers in brainstorming."

"You can pull back," Griffin calls to the room at large. "We've seen enough for now."

Gumley strides forward, controller in hand. The view on the screen slides to the right as the drone turns in midair. The little copter buzzes back across the empty space between the two cliffs and for a second my non-stomach drops. I was never a fan of heights. I went out on a first date with a session bassist one time and he took me to an outdoor rock climbing wall, like we were on a second-tier dating show being forced to do something "active" instead of having two drinks and quickly realizing that we have no chemistry except for some vague contempt for each other like normal people. I got about three feet off the ground before my fight or flight kicked in and I clung like a splayed cat to the side of the rock wall, and I thought to myself, *Why am I on a date with a session bassist?* We never went on a second date, but he ended up playing on *Canary* and laid down his part in one rock-solid take, so there's that.

"Wave to Peter," Griffin says.

The drone swoops over a rocky ledge, and I catch a glimpse of a very odd scene. One guy—Peter Larkin, I presume—is standing over another guy. This second guy might be dead. Or sleeping.

Griffin taps the sleeper's face. "Who's that?"

Gumley clears his throat. "Wayne Krupp Junior. Peter Larkin's best friend since fourth grade. Son of the owner of a hardware store in Wofford Falls. Undiagnosed narcoleptic. Functioning alcoholic. Well-liked in town, if viewed as a bit of a blabbermouth. Never married. Currently resides at—"

"Okay, Brandt, thank you," Helena says. There's a moment of silence I can only describe as mildly uncomfortable, a pause that might be pregnant, though I'm never sure exactly what that means. The Belmonts glance at each other. Finally, it's Griffin who turns to King Douche.

"I guess we're both just a little bit confused, here, Brandt. This undertaking is for Peter Larkin *alone* to complete. Did you make that clear?"

Brandt gazes back placidly. "You told me to emphasize the fact that he would need to fight his natural inclination to call the police."

"I said *underscore*," Griffin says. "*No police* is kind of a given, though, right? Table stakes, for pretty much everything we do?"

Helena drains her glass and swipes the back of her hand across her mouth and hands the empty glass to Gumley. Then she giggles. "Peter Larkin brought a friend. A little pal. A *buddy*."

"If I was supposed to imply to Larkin that he had to do this completely solo," Gumley says, "then I missed that."

"So he could be bringing any number of pals and buddies along for the ride."

"Wayne Krupp's not a cop," Gumley points out. "He's mostly just a jackass, from what I can tell."

Griffin rubs his eyes and turns to his sister. "Am I too literal? Is that a problem with the way I communicate?"

"Your communication problems are...kaleidoscopic," Helena says. "It's too much to unpack for right now. Too much!" She's practically swooning at the screen. "*Look* at it."

A few feet away from the two guys on the cliff's edge is what looks like a pile of junk, but as the drone gets closer it pulls itself together before my eyes—like it's really moving, even though I know it's not—into one of those found-object sculptures. The drone hovers over it for a moment, and it gives me a shiver.

"*The Insomniack*," Griffin intones with semi-hilarious reverence.

The three of us take it in.

It shouldn't be frightening, or even all that odd—it's just a bunch of stuff that, taken on its own, isn't very scary. I see a bed frame, a radiator, a sink. Maybe a fire extinguisher? Nice pop of color, there. It's the stuff of anybody's apartment, anybody's life. Or death—I think I caught pieces of a coffin in there too. It's the way they're combined and reshaped into something new. Created, not made—same feeling I got from that new sculpture I checked out in the gallery.

"I think Larkin's understanding of his task is almost intrinsic," Griffin says. He's getting hyped. "I mean, the fact that this is only the first of three stages. This piece has a complete arc to it that also seems to exist within the framework of something larger."

"It's act one," Helena says. She's got that slightly husky, I'm-high-and-this-is-very-deep vocal thing going on. "In narrative terms." With the drone paused on a bird's-eye view of the sculpture, Helena runs her finger along the bricks at its base. They've been stacked at odd angles. Hardened wax is captured oozing out from between them like congealed cheese. "You can see how everything's leading into everything else, compositionally, but it still feels like a..." She trails off with her finger on the bed frame, which connects the bricks with an old-school radiator in a way that looks weirdly seamless.

"Pedestal," Griffin suggests. "Platform?"

I can see what the Belmonts are getting at. The sculpture is its own thing, but it doesn't yet contain another world. Its boundaries are undecided, or maybe just unmapped, like the boundaries of the museum. Everything juts out of everything else in a way that almost makes it seem half destroyed, like a replica of a—

"*Ruin,*" Helena says. I shiver. Sometimes the borders between us get fuzzy and she speaks with my voice. I've been here too long. "That's what's so perfect about it. That's why it succeeds where everyone else has failed. It's like Larkin visualized it in reverse, whether he meant to or not. He deconstructed as he worked. A chess game."

The bricks and the twisted bed frame and the radiator form a sort of framework for the pieces of a disassembled coffin. Struts and supports to nothing at all rise from the base. It could be the collage assembly of some grand table for a whimsical feasting hall. Massive nails bristle. Typewriter keys sparkle in the morning sun.

"It's waiting for more of itself," Griffin says.

So much of what they say is one big eye-roll, but I see what they're getting at with this sculpture. Bits of a ragged tarp blow in the wind. Purposeful tatters can be so cringe-inducing, but here they work. They make it sadder than it ought to be.

"It itches in the back of my mind," Helena says. "It's connected to something."

"Father?"

"Something he dreamed up, seeing it come to life." She rubs the back of her head. "It makes my spine warm."

I know what she means. *It's connected to something.* The way the morning light hits the sculpture and sort of gets channeled down all these metal bits and into the ground—takes me back to the corner booth at the Sip 'n' Sup diner in my hometown of good old Hart Springs. They had one of those old-fashioned mini-jukeboxes in every booth, but who has actual quarters on them ever? So all I did was flip through it with my cousins, and if something sounded interesting we'd just stream it. I used to meet my cousins, Sheena and Allie, there every Thursday. It was the first place I went the day I got my license. I picked them up in my mama's Buick LeSabre, you ever drive one of those? It's like steering a boat down the street. It feels like you're about to sideswipe every mailbox. You have to pull over to the shoulder to let other cars through. We'd get to the corner booth right after school and camp out there till dinner. Vanilla Cokes and disco fries and the Sip 'n' Sup's special jalapeño poppers, which were definitely courtesy of jolly old Sysco (America's Restaurant!) but were somehow magically delicious in that booth. *Get yer grubby hands off that last popper, Sheena.* I think I must have a special sensitivity to light because what I remember now is the way afternoon turned to nighttime and the shadows slid from the wooden-slat blinds across the vinyl seats and Allie's crop top while the poppers disappeared and the Vanilla Cokes flowed and the poor old lobsters moved slowly around their big water tank by the door of the diner, claws rubber-banded, silent desperation in the way they crawled back and forth over each other. It wasn't so much that we were young and free in the way that people like to romanticize that shit, like we have our Whole Lives Ahead of Us (although that was true for Sheena and Allie, at least). Our exhilaration wasn't just a product of the endless soda refills and the freedom of having a driver's license. It was in the way the afternoon crept on and we hunkered together in our corner-booth bubble, alone together. Stacking the sugar packets, dragging fries through ketchup, asking for more clam chowder and oyster crackers, hold the chowder. There was, back then, a breaking-away from the Hart Springs we knew before we knew anything else or had been anywhere else. Every Thursday was like fifty coming-of-age tales rolled into an afternoon in a diner booth. We navigated a dozen narrative arcs at once and cracked our character development open for each other to see. And what I'll always remember is that light, changing to dusky beer-colored stripes in the winter, and lemony sun in spring, as the sugar packets scattered across the Formica table in disarray and the waitress, increasingly irritated, quit refilling the sodas. I'll always remember the day Sheena told us she'd fucked Jackson Kemper too, but that's not as poetic as the afternoon light trapping our most hopeful years in a booth-shaped memory globe.

The drone moves toward the forest beyond the cliffs and the sculpture disappears from view. But the sculpture sticks in my mind because it filters light in the same way as the diner booth. It made it feel like it meant more than it actually did. It didn't scoff at your melodrama—it was there to facilitate. Light you wish you could see again. Thanks to that weird sculpture, I think I just did.

The art I consider mostly "good," I've learned in the years I've been cooped up in here with nothing to do but look at art, latches onto your existing thought patterns and reconditions them without changing what those thought patterns already do to your emotions. Like, this found-object sculpture somehow glommed onto the memory of diner light and wrenched it into this moment without taking any of its power as a treasured sense-memory away from me. Now it moves in two directions instead of one. Could it do that for everybody? I have no idea. There's no reason to assume it's imbued with any more strange power than it would be if some kid nailed a bunch of junk together and called it a sculpture. All I know is that I've never really felt this way about the other sculptures the Belmonts have owned over the years.

"And we haven't even gotten to the good part yet," Helena says.

"Well. That was pretty good."

"I mean the way he's working in conjunction with his sister. The intangibles of all this."

Sister. That's gotta be you, lady.

"The acts of creation Father intended for *us*," Griffin says quietly. There's another bun-in-the-oven pause. I've so rarely heard them speak of this, and I only know the barest sketch of what they mean. This whole, um, paradigm—a sculptor and a painter, working together on the crazy shit Marius Van Leeman laid out a few hundred years ago— was intended for Griffin and Helena. Makes sense—here you go, kids, a blueprint to follow. Except they could never pull it off. This is all way before my time (and, like, before Abraham Lincoln's time), so, context clues, et cetera.

"We could have done it ourselves," Griffin says, his excitement beginning to curdle.

"With what?" Helena says. "More time? This is the way. This is the *only* way."

"You're so *accepting* of our failures," he says in mock-admiration.

"Oh, come on, Griffin." Despite being half-sozzled on whatever mind-altering compound she mixed for herself, Helena can slip into pointed articulation with the best of them. "There's nothing more use-less and ugly than festering bitterness. The reason I'm so accepting is, I look at it like this: It's not a failure, it's a *gift* to be able to realize you're not capable of a certain act of creation, and to redirect your energies into finding the ones who *are* capable of it. Mired in bitterness, we may never have found Peter and Betsy in the first place."

Betsy. So that's your name.

Helena, by the way, is completely full of shit. Except for the part about redirecting energies—I've seen her redirect her own bitterness not into the Zen-like acceptance she just preached to her brother, but into pure viciousness.

Do you know what it's like to have the flesh of your face removed while you're still alive? I do, thanks to Helena and that curved knife on the table in their sanctum. And in her eyes, before the tears and the pain and the sheer panic blurred my vision, I saw her fucking redirec-tion. She can talk the talk, and slap on her practiced veneer, but her own bitterness and failure is a white-hot supernova in the core of her being. She lets it feed on itself, mean little electrons spinning and spinning in a frenzy around the supernova, like a sword power-up in Zelda, until she's practically hovering above the plush carpets. Then she can redirect it into sadism toward her latest obsession.

Let me tell you, the worst part is the split second before the blade sinks into your skin. It's like being at the dentist, when you brace yourself for the needle, knowing you can't do anything about it—times a million. It's simply something that is happening, and you are completely dehumanized and devoid of agency. You are nothing but a thing that accepts torment, a pinned butterfly who still feels things.

I'm full of shit—the worst part is the peeling-away of your skin. I don't know if I have a high pain tolerance or what. I read that the witches they used to burn at the stake (which the Belmonts could very well have witnessed for all I know) would either die of smoke inhalation or go into such severe shock before the flames consumed them that they only suffered briefly, at the beginning. It sounds weird but you can acclimate to the feel of a blade intruding upon your body. Then, just when your racing thoughts are like, I can deal with this, I've reached a new plateau in courage and acceptance and pain tolerance and all that, every nerve ending on the underside of your skin starts burning and scorching and popping away, one by one. And the worst of all is the knowledge that there is no coming back from it.

I'll save you from what's coming, Betsy. I'll find a way.

"Let's see what she's up to, our prized muralist," Griffin says.

He leans forward and messes with a tablet computer on the desk. A new image comes up to fill the main screen, and there you are, Betsy Larkin. It's nice to put a name to your face, which I hope you get to keep.

Together, the Belmonts regard their captive. The image trembles a bit as what's left of Leif, huddled there in the darkness, tries to hold the camera steady. I wonder if you've been able to communicate with him. It. Whatever.

"*What* is she doing?" Griffin mutters.

On the screen, you're lying in what looks like a hammock. The long wires that suspend the mesh a foot above the hangar floor descend from some dark place in the high unseen ceiling. It's like a part of some elaborate staging, the mechanism in *Phantom of the Opera* that allows the phantom to soar above the audience (is that a thing that happens?).

"Napping," Helena says. "Maybe it's part of her process."

Griffin shoots her a look. "She needs to be working. She's falling behind."

He heads for the door to the underground war room.

"Are you going to make a speech? I seriously can't wait for this," Helena says, at his heels. "Like, I'm genuinely excited to see what comes out of your mouth."

"I just have to get her on track."

"Your big speech. Your halftime pep talk. Your St. Crispin's Day. Your *Braveheart* moment. Gentlemen in England now abed will think themselves accursed, et cetera."

They exit the war room while Gumley, still lurking in the shadows, comes forth to straighten the chairs and fiddle with the monitors. The Belmonts bypass the malfunctioning elevator—its entrance bricked over entirely by a construction squad from the KPM. For some reason these bricks are schoolhouse red, which clashes dreamily with the insane-asylum cinder-block aesthetic of the rest of these sub-sub-sub-basement corridors. Way down here being essentially the one place the Belmonts' ever-evolving aesthetic demands never really crept into. There are bare bulbs strung above and cold gray walls and that's pretty much it. I follow them, above and around, everywhere and nowhere. This way of being didn't exactly come naturally, after twenty-seven years of mostly walking upright on two legs. What's so hard to get used to when you first find yourself deceased and occupying a man-made space instead of some floaty blissful afterlife is the out-of-body mechanics. If you think you just drift around like a sentient balloon, or control yourself with your mind, you've got another thing coming. The very first orgasm I ever had brought on the curious sensation of the room around me getting larger and smaller. Walls expanding, pressing outward, and then closing in as I rode the waves. At first, being dead is kind of like that—overwhelming to the senses while at the same time set free in a space that doesn't make any rational sense. Because it doesn't contain you like it did before, a moment ago, when you were under the pearl-handled knife. It's like the montage scene where the astronauts in training first get acclimated to zero gravity, except I didn't have floating water droplets to drink or wonder in my eyes.

We pass the bricked-up, useless elevator. The muffled sounds of what's trapped behind the bricks leaks out into the corridor. Helena and Griffin pass by casually but I know it's gripped their minds as it still, somehow, grips mine. The lingering presence behind the bricks implants the image of a dead horse on a scaffold being lowered from a great height into a vast and lonely field. I hate it. We all pass quickly as the horse falls away. I follow them into the working elevator at the end of the hallway. Tight squeeze with three of us in here. Like I always do when I join Helena and Griffin in a small space, I attempt to make myself known to them. It's automatic by now, all the obligatory ghost shit. I try to rattle the elevator car, shake it from side to side, but it's like I'm shouldering something that absorbs me partway so that we coexist in space, rather than repel like matter should. It's maddening, even after all this time. Soft Muzak plays, Griffin's HILARIOUS little joke, "Girl from Ipanema" on a never-ending loop. At least we're in elevator two—elevator three is "Escape (The Piña Colada Song)." Nobody likes getting caught in the rain, what the fuck.

I hit them with a total banshee scream. From my perspective it's deafening. They don't react.

Griffin whistles idly. Helena closes her eyes.

I shift my presence so that it expands and contracts. I'm everywhere at once, a thousand elbows ramming the elevator's gold-leaf siding, appropriated from some art deco skyscraper in Manhattan. If there was any justice in this world or the next, they'd be cowering at the onslaught. The cacophony would be driving them mad. Their ears, eyes, and noses would be bleeding. The lights would be flickering as the madness intensifies.

Griffin sniffles and scratches his nose. "Girl from Ipanema" prances merrily across the xylophone.

I have wondered, over the years, if there are others like me. Forced, through whatever occult chicanery the Belmonts tripped ass-backward into, to stick around the site of their awful deaths. All the existential torment of an unfree soul, none of the haunting privileges. But in all my explorations of the museum, I've never stumbled upon so much as the hint of another me.

I wrap my hands around Griffin's neck. Choke the life out of him. Nothing happens.

Frustration builds. I scream, but not to scare anybody. Because it's the only thing that feels good right now.

The golden doors open. Together they step out of the elevator, and the doors shut noiselessly behind them.

We've emerged into a long gallery lit by fake candles in sconces that give off a washed-out, tentative glow. *Spoiled*, whispers the voice in my head. *Spoiled.* The floor, once pristine tiles of polished Italian marble— I remember this wing's completion—is interrupted here and there by tiles that have become *wet*. That's the only way I can describe them— seemingly at random, several dozen once-solid, horrifically expensive floor tiles have melted to a viscous marbly goo. Griffin takes Helena's hand to guide her across a maniacal hopscotch pattern of these strange new tiles. *Spoiled.* The gallery smells of wet paint gone rancid, as if it had been mixed with eggs for thickening and sat exposed for years.

Helena's footwear, some curious combination of house shoe and high heel, trails along one of the runny tiles and drags a strand of melted marble along with it.

"Shit," she says, her reaction time slowed by some internal dreaminess, the lingering effects of her cocktail.

"We'll get you another pair," Griffin says.

"There is no other pair of these," Helena says. "Why did we come this way?"

"I thought, given your state of mind, you might enjoy a visit to an old friend."

There are small square paintings hanging on the walls, some no bigger than postage stamps, surrounded by heavy ornate frames a hundred times their size. I can barely remember what happened here, who the artist in question is. The smell, as we approach the paintings, is infused with a bland chemical odor. Cheap industrial cleaning supplies. The odor of a drab office, a 1980s cubicle farm, back when you could still smoke indoors. Yellowed papers tacked to peeling walls, the never-ending hum of the giant copier, flimsy metal drawers slamming shut, burnt coffee in the break room, a water-stained popcorn ceiling. *Spoiled*, says the voice, gentle as a dandelion shedding its spores.

"Ah!" Helena says, leaning in to examine the first in the series of tiny paintings. "I haven't thought about her in a long time."

I haven't either, and now I remember why I blocked it out. Kalina Godfrey, painter of intricate miniatures of the saddest places. Not sad like cemeteries during funerals, or NICU wards, or the aftermaths of bloody battles. Sad in a way that is never dramatic, never a heartstring-tugger. Not poverty porn, either, which I've seen my share of in here, barf—and not photos of urban blight. But still done in a way that eats at your soul, though it munches at the soul with more of a nibble.

The first painting is the size of a Triscuit cracker and is enveloped by a frame of such fearsome beauty that the juxtaposition makes me want to start screaming again. I lean in close, along with Helena, and find myself drawn into the image as if it were a tunnel and not a 2D visual. Every detail perfectly placed, every line photorealistic. Kalina Godfrey's remarkable style comes back to me now in force. It's the generic office I smelled a moment before, a dead place not given life but captured fully in its deadness. Everything from filing cabinets to cubicle walls to standard-issue beige carpet is rendered with a slight tint of yellow, like an old newspaper. There are no people, just things, and the things are so depressing I want to jump out of my nonexistent skin. Helena moves to the next painting in the row while Griffin hangs back, alternately smirking and checking his phone. I follow Helena, remembering more and more. How they stuck her in this place, Kalina, with no explanation, ever, of why she was here or what she could do to gain her freedom. They didn't interact with her, had the KPM slide her food and all the painting supplies she could ever require through a slot in the door to her large and sumptuous cell. There was no one, ever, to answer her screams, demands, pleas.

Imagine it: being abducted out of the blue, dosed with a powerful sedative, waking up groggy and disoriented in a room the size of a three-car garage and decorated like a lounge in a New York City apartment from the 1920s. Now imagine trying to get your bearings in such a place without hearing another human voice for the rest of your life. Kalina, like me, was an experiment for the Belmonts, testing the limits of what an artist would produce—exclusive paintings that could be created under no other circumstances on earth, because the circumstances were both extreme and controlled entirely by them. Deprivation, confusion, terror, and a downward spiral while they delivered to her room, daily, the best oil paints, horsehair brushes, and supplies money could buy.

Kalina Godfrey lived this way for two years and seven months before she gave up. (How long will you last, Betsy, if I fail to free you?) She completed thirty-seven new paintings before she started to cut herself, and they're all on display in this gallery. You'd think they'd be a linear progression of mental disintegration, like one of those Faces of Meth billboards they put up in Hart Springs when I was growing up. But Kalina didn't roll like that. Looking at these paintings, you would never know she was under duress. Not a single crack in her style or technique. Right up to the end, she kept rendering her little tiny slices of drudgery. Why?

Thinking about this as I move along the series of badly overlit office spaces is the most disorienting experience. The lack of deviation, even while she was flaying herself alive in here. Yet not a drop of blood mars a canvas. Willpower, or just insanity in a different form? Helena and I move along the row of paintings together. There's the corner of a paper shredder, an exit sign, an empty table with a manila folder on it, all depicted in miniature, perfect down to the last paperclip.

The final painting, number thirty-seven, is no more or less interesting than all the others. There's no final statement, no attempt at summing it all up—the art or the life—with any kind of open-ended flourish. It's a painting of a plastic desk organizer. There are a few pens and highlighters in it. A staple remover. That's it. That's what Kalina painted with wrists hacked to bits with a sharpened palette knife. Bleeding out, goodbye cruel world, here's something I saw at a Staples once.

The Belmonts siphoned decades of life from this sad, spoiled energy. One of their most successful experiments.

Helena runs a finger along the edge where the frame meets the canvas. "Think of it," she says, her voice introspective but still laced with honey.

"I have." Griffin, inspecting his nails, probably regretting he took her through this place.

"Kalina Godfrey's last act," Helena says, "*this.*"

"Mmm-hmm," Griffin says. His eyes stray toward the door beyond the series of paintings.

"We did this to her." Helena steps back, takes in the series as a whole with a quick turn of her head.

"She did this to herself," Griffin reminds her.

Helena turns to regard her brother. "I don't know if it's courage or something else. Maybe it's the opposite. Pure fear." The note of wonder in her voice is searching, almost pleading. "To do what you've always done when your circumstances are so different, so intense. To simply continue. Why no deviation? There's not a single line out of place. Taken away from everything you know, everyone you love, and given no answers and no human contact for nearly three years." She turns to take one more look at the desk organizer. "To keep producing your work at more or less the same rate, in the same style." She shakes her head. "Is there something I'm missing here? Something I'm not seeing? Something hidden in one of these paintings?"

"There's nothing," Griffin says. "None of it means anything at all." He sounds almost proud. And I'm inclined to agree. All that's left of a life completely destroyed is a series of paintings that speaks to an unchanged state of mind. How is that possible?

When they took me, for example, my voice became the voice of someone totally different, my discomfort and fear in the booth coming through in quavers and missed notes. That's why my end was accelerated, I believe. My arc was too predictable. I was scared and useless and failed to make much of a dent in their mortality.

But Kalina? What happened to her terrifies me. The strength, if that's indeed what it was, to churn out these precise little slices of signature drabness while her mind quite understandably came apart. I know why I don't ever come through here. I don't like to think about it. And whatever leaked in from the installation wing to whisper *spoiled* and disrupt the floor tiles and mix its rank smell with Kalina's paintings further highlights how straightforward her effort was. She was, until the end, in some way, always herself.

Griffin's ennui in the face of all this seems like a put-on, but with him, who knows. Helena, gripped by the cocktail's effects, is still sputtering out her wonder. She walks to her brother. I retreat from the paintings on the wall.

"Why are you being so weird?" Helena says.

"I'm not being weird."

"You are. Why did you bring me here?"

"It was on the way. How does this place make you feel?"

"Confused. This series of paintings is ours and only ours. But could it only have been produced under the circumstances we provided? Or would she always have made these paintings if left completely alone by us to pursue her life's course, surrounded by her comforts and her family? What is it that makes these paintings uniquely ours?"

Griffin shrugs. "They're hanging in our home."

"So art is art if it hangs in a museum."

He laughs. "That cocktail has reduced you to a dorm room philosopher." He gestures at the paintings. "I thought you'd have a more interesting perspective on this right now. I was wrong. It's no fault of yours. Now, let's move along. The smell of this room is going to cling to my shirt."

She giggles. "The smell of your face clings to my face."

He turns and heads for the door. "You've been mixing those drinks too strong."

I take one last look at the paintings. The bland realism infects me. Break room refrigerators full of Baggies and Tupperware with Sharpied names, off-white blinds on inner office windows, stains of unknown origin, recycling bins full of paper. They found Kalina sprawled out on the floor in front of her easel, that desk organizer painting clamped neatly into place. The last thing she ever saw.

Griffin palms an iPad-size screen on the wall next to the door. The system reads his prints and the lock springs free with a friendly little click. That's the last friendly thing we'll experience for a while. Beyond this door is the installation wing. Diaper Wall Guy's final resting place. The inner sanctum of the private collection.

The voice slithers out as Griffin opens the door and takes Helena's hand. *Spoiled.*

"Hello, friends," she says. I think of the KPM's recent sweep through this wing on the way back from your chamber. Laser sights in motion, tactical douchebag-speak deployed, double-time. Lots of *coverage* and various sixes being watched.

Griffin consults his notes app and speaks some runic bullshit with a surprising degree of conviction. Here's what I've learned from watching them over the years. When you've got billions of dollars at your disposal, lots of weird shit that's basically fairy-tale stuff and fantasy novel cover art to normal human beings is at least sort of attainable. A VERY small degree of it, anyway, the tiny slice of the bullshit pie that's actually "real" in some sense. But not because of any concerted effort or skill, which, like everything associated with billionaires, is so goddamn frustrating to witness. When I went to music camp in the summer before tenth grade there was a boy who said his name was Wyltwicky, and who told us he was a practitioner of black magic. (Note that his real name was Kevin and he was a bassoon player from

Grand Rapids, Michigan.) Wyltwicky read everything out loud backward in these jarring declarative statements—for example, there was a road that cut through the camp to separate the cabins from the dining hall, and just before you got to the crosswalk was a sign that said STOP! WATCH FOR CARS. And so every time we approached, in all our bug-sprayed glory, Wyltwicky would yell out, "SRAC! ROF HCTAW POTS," because Wyltwicky claimed that speaking backward was the key to building spells and incantations, so he had to practice as much as he could, until it became second nature. I tell you this to highlight the fact that Kevin and Griffin Belmont have roughly the same understanding of "magic." Throughout human history there have been a million Kevins. Outcasts lusting after power. Goth kids who watched *The Craft* one too many times. Actual satanists and Luciferians. Cultists and ritualists and Kabbalists of all persuasions and quirks and obsessions. Snake handlers and voodoo priests and crystal worshippers and Tarot card readers. Wiccans and various blood-drinkers and those two girls who really believed in Slenderman.

The difference, like anything else in this world, comes down to money. Griffin and Helena have the means to find all sorts of ancient and obscure bits of knowledge for which they pay more than 99.9 percent of human beings will ever make or see in their lifetimes. Most of it, even in this rarefied air so high above the Kevins of the world that you can't even see them from here, is still bullshit. But get your hands on enough of this stuff—and the Belmonts have libraries and galleries full—and something real is bound to slip through. I sometimes imagine them climbing misty mountains to gain audiences with old dudes in lonely hermitages, but I suspect it's more like meeting shifty brokers in hotel rooms in Macau and handing over suitcases full of cash and getting, like, an Annabelle in return.

The incantation Griffin speaks now, as they cross the threshold, is like a mute button for the installation wing. I've seen it performed before to keep the worst of this place at bay. They pass through the darkness, holding hands, and the sour smell drifts around us as if it were alive, which I suppose, in some sense, it is. These installations are a lot of things—mainly trapped, unpredictable, and animate, through a combination of luck, a twelfth-century text they stumbled upon, and torturing the shit out of the artists to siphon off their borrowed time. Whatever sour combo of trickery and repetition they managed to perform manifested in odd ways that bounced off the artists' original intentions. Normal people might call what's here monstrous, but I have some sympathy.

The Belmonts hold their breath. Griffin clicks on a powerful flashlight. A floor full of numbers appears out of the darkness. This end of the long gallery used to be devoted to one man's quest to paint tiny numbers in an outward spiral from zero. They left him in the spot he died of starvation and let him rot. Now his bones are scattered around 4,398,523. He was naked when he died. He kept trying to eat his clothes so they had him stripped. The numbers speak of endlessness and futility. We've all got a spiral that begins at zero and ends abruptly. It's no accident that the pattern makes a drain. It smells like death in here still, like the odor of half-rotted flesh was trapped at the precise time the artist began to decay and never faded. I don't know why I'm not immune to this. I hate it here, this glimpse it gives of what comes afterward. There is laughter when the spiral begins to move, and then we're walking along an endless concrete expanse beneath a sky missing a sun yet not entirely dark. The gray smear of a threatening storm that will never come. There we are, millions upon millions of us, painting our numbers in widening spirals until we collapse and lie still. Some of us won't make it past fifteen. Some of us will paint up into the millions. There is no beginning and no end to this place. It lingers as the Belmonts move in, the numbers nipping at their heels. They whisper quietly to each other. Depression sets in and I remind myself that the effects of this installation have actually been muted, that it would be much more potent without Griffin's lucky incantation. I have witnessed a KPM guy turn his handgun on himself immediately after glimpsing this. They left him here to rot too, just to see what would happen. Nothing did.

Now they step over his bones and into a long, narrow tunnel made of gorgeous wood, teak or something, like the walls of a high-priced Scandinavian guesthouse. Inside this tunnel used to be a block of ice and a fan. Those things are gone now but the cold lingers. Baby monitors hang from the ceiling. Somewhere in this place—a walled-off nook even I haven't been able to find—the artist still lives, and it's her voice that comes from the baby monitors now. Utter gibberish. I suspect she's been kept in the dark and force-fed and denied the means of suicide by KPM monitoring. I can't quite remember her name. Lena something. She was never famous, had no family, and was a heroin addict. I suspect everyone has by now forgotten her, chalked her disappearance up to the drugs or the streets and moved on. I think that's what this piece might be "about," trying to make people remember. The tunnel seems to expand and contract. Without the muting, the artist's voice would move through the tunnel like an infection through a bloodstream. The baby monitors drip with condensation. There's a humid dampness here.

We emerge from the tunnel and the flashlight plays along a series of monoliths. Not reflective and black like in *2001: A Space Odyssey* (which Helena, I shit you not, watches like once a week—maybe Griffin's right and she's making those cocktails way too strong), but withered and weak. Monoliths barely clinging to life. The opposite of imposing. Sad things that once maybe tried hard but always came up short. Griffin's light plays along the first monolith. It's been graffitied. I can't remember what the point of this installation was, but it says, in blue spray paint, THE DOCTOR REMOVED THE DEMON FROM YOUR WEE WILLY WINKY AND NOW IT CAN'T GET HARD EVER AGAIN :(

As we pass through the dead forest of weak, drooping monoliths, I recall, very suddenly, a castration I never witnessed. It's simply what's present in this part of the gallery—a free-floating scene trapped here forever and placed in our minds as we pass through. A man's penis stretched out on a chopping block. A cast-iron pan heated on an open fire to cauterize the wound. The old west stretching every which way into the distance, an empty American plain with monoliths dying all around. A distant speck of a horse frozen mid-gallop. Even muted this exhibit contains so much energy it can barely be contained. This artist was on the cusp of greater fame, I remember—which became the Belmonts' go-to place in any given career to work on. Something about this transition point being fertile ground. I remember this manifesto now, and the artist, an Italian guy, a real two-fisted macho type. He did these revisionist western motifs with familiar elements from pop culture, repurposed with the intention of creating a way in for people that felt comfortable, referential. Then the rug-pull, according to the *Art Forum* I read over Helena's shoulder, was the real reckoning with the brutality and unfeeling savagery of colonialist history. Except there was also this reckoning with his own history of abuse, and the whole thing was pretty muddled, in the end.

Griffin and Helena stop in their tracks before a monolith that's actually curled itself down to the floor as if in full emotional collapse. The scene the artist may or may not have intended to evoke surges and the room goes black. There's the crackle of the fire, the shackled man, gagged and bound, with his member outstretched. A man in a black hood delicately takes a piece of foreskin between thumb and forefinger and with a long needle pierces it to fasten the penis to the chopping block. The bound man screams. *The doctor removed the demon*, says a voice like a tour guide. *Your wee willy winky can't get hard.* The man in the mask holds up a blade that catches the firelight and blazes with orange. *The doctor removed the demon from your*

wee

(the blade comes down)

willy

(the severed penis inches toward its pinned head, leaving a slug's trail of blood on the block)

winky

(the bound man strains against his bonds and makes gurgling shrieks behind his gag while the masked man unpins the penis from the block and tosses it into the fire)

I can't shut it out. I think of growing up, of all my plans hatched with Sheena and Allie in the booth at the Sip 'n' Sup. I was so focused on my career. I was on my way. I loved to sing. I was making it work. I was going to scratch and claw my way to the life I wanted. So much hope. And now I'm here. With *them*. Seeing such awful things. Maybe forever.

Griffin speaks the muting words again, but it's too late. Next to him, Helena vomits. He leads her beyond the monolith forest, then taps his watch and issues a command.

"Cleanup in the installation wing."

There are more works of art, of course. But Griffin, done with his little tour, bypasses a dozen more installations looming in the darkness by heading for the ostentatious door. Helena pops a mint, then presses her palm against the screen embedded in the wall. The door clicks.

We step into the hangar and the door shuts behind us. I sort of blob out to the shadowy edges of the room. I've still got the forlorn plains of the old west stretching out in my memory, though now the small group huddled around the firelight is an orange blot in the distance. Still, for whatever reason, the plains themselves are almost as awful to comprehend. They mix, in my vision, with the haze of this massive windowless space, and for a moment I see you, Betsy, crouched in the firelight of that desolate torment, alongside the man in the hood and the man in shackles. And then he's gone, and there's only you.

"Hello there," Griffin says. He tries to juice his tone with the appropriate amount of normal-person greeting, but from him it just comes out as slightly sarcastic. It's funny how broken he is in so many ways. Like, he can approximate how he should feel at any given time, but the expression of the feeling comes out all wrong. Whatever channel he's tuned to, RICH TV or whatever, is just slightly out of focus. A little fuzzy.

"Hey, B," Helena says. Their shoes echo oddly in this place as they walk, as if the sound has been trapped in Tupperware containers and released a little out of sync with their actual footsteps. *The doctor removed the demon* echoes in my head, that tour-guide intonation, the nearly soundless descent of the gleaming blade down to the wooden block.

Spoiled.

It's nice to see you again, Betsy. I saw your brother today, for a second, from a drone's-eye view. He looked unharmed. He's working on a sculpture. I wish I could say *I've got your back, I'm going to get you out of this,* but I can't even make you aware of me. It would be a joke.

The little round coaster-size objects—painting excerpts like donut holes—are exactly where the KPM left them, scattered around the vast concrete floor. If there's a pattern I still can't see it, but it doesn't really matter, because you've already begun some kind of elaborate connect-the-dots scheme.

Being careful not to smear the wet paint, Griffin skirts the easternmost edge of the burgeoning floor-mural. (This room is so big I can only think of it in terms of directions on a map, *the southwest quadrant.*) There's a skeleton to it all now. Like how a real estate agent tells you a house has "good bones." You've started painting in shades of gray—no bright lines, no solid fields of color, no spatters and drips. Just the bones to link the canvas coasters like fluid tree branches. In the center of the mural is a workbench on wheels, and stacked upon it are several large palettes smeared with grays you've mixed in small increments from white to black. Tubes of paint are curled and empty, discarded at the base of the workbench. There are wicker baskets filled to the brim with fresh tubes of every color imaginable. I spy cadmium red, phthalo blue, primary yellow. All acrylic—I know by now that oils would end up a smeary mess on a concrete floor.

You're next to the workbench, lying in the hammock. You haven't opened your eyes to look at your visitors, which must be driving Griffin up the wall. One thing he has a tough time shrugging off is the lack of acknowledgment from his captive audiences. You've got a gorgeous mess of lavender-gray hair and big glasses that make me think it's a toss-up between hip eyewear and a serious vision problem. Your jeans are spattered with blots of color. I think I would like to be your friend.

The thought of a friend, a casual acquaintance, *anyone at all,* makes me well up. I can't cry but I can get stuck in the feeling of tears coming on. An imminent sob. All tension, no release, like everything else in my non-life.

"What's going on?" Griffin calls out, stepping between the bones that link the coasters, approaching your place in the center of the mural. "You've barely gotten started, Betsy. Is there a problem?"

He's still got a ways to go and his voice bounces around the hangar. Something shifts in response in the darkness at the margins of the room. You don't open your eyes.

"The artist sleeps," Helena says.

"Talk to me," Griffin says. "I'm here for you. *We're* here for you."

You don't stir. Helena laughs softly. "Off to a good start."

Griffin's face twists into anger, and he begins *stalking* toward the hammock like a jealous husband. Then he takes a breath and softens once again. He bypasses the hammock and stands by the workbench, taking in your arrangement of the material. Helena joins him and picks up a square, coverless book. Ragged bits frizz out of the binding, like it's been torn from a larger work. I recognize their father's neat calligraphy, his precise diagrams. Say what you will about Marius Van Leeman, the man's penmanship and design sense were impeccable. The exposed front page says

Reprefentations of the Falls—
An Appendix—
To Be Performed in Conjunction With the filent Hymns

"*Performed*," Helena says. "I could never really get that part right."

"She's not doing much in the way of performing now," Griffin says, gesturing to your prone, hammock-bound form.

Helena genuflects. "The floor is yours, oh Captain my Captain."

Griffin clears his throat and looks around. Then he nudges your shoulder. The hammock swings. You stir.

I send vibes your way, willing you to open your eyes and acknowl-edge him so he doesn't have Gumley come in here and rip off your toenails. I try to mount a distraction, let loose with a couple of shrieks, reach out to rattle the workbench, but of course nothing happens. Helena's got her arms folded, watching it all play out. She sways a little on her feet.

"Act four, scene five," she says.

Griffin nudges harder. "Betsy. I need to talk to you. Can you sit up, please?" I can sense the strain in his politeness, like a gossipy neighbor being "nice."

There's a tipping point here, a moment where Griffin's about to abandon any pretense of being on your side and let his cracked eggshell veneer of gentle handling fall away to reveal the viciousness. But then, thankfully, you open your eyes. You slip a finger underneath your thick lenses to pick at some sleep crusties. Then you sit up, blinking, glancing around like you're totally disoriented. Your eyes play along the mural you've just begun to create. I'm astonished at the change that comes over you. A hunger washes over your face. Pure desire. You look at Griffin, almost pleading.

He grins. "Well, hey there. Welcome back from the land of the somnambulists."

Helena smirks and nearly chokes on her own held-back laughter. She shakes her head, coughs, and mutters something about "douchebag vocabulary."

You turn to glance at the paints spread out on the workbench. You press your palms together in your lap and rub them and clasp your hands until the skin pales.

"This is a safe space," Griffin says. "Is there something bothering you? Something you need to get off your chest?"

She turns back and looks at him as if for the first time. Blinks herself fully awake and alert.

"You took me," she says.

"I sincerely apologize for the drastic interruption of your life. It must have been very jarring."

"You took me here to paint."

"We took you here to set you free, Betsy." He glances at Helena.

I can see the wheels turning. Then he kneels down to meet your eyes, grips the edge of the hammock in his fists. "Listen. Our father—the man who wrote the book we gave you, the book that's right over there—was just like you. Gifted. Ahead of his time. Horribly misunderstood by the people in the very same town. The ones who whisper about you now are the descendants of those who hunted down our father like a dog and murdered him because he was capable of so much more than they were, and they were jealous and afraid."

"We know about what you did to the Dutch Reformed church. What happened fifteen years ago."

You turn to regard Helena.

"We know how you've been shunned since then. And it's not fair, Betsy. Neither is what your brother's done to you—"

You shake your head. "He hasn't done anything to me. Anyway, it's for the best." Her mouth is dry, her voice scratchy.

"*What's* for the best," Griffin says, "artificial boundaries? Tethering your immense talent to meaningless forgeries? And for what? So some uptight pearl clutcher's sensibilities don't get offended. God forbid a *real* artist, a *generational talent*, comes around and snaps people out of their stupor." Griffin indicates two of the nearest cutouts on the floor, those canvas coasters with peculiar imagery. "*This* is the real you, Betsy." He leans down and picks one up—it's the antlers. "Right here." He stares at it, mesmerized. Sweat beads his forehead.

"Griffin," Helena says. Then she comes over, takes it from his hand, and drops it back down to the floor. Griffin blinks his awareness back. He swipes a sleeve across his wet brow and turns back to you.

"So much incredible energy," he says. "Wholly unique ability. And this place exists for you to let it out. To unleash what your brother and everyone else wishes you would just keep buried until you die. Well, Helena and I don't believe in that kind of limitation. Neither did our father."

He lets that sink in. He's smiling at you. He reaches out to lay a gentle hand on your shoulder and you recoil. He frowns.

"I want to see my brother," you say.

Griffin sighs. He shakes his head. It lasts longer than a normal head-shake session. I count seven, eight shakes. It's bizarre. "Betsy. Your brother's kept you in a *prison* for fifteen years. Imagine the progress you could have made—the artist you could be—if you'd been allowed to create freely this whole time."

You shake your head, but it's feeble. I can see that you're thinking, but I can't figure out your angle. Is this asshole really making some kind of sense to you?

Griffin leans in. "What you've done so far is beautiful. It's a miracle. It's freedom." Beat. "Right?"

He makes a sweeping gesture to indicate the floor all around them.

I loosen up and spread out along the ceiling, at least twenty feet above your head, to get the full picture of what you've been working on since you got here. At least, before your little nap break that sparked this visit from the Belmonts in the first place. Up here, I can see that you're not just playing connect-the-dots with your little coasters. There's a flow to your lines that's not apparent when you're down at floor level. If I back up as far as I can, press myself into the ceiling, the whole thing falls into place.

It's a waterfall in its infancy. A sketch. Just enough feathery curves to indicate flow and churn. Not yet a torrent but the inner workings of a deluge, built from the inside out, pouring down over the coasters. The impression of a waterfall built from nothing more than lines and negative space.

"You're off to such a wonderful, incredible start," Griffin says. "So why did you stop?"

You shrug and avert your eyes.

"Did it hurt you, in some way, to do this?"

Helena folds her arms, watching intently.

You shake your head. "No."

"Then what?"

"It felt good," you say, and for some reason the way you say it breaks my nonexistent heart. "Really, really good."

Griffin is taken aback. There's a long moment of silence. "Oh," he says. "I'm glad. We want you to feel good. Now, do you think you're ready to keep going? There's a lot of work left to do."

You cross your arms in front of your chest, grip your shoulders, and hug yourself as if you're freezing. You rock back and forth in your hammock, eyes sweeping across the floor. Then you look from Helena to Griffin. I can see helplessness in the way you know what you're going to do.

"It's going to happen again," you say. "If I keep going. And I made a promise that it never would."

"A promise to whom? Your brother?" Griffin makes a show of looking around. "He's not here to impose his limitations, Betsy. It's only you, and me, and Helena, and my father's book. And you're free to interpret what's in that book any way you like. That's the whole point. It's what he wanted. What he *demanded*. Be free. Create."

You rock back and forth, back and forth, squeezing yourself.

Helena kneels down beside her brother. "Years ago, in Andalucia, we knew an artist." She's dropped into her smokiest register. "A painter, like you. Commercially successful beyond her wildest dreams. A critical darling too, at least for a while. At the forefront of the movement she's become synonymous with. To the casual observer, it seems that such metrics and appraisals, once they are reached, become static. But there's always an ebb and flow. Fortunes fade, talents become misapplied, certain skills atrophy in favor of shallow provocations. Except with true geniuses, like this painter, all of those layers—the surface static, the ebb and the flow beneath, the private doubts and tribulations—existed in their own atmosphere, which she compartmentalized. An entire life's hopes and dreams and successes and failures, tied up with a bow." Helena mimics giving you a small gift. "It was only after she died that we discovered an alternate path, hidden from everyone in her life, in a second studio hidden beneath the first like fossilized remains. An entirely unprecedented course she charted in secret. A second artistic development. The true movement, a personal renaissance explored in private, completely free of the strictures of the marketplace or the whims of the public's taste. Separate, even, from the painter's own seemingly hard-fought evolution."

"Total, mind-blowing purity," Griffin says.

"And this is what we're offering you now," Helena says. "That same path. Unchain your ability. Unleash yourself."

And you, with tears in your eyes, un-hug yourself and plant your feet on the floor. You stand up, go to the workbench, select a brush, and swirl its bristles in a jar of murky water.

I think of your brother on the edge of the cliff with his sculpture.

I think of Marius Van Leeman in his dusty, ageless chamber.

It won't be long now.

Don't do it, Betsy. Tell these freaks to go fuck themselves.

Instead, to the Belmonts' delight, you crouch down with your brush. Your hand, fluid and graceful, reconnects the tip of the brush with an interrupted line. Your tears fall to the floor. Your body heaves as you work. I can hear you breathing. There are bags under your eyes that give away the sedatives and stress of the past twenty-four hours, but your expression is one of pure focus. You inhabit grace. I wonder if they've got another Kalina Godfrey on their hands. Speaking of hands, it's a pleasure watching yours move. You're not squinting one eye and lining up your shot like a pool player. You're just going for it, and I get the sense that your hands are working almost independent of the thoughts that are driving this mural you're painting.

Griffin and Helena watch you work like proud parents. Then, very quietly, as if noise would break the spell, they head for the door. Their footsteps recede, and they're gone.

There's something all-consuming about your flow state. It's like watching advanced yoga poses. I come down from the ceiling to take a closer look, following the gentle arc of your wrist as it bends to move the tip of the brush along the smooth concrete.

Then, suddenly, you deviate. The way your upper body is moving with that gentle hypnotic sway is unchanged, but the flow state evolves at the tip of your brush. Quickly, without skipping a beat or even lifting your brush from the floor, the line becomes much more complex. It's like you've switched to calligraphy on the fly. In a matter of seconds, a word emerges from the spray and the curve of the falling water.

Hello.

There's a moment in the vocal booth, usually after nine or ten takes, when it's two A.M. and you've come out the other side of exhaustion and the words you're singing don't make sense anymore—they're just subdivided little melodies, nonsense arranged as notes, no more musical than a little kids' improvised song—and the absurdity of what you're doing takes hold. Commanding your voice to do this elastic, emotive thing into a microphone, so that an engineer can pretty it up and sand down the rough edges to make a song that just might buy you the time to do it all over again. Sometimes a moment like that disintegrates further and everybody calls it a night and you go home wired and frustrated and sleep badly and let all your doubts force-feed you the knowledge that you totally suck. And sometimes, when you're about to slide down that suck-slide into suck-land, you ask Gary for one more take, and he swivels in his chair and runs the track, and for reasons beyond your comprehension you pull it together and nail the take and he looks at you like *Holy shit, that's the one.* It's times like these when your doubts can fuck themselves because there's something in you that knows, instinctively, how to wrench up your talent from the depths of nervy frustration. You get all buzzy and light and happy, the best you can possibly feel sober. It has nothing to do with how the song might come out, or the album, or the tour. It's the most in-the-moment you can get, there in the booth, with Gary suddenly animated and bopping around at his Pro Tools setup.

I've thought a lot about this infinite feeling over the years, but just like the faces of the people I used to know, it's faded to a shadow of itself. I considered it lost and gone forever, until now. Now my whole spectral self feels shimmery. It's like there's real sun on my face, a megadose of vitamin D. Choirs of angels. A 2010 EDM drop injected into my veins.

I don't know if you can hear me, or how we're going to talk, but for now, just the fact that you know I'm here is enough.

Hello to you too, Betsy Larkin.

You flick your wrist, the brush slides across concrete, and the word vanishes into the waterfall.

PART THREE

THE WORM & THE DOGSBODY

12

Lark wakes at dusk, dragged from sleep by a chime that comes from everywhere and nowhere. He sits up in bed, works his tongue around the inside of his dry mouth. His teeth feel slightly out of place and he thinks of dental impressions, biting down, molars and incisors thrown out of whack. It takes a moment to come back to himself—the chime had been in his dream, too, echoing through a vast concrete hollow, a bunker the size of a hangar where a cloud hovered just beneath the ceiling, trapped and bloated with rain it could not expel.

"Doorbell," he says out loud to merge the chime with reality. He rubs his eyes. Goop clings to his fingers. His sheets, soaked in sweat, twine around his legs. He moves to extract his limbs and discovers that he's sitting in a puddle. His damp underwear clings to his thighs. There's a sticky heat to the moisture, a tang sharper than sweat.

"Jesus," he says.

Apparently, he's wet the bed. Something he never did as a child.

The doorbell rings, insistently, twice.

He rushes up through a bedroom sunk deep in the gloaming, the late-afternoon light of depression naps. His sparse furniture is indistinct. Dresser, desk, bed. A monkish, ascetic arrangement at odds with the visual clamor of his studio. One of Betsy's abstract originals from her early twenties hangs on the wall. The subject is their father. The painting seethes with nervous energy. It had been a running joke for a while—how could anyone sleep with *that* in their bedroom, staring down at them? Whatever the opposite of Zen is, the painting oozes. But after a while he just got used to it. He moves past it now, registering its patchy fields of color as the hints of a dim figure, deconstructed and remade.

In the bathroom he peels off his sodden boxer briefs and tosses them in the bathtub. They land with a wet plop. The doorbell rings again. He grabs a used towel from the hook behind the door and dries himself as best he can—his impromptu dance is all elbows and knees—and drapes the towel over the shower curtain rod. Then he slips into a fleece bathrobe and heads downstairs. Crossing the living room, he registers Krupp folded into a Z on the sectional, half covered in a wool throw. Out the windows, his wire-and-wood sentries sprout from the lawn, guarding the no-man's-land between forest and house. He pauses by the front door. A slender figure is visible through the beveled glass, radiating impatience. He opens the door.

"Asha?"

A shiny vinyl duffel is slung over his art agent's shoulder. She hands him a white cardboard box the size of a microwave and just as heavy. It's stamped FRAGILE.

"This was on your porch." She steps past him into the living room. "The drive up from the city was ludicrous, let's never speak of it. My GPS had me turn left off the exit, then kept redirecting me around your tragically institutional-looking high school and back into some hilly development that could have been charming, but managed to feel like Levittown circa 1957. Developers who lack vision on such a scale ought to be rounded up and shot. It takes *effort* to ruin a perfectly acceptable landscape. Wouldn't you think standard practice would be to let the designs be informed by their surroundings instead of simply plunking down ready-made A-frames and ranches?" She slides her duffel off her shoulder and sets it down on the floor. Krupp stirs, groans, and turns his back on the room.

"Um," Lark says. Then he shuts the front door. "Hi."

Asha puts her hands on her hips and surveys the room. "A bit gloomy in here, yes?" She pauses to regard Lark with the careful scrutiny of someone who appraises and judges for a living. He's conscious of the smell of bed-wet. "Were you sleeping? It's *dinnertime*, Lark."

He pulls the robe tight around his body, as if that will trap the odor. "I was up all night."

He feels himself waking up, the events of the past day and night crashing into his brain stem like a stimulant. His heart revs up. There's still so much work to be done. His phone's plugged in upstairs. He needs to see if Gumley's been trying to reach him, if there's another video of Betsy. He didn't mean to sleep for so long, it was just supposed to be a quick nap before—

"Lark."

"Asha."

"I'm going to ask you a question, and once you give me an honest answer, we can move forward."

"Okay."

"Did you urinate on yourself?"

"No."

"Lark."

"It was an accident."

"All right. First, I want you to go upstairs, take a shower, and put on fresh clothes. Have you eaten?"

Lark tries to remember eating anything, ever. The taste of food, the act of lifting it to his mouth. "Not lately."

"I'll order something. Sushi?" There's hope in her voice.

"They do sushi at the Chinese place."

Asha shudders.

"They've got pad thai, too."

"That sounds like an abomination. I'm serious about the gloom, Lark, can we burn some paraffin oil, or whatever you do for light this far north?"

"Asha, what are you doing here?"

He sets the box down on the end table next to the sofa and clicks on a floor lamp. Krupp makes a noise and pulls the blanket over his face. On a hunch Lark rips off the packing tape, opens the box, and removes a slab of Styrofoam. Eight bottles of caramel-colored liquid poke up from cushioned dividers.

Gumley's employers' single-malt scotch. He remembers the peat-bog fumes, the leather volumes lining the walls, the stern onyx falcon…

"Your friend called me," Asha says. "Wayne." She points to the bony mass underneath the blanket. A grumpy collapsed tent. "This one, right here, I presume. I came as soon as I could, but as I was saying, the route was circuitous, to say the least."

Lark lays the Styrofoam back into the box, covering the bottles. "What did he tell you?"

"Everything. What happened to your sister. What they're forcing you to do. That awful book. The sculpture you began last night. So, I thought, either my favorite client is in a truly desperate situation, or he's having a complete mental breakdown and has somehow convinced his odd little friend to share in his overwhelming paranoia. Either way, a trip to the northern wasteland was in order. I took the Saab. Full disclosure, I've been microdosing psilocybin for seven weeks now. I don't think it does anything, but Justine swears by it."

"I'm your favorite client?"

"Unequivocally. Since day one."

Lark knows she's lying. Asha has twenty-seven clients, including Felicia Raymond, whose mixed-media works were shot into space as possible cultural outreach to potential alien life-forms, and the estate of Yvonne Baker, whose *Infinite Margarine* series sold at Sotheby's for $87 million.

It could be the messed-up sleep schedule, the sheer backloaded trauma of the past day and night coming down on him, but Lark feels swept under by a grateful emotional surge. He realizes now how alone he's felt in all this, even with Krupp along for the ride. Alone and flailing, driven solely by the fear of coming up short and killing his sister. The dim room blurs behind tears that come on suddenly.

"Lark," Asha says, folding her arms as if to shield herself from the outpouring of emotion. "Why don't you go get cleaned up and I'll order that"—she pauses to consider her word choice—"*Asian fusion* you mentioned."

"I had to work so fast last night," he says, "I didn't even have time to stop and think. They sent me a video of Betsy in some *place*. I don't know what they're doing to her."

"All right," Asha says, glancing around the living room with lips pressed tightly together. "I understand. Let's just take a moment, then."

Lark follows the turn of her head as she scans the mild clutter of the living room. More of Betsy's early work adorns the walls—a strange period, when his sister was first realizing the depth and range of her gift, yet struggling to keep it out of her work. Her paintings of that period are, at first glance, painfully *normal*. But to Lark's trained eye, well versed in the way his sister's brain pours out onto the canvas, it's the struggle to suppress the awareness of who she really is that makes these paintings so interesting. The conflict between the blossoming of something she would not come to grips with for several years and the luminosity of her talent. That Central European expressionist bent he's always favored, the passage of sick-complexioned mannequins through light that settles like a fever.

Lark sinks down in a leather armchair trucked home from Wrecker's ten years ago. A thick biography of Edward Hopper rests on its arm. The cover of the book, of course, is *Nighthawks*. Lark holds it in his lap, opens to a random page, lets a dry passage detailing Hopper's office paintings wash over him.

"Betsy's book," he tells Asha. "She was in the middle of a Hopper thing."

He imagines his sister's studious attention to the book, late at night in this very chair, peppermint tea gone cold. The status quo of this captured moment makes fresh tears come on. How he longs for normalcy, routine, the daily worries of their shared existence. Instead, Asha's up from the city, Betsy's gone, and *The Worm & the Dogsbody* awaits.

Asha pulls up a seldom-used wicker chair, crosses her legs, folds her hands in her lap, and looks at him expectantly. It takes him a moment to realize that she's determined to *listen* to him. Her pupils are black saucers and he wonders if she accidentally macro-dosed on the way up. Or it could just be the light in the room.

"Tell me about it," Asha says gently.

"About what?"

"Anything. Her."

"It feels like she's dead if I talk about her. Like I've already failed. Like I'm remembering."

"She's not going to die. I'm going to help you."

He grips the Hopper book tightly, grateful for Asha's conviction. "I never told you about this before." He swipes a finger along the underside of an eye and it comes away wet. He points at the blanketed lump on the sofa. "Krupp's the only one who knows the whole story."

As if some part of him is listening deep within a dream, Krupp stirs, mutters, and lies still.

"My father was out of his league as a parent after our mother died," Lark says. "I mean, he probably was before too, but I was too young to remember that. When I say *out of his league*, that's me being polite about it. For me, it was just unpleasant. But for Betsy—there was nothing there. It was like, she made him uncomfortable. Freaked him out. This big tough guy, a carpenter who worked his way up to site manager. Big Tom Larkin, doing his best to not ever be in the same room as his own daughter.

"Betsy used to get these fevers. Spells where she'd be totally out of it for a week, talking nonsense, painting the pages of books with her fingers, rearranging furniture. And my dad would just leave the house, go to a buddy's place, maybe get a hotel near the job site, I don't know. Like he was hoping maybe she would just die and get it over with." Lark pauses, looks down at the book in his lap. "I try to put myself in his shoes. I've tried over and over again to give him the benefit of the doubt. A single dad, an old-school guy with two complete fucking weirdos as kids. Maybe if Betsy was the prom queen and I was following his footsteps in the trades, he might've been able to find it in himself to at least fill the role of a father. If we all ran on autopilot. But we didn't."

"My father was a narcissist," Asha offers.

"I don't know what Big Tom is." Lark shakes his head. "That's what's so hard to explain about this. He wasn't really *abusive*."

"I'd say that kind of neglect is a form of abuse."

"I never thought of it that way. I know people who suffered through awful shit. This wasn't that. He never hit us, never got wasted and screamed at us. As far as I've been able to understand it, he just gave up. Checked out. Never bothered to put in five minutes to try to understand what was going on with us, ever. Just did what he had to do to keep us alive. But, I think, if he could have gotten away with letting us die—I'm talking *indirectly*, like if there could have been some perfect circumstance where we could have been found dead in an accident, and he could have been one hundred percent not culpable, legally—he would have found some satisfaction in that. All wrapped up in a neat bow. Or, if not satisfaction, it would have been like a giant shrug. I've always imagined him going to work the next day after Betsy and I were found dead, and all the other people at the site, all those union guys, Local 87, the electricians and the welders, slapping his back and giving him that sort of wary respect for coming to work, like *This is the way he copes, Big Tom Larkin.* Like he's a classic stoic on the outside to hide his emotional turmoil. Just gonna plow ahead with his life, the tough sonofabitch. *Give him some space.* But what they would overlook because they grafted that persona onto him was that he wouldn't feel anything at all. He wouldn't be at work to keep himself from going crazy at home, peeking into our bedrooms and weeping, he would be at work *because it was a workday*, and that's what he always did."

"What would he do when you engaged him directly?" Asha says.

"Imagine someone pretending they're looking at you, but they're really looking just over your shoulder, like this"—Lark shifts his gaze slightly, lets his eyes go slack so that one of Betsy's paintings goes blurry—"and then I can nod when it's sort of appropriate, and make my mouth move to say things that are sort of like the bare minimum you could say that would still count as a human response. Or sometimes just not say nothing at all, until we learned not to try to talk to him in the first place." He shakes his head. "Imagine looking at the walls more than you look at your own kids. Sometimes I used to wish he would just fucking hit me, you know? At least then I would know where we stood."

Asha drills him with her dark eyes. "What about all the little things you have to deal with when you have kids? What happened when you skinned your knees?"

Lark shrugs. "I knew where the Band-Aids were."

"Emergencies?"

"I figured out what to do. Every time Betsy had one of her fevers, it wasn't like my dad sat me down and told me I'd have to step up and take care of her because he had to go away for a while. He just wouldn't be around, so I'd bike to the store and get chicken soup and try to make her eat, and get her to lie down when she wanted to roam the house with paint on her fingers, and sit up all night trying to talk to her when all she did was spout nonsense about horses and cows."

Asha's eyes stray to the walls and sweep across Betsy's work.

"She was a kid when she made those," Lark says. "Actually, it would have been about the time I met you, in the East Village. I took off right after high school, when Betsy was fifteen and I was eighteen."

"Almost twenty years ago," she says quietly.

"I couldn't wait to get the fuck out of this place," Lark says. "I had tunnel vision for the city. I told myself she'd be okay. It's not like he was physically abusive, or anything, right? I rationalized it a million different ways, mainly because nothing was going to stop me from getting out. It wasn't an agonizing decision. I just left." He pauses. "I left her here alone. With *him*. And I didn't come back for three whole years, because I was a selfish piece of shit, and—"

"Lark—"

"I was afraid, Asha. I know this sounds starry-eyed and lame, but that was a magical time, when I first got to the city. Scavenging during the day, working all night, living in that shitty squat in Bushwick that smelled like a gas leak for two years. Then we sold my first piece for more money than I'd ever seen in my life. I got swept up in things. And I was afraid if I went back up here, it would break the spell, and I'd be back with *him* in this weird little nightmare world. The person I'd become down in the city would be poisoned by the person I was. And it would all go away—the work I was doing, the name I was making for myself, the whole scene. *You.* Everything. Gone."

"You know," Asha says, "the de Laurrentisses still have that piece of yours. *Borderline Exigent.* And they're notorious flippers, so it speaks highly of your earliest work. I always knew, with you." She shakes her head. "I'm sorry. Continue."

"The day I turned twenty-one I woke up in somebody's loft just before dawn. My heart was pounding. It was raining out—there was a view of the Queensboro Bridge, looking smeared and post-apocalyptic. A Francis Bacon bridge. I don't remember what I'd done the night before—"

"Drugs," Asha says with authority.

"Well, yeah, but I mean, which ones, I don't remember. All I knew was, I needed to get back to Bushwick. I was in a cab when the sun came up—ever since that sale, I'd started taking cabs—and when I got home I saw that I had a bunch of missed calls from Krupp. I couldn't make any sense of his messages, because I was really hungover, and I found out later that he was hair-of-the-dogging, and it was just a bunch of frantic babbling. So I called him back, and that's when I got the story.

"Betsy and I hadn't spoken in ages, it was one thing after another down in the city, I don't know. Like I said, I was pretty disconnected. In the first few months, Krupp would see her out and about every few weeks, getting groceries or whatever. Then that stopped, so he went around to the house, made sure they were both still alive. He did that every couple of weeks, just to make sure nothing crazy was happening. I was pretty content with the status quo, Krupp just kinda mentioning that they were okay, that Betsy was shut up in the house but definitely alive and all that. I realize that sounds callous, but you remember what a whirlwind those days were for us. It seemed like a different life up here, one I could barely even remember, maybe one lived by somebody else entirely.

"Anyway, that was how it went for a few years, until this call with Krupp on my twenty-first birthday. He tells me that during the night, Betsy ventured out of the house and into town for the first time in three years. She brought a bunch of paints and brushes and went to the western edge of Main, over to the little strip of historical buildings. The printer, the courthouse. *Washington slept here.* All that pre-revolutionary tourist shit, the historical markers. And she just starts painting a mural on the side of the old Dutch Reformed church. This three-hundred-plus-year-old building, she just starts *painting it,* right there, in her goddamn pajama pants and a sweatshirt.

"At first nobody noticed, because it was the middle of the night. So she had hours of uninterrupted work time, and when daybreak rolls around, the mural is already pretty big. The town started to wake up, go about its day. You've always lived in the city, but imagine how jarring it would be in a place where everything's the same, every day, to start your day and step outside and see Betsy Larkin defacing the side of this town landmark with a huge, impressionistic painting of Big Tom's face."

"Incredible." Asha applies lip gloss from a golden tube. "The psychological underpinnings are writ fairly large, here."

"Anyway, Krupp's freaking out completely, telling me I have to get my ass back up here *stat,* like just hop in a cab and tell the driver to step on it all the way up 87, don't even fuck with a train, because the mural and the vandalism element is only half the story. I say, what's the other half? He says, you just gotta see it. I say, why isn't anybody stopping her? He says, you just gotta get up here now. So, I hightail it back upstate as quick as I can, the most expensive cab ride of my life, from Bushwick straight to the Dutch Reformed church in Wofford Falls. It's midday when I get up here and she's still at it. Totally feverish.

Painting like a girl possessed. And the thing was, the likeness of *him*, our father, was incredible. He was staring right out of the side of the church, gazing off beyond me at something else, like he always did. It was amazing.

"In those days I soaked up art like a sponge. It wasn't like I went to college for this shit, so I went to the Met, and MoMA, and the Whitney, and all the galleries, and the underground DIY spaces where there'd be hardcore shows in one room and art in the other. I just absorbed. I'd stare at the old masters for days on end and give equal attention to Basquiat rip-off number fifty seven in a sweaty basement in East Williamsburg."

Asha un- and re-crosses her legs, folds her hands, rests them on her thigh. "You'd seen a lot of art, is the point here."

Lark sets the Hopper book on the floor and leans forward, meeting Asha's saucered eyes. Imploring. "But nothing like this. It wasn't just that I'd never seen anything like it, it was more that I'd never *felt* anything like it. What she got across to me, personally, in that mural on the side of the church, is hard to put into words, but I felt everything she'd been going through the past few years, alone in that house with him. The hypnotic indifference. It was like I was being filtered through his eyes, and I saw a blankness to everything. Betsy had somehow given me this glimpse inside his head—like she'd cranked up the empathy and reproduced it in this mural so effectively I was seeing the world like he did. And the way he saw things made me feel like I was nothing, like the world was nothing, like there was no point to anything and love and hate could both be met with a shrug.

"It was this pathological thing, and it was so sad. I've never had a suicidal thought, but in that moment, standing there on the sidewalk, it washed over me, this idea that I could end my life. And it was followed by the thought that that might be too much work, that it's easier just to keep going. And while I'd been working nonstop in the city, and meeting you, and starting to sell sculptures, she'd been soaking up my father's horrible blankness."

It's fully dark outside the house. The wire-and-wood sentries are invisible from where he's sitting. Asha, more patient and accommodating than he's ever seen her, nods for him to continue.

Lark swallows. His heart pounds. "Even telling you this now, I can feel this wave of anxiety. What living like him must be like. The color and the saturation and the volume of everything turned all the way down."

"So you're standing there outside the church," Asha prods.

"Right, and that's when I see what Krupp couldn't describe over the phone. It looks like half the damn town is overflowing from the churchyard, to the sidewalks, into the road. Entire families. A few hundred people by now, packed into the streets. At first I'm like, this is crazy, everybody and their mother turned out, but nobody's doing anything to stop her from defacing this jewel of a wonderfully preserved building. And then I realize it's because they're all in a trance. They're under the spell of the painting. Mesmerized. Obsessed with it. Paralyzed by what she's creating right in front of them. That's when the smell hits me—people are pissing and shitting themselves because they've been there for hours, just staring up at the side of the church."

He thinks of Eddie the Can Man. "There's a whole crew of little kids with their bikes, just totally gobsmacked and out of it. Old people swaying. A few people making this low moan. A few others crying."

"So what did you do?"

"I didn't do shit," Lark says. "I couldn't. I started to walk up, fight my way through the crowd, to talk her down or drag her away if that's what it took, but at that moment I stopped breathing. I don't mean my breath caught in my throat or my heart skipped a beat. There was nothing metaphorical about what happened. The things my body did to keep me going—oxygen intake, et cetera—just hit pause. The mural flipped my off-switch. This part's a blur. I remember my father's face taking shape, and finding beauty in what Betsy was doing like a ribbon in a dream that was curling through the air, and feeling like I was chasing every brushstroke she made, but the ribbon was always out of reach. The whole time I'm just standing there, like everybody else, right? But my mind was racing. It wasn't a dull kind of trance. It was active. Years passed in a heartbeat. Her technique stirred my brain, like she was reaching in with a wooden spoon and mushing it around. I remember being at least semi-aware that I was in the grips of a profound and untamed energy. Then the heat started to rise. The ribbon I was chasing lit up and burned bright like the trails of a sparkler. I snapped out of it, along with everybody else, and found that it was nighttime. And the church was on fire. I watched the mural burn, and the roof cave in on itself, and nobody came to put it out. I found out later that Assface Hank—he's the local sheriff—"

"Of course he is."

"—managed to lead a few people in to burn the church from the inside."

"Sounds drastic."

Lark shrugs. "I don't blame them. What are people supposed to do in a situation that has no precedent at all? Honestly, I feel like the next step would have been to shoot Betsy, so I'm actually grateful for their restraint in the moment."

Asha considers this.

"So when enough of the fire had engulfed the wall with her mural on it, and everybody came back to themselves and sort of slunk away to clean up, I grabbed Betsy and took her home. My sister was obviously not in a good place. There was a lack of hygiene. She was way too thin. Her clothes were covered in paint, and her skin was too. She was so weak and depleted she could barely stand up. It was like she focused all her energy on the mural, and afterward she was just a husk. I tried to talk to her, to ask her what the fuck had just happened, and how she did it, and it was like talking to somebody raised by wolves. Like she'd gone feral. I mean, she was still my sister, but a million degrees away from the person I left there three years earlier.

"When we got to the house, my father was watching the local news and eating a bowl of cornflakes. He turned to look at me when I walked in the door and his expression didn't change. At all. Keep in mind I'd been gone for three years at this point. There was a little driblet of milk on his chin and I watched it drip down onto his shirt. In that house, growing up, Betsy and I had rooms upstairs and my father slept on the first floor. I took her upstairs and the second I got up there, I knew something was really, really wrong. The first floor looked exactly how I'd left it, but the second floor was everything Betsy had been grappling with here alone, spread out and scattered everywhere. Half-finished paintings on whatever she could find. Canvas and cardboard and wood and bricks. Pages torn out of coffee-table books. The whole place smelled like rotten fruit. I knew right away that my father hadn't bothered to set foot up there in years.

"I don't know how long she'd been fending for herself, but it clearly wasn't working. There was a total disconnect between my sister and my father. I couldn't believe it. How could they be occupying the same house together, you know? But living lives so separate that she was going through some insane metamorphosis upstairs and he was down in the living room eating cornflakes?

"So I got her the hell out of there, and bought this place"—he gestures into the air around him—"with the money from the rest of the *Citadel* series."

Asha raises an eyebrow. "That was enough money for a *house*?"

"Enough for a fixer-upper in the woods outside of Wofford Falls, yeah. So long story short—"

"Too late for that," Krupp says from under the blanket.

"—I owed her. I ran away, and she spiraled, and my dad didn't give a shit. He got just as lost, I think. So I never left again. I give her a safe place to work. I make sure she eats and sleeps. Has actual human contact. It's not a bad life, for either of us. And here we are." He shakes his head. "*Were*. Until yesterday."

"And her work itself, these days…" Asha prods.

"Forgeries, entirely," Lark says. "It's the only way to keep her, uh, *gift*, contained. Strict imitation. Perfection. An obsessiveness you wouldn't believe. Talent I don't understand even a quarter of, laser-focused. Given boundaries. Existing inside a fucking fence. Still, there's always a little piece of the true Betsy that slips itself in. The turning. But it's mostly contained."

Krupp sits up. There's a red imprint in his cheek, an indent from the bunched-up blanket. The flesh of his throat is the color of a plum in two distinct blotches where Wrecker pressed hardest. He rubs his hollow eyes. "Morning, everyone. Asha, hey. Thanks for coming on short notice. Nice to finally meet you. I like your hair. Very, um, something." He turns to Lark. "I got her number from your phone, if you're wondering." He pulls an arm from beneath the blanket and holds up Lark's phone.

Asha looks from Lark to Krupp. She smooths an imaginary wrinkle atop her thigh. "All right," she says. "Now that I'm here, I think it's time we boiled this down to the essentials. Betsy's been abducted. You've been given a task. Quite understandably, you've been operating as if the latter is the key to the former."

"I don't have a *choice*, Asha."

"But you do have *options*."

"This is why I called you," Krupp says, proud of himself. "An outside perspective. City mice and country mice, joining forces. Unstoppable mice-pals. Sorry. Keep going. Nice robe, by the way, Lark."

"I have to finish the sculpture," Lark says, getting to his feet. "You guys can help me do that, or not. But it's the only way."

He supposes Asha could be right about options, but he's committed now. *The Insomniack* rises on that lonely outcrop, awaiting *The Worm & the Dogsbody*, and he will see it through.

There's that old tingling in his gut that has nothing to do with Betsy.

"You're blowing up," Krupp says, tossing Lark his phone.

"As am I," Asha says, retrieving her own phone from her handbag. "Oh my God." She holds up her screen for Lark and Krupp to see. At the same time, Lark opens the message on his phone from another unknown number. Krupp scrambles within the folds of the blanket and comes up with his own device.

"Shit," he says softly.

They've all three received the same pair of photos. In the first, Betsy's face is framed in close-up. A curved, pearl-handled knife juts into the frame.

In the second photo, the tip of the knife pierces the skin of Betsy's neck, drawing out blood that trickles like the newly birthed waterfall, but darkly, with no sun to hit it in Betsy's prison.

13

The worm and the dogsbody," Asha reads aloud. She's in the passenger seat of Lark's truck, shining her phone light on the psalter open in her lap. Krupp, sandwiched between them, has the glass jar containing Lark's birthday gift from Betsy wedged between his feet. They're en route to the Backbone. Asha needs to see the sculpture.

Lark wraps his sweat-slick palms around the steering wheel and tries to keep them from sliding. His eyes are pinned to the road that winds up through the hills. The blade sinking into his sister's neck is superimposed over the windshield. A ghost on the nighttime highway. He can't blink it away. It's just a small nick as captured in the photo, but what happened in the moments after the picture was taken? Did the blade withdraw, or did it sink in farther?

You are fucking this up, Larky boy.

How could he have slept so long? For that matter, how could he have *pissed himself*?

"The lowliest creature of the foil"—Asha shakes her head, corrects herself—"*soil.*"

"Lark," Krupp says.

"Giving one yet lowlier still a task at which it will toil until the firmament collapses and the heavens darken and the—"

"Lark!"

The blade floating over the two-lane blacktop recedes as Krupp's voice inflicts some damage on its spell. Betsy's neck fades into the night.

Lark pulls onto the shoulder and clicks on the hazards. His tired brain grinds against itself.

"What the hell?" he says. Asha looks up from the book and kills her phone light.

Lark turns to his passengers. "I'm not supposed to be here." The headlights illuminate a yield sign and a bend in the road. A soggy McDonald's bag is clumped against the guardrail. Lark points straight ahead. "That's the ramp to 17—it'll take us to the bridge."

Asha looks back at him blankly.

"We're heading east out of town, toward the Hudson," Lark explains. "The sculpture, the Backbone, the creekbed, the cliffs—they're *west*, on the way to the mountains. We're on the wrong side of town. Somehow."

"So," Asha says, "you went the wrong way."

"No," Lark says, laughing at the absurdity, "I didn't. I took Market to Prospect to Miller. I've done this a thousand times."

"Since we were kids," Krupp adds.

In the darkness of the truck's cab, Asha's massive pupils still gleam. "This was overshadowed by everything else that was going on," she says, "but what I was telling you when I first arrived—it took me twice as long to get to your house as it should have. Once I got off the exit, my GPS kept rerouting me to nowhere, like it got stuck in a glitch. Or the satellites went offline."

"Magnets," Krupp says. Lark stares at him. "Something magnetic."

"I wasn't using a *compass*, Wayne," Asha says.

"Call me Krupp," Krupp says. "Wayne's my dad."

Lark gazes out into the darkness of a late-winter evening that would be early spring most anywhere else. The McDonald's bag, it occurs to him suddenly, appears to have been planted. He can't pinpoint the source of this notion, but there's something inorganic about the whole scene, lit up like a museum exhibit—*roadside, 21st century, upstate NY*. Something else crowds his thoughts—the waterfall springing from nowhere, bursting forth from the dry centuries. Today's deep sleep, despite his nerves being on a razor's edge, his day loaded with tasks yet to complete. Waking up in a puddle of his own piss...

A sudden stark vision comes and goes—the world as a painting, a perfect forgery down to the last blade of grass, and Betsy's turning landing squarely upon Wofford Falls itself.

"I just need to turn around real quick," Lark says, unconvincingly.

He three-points it and heads back the way he came, or so he hopes.

"What do you think, Asha," Krupp says, tapping the book in her lap. "Can we actually make this thing?"

"Give me some time to make sense of it," Asha says, turning her light on and resuming her study of the psalter.

"Hey, Krupp," Lark says, "why'd you call Asha in the first place?"

"Don't talk about me like I'm not here," Asha says.

"Why did Krupp call you?" Lark redirects.

"You enlisted *me*," Krupp says, "so I figured anyone non-law-enforcement was fair game."

"Yeah, but I mean why her specifically." He shakes his head. "Asha. You. Whatever."

"I'll venture a theory," Asha says. "You needed an outsider's perspective—someone with an eye for the work we'll be doing, but without the emotional ties to this town and its inhabitants. Since Lark's existence up here is rather *hermetic*, I was your only option."

"That," Krupp says, "and our other friends are complete fuckups."

Lark hangs a quick left on Miller, past another figure of wire and wood that he donated to the library. This one seems to beckon to weary pedestrians to take a load off on a rust-flecked bench. There's a plaque on the seat commemorating his gift and a spotlight planted in the mulch that illuminates it from below.

"I think it's more like, you wanted to put together a team," Lark says.

"It has nothing to do with that."

"You've *always* wanted a team." Lark explains what he's getting at to Asha. "Ever since we were kids watching GI Joe, he's always wanted to assemble a crew of operatives with different skills. Explosives, spy shit, knives, telekinesis, safecracking."

Krupp squirms in his seat. "Shut up."

Lark can't help the laugh that escapes. Krupp's embarrassment is palpable. It's like he just told Asha that Krupp still plays with action figures. Like they're kids on the bus with an older girl they're trying to be cool around. "I guarantee you he's got a list of possible code names for us in his notes app."

"Let's talk about how you just went the wrong way, Lark. That was weird."

"Marauder to Eagle, over."

"*Shut the fuck up!*" Krupp hits back with venom.

A thick silence hangs in the wake of his outburst. Lark can sense his coiled energy, his wiry body curling inward, the rage of a cornered animal.

"I'm sorry," Lark says. He can't remember the last time Krupp took something the wrong way.

Krupp takes a few deep breaths. "I'm sorry too," he says, sounding stunned by his own vehemence.

"It would be an order of magnitude easier if this book supplied an itemized list," Asha says, pointedly breaking the tension. She flips through the psalter with authority. "How maddening. Though I'd be interested in its provenance. I'd love to get Justine's appraisal. Anyway, it looks as if it's all subject to interpretation."

"Yeah," Krupp says, "but it was easy to interpret *The Insomniack*."

Lark thinks of the radiator, the cast-iron pan, the coffin. "More or less."

"Let's zoom out and consider the theme," Asha says, her eyes scanning the tiny, crabbed text. She flips to the diagrams. Lark hangs a left on Miller, past the oldest beer hall in the Hudson Valley—now an apartment building—and glances over at the psalter.

"Jesus," he says.

"I doubt that," Asha says quietly. The diagram practically throbs on the page. Organic rather than geometric. Amoebic shapes, the etchings and shadings of some early anatomy textbook, oversize organs and offal in weird bloodless array. Soft rather than precise. Alive with sketched energy, beating and writhing like a body turned inside out.

"So," she says, "as far as I can tell, the idea here is that a hierarchy can always be created. Even when you think you've reached the bottom, there's always a lower place. A lower form of life. I guess this Van Leeman, three hundred years ago, conceived of a worm as both low on the food chain, and *literally* low, as in—dwells underfoot, in the soil."

"I figured he meant worm as in *demon*," Krupp says.

Asha shakes her head. "I think he would have used *snake* if there was any kind of satanic overtones. Which I don't really see here. This doesn't seem like a text in opposition to any sort of Judeo-Christian framework—it seems like its own thing. We're not summoning the devil, here, as far as I can tell."

"This is going to sound weird," Krupp says, "but I kind of wish we were. I mean, not literally—I just mean that kind of thing would be easier to understand. Devil worship, pentagrams, blood chalices. A stolen piece of hair. A fucking chant or two. Cliché but at least I *get it*."

Asha eyes his Danzig shirt. "Anyway. What I believe we would have to do to create the easiest representation of this concept is get a preponderance of worms—"

"A bait shop," Lark suggests. Ahead, a hatchback with its flashers on is pulled over on the shoulder, jutting halfway out into the road. They're on the Miller Avenue Extension, which curves like a ladle scooping up the south end of town, skirting Main Street entirely. One time Lark and Krupp, underage-drunk on malt liquor forties bought with couch-scavenged coins, streaked for half a mile down this forlorn road on the coldest night of the year. Lark recalls an argument about whether it was okay to wear shoes, if footwear counted as clothes and thus negated the streak. In the end they ran it barefoot and no cars passed them. This engendered further discussion, still not settled to this day. If you streak and no one witnesses your naked ass, did you really streak at all?

"Marky Mark's Bait and Tackle over on 34 South," Krupp says.

Lark slows to pull alongside the stopped car.

"And then, perhaps, some sort of dirt sculpture," Asha says. "Worms eat dirt, as I understand it."

Lark stops and rolls down his window. There's a woman leaning against the hood of her car, staring off into space.

"You okay?" he calls out.

Startled, as if she didn't hear an F-150 cruise up and stop a few feet away from where she stands, the woman recoils. Her long hair obscures her face.

"You need help?" Lark calls out again. He can feel Krupp and Asha watching with great interest.

The woman shakes her head slowly. She's backlit by her headlights, strobed red by the flashers. "I don't know how to get home," she says, maybe to Lark, maybe to no one at all. "To my babies."

"Okay," Lark says, "where's home?"

Now she looks at the truck. The light on the left side of her head makes a half-moon of her face. Her eyes are bright, searching, wet.

"There." She points off into the distance, in the relative direction of downtown Wofford Falls.

"Like, by the Stewart's?" Krupp asks.

"Yes!" Suddenly animated, the woman takes a single step toward the truck. Now Lark recognizes her as one of the checkout clerks from the Price Chopper over on 9 West. Sandy, he thinks.

He's struck by the sudden urge to roll up his window and peel out. *Calm down*, he tells himself, *it's just Sandy.*

"You need to backtrack," Lark says. "Try again. That's what I did, just now."

"My youngest, Peyton, has a chest cold," Sandy explains. "I just went to get some cough syrup. But then the pharmacy wasn't—I couldn't find it." She takes another step toward the truck. "My babies are home alone," she says, pleading. "And now I'm *here*." She raises her arms, *here* as in the shoulder of the Miller Avenue Extension, where there's nothing but a guardrail and a ditch full of poison ivy and a shopping cart or two.

"Just try again," Lark says. It sounds feeble, almost mocking. It's no help at all. His foot trembles, hummingbird-quick, desperate to hit the gas.

"Geographical dislocation," Krupp says quietly, quoting the subtitle on the cover of the psalter. "You did this."

Lark cuts his eyes at his friend, sharp and sudden—Krupp's usage of *you*, the implicit accusation that Lark and Lark alone, through his sculpture, is responsible for this new wrinkle. As if Krupp hadn't been at his side through all of it. For the second time since they got in the truck, some strange new facet of Krupp has emerged. He feels, suddenly, alone. And culpable.

Normal Krupp? Normal Krupp would have said *we.*

"Lark," Asha says, low and measured. "We need to go."

"Hey!" Sandy says, nearly at the truck's window now. "I know you. Mr. Larkin, right? You're a Price Chopper Advantage member."

Discomfort prickles. He's caught between Krupp and Sandy—responsible, perhaps, for everyone's predicament. The last word of the Gold Shade's Saturday revelers runs through his head: *asshole.* Along with Wrecker's parting shot: *I never want to see you again.*

The town baring its true feelings for its most famous son.

"Yeah," he says. "Hi, Sandy."

"It's Sally."

"Hi, Sally," Krupp calls out.

She peers into the truck's cab. "Wayne Krupp? Gotta be."

"We really have to go, Sally," Lark says. "Just take Miller back the way you came. Keep trying."

"No, that's what I just did!" A hysterical edge rises. She curls her fingers around the lip of the open window. Cigarette-breath puffs into the truck. Lark remembers now, though he can't see it: She has a chain of dolphins tattooed around her wrist like one of those Pandora bracelets. Inked fishy charms. "Help me," she says. "Take me with you. I'll show you that I'm not crazy."

"We don't think you're crazy," Lark says.

(*You did this.*)

The wind picks up. A crumpled candy wrapper tumbles past, along the shoulder, and disappears into the ditch. Dark strands of Sally's hair get lifted by the breeze. They float, sideways, then fall away.

"I need to get home," she says. "Please."

"Just turn around and head back on Prospect. Prospect's where it should be. There are people at the library."

"It's craft night," Sally says, like *duh* there are people at the library. "Please," she says, "take me with you."

"There's no room," Lark says.

"I'll ride in the back."

"We gotta go, Sally. I'm sorry. Just—get to the library. Someone will help you."

"I'm asking *you* for help, Mr. Larkin."

"Hop in the back," Krupp says.

Lark opens his mouth to protest, but instead finds himself rolling up the window, slamming the truck into drive, and leaving Sally in the roadside dust that swirls up as the F-150 peels out.

"What the fuck!" Krupp says. "She needed our help."

Lark forces his eyes down on the road ahead, keeps them away from the rearview. Sally is screaming after him, something he can't make out. *Asshole.*

"That was the right decision," Asha assures him.

"*You* don't live here," Krupp says to her, that un-Krupp-like viciousness returning to his voice. An anger seemingly borrowed from another person entirely. "We help each other."

"What did you want me to do?" Lark says. "Take her with us? Drive her around? Add her to the *team*?"

Krupp mutters something and shifts in his seat.

Lark turns off the extension, picks up a winding stretch of 212, feels the truck meet the new gradient with an eagerness he's always appreciated. A truck that *wants* to climb higher.

"I can't make this out of worms," Lark decides, all at once, out loud. The moon, almost full, moves through the upmost reaches of the roadside pines, zipping across the windshield like a Méliès moon with modern production values, a stage prop fixed to the night sky while the world swoops and dips around it. Lark half expects it to grimace. "There has to be solidity to it. Form beyond just the thing. I'm not Damien Hirst."

"I understand," Asha says. "Organics aren't really in your wheelhouse. But I don't know if you have much of a choice here."

"I need a way to adapt what's in that book to what I do," Lark says.

Asha bends to the psalter. Krupp's head lolls back against the seat. A moment later, he's snoring.

"Is he sleeping?" Asha says.

"He does that." Lark slows as the road dips. His brain tingles. A warning, an off-kilter rhythm, a disruption in the road he's been driving since he got his license. His headlights sweep across errant landscape, stray trees, an out-of-place guardrail that reflects dully and without purpose. He tightens his grip on the wheel. Maybe, if he white-knuckles his way through this disruption, it will smooth out into the geography he understands.

You did this you did this you did this—

"Cattle," Asha says abruptly, and he glances across his slumbering friend to the passenger seat.

"Like what," Lark says, "like *cows*?"

"I think that's the way," Asha taps a page in the psalter as if punctuating this decision. As if anything in the old book could be so neatly expressed. "Which means you'll have to become an upstate Damien Hirst after all. Sorry, Lark."

Lark swings his attention back to the road that ought to be winding ever higher into the Catskills, but has begun to slope down toward a forlorn-looking tree removal service housed in a dilapidated old warehouse, which he knows to be on the northern outskirts of Wofford Falls. At the same time, his scrambled thoughts organize around Damien Hirst: tiger sharks floating in vats of formaldehyde, rotting heads, maggot-infested glass cases.

"If you say so," he says.

Krupp begins to snore. Lights appear. Lights that should not be. The old brewery building looms. The sagging porches of old homes long ago sliced into cheap apartments with shared kitchens. Wofford Falls, clawing him back down from the mountains. The inexplicable embrace of roads given new destinies.

"Motherfuck," he says. "I did this."

"I take it we're not where we want to be?" Asha says.

Lark feels the nerve-jangling rage of his Lost Year nipping at him. "Not even close," he says. The world outside the windshield takes on a cinematic blur, a rotoscoped quavering like two flat planes moved out of sync. Then they snap back together, shoved into place by the figure who bursts out the door of the Gold Shade and stagger-steps into the middle of the street.

Lark hits the brakes. Asha's arm darts out to keep Krupp's head from face-planting into the dashboard. He lays on the horn. "Jesus Christ, Eddie!"

Eddie the Can Man, slack-jawed and swaying in the headlights, flips Lark's truck a double bird. Lark rolls down the window and leans out. "What the hell are you doing? I almost hit you."

Eddie takes a moment to process the voice coming from the window of the truck. Then a sly, downturned smile shifts his scraggly beard. "Burn the witch!" He glances back toward the Shade, transfers one of his middle fingers in the bar's general direction, then crosses the street to reunite with his shopping cart.

Lark spots a hulking figure in the doorway, pulls up in front of the bar, and throws the truck into park. "Ian!" he calls out the window.

Ian's standing with massive arms folded, watching Eddie go, affecting a bouncer's mean-mug and stance. The sleeves of his leather jacket ride up his forearms.

"Hey, brother. I had to toss his ass out."

"I almost nailed him."

"I'd be more sorry for the psychological damage that'd leave you with than the physical fucked-up-ness for Eddie, getting a face full of F-150."

"I don't even want to know what he did."

Ian shrugs. "Weird shit going down, people act one of two ways.

They man up, or they think they got a license to act dickish with impunity." Ian peers into the truck. "Krupp reformatting," he says. It's more of a matter-of-fact statement than a question. A thing he just noticed.

Asha leans forward. "Hello." She waves to Ian.

"Hey there."

"Asha, my agent," Lark says, "Ian, my old buddy. He owns the yarn and tea store."

"That sounds unbearably charming," Asha says.

"It's painfully twee," Ian agrees. "I fucking love it. Anyway, Beth Two's got a safe space sort of thing going inside. Making the Shade a refuge. What else are people gonna do, call 911? Assface Hank's off on goose chases."

Lark's mind whirrs. He thinks of cattle. More specifically, a lone cow, standing in a field, transferred, somehow, to the sculpture...

Organics aren't his wheelhouse indeed.

He turns to Asha. "Watch Krupp for a second."

"Where are you going?"

"I need a drink."

"*Now? We don't have time!*"

He puts the truck in park, kills the engine, and hops out. Ian turns his head and blows out a floral cloud. "Fuckin' lavender, you believe that?"

Lark claps him on his meaty shoulder. "How are you, Ian?"

He thinks for a moment. "There's a lack of clarity." He shakes his head. "You know, Eddie was a real aggressive shitstain just now. Even for him."

Lark glances back toward the truck and lowers his voice. "Krupp had a moment, too. A little while ago. He lost his cool, snapped at me like he wanted to bite my head off. It was weird."

"Aggression's general all over town. I walked here just fine, but people been straggling in, freaked as fuck, telling stories about getting lost. Tell me this, Lark, how's a guy like Terry Haverchuck getting lost? He's been here his whole life, same as me."

You did this. "I don't know," he says.

Ian seems to regard him for a beat too long. Then he shrugs. "Let's get you that drink."

Lark shoots another glance at the truck and sidesteps under the eaves of the bird-shit-spattered awning. "Listen, Ian. You still got that piece?"

"You talking about my uncle Burl's Magnum?"

"Yeah, the Dirty Harry gun."

"It's in my shop."

"Um." Lark feels suddenly like he's overstepped, like he's being as much of a dick as Eddie the Can Man in a different way. "Can I borrow it?"

Ian slides his vape into the pocket of his jacket. "Tell me something, Lark. You roll up with Krupp and your agent in Shifty—"

"In what?"

"Shifty. The F-I Shifty. The truck."

"Did we used to call it that?"

"I did."

"I never knew."

"The point is, there's something you're not telling me."

"Just, can I borrow the gun or not, Ian?"

"You realize there's never a good time for somebody to borrow your gun without saying why, but right now is *really* not a good time, right, my dude?"

"I do realize that."

"You wanna shed some light on your whole deal, here?" He thwacks a palm against the door. "Because there's some pretty scared people been popping in and out all day. If you got some insight, we could all use it. Like why you think you need to be strapped. For example."

"I don't have any insight that's gonna help anybody right now."

Ian ponders Lark's carefully chosen words. "If you say so." He turns and Lark follows him into the Shade. There's Beth Two, the fossilized crew by the jukebox, and a few stragglers kicking around the booths.

"The prodigal son!" Angelo calls out as Lark enters.

"Shut the fuck up," Jerry says.

"Anybody heard from Del?" Constance says. The old blue-hair brings her iced Chardonnay to her lips, pinkie up, and leaves a red crescent of lipstick on the glass.

"Probably taking a shit at the Burger King," offers Jerry. He's eating handfuls of cherry tomatoes from a Tupperware container. "I says to him once, Del, you got issues with the plumbing at your place? He says to me the walk to the BK gives him more time for the loaf to cook." Jerry shakes his head. "Fucking vulgar."

"Maybe he got out of town," Constance says.

"Roads are bad," Jerry counters, tomato juice dripping down his chin.

"Roads ain't being *roads* no more," says Angelo as Beth Two slides a fresh Fernet in front of him. "If he got out he's one of the lucky ones."

"It's that nuclear power plant," Constance says. "I warned them, back in '89. Look what happened to the Russians."

"Ukrainians," Beth Two says. "Chernobyl was in Ukraine."

"It's all *Soviet*," Constance says. "People say it's better here, I don't believe that. You think it can't happen. I've got news for you. Look around."

"The plant's in Fredericksville," Angelo says. "A hundred miles away, dingbat."

"I know where it is." Constance sips.

"And two," Angelo says, "I never heard of nuclear radiation acting like this."

"The things you never heard of could fill Yankee Stadium," Jerry says.

"We don't know what it can do," Constance says. "We can't even see it."

"That's crap," Jerry says. "This ain't nuclear."

"Whatever it is," Beth Two says, "we'll get through it together. Why don't you play some songs, Jerry."

Ian takes a seat and taps a fingernail against a glass of the house red. Lark leans on the bar and waits for Beth Two. It might be his imagination, but he thinks she's stink-eyeing him. She tosses her bar rag into the netherworld of half-hidden bins and comes over.

"Hey, Beth," he says. "You still have that .38 special under the register?"

She narrows her eyes. "You got nerve, Lark. Bringing your goddamn sister out and about, bringing her to *my bar*, right before everything starts to go to hell? Like we can't put two and two together. Like we got short memories, don't know what happened last time she got loose."

"That was fifteen—"

"Don't give me that shit!" Lark has no idea if Beth Two is pitched a degree or two higher, like Krupp in that slippery moment, or if she's righteously, organically pissed at him. "Terry Haverchuck was just here. He can't get out to the farm to see his girls. He's falling apart."

"He's been falling apart in slow motion since Jamie-Lynn left him," Lark points out.

"Fuck off with that," Beth Two says. "Don't change the subject. Your sister came in here with bad energy. I felt it from ten feet away. Everybody did."

"You take a poll?"

"You know you act like you and her have diplomatic immunity," Beth Two says.

Lark tries to interpret this and Beth smirks at his silence. "You surprised I know about that concept?"

"No, I just—I don't get what you mean."

"What I mean is, level with me, Lark. What did that witch do this time? Are we gonna have to burn the whole fucking town to the ground to get rid of whatever evil curse she sprung on us?"

"Beth, for one, that's ridiculous. And two, can you trust me, here? You've known me forever. I just need to borrow that gun."

She laughs. "Unless you make a solemn vow that you're using it to put two in your sister's head, no fucking way."

"You bastard."

Lark wheels around at the venomous interjection. There's Sally, striding across the barroom, turning the heads of the stragglers in the booths. Her eyes are wild. Her boots clomp with savage intent. *"You motherfucker."*

"Sally—"

"You ditched me back there on the road because you were in a hurry to *get a drink*?"

"I'm here for something else," he says, flashing his empty palms to demonstrate the lack of drink.

"This selfish asshole," she raises her voice, proclaims to the bar, pointing a trembling finger at Lark. The regulars quit murmuring. "Saw me out there, alone, on the side of the road, and I begged him for help. My youngest is sick and I was just trying to get some medicine but the roads"—her hysteria overtakes the words and she catches her breath—"they brought me to the wrong place, to the middle of nowhere, outside of town, and then back here, when all I want is to get to the goddamn CVS."

"Jesus, Lark," Ian says. He gets up from his seat and goes to usher Sally gently to a barstool. "It's okay," he tells her. "Take it easy. We'll figure it out."

"The CVS that's not where it's supposed to be!" Her voice edges into ragged dissolution. Ian goes behind the bar and gets her a glass of water from the good tap.

"His sister was here," Beth Two tells Sally. "Betsy Larkin. Out and about doing God knows what."

"It ain't God knows anything about what Betsy Larkin is doing," Jerry says with a smug certainty that makes Lark want to bash in his red, mottled nose.

Eddie the Can Man's voice echoes in his head. *Burn the witch.* "Betsy has nothing to do with this." Lark tries not to shout, but it comes out nervous, defensive.

"Quite the coincidence, though," Angelo points out.

"Take it easy, everyone," Ian says. Sally chugs her water and it runs down her chin and darkens the front of her gray top.

"Help us, Lark," Beth Two says. "Tell us what's going on out there. Tell us what we should do."

"Stay put," he says. It sounds like feeble, tossed-off advice.

"My Peyton is *sick!*" Sally says. "I can't sit around a bar."

"Hey man." Ian puts a hand on Lark's shoulder and steers him toward the door. "Let's go outside."

"Listen to me," Lark says quietly. "Try to keep everybody calm. They're better off here than out there getting lost."

"You want me to babysit the Shade crowd while shit goes down?"

"Just to make sure nobody gets hurt."

"*Are* people going to get hurt, Lark? Why do you need a gun so bad? What else is coming?"

"I don't know."

"But something *is* coming."

"Yeah," he says at the door. "Something's coming."

14

It didn't click for me until you mentioned Hirst," Asha says. "It was like you *invoked* him, and everything fell into place. I was conceiving of the worm and the dogsbody much too literally, which I blame on Justine's recent obsession with a certain kind of cranky Russian formalism. You should see the *angles* in our town house, it's like I'm always being poked and prodded. But that's neither here nor there. What I'm getting at is, Hirst's work floats over what the psalter is asking of you, conceptually." She shakes her head. "I'm not expressing this properly. Justine and I speak a different sort of language, I've become accustomed to a certain—now it sounds like I'm blaming her for everything, but I assure you—never mind."

Lark takes a hard right on what he hopes is the road that will take him past the skate park where the Czerpak kid just OD'd, the one-story Midway Motel, Ian's newly sober sister's newly shuttered bakery (which, depressingly, sucked). He thinks of Asha's pupils, round black pools, and wonders if she re-upped her microdose since they left the house. He's suspicious of her sense of wonder, even though it's justified. The echo of the waterfall churns through his mind. *You did this.* "Can you boil this Hirst thing down for me?"

"Hirst's work is executed by dogsbodies. He's a factory operation, assistants in Mexico doing the assembly, the sourcing, while he squeezes out the conceptual juice from his house in some druidic UK hinterland."

"So you want me to—" Lark is struck by deep resonance. "Goddamn."

"What?"

"It's like I told you—my sister's a forger. A Method actor. She *becomes* artists."

The jar with his birthday gift is still sitting in the dark, wedged between Krupp's feet.

"And now you're asking me to do the same thing." He shakes his head. "But that's not me, Asha. You know that."

Asha lets out a sigh as only she can—clipped and brief and haughty and sympathetic, all at once.

"Lark, I don't know how else to say this. You know I have your best interests at heart, yes?"

"Yeah, I'm your favorite client. Hold on." Lark hits the brakes as shining eyes, hovering for a moment at the edge of the road, float smoothly across it, attached to a bounding silhouette. "You always gotta look back the way it came," Lark says. "Where goes one deer, more follow."

"Syntactically a nightmare," Asha says, but her heart's not in the insult. The wonder's there. She keeps her wide eyes on the empty road. No deer follow the first. Krupp snores softly.

Lark eases his foot down on the gas pedal. "Anyway."

"You're a rare talent, Lark, but you don't possess the rugged individuality that you've internalized about yourself over the years."

He laughs. "I've never pretended to be anything special, Asha. You know that."

"What I mean is, your outsider bent—"

"None of this is an *act*. I don't do acts. It's just the way I live. The way I work."

Asha seems to brace herself, then the words come in a torrent. "You should be able to slip into something Hirst-adjacent now with ease, is what I'm saying. You're not an innovator, Lark, and you never have been. You've done quite a bit of self-mythologizing in that regard. I am being completely honest when I tell you that your work is a lot of wonderful, rare things, but it doesn't have that, I don't want to say *stamp* of true originality of—"

"Your other favorite clients?"

"It doesn't have the *frisson* of the new," Asha continues. "It lacks reverence for influences, of course, and that's sort of tonally admirable, but it's also wholly separate from the generational boldness required to—"

"Have your work shot into space?"

"Well, yes," Asha says, sounding relieved that he drew the parallel. "Felicia's not nearly as formally gifted as you are, but, conceptually speaking—Justine calls her Le Petit Oeuf, meaning—"

"I know what the fuck that means, Asha. Thanks for the pep talk." He realizes he's speeding and doesn't care.

"You may resent it at the moment," Asha says, "but a pep talk is exactly what this is."

Lark wishes Krupp were awake to hear this shit, but he's also equally grateful for his friend's momentary oblivion. The crack team Krupp's been craving all his life isn't exactly gelling, here. The mission, such as it is, is in free fall. Maybe they would be better off with the old deadbeat crew. Maybe he should swing by the Old Forge, an even divier dive than the Shade, and see who's prowling around.

Lark zips through the intersection where the CVS and Nico's Pharmacy (est. 1907) stare each other down. At least, he thinks, the CVS *should* have been there, a bright blot of commerce at the edge of town. He wonders if Sally's moved on from the Shade, if she's managed to blunder her way to this corner, or if she's still sitting at the bar sipping water and talking shit about him.

Next to him, Krupp's head tilts forward and then snaps upright like a zombie come alive. A cheap effect.

"What's going on?" he says.

"Asha was just telling me that my work is derivative garbage. I'm beginning to suspect I'm not her favorite client after all."

"He's taking it the wrong way," Asha tells Krupp. "And that's not what I said."

"Don't talk about me like I'm not here," Lark says. "Also where *is* here?"

"We're on Granger," Krupp says, pointing. "There's the animal shelter."

"That should've been back there," Lark says. Dislocation creeps into his blood, carves his thoughts into snippets.

"I was saying a suitable modern interpretation of the worm and the dogsbody might be to do something kind of homage-y but also slavish, and Damien Hirst's work fits the bill perfectly."

"I agree," Krupp says.

"You don't know who Damien Hirst is," Lark says.

"Cow head," Krupp says. "Shark. I have the internet."

"There's the sign for 78!" Lark says. "We've been on this road forever."

"So where are you *trying* to go?"

"The old homestead."

Krupp coughs into his hand. "Your father's place?"

"Why on earth would you want to go there?" Asha says.

"Guns."

15

The old homestead comes into view at last. The clock on the dash says 9:37, but Lark suspects the minutes are ticking by too slowly, like time's stuck in primordial ooze, dragging itself out of the bog with great effort.

The house where he and Betsy grew up, where Big Tom Larkin still resides, sits on a patch of unincorporated land between the western edge of Wofford Falls and the trailer-strewn reaches of Meisnerville. He nears the end of the gravel drive cut into the woods and takes careful stock of the yard, which he pays Jamie-Lynn's ex-husband Terry to take care of. Lark entertains a brief fantasy of nature reclaiming this place, vines rising up to strangle the siding, roots bursting through floorboards, branches dismantling the roof. Big Tom himself, recliner and man fully enveloped by a massive flytrap, the TV glow illuminating his final devourment.

He parks the truck but doesn't yet kill the headlights.

"Here we are," he says. The house, a modest split-level, suburban in spirit despite its seclusion, seems to long for some neighbors. In a hazy past he can scarcely imagine, his mother and father had the place built as their forever home. He wonders, if Big Tom could have seen the future, would he still have married his mother, had two kids, tried to build any kind of life at all?

"After everything that happened here," Asha says, "why did you settle down in Wofford Falls? You and Betsy could have lived anywhere."

"Ha," Krupp says, like he already knows the answer, which he does. "Betsy wanted to stay close."

Asha's taken aback. "She still has a relationship with your father?"

"Something like that." Lark kills the engine and the front of the house goes dark except for a lamp in an upstairs window. Betsy's old room.

"Plot twist," Krupp whispers to Asha, nudging her arm.

Lark opens the door and steps outside. The gravel drive feels spongy beneath his boots. The air's acrid with trash burning in Meisnerville, a Sunday-night firepit. Crickets join in chorus from the underbrush. There's something *summery* about the atmosphere here. The air's so cold he can see his breath, but Lark's hit with a wave of nostalgia for cruising to the docks on Bernard Lake, where the fireflies congregate so thickly it's like a shower of sparks from some invisible arc welder. His memory-trigger's become unpredictable. Too many wires crossed, and it's going to get worse before it gets better. This much he knows. He glances across the hood of the truck to Krupp, who pops out the door and stretches his arms above his head and tilts his upper back to one side until his joints crack.

"You guys don't have to come in," Lark says.

"Can't pass up a chance for a chin wag with Big Tom," Krupp says.

Asha kicks at the gravel with an impractical shoe. Lark wonders, when she woke up this morning, how she imagined her night going. An art opening downtown, some late-night eats at the Odeon (he always imagines her traipsing through a simulacrum of some lost Reagan-era downtown scene), a cucumber mask before bed.

She folds her arms. "How many guns are we talking about here?"

"He's got a few hunting rifles kicking around. One for each of us."

"And we're just going to take them?"

"*Cattle*, Asha," Lark says, his patience wearing thin. "Damien Hirst shit. Cow heads, right? Those *organs* in the psalter—how else are we supposed to get them? Go to a farm and ask nicely?"

Just ahead, the old front porch proudly bears its fresh coat of paint, its new roof, the double-wide swing straight out of a *Country Living* spread. As long as Betsy's intent on forging something with their father, Lark will pay the roofers and painters, the landscapers and the home health aides and the cleaning service.

He raises his eyes. There's movement behind that upstairs window, the flutter of a curtain, a silhouette in passage. He takes a breath, lets it out, and walks up the porch. A moment later, they're all three standing at the front door.

"Been a long time," Krupp says, running a hand along the brass fixture that outlines the bell. Lark produces a key, unlocks the door, pushes it open. They step into a darkened foyer. He can hear Asha's sharp intake of breath.

The smell is overpowering.

Oils, mediums, fixatives. The same odors that waft up from Betsy's basement studio. At her request, Lark supplies their father with the same materials.

He feels for the panel, flicks all four light switches up.

"What *is* all this?" Asha asks, stepping into the living room.

"Penance," Lark says. "As best as I can figure it."

The walls are covered in paintings. Not an inch of the original wallpaper, chosen by his mother so long ago, is visible. There are hundreds of canvases, bits of cardboard, scraps of wood, all of them hanging over one another, overlapping in mad assembly.

Every painting is a representation of Betsy.

There are rudimentary attempts from a decade ago, swaths of color and childlike, stick-figure formations. There are blotchier, semi-competent renderings from his father's middle period, when Big Tom actually began to bend himself to his endless task and apply his silent energy to representing the daughter he barely bothered to speak to. And then there are the recent abstractions—at first glance a regression—but give any one of them a long enough look and you'll see Betsy emerge as if from a sandstorm.

"So he's going for an outsider effect," Asha says. She turns in a circle to take in the entire room. All that remains of its original layout is Big Tom's recliner and television. "That self-taught Henry Darger mythology, minus the...little girls."

Lark can't help but laugh. "I'm pretty sure Big Tom's not consciously *going* for anything."

Asha approaches a painting from his middle period, in which Betsy's face and hair blend into the backdrop, a haze of oily wash reminiscent of a Cézanne sky if you squint a certain way. "Say what you will about the technique, but I have to disagree," she says. "There's intentionality behind all of this."

"Looks like you've got a new favorite client," Lark says. "No charge for the referral."

"You've been holding out," Asha says, "biographically speaking. I had no idea this creative energy ran in your family to such a degree."

The popcorn ceiling creaks. Big Tom's moving about upstairs. Lark imagines him stepping back to regard a canvas with the same placid non-engaged way he used to let his eyes drift lazily over his children and then out into some thousand-yard abyss. You could talk to him for hours, and his eyes might stray over you at intervals of five, eighteen, forty-two minutes, completely independent of what you're saying, or how you're saying it. Driven, it always seemed, by some randomization tool embedded in his brain.

"It didn't," Lark says, moving toward the passageway to the kitchen. He notes the dust clumped in the corners, feels the grittiness of outdoor dirt under his boots, and resolves to find a new cleaning service. As always, there's the mental tug-of-war between his sister's insistence on their father's comfort and his own petulant urge toward *FUCK YOU, BIG TOM*. Hovering over those clashing impulses is the knowledge that he'd rather not know what Betsy is getting out of all this.

What she's been doing, or saying, to nudge him toward such single-minded artistic expression—at odds with how he lived his entire life, before Lark came home and took Betsy out of this place.

Back when he thought they were done with Big Tom. When he thought he'd be taking Betsy back to the city with him, helping her launch her own career. In some alternate reality, they ascended together, both of them repped by Asha Benedict, each carving out a niche, though Betsy, with her raw talent, would undoubtedly eclipse him.

He moves through the kitchen. His father's dishes are piled in the sink: remnants of the food delivered by the service, prepped by the home aide. The fridge is plastered in sketches—studies of Betsy from every angle. A study in obsession, if you can call it that. Lark's pretty sure it's something else, something more akin to a compulsion imposed upon him. Externally driven. Because there's no way this dedication comes from anywhere within Big Tom, which Lark imagines as nothing more than a yawning void.

"Hey, Lark?" Krupp calls from the living room.

"Be right there," Lark calls back.

He opens the basement door and reaches for the string dangling from the bare bulb. There, hanging on the wall of the landing, where they've always been, are his father's three hunting rifles: one black and tactical-looking, one classic wood-grain stock, and one camouflage. They look no worse than they did a decade ago. He doesn't know much about guns—there was never any pretense that Big Tom was a hunter because of its father-son bonding potential—but he figures your basic rifle is kind of plug-and-play.

"Hey Lark!" Krupp calls again.

"One second, Krupp!" he calls back. He takes the black rifle off the wall. He doesn't know why he expected a clackety thing, a toy, but it's heavier than anticipated. This firearm feels like *material*, something hefty he'd turn into something else. Except he'd never use a gun in a sculpture. Too much metaphorical weight.

He practices sighting down the barrel, jams the stock against the meat of his right shoulder. The last time he shot a gun was with Krupp, in Ian's vast backyard. They'd been seventeen, and each beer they finished had been balanced on a wooden fence, sacrificed to the target-shooting gods. That gun, Uncle Burl's rifle, had been a .22. Lark has no idea what the caliber of this one is.

He pulls the other two rifles from the wall—*three of them, three of us*—and cradles them in his arms, twenty-five pounds of metal and wood. It isn't until he heads back through the kitchen that he hears his father's voice.

Big Tom must have come down the stairs. Which is why Krupp called to him. Lark hurries back down the hallway. Sure enough, there's Krupp, Asha, and Big Tom, standing at opposite ends of the living room like they're playing a party game.

Asha regards the old man warily.

Krupp, on the other hand, is grinning.

And Big Tom? To Lark's utter astonishment, he's *talking*. And it sounds friendly and welcoming, like he's glad to have unexpected houseguests upon a fine Sunday evening.

"Ah!" Lark's father turns as his son enters the living room. "There he is. Hello, Peter."

"He called you Peter!" Krupp says, giggling. Lark shoots him a glare then turns back to his father. He tries to remember how long it's been since he set foot in here. Eight months ago he let a worker in to replace the boiler. Big Tom had sequestered himself upstairs the whole time. He notes that his father has retained his massive presence—at six-four, it would be difficult not to—but looks almost *healthy*. His graying hair is neatly combed, his face freshly shaved. His T-shirt and jeans are spattered with fresh paint, not food or old sweat stains.

"Dad," Lark says, giving his father a curt nod. He notes how self-conscious an armful of rifles can make you feel, especially on a surprise visit. But his father doesn't say anything about them. Instead, Big Tom gestures toward the sofa, covered in a floral sheet.

"Please," his father says, actually meeting his eyes, "take a load off."

"We can't stay," Lark says, fighting to speak through sheer astonishment. He has to tighten his grip on the guns to keep them from hitting the floor like so many cinematic coffee cups. This is the first time in his entire life that his father has ever invited him to sit down and "take a load off."

It only took thirty-six years.

Asha regards the whole scene with great microdosed interest. The only thing she knows about Lark's father is what she's just been told—and now here's the man himself, at odds with the story she'd just heard.

Lark wonders if he's walked into some massive gaslighting scheme, that his father is playing a cruel prank on him, making *him* look like the crazy one...

"What a shame!" Big Tom says, gregarious and genuinely bummed. He eyes the rifles cradled in Lark's arms. "There's ammo on the top shelf of the coat closet." A wry smile appears on his smooth face. "It's funny you'd show up now, like this—I was just thinking of that time we were stalking that whitetail up in the woods outside of Shelby. God, Peter, you must've been fourteen. Anyway"—Big Tom turns to Asha and Krupp to illustrate his point—"I'm talking Bambi on steroids. And so Peter, unbeknownst to me, brings along this portable video game for all the downtime, right—"

"What the fuck," Lark says, "that never happened."

"Whoa!" Big Tom, pretending to be shocked and appalled. "Language, Peter. We have guests."

For the first time, Lark thinks he truly understands the emotional overload that triggers one of Krupp's reformatting snoozes. The utter inability to process an event. Better to simply remove yourself from the proceedings entirely, let other people deal with it, resume your waking life when it's in the rearview. It's not weakness. It's genius.

"How 'bout those Mets, Big Tom," Krupp says.

Lark's father regards Krupp with a smile that comes on suddenly. He doesn't say anything at all, just beams that smile across the living room. "Wayne. It's not baseball season for another few weeks."

"Krupp," Lark says, "would you mind grabbing those boxes of ammo from the closet?"

"Phosphenes!" Big Tom says. The triumph in this exclamation makes Lark feel unmoored, as if his feet are about to leave the floorboards of his childhood living room, despite the rifles weighing him down. His father stands there, beaming.

"Come again?" Krupp says, totally engaged in this moment, making no move to retrieve the shells.

"Those colors and shapes you see behind your eyelids, when your eyes are closed," Big Tom says.

"Phosphenes," Asha says.

"Yes," Big Tom says, nodding respectfully. "I just learned that they had a name." Big Tom shakes his head at the wonder and the beauty of it all. "Isn't that a great word?"

Lark's heart begins to pound. He can't map this person onto the blank slate of a father he'd always known. It simply does not scan. He struggles to remember a moment when Big Tom expressed any intellectual curiosity—or *any kind* of curiosity—at all. He's not exactly a word-a-day-calendar kind of guy. He's an empty vessel, disconnected from his children out of some spite or sheer disinterest or something worse, something Lark never came to grips with. At thirty-six, he's gone so far down the path of resignation that he's actually becoming more like Big Tom in his dealings with the man. Going through the motions of long-term care solely out of respect for Betsy's wishes. He almost has to smile. He's never really framed it to himself this way before, but he supposes that becoming your father is inevitable.

"What the hell's going on here?" Lark says to his father.

Big Tom throws his head back and laughs, like he's the kind of guy who holds court down at the Shade, a legendary yarn-spinner. "I'm just feeling good!" Big Tom says. "I've had a sort of breakthrough on a piece I'm working on. In fact, I've been meaning to talk to you about this."

Lark shakes his head. As if they've ever had heart-to-hearts about *process* before.

"It's such a natural high, right?" his father says. "You're stuck for a week on something, and all those doubts creep in, and it starts to gnaw at you, how terrible you are, what a fake, what a joke. And you just feel so listless and *gray*, standing there at the canvas—"

"Dad," Lark interrupts. This is too much. His father's words are the words of a different man entirely. How impossible this is, to affect a rapport where none ever existed. Why is he being granted this glimpse into what could have been?

Lark can barely hold on to the rifles, suddenly weak at the prospect of what such a life might have held for him. And for Betsy. For Big Tom himself! Because, in the end, what was the point of such disconnection? And now that they're decades removed from living together in this house, who's really at fault anymore?

"Oh, and but then!" Big Tom says, lifting a finger to illustrate his point. "Right when you least expect it, *BAM*. You find the rhythm again. The missing piece. Whatever you were lacking just falls into place, and you can *work* again. It's not like the doubts all melt away, or you feel like you're *good*, or anything. It's more like you just resume your focus, pick up where you left off, and all that other stuff about whether or not you're doing something worthwhile just stops mattering." He smiles. "You know? You must have experienced this. I've been meaning to talk to you about it. I'm sorry I haven't called—"

"You've *never* called!"

"—I've just been busy."

"Wait," Asha says, "I'm confused. Mr. Larkin, that story you told about taking Lark—Peter—hunting. Is that a total fabrication? Because on the way here, Lark led me to believe things like that never happened. That your relationship was far different than the picture you're painting now."

"Shut the fuck up!" Krupp yells. He turns to Asha, face flushed, breathing hard. "What kind of question is that for a man in his home? And what do you know about any of it? Stay out of things you don't understand."

Lark feels like he's been sucking down whatever expensive psilocybin tincture infusion Asha favors.

Angry Krupp.

Jovial Big Tom.

"Man," Lark says to Krupp, "do not talk to her that way." Krupp swings his eyes over to Lark and there is such un-Krupp-like rage in the way his mouth curls into a sneer, like he's a *Clockwork Orange* droog out for a night of the old ultraviolence. Affecting an absurd air of menace. It's a reprise of his outburst in the truck, except that had been a cloud that passed over him quickly and left him apologetic in its aftermath. This time the cloud lingers.

"Boys!" Big Tom says.

Krupp's shoulders are hunched, his neck diminished, the flesh of his perpetually cold arms blotchy and crimson. The bruises on his throat are a livid violet. On such a scarecrow of a man the effect is of transmutation, the prelude to a full-moon emergence, all sprouting hair and thickening nails.

"Lark," Krupp says, "did anybody ever tell you that you're a truly entitled little shitbird of a man?"

Asha grips the back of Big Tom's worn-out armchair like it's a railing on a wave-tossed ship. She averts her eyes, almost shyly, to study a particularly abstract Betsy.

"Snap out of it," Lark says. "It's me, man. It's Lark. What's wrong with you?"

Krupp drills him with a pair of stone-cold eyes. "You didn't give a *shit* about the Red Vines. And the jar. And the candy shop."

The rifles weigh a ton. His arms are sore, stuck in an unnatural cradle pose, palms up. "What did you want me to say about it? It's a *jar*, Krupp."

"Boys!" Big Tom says again, beaming his radiant positivity between them. Lark can sense it curdling, the wrongness of this other man, this spirit inhabiting the shade of his father.

Lark faces his best friend down. "Get the ammo from the closet so we can get out of here, Krupp. We're wasting time."

"Just a *jar*?" Krupp, stuck on this, a splinter in his mind. "Me and you, every day after school, Lark!" His voice goes up an octave and becomes hysterical. "Sliding dimes across the counter!"

"Yeah, man, we've been over this! Jesus Christ, what is it with you and the candy store?" He crosses the room and dumps the rifles onto the armchair, then heads for the front hall closet. "Never mind, I'll get it myself."

Krupp grabs him by the upper arm, sinks his fingers in, stops Lark from passing by. His fingers seek to find some hidden softness, some pressure points Lark never noticed before, and they dig in hard. Krupp gets close, grits teeth. "Everything we've been through together, and you treat me like I'm charity work to you."

Lark tries to shake free. He is conscious of both Asha and his father watching this unfold. A hint of stale urine wafts up as if activated by this situation.

"You're my best friend, you fucking asshole," Lark says. He puts his shoulder into it and wrenches himself free.

"Language!" Big Tom says.

Lark's eye catches Betsy's in a canvas hanging by the closet. It's a close-up of half her face in tight impasto swirls that together add up to a mature and sensitive evocation of his sister. Inside her eye, reflected, Big Tom has sketched in, with the tip of a thin brush, a torrent of water cascading down from high atop a rocky cliff.

Betsy, seeing what he saw from his vantage point at the Backbone, painted by his father.

"Dad," Lark says, still in disbelief that he's actually addressing the man directly, "when did you paint this one?"

"Hey!" Krupp says, as he moves to reclaim his grip on Lark. His skinny physicality, his lanky mannerisms, seem to have taken on a new substance. There's something hard and grim about him. Lark thinks of Krupp's tenderness with the jar. *Maybe you and me could share custody.* Lark had brushed that notion away, half considered, and moved on. He wonders, not for the first time today, if on the spectrum of assholes, his own life might be weighted more toward the asshole side. If what he'd always chalked up to an artistic temperament has simply been an excuse to live inside his own head at the expense of forging real connections.

"Ah!" Big Tom says, this professorial quirk beamed in from some other personality entirely. Lark could swear his father's eyes are *sparkling*. He lifts a hand to block Krupp's advance. "That's the one," Big Tom says. "I'm so glad you noticed. That's the breakthrough I was telling you about."

"Motherfucker!" Krupp says, batting down Lark's parry with a hammer-fisted street-fighting move. Pain reverberates up Lark's arm. He backs away quickly, under Betsy's unflinching gaze.

Asha scoots to the corner of the room, out of the fray.

"Boys!" Big Tom says.

"What the fuck, man, get off me!" Lark says, fending off another flailing haymaker from Krupp.

"You left me!" Krupp says, lowering his fists to harangue instead. "And when you came back upstate you were such. Hot. Shit. You know what I think? I think you *like* being the big-ass fish in a small fucking koi pond. You get to be Wofford Falls's very own homegrown famous artist, with your work on the library lawn—"

"I *donated* that because they *asked* me to."

"It doesn't matter!" Lark has seen Krupp, in his happiest moments at the Shade, getting worked up about the finer points of crossover thrash metal and the fluid boundaries of the genre as a whole. This, now, is some devilish inverse, the core of warmth and good-natured discussion turning sour, cold, *pointed*. "In New York you're just another face in the crowd, anonymous sculptor number five thousand two hundred forty-three, who gives a shit."

Lark turns to Asha—for what? Some interjection on her part, some defense of his cachet? He's instantly ashamed of the impulse. She shrugs.

"It's not like that," Lark says. Krupp's breathing hard, his shoulders heaving up and down like knobby pistons. "You *know* it's not like that."

"I don't know anything about you," Krupp says, more subdued. "Except that you're not who you used to be."

Asshole.

You did this.

"Yeah, well, we can't all be the exact same person we were at seventeen." Lark knows he should check the impulse, but he gives Krupp's Danzig shirt an overt nod.

"I remember bringing a plate of oatmeal cookies to you two when you'd come here after school to play Nintendo," Big Tom says, smiling wistfully.

Lark turns on him. "That never happened! You never gave a shit what I did! And I had a PlayStation!"

"Oatmeal cookies are delicious if done correctly," Asha offers from the corner of the room, surrounded by loose color field Betsys. "Sans raisins, in my opinion."

"Fuck you, Lark," Krupp says, taking him by the wrist, twisting, then letting him go and stalking past him to the closet, wrenching open the door, rummaging around a high shelf until he comes down with a box of ammo. "Let's just go."

Lark watches his friend come back to himself. Krupp turns, holding the box of 12-gauge shells, the ruddy blotches fading across his face and arms.

"Well!" Big Tom says. "I'd better get back to work."

Lark glances around at the years of accumulated studies of his sister, in several styles, from every conceivable angle, created for no apparent purpose. "You on a tight deadline?"

Big Tom's smile fades. He peers off into the middle distance, beyond Lark, beyond the walls, gazing unblinking at something Lark can only guess at. "Betsy doesn't like it when I stop working."

Lark glances at the painting of his sister's magnified eye. The waterfall, finely cascading across her pupil, strikes him as a conduit. There was always something about his father's compulsion he didn't ever want to fully engage with. Framing it as penance—some self-derived act, a dour, plodding procession of freaky atonement wholly owned by Big Tom himself—saved him from having to consider its more likely origins.

"Dad," he says, heading back to the armchair, scooping up the rifles, "does Betsy *make* you do this?"

Big Tom's face sags, then seems to *congeal* back into the doughy, unremarkable mass that Lark's always known. It's like a reverse Polaroid, the way his father's features regress toward blankness.

"Wait," Lark says, as indifference overtakes Big Tom, pulls a hood of disconnection around his head and yanks its drawstring tight. The normal-ish man he'd just discovered in this house, occupying his father's body, living his life, has vacated the premises.

"Hey, Lark," Krupp says quietly. Lark turns. His friend is standing there, downcast, barely meeting Lark's eyes. "I'm sorry, man. I don't"—he shakes his head, some internal bitterness clawing at

him—"I don't know what happened. I didn't mean to snap like that."
He regards the box of ammo in his hands as if seeing it for the first
time, looks up and connects it to the rifles Lark's cradling. "Right," he
says. "Cows."

Lark takes a deep breath—inhaling the life he'd just glimpsed, an
alternative slice of a Big Tom full of humanity and a Krupp brimming
with resentment—and breathing it out. With his next breath he takes
in things as they actually are and have always been: Big Tom lost to
some netherworld and Krupp, loyal as ever, by his side.

Asha, backed into the corner of the living room, stares at a painting
high up on the wall above the television. The top of the canvas touches
the ceiling. "I have an idea for the sculpture," she says. Lark studies
the piece that's caught her attention. It's a bloodred Betsy, seated like
Francis Bacon's pope on a chair that tilts slightly forward. There's no
overt indication of wounds—her clothing is intact—but there is a
wrongness to her body and posture that suggests internal trauma. She
is openmouthed as if about to speak. The canvas is swept in a crimson
wash, haphazard strokes with a large wet brush left to dry. Lark turns
away. He doesn't want to know what this sparked in Asha.

He turns his back on his father and leads Krupp and Asha through
the front door. Outside he breathes in fresh air and realizes how sti-
fling it is in his father's house. In the darkness of the yard, moonlight
glints off the hood of the truck.

"Your father..." Asha says quietly, trailing off.

"He's not really like that," Lark says.

You did this.

"The man I told you about earlier, the man I took Betsy away
from—that's my father."

Krupp hops down from the porch and heads toward the truck,
shaking his head. "Whatever, man. I remember the oatmeal cookies."

Lark watches his friend melt into the darkness. "He's different too,"
Lark says to Asha. As far as he can tell, her personality's been unaf-
fected by the dislocation he's wrought. They're the ones holding it all
together now, and they've got to keep an eye on Krupp.

"You know what?" Lark says, struck by the thought of Krupp with a loaded gun, losing his shit. He glances out toward the truck and waits for Krupp to open the door and slide inside the passenger seat. Then he sets two of the rifles down on the porch and stands up, holding the black tactical gun with the scope. "We probably only need one."

"Fine with me," Asha says. Her voice is laced with uncertainty. Lark can sense her scrutiny, her caution. She looks back at the living room through the window. It's empty, his father presumably gone back upstairs to Betsy's old room, the nexus point of his compulsion. "First you told me your father's paintings were penance. But then you asked him if Betsy was making him do it..."

"It occurred to me in the moment."

"—did you mean *making him* in the same way she made you and all those other people paralyzed at the sight of the mural on the church? Some kind of hypnosis, perhaps something that she doesn't even have full control over?"

"I don't know how I meant it."

"You spoke of her turnings," Asha presses. "Her abilities leaking through her forgeries. If your father has no agency in the matter of his paintings, if your sister has somehow tethered him to this rote behavior, then maybe there's more leakage than you know about."

"It was just a passing thought, Asha."

"Or maybe she's simply dangerous, Lark."

"She's not dangerous, okay? Her entire life is course correction. It's fucking brave, and difficult. She's appalled by her lack of control. Wouldn't you be? If there was something inside you that even you didn't understand, that was capable of doing impossible things?"

"Things that hurt people."

"You know who hurt people? Big Tom Larkin. I'm telling you, what you saw in there wasn't him."

Asha hesitates. "I believe you."

And in that hesitation, that little pause, Lark is flooded with a fresh anxiety. The shot nerves of a sudden reevaluation—the notion that maybe he's been gaslighting *himself* all these years. That the versions of his father and Krupp that are breaking through aren't so far off from how they've always been. That maybe his inability to step outside himself for too long has smeared the lens through which he's always seen his best friend, his father, his hometown. The rifle, so alien in his hands—the first time he's held a gun since he pegged bottles off a fence two decades ago. Had there been a moment, that day, when Ian and Krupp had stolen away to talk about him? Or met each other's eyes in unspoken agreement about some deficiency in Lark's character?

How much of our personal history is revisionist?

For the first time Lark is worried that the answer might be *All of it*.

Poised on the knife's edge of this gnawing uncertainty, Lark waits for some affirmation from Asha. *You and me, Lark. Let's do this!*

None comes. Asha slips a fingernail inside the sleeve of her leather coat and scratches at her wrist. Crickets chirp. Inside the truck, Krupp moves like he's swatting a hovering bee. The porch creaks and the swing moves, just a little. Loneliness comes over him then. He feels that something inside him has been put together wrong. He should be thinking only of Betsy, and instead he's settling back into the comfort of an angst for which he's much too old. Narcissism, it turns out, comes in many forms.

Asha turns to head for the truck.

Krupp begins to scream.

16

Krupp staggers back from the open door as Lark and Asha reach him.

"Fucking Christ!" He bends at the waist, heaving. He drags the back of his hand across his mouth.

Inside the truck, the dome light is on, and the jar is sitting on the passenger seat as if it's waiting to be buckled in. Inside the jar, the birthday gift, the turning-come-to-life, has taken on considerable weight and mass. As if influenced by the jar itself, the turning has incorporated glassy transparencies into its bloated-matchbox corporeality.

Lark, careful not to get too close, peers in as if at some biting, gnashing zoo animal whose cage isn't as secure as it might be. Spielbergian wonderment, the slowly dawning golden-hour *OH WOW* on a kid's face, here twisted into a kind of astonished fright. Its glassy prison has been subsumed, woven into the turning's makeup. What was once a twisted slice of *Nighthawks*, a sickening hole-punch of Betsy's talent, has mostly shed its former skin. Looking at it now there's almost nothing of that sterile painting left, no evocations of that mannequin-staffed diner, that empty sanitized street, that midcentury diorama of things left unsaid.

There is no *inside* or *outside* the jar anymore. There is only the birthday gift claiming its space, growing, impossibly, into the glass. Lark recalls learning at the dismal terminus of some lost internet rabbit hole that everything glass on earth is very slowly dripping like lava, moving on a geologic scale invisible to the human eye, settling toward its base. If left unbroken for millions of years, the glass will eventually glob down and thicken. The materials we take for granted as reliably solid are actually anything but. He's pulled inspiration from this over the years, especially in the earliest days, his New York days, when a much-remarked-on fluidity defined his work.

Maybe it's just the general self-reflection that he's stuck in, this hall of mirrors turned inward, but it strikes him now that the birthday gift's hybridization with the jar is a more beautiful and complete piece of art than anything he's ever created. Organic, mindless, and also free of doubt and hesitation. There are filigrees of its original makeup encased in the glass—long tendrils of what the woman in the red dress used to hold, stretched beyond recognition. Some of them have pierced the glass entirely and jut out like frizzy hairs. There is no discernible cracking or breakage, as if the birthday gift has managed to slither through the glass on an atomic level. What he thinks of as the "meat" of the object, the plump center, has grown to the size of a large human heart and taken on roughly the same shape, though its color is still that sickly chartreuse from Betsy's original. Its miasma fills the cabin of the truck. Krupp has backed away, halfway to the porch. He's shaking his head, moaning *No no no no no.*

The air pouring from the truck reeks of a variety of odors, all of them rotating in a way that reminds Lark of those bulbous pens loaded with a dozen shades of ink you click into place one by one.

Click.

The stench of fixative spray, vaguely peanutty.

Click.

Damp, musty, subterranean space. Instantly Lark pictures the vast cavern his sister is being kept in.

Click.

A hint of Betsy's up-all-night body odor makes his heart leap.

Click.

Spoilage. Something rotten, crawling with maggots, cloying and decayed. Lark retches. Asha recoils, cursing.

"Shoot it, man!" Krupp yells from the porch. "Blow that thing away!"

The filaments that poke through the glass begin to waver, bending languidly in unison like wheat in a gentle breeze. A shadow creeps across the upholstered seats, as if the light source is elsewhere, not the dome light at all. That low hiss implants itself in his mind once again, more audibly than last time—that phonetic matter-of-factness. This is a word. Here you go. Behold its shape.

Hiss.

Krupp's suggestion to shoot it strikes him as cruel.

"I can't do that," Lark says back. It would be like shooting Betsy herself.

"Come on, man," Krupp says, "*look* at it."

The hissing dissipates. The word in his mind scatters like pollen in the wind, replaced by total blankness.

"What. The fuck. Is that," Asha says, at last, from well behind Lark.

Krupp's laughter is grating and forced. "You better hope Betsy Larkin never gets you a birthday present!"

Asha approaches with caution. "Lark?"

"It's a gift," he says. "From Betsy. One of her turnings."

"Oh," she says, resting the back of her hand over her mouth as if to hide some unseemly reaction. "I'd imagined them to be part of the forgeries themselves."

"It was. This one's from *Nighthawks*."

"As in, Hopper."

"Yeah."

"But now it's here. Like this."

"She put it in a box for me."

"Lark. I really don't think you're seeing things very clearly regarding your sister. These borders around what she's capable of are fairly porous. I mean, *look* at it."

"She connects with people in strange ways. I guess I'm just used to it."

Asha wavers between diplomacy and disgust. "Well. It's certainly…
potent."

"It's fucking *alive*," Krupp says, like he can't believe he has to be the
voice of reason yet again. "It's growing up, or something." He retreats
further into the shadows beneath the eaves of the porch. "Come on,
man," he begs, "just shoot it, please?"

Lark's attention is torn between the turning that's not so much *in*
the jar anymore, but *of* it, and Krupp's dim presence, retreating slowly
then quickly, all at once, his footsteps thudding on the porch steps.

Hello?

The word makes itself known in his mind. He whips his gaze
around to the jar. It throbs. Breathes. The glass bends convex, then
concave. Before his eyes it learns to be supple in its machinations.
Cilia catch a breeze from another world, blowing in on a slipstream
he can't feel. Bile rises in his throat. His heart pounds. The word in
his mind—*hello*—goes staticky like a radio station just out of range
while at the same time the truck's dome light flickers. The voice in his
head isn't Betsy's—it's no voice at all, a representation of a word, syntax
without tonality, but he can still detect a searching warmth to it. Intention in its outreach.

"Lark," Asha says, gesturing urgently to the darkness of the porch.
A dry click comes across the clearing, followed by the metallic snap of
the rifle's breech.

"Shit," Lark mutters. Then shouts. "Krupp! Put that down!"

His own rifle, unloaded, is nothing but deadweight in his hands. A
blunt object at close range, but useless as a firearm.

"Fuck you, Lark," Krupp calls back. "You smell like piss."

Hello?

More insistent, this time. The shape of the word etches itself behind
his eyelids. A pain, a *good* pain, like the deep muscle soreness after a
long day in his studio, rides the word like comet's tail.

"Can you hear that?" he says to Asha.

"Hear what?"

Krupp stomps down the steps and crosses the clearing and comes to the edge of the light cast through the truck's open door. The rifle's a dark slash across his torso. His finger's extended straight out along the barrel, just above the trigger guard. *Trigger discipline.* Lark remembers teenage Ian showing them the ropes, a cigarette wiggling between his lips as he demonstrated the no-bullshit gun safety imparted to him by his uncle. The ammo box is wedged up in Krupp's armpit.

"Would you get hold of yourself?" Lark says, backing up so his legs hit the running board. Behind his back, the jar gives off its distinct, rotating stenches.

"Look," Krupp says. "I know I flew off the handle back there in your dad's house, but this isn't that. This is me making the right call. That thing is cursed."

Hello.

Krupp raises the gun and aims it straight at Lark. "Get out of the way."

"Krupp." This moment, above any other, shimmers into unreality.

You and me, sliding dimes across the counter.

Krupp and Lark. Saturdays at the Shade. A thirty-year friendship. All of it flowing down into the black hole of the rifle barrel, a relationship as twisted up as the turning-jar, as corrupted and unrecognizable.

"Krupp," Lark says, putting a hand up in an absurd facing-down-a-gun gesture. "Listen to me. You were right back there, earlier, in the truck, with Sally. I did this. Me. Nobody else. I'm responsible for everything that's happening, and I'm sorry. But I can't let you do this. That's *Betsy* in there."

Krupp's mouth drops open. He blinks violently as if expelling a foreign object from his eyelid. Then he laughs—too high, too loud. "Listen to yourself! I suggest you take a good long look at that little abomination behind you, because it sure as shit isn't Betsy Larkin."

Krupp steadies his aim, sights down the barrel.

"It might be!" Lark says. "It said something to me before. I can hear it. And it smells like her."

"It smells like *shit*, Lark!" Krupp steps forward, keeping the gun trained on Lark's heart. Lark's body feels light and vaporous. "It's a nightmare Pixar monster that some rogue animator put in before she went fully off the deep end. Okay? No offense to Betsy, but this is a forest for the trees situation, and you're way too lost in the trees to see it. What your sister does isn't *right*, Lark. It isn't *good*. Sure, you guys manage okay together, draw these little imaginary boundaries around her talents, keep it all in line, but you guys aren't together right now, are you? You're apart for the first time in what, fifteen years?" He shakes his head. "Here's the thing. I was wrong before, in the truck. *You* didn't do this. You didn't do shit, except waste your time making some weird-ass sculpture up on the Backbone. *She's* doing this, you dumb bastard. Think about it. She's always been more—"

Abruptly, Krupp goes boneless and slack. The rifle falls from his grasp and hits the dirt a split second before his body crumples. He lies there, sprawled out, still. Asha stands behind him, the butt of the third rifle hovering in the place Krupp's head occupied a moment ago. She holds her position, a monument to some lost wartime hero.

Lark uses his foot to slide Krupp's fallen rifle out of the way, drag it back toward the truck, out of reach. The feeling of lightness in his body remains, the unreal gloss. Krupp had been pointing a gun at him, and now he's lying still.

"How hard did you hit him?" Lark says.

Asha drops the rifle. "I don't know." Her eyes are wide, searching. "I've never hit anybody with a gun before." She turns up her palms and looks at them as if they struck out on their own, independent of her will.

Lark goes to his knees and turns Krupp over on his back.

"Are we supposed to move him?" Asha says.

He places two fingers alongside the big vein in Krupp's wiry neck, just under the jaw. "There's a pulse," Lark announces.

"Thank God," Asha says.

"And he feels really hot."

He lingers against Krupp's feverish skin, a furnace in the late-March chill. Something falls away inside him and he looks up at Asha's dim figure, and his heart opens up.

"He pointed a gun at me," Lark says. "We've known each other since fourth grade."

A photograph exists, somewhere in his attic, of young Lark and Krupp, crouched together in the mulch of a flower bed, pointing out the pistil and stamen in a brilliant amaryllis, totally psyched on discovering that week's unit in science class in the wild. It's one of a thousand off-the-cuff documents of their adventures over three decades. The thought of it makes him feel nervy and reckless, like he can't believe what just happened, and at the same time like there's nothing left to lose. Which is a lie. There's always more to lose. Entropy, insatiable, gnaws life to the bone.

"I honestly thought he was going to shoot you," Asha says.

Lark considers this. *Would* Krupp have shot him? A few days ago, he would have thought the idea laughable—the kind of thing they'd mock-debate two pitchers in at the Shade. *What if you had to shoot me in the leg, like in* Speed? Now he's not so sure. There's a state of being he drifts into around the midpoint of a new sculpture, moving from the side yard to the studio, from shaping to assemblage—a sense of tenterhooks and possibility. It's less a nebulous *anything can happen* than the notion that whatever path fate chooses for him, he's an adaptable enough artist to navigate. But here, the very act of creation breeds unpredictable destruction. It's like being a hamster on a wheel that's sprouting other grotesque wheels as he races to nowhere.

Focus, he thinks. "How long has it been since we all got those photos of Betsy sent to our phones?"

"I have no idea."

Lark understands where she's coming from. Time's gone as elastic as the roads, stretched and compressed in unequal measure. It feels like it could be three in the morning or dinnertime. He slides a hand beneath Krupp's clammy-hot neck, where the bruises from Wrecker's grip have gone a dull eggplant, and moves his hand up to the back of his friend's head, where he can already feel a tough fleshy knot forming. Krupp's been concussed on four previous occasions. (Flag football, broken step stool, ice storm, swinging door.)

"All right," Lark says, trying to sound decisive. "Let's get him in the truck."

Asha stares him down.

"We're not gonna just leave him here," Lark says, gesturing out into the darkness.

"Of course," Asha says, in a way that makes Lark think she was trying to justify ways to do exactly that. "What about your birthday gift?" She points into the truck's open door. Lark glances into the cab.

The turning-jar responds with a throb of recognition. The glass goes convex and puffs out the smell of cadmium red. The cilia, those brittle-sharp dendrites that pierced the glass without breaking it, quaver at stop-motion speed. A low hum comes across the gravel and at the same time the word *hum* draws itself into his thoughts.

Lark slides his hand out from under Krupp's head and goes to the truck bed. A quick rummage yields a paint-spattered towel and an empty NY Giants duffel bag (provenance: Sports Plus, Hudson Valley Mall; shoplifted by thirteen-year-old Wayne Krupp Jr. in a truly madcap incident involving a mall cop complete with Segway).

Asha eyes him nervously. "Should you be wearing gloves?"

"How the hell should I know?"

He holds his breath and leans into the truck. *Hum* erases itself, except for the *H*, so that *Hello* can redraw itself.

"Sorry, Betsy," he says. Then he drapes the towel gently over the turning-jar, like he's silencing a pet bird for the night. He hesitates, then grasps it on either side. It does not feel like glass, or like anything organic. This hybridization is soft but firm, with quicksand-like give. The cilia quaver beneath the towel, those extensions of what the woman in the red dress holds feeling out their new prison with invertebrate curiosity.

He zips the towel-covered gift into the duffel bag, and instantly the churning, rotating odors dissipate. He snaps back to alertness.

"When Krupp wakes up," Lark says, depositing the duffel into the bed of the F-150, wedged between sculpting tools, "tell him we chucked it in the woods. Don't tell him it's here."

He grabs the rifle with the scope and sets it down next to the duffel.

"*Chucked*," Asha practices, expelling the word with distaste. "Hello, Wayne, I hope you're all right. Yes, we chucked it into the forest."

"*Woods.* Help me get him in the truck."

Together, they manage to lift Krupp and maneuver him into the cabin. He flops on the passenger seat, and his dangling arm breaks Lark's heart. The deadweight of him, the floppy non-Krupp-ness.

"Where to now?" Asha says when they've climbed in after Krupp and wedged him between them.

Lark pulls his door shut. "The farm."

"*The* farm?"

"Jamie-Lynn's farm."

"Who's Jamie-Lynn?"

Lark shifts into reverse. "Another old friend."

17

How come you never got married?" Asha's eyes flick metronomically to the rearview like she's just spotted a tail. *Black sedan, two cars back.* Except they're alone on Route 34, heading north from the old homestead along the Meisnerville line, loosely defined by the Greatkill Creek that snakes up from Poughkeepsie, a thin squiggle dropped like blue thread on a map. Jamie-Lynn's inherited family farm is in the uppermost reaches of Wofford Falls, near the county line, nestled in a patchwork of agricultural desolation.

"I don't know, Asha, how come *you* never got married?" Lark steers around a fallen branch, thick with leaves, that lies across the lane. Krupp is slumped openmouthed against his shoulder. Lark wonders if at some point behind consciousness, Krupp transitioned from *knocked out cold* to *reformatting.* It's a comforting thought: His friend isn't hurt, just taking a breather.

"Justine refuses to sign a prenup," Asha says.

"Gotta protect that Felicia Raymond space money. Prenup a sore spot for you two?"

"It's an ongoing conversation."

"Seems like a dumb sticking point to me. You love each other, right?"

Asha does her single-note, nasal laugh. "Of course you'd approach it from the *it's only money* angle."

"I'm not approaching it from any angle, just making an observation. Don't you trust her?"

"Of course I don't trust her."

Lark shakes his head. "Your world is really something." Quickly he adds, "I do understand that your world makes *my* world possible. So, thank you."

"You really love it up here, don't you?"

"I do," Lark says, as Krupp's accusation echoes in his mind: *You love being a big-ass fish in a small fucking koi pond.* Weary strain settles in his forehead. That out-of-body lightness takes hold. On the side of Route 34 he spots a glowing pair of eyes low to the ground: fox eyes, bunny eyes, raccoon eyes. Beyond them the shoulder plunges to the burbling Greatkill, drinking up snowmelt. Asha's gone quiet, and Lark wonders at the thrust of her questions as more of the revisionist history he's been dosing himself with falls away. "Well," he says, "I don't know."

"Don't know what?"

"If I love it here. Or if it's just, you know. Where I ended up."

Asha brushes a strand of Krupp's scraggly bangs out of his closed eyes with a tenderness that strikes him as almost romantic. "I can get to Staten Island in thirty minutes," she says, "to my parents' house in forty. And I can count on one hand the times I've been back in the past ten years. They've never met Justine."

"Do they miss you?"

Asha shrugs. "I have siblings." She's quiet for a while. "You know, I wasn't totally up-front with you before. When Wayne called me—yes, I was incredulous at the story he told, but I didn't even care if it was true or not. I've never been up here, Lark. We've only ever seen each other in the city. And even that's been infrequent over the past few years."

"I realize that." He wonders what she's getting at. At the same time he can swear he hears the creek, as if its burbling, mellow rush has been amplified by spring rains that haven't yet come. It occurs to him that the Greatkill might now be feeding the burgeoning waterfall across from the Backbone. The geography untangles itself in his mind, shifts and re-forms tectonically: water flowing up in defiance of all laws, bursting from the cleft in the rocks, pouring back down to join itself in an endless loop. He shivers, not because it's impossible, but because it *doesn't* seem impossible to him now. A pair of headlights come and go and he could swear it's Sally behind the wheel, still searching for the way home. But then she's gone and the truck's alone on the road once again.

"I'm not sure you know how hard I was working to prove myself back then," Asha says, "back when we sold the first *Citadel* pieces."

Those days come back to him in fragments, as they always do. More revisionism: When he thinks of Asha back then, it's as he sees her now, as if she sprang fully formed from the nexus of art and commerce, uptown and downtown. But that diminishes the work. While Lark was sowing the seeds for the manic blackouts of his Lost Year, laying the groundwork for that regrettable plunge into oblivion, Asha was doing the opposite. Building bridges instead of burning them. He wonders how often, in the bleary haze of a morning after, she made calls to repair damage he'd so blithely inflicted. Her invisible hand, clearing lanes from afar, managing deals he'll never know about, just to keep him afloat. He might have carved his niche, but it's Asha who kept its edges from caving in.

"I do know that," Lark says. "I do. Sometimes those days just run together for me. I don't mean to be ungrateful."

Asha makes a breathy noise he interprets as frustration. "I'm not asking for gratitude. Your thanks is implicit in the money. I just don't know who lost track of how close we used to be, or if we're both guilty of this whole relationship calcifying in the way it did."

"Relationship," Lark says. He's not sure why. Maybe just to repeat the word out loud, see how it sounds.

"You play the rugged individualist. I play the exasperated mother hen, nudging you into place. We hang up, talk again in a week. Twice a year we have coffee at that diner in the West Village you insist upon, I assume to demonstrate your commitment to salt-of-the-earth cuisine, like it's all you know up here, so God forbid you come to the city and let me take you for a half-decent cocktail and some good tapas." She taps a fingernail on the dash, scratches lightly down the glove box cover, folds her hands. Lark wonders if she's re-upped the microdose, if it leaves her overly reflective. "I know you think I was just feeding you a line, about you being my favorite client. And I was. But there's something real behind the sentiment. I don't mean you're my *favorite*, I just mean—there's history there. We shared something back then. Right?"

"I remember," Lark says, feeling nostalgia settle in at the back of his neck, melt down his spine, "the night we opened with *Citadel*, in that warehouse by the West Side Highway, that no-man's-land by where you return a U-Haul. You made me get a suit."

"Oh God. I knew you were going to bring this up."

"But you didn't go with me to get it, you just said, *Get a suit.*"

"I was afraid you were going to wear something tie-dyed and ill fitting. I was nervous."

"And then when I showed up in this suit I got—"

"At the *Salvation Army*—"

"You dragged me into this closet full of old air conditioners and made me hide."

"You looked like David Byrne in *Stop Making Sense*."

"So you sent some intern from NYU out to get me some slim-fit jeans and a blazer."

"It was a vast improvement."

"I looked like a suburban dad who plays guitar in a local blues band."

"That was still better than you've ever looked, before or since. Remember the *Art Forum* spread?"

"You mean the only profile they ever did of me? Yeah, I kinda remember that."

"You looked ridiculous in that. Like a, a *beaver*."

He laughs so hard he has to slow down so he doesn't plow the truck nose-down into the Greatkill. It feels unbelievably good, working out knots inside his head he didn't even know were there. He's been a clenched fist for days. Now he remembers how Asha used to make him crack up, huddled in the leopard-print corner booth of Merle & Bess, eyes shining with cheap gin and tonics, foreheads tinted Cindy Sherman by the stained-glass lamp. Asha's laughing too.

"A *beaver*?" he says at last. "What does that even mean?"

"You had"—pausing to wipe her eyes—"you had on that brown striped cardigan thing that looked like a beaver pelt."

"Okay, first of all, that was a very classy garment I picked up in Uptown Kingston."

"I think it even had a flat tail-type thing coming off the back."

"It did not."

"The better to thwap the dam with."

"Is that what people who live in the city think beavers do? Thwap dams?"

Asha lets out one more fairly unhinged cackle, then settles back in her seat. Lark takes a left off 78 onto a road with no name, crowded by trees, tunneled by overhanging branches, that should be one lane but somehow acts as two.

"Goddammit, Lark," she says, "I missed you."

"I missed you too."

Perhaps no two people can ever evolve and still give what's needed, always and forever. Perhaps that's too much to ask of anyone.

His thoughts are interrupted by a wooden fence that juts suddenly up from the road.

He hits the brakes and turns the wheel into the skid. Asha grabs the handle above the window. Krupp stirs. The side of this abrupt fence scrapes the truck and at the same time reveals itself as no more than an *excerpt* of fence, a cutout, like one of Betsy's turnings. A section removed cleanly and deposited half a mile from the entrance to Jamie-Lynn's farm. He regains control of the truck. The fence disappears in the rearview.

"I take it that wasn't supposed to be there," Asha says.

Krupp mutters insensibly. He lifts a hand to his face before it falls back into his lap. Lark wonders which version of Krupp will wake. He thinks of the rifle, the turning-jar.

And then the horse comes out of nowhere, bounding up the road with flared-nostril equine terror. Lark pulls to the side as best he can as the animal stumbles, its stride too long and loping for uneven pavement, then regains traction and churns into its gallop. It's the white Arabian, Jamie-Lynn's favorite, the one she broke herself instead of delegating to her father's ancient farmhand. Asha gives a cry of disbelief. The horse rears up. Asha covers her face. Shod hooves come down hard on the hood of the truck and the cab dips. Lark catches the horse's wide, unblinking eye. The horse snorts and its hooves slide down the hood, leaving dents in the metal. The smell of horseshit and hay, stables and fields, comes through the truck's open vents. Lark braces himself for another rearing-up, for the hooves to splinter the windshield and come down on their collarbones. But the horse, blinded by fear, doesn't spare them a look, just shakes its mane and gallops on down the nameless road. Lark and Asha, breathing hard, wait for the animal to recede into the night.

"That was Willa," he says. "Jamie-Lynn treats that horse like a member of the family. There's no way she'd fuck up and let it get free, unless..."

"The fence came down," Asha guesses.

"Yeah," Lark says. He thinks of the fence-excerpt rising from the road. A better way to express what happened to the fence than *came down* would probably be *teleported*, but he can't bring himself to say the word out loud. He remembers a teleportation obsession he and Krupp went through in fifth grade, zooming action figures to chairs in different rooms and claiming that once a portal existed it could only be shut by the person who made it in the first place, resulting in an invisible web of conflicting portals. Wayne Krupp Sr. would walk through the portal-web and the boys would giggle and he'd shake his head and grab another High Life.

Lark's phone vibrates. His heart sinks. He knows what he'll find on the screen before he looks. He glances at the phone. "Shit."

"Betsy?" Asha says.

"We gotta get this done."

"Is she okay?"

Lark holds his phone across a slowly stirring Krupp to show Asha the screen. He tries to wipe it from his mind. The tip of the knife creeping toward Betsy's left eye...

"Dear God," Asha says.

"Let's just do this." He throws the truck into drive.

"Wait," she says. "Let me see that."

He hands her the phone.

"There's some kind of uncanny-valley effect going on here," she says.

Lark keeps his foot on the brake, fights the urge to step on the gas, and peers at the screen as Asha holds it out. She moves her finger to the side of Betsy's face.

"Here," she says. "The way the knife's inserted into the frame. It looks like a Gigi Palmetto collage, a digital portmanteau that draws attention to its own artifice."

"Jesus, Asha, what the fuck."

"It looks *Photoshopped*, Lark."

He takes a breath, lets it out, and tries to clear his head and examine the photo. It's one of those situations where he wouldn't have noticed it if she hadn't pointed it out, but now he can't unsee it. There's something slightly off about the planes, as if the knife is entering the frame from a skewed reality.

"So," he says, "if these are all fake, then she might already be dead for all we know. Or she might have escaped. Or—"

"Or else Krupp is right, Lark. It's worth at least considering the possibility."

"Krupp's right like two times out of ten."

"What he said, right before I hit him. *She's* doing this."

"That's bullshit." He grabs his phone and hits the gas.

Krupp begins to thrash like a little kid in the throes of a night terror. Outside, glowing eyes line their path like luminary candles. Trees reach out across the nameless road to scrape the sides of the truck. Was it always so overgrown and wild up here? Lark can't remember. The road narrows, the pavement turns to dirt. He tries not to think of Betsy's pupil on the verge of being sliced. This conjures up an unwanted image of Gumley and his acolytes sitting around a screening room while *Un Chien Andalou* flickers across their rapt faces as they field-strip their AR-15s.

"I'm just asking you to consider the possibility." Lark can practically feel the psilocybin surge in her sudden thousand-yard yet dialed-in struggle to relate her deepest realizations. "If she's compelling your father, if she's trapped him in this current routine of his, it's not such a stretch to extrapolate other profound effects on your town. Between your story of the mural, and this turning's evolution here with us"—he can swear she shudders—"I feel a darkness in her, Lark. I'm sorry."

"There is no darkness. Stop talking about this. They *took her*, Asha. Nothing's changed."

"I know you think she means well. All I'm asking you to consider is, with all her abilities, what if she really doesn't?"

He rounds a bend and a scarecrow comes into view, stuck up in the pine branches like an ornament. Startled, Lark slows down without stopping completely. He tries to remember if Jamie-Lynn's is the kind of farm that would employ a scarecrow.

"Oh no," Asha says. Krupp's head moves from side to side. A strand of drool whips across his cheek. Asha shrinks back against him, away from her window. Lark peers out. A new smell comes through the vents: something unclean.

It's not a scarecrow in the trees.

"Oh God."

It's an old man, dangling like a soldier trapped in barbed wire, splayed in the nonsense angles of the dead. He's wearing flannel pajamas. The plaid top, lifted coyly by a branch, exposes the sagging skin of his belly. His sightless eyes stare across the road. Above his head, stuck in the tree, is a pillow.

"It's the farmhand," Lark says, trying to recall the man's name. "Forester."

Asleep when it happened, he thinks. Shunted like the fence. Waking in pure fright, if he woke up at all. Lark doesn't stop to investigate.

If the man is crucified in some way, or his body broken, he doesn't stay long enough to confirm. The road ahead glitters like a galaxy. The truck crunches broken glass.

"What happened here?" Asha says.

The truck bumps over piles of soil. A rooster pecks through the dirt as they pass.

"They have a greenhouse," Lark says.

The truck rounds the last bend and the looming trees retreat. There's a natural rise in the land that gives Jamie-Lynn's farm a stately perch to look out on thirty acres of fields and stables.

The lights are on in the old house, bright-yellow squares giving shape to the darkened structure. Except the building's form is incorrect. There are windows as high as a castle turret, bright slices in the night where no windows have ever been. Lark stops the truck. The feeling that something inside of him is put together wrong, that the way he perceives things has always been wrong, is now writ large before him. The twisting of his father's personality, Krupp's newfound rage. Corruption within and without. The house itself, burst apart and put back together in some new way, like the old man dangling from the tree. Next to him, Krupp's muttering takes on a fresh urgency. The headlights, trained on the porch, shine through a gaping hole where the front door used to be. Not a hole punched by sudden violence or a piece of runaway farm equipment. This opening is neatly carved in a shape Lark recognizes from somewhere—a diagram in the psalter, he thinks.

The house, once a neat Colonial, tilts like a decrepit old barn. The lighted windows shudder.

"Over there!" Asha points.

A woman comes running from the dark side of the house, waving her arms above her head. Hailing the truck.

Lark opens his door, propping Krupp up straight before he hops out. "Jamie-Lynn!" he calls out.

She stops running at the edge of the headlights' beam. Lark reaches into the truck and clicks on the brights. Jamie-Lynn shields her eyes and turns her head away. She seems tentative, unsure of herself. "Lark?"

"Jamie-Lynn!" he says. "You okay?"

He feels stupid the second he asks. She's wearing black stretch pants and a sweatshirt that says HAVERCHUCK FARMS underneath a nifty logo of a cartoon thresher. One of her schemes to monetize what's left of her parents' farm operation: "day at the farm" packages for tourists and kids. Pick berries, ride a horse, milk a cow.

"The girls are gone!" she says. She's still skirting the edge of the light, moving oddly, like she's desperate for Lark's help but doesn't want to get too close.

"Terry?" Lark says automatically.

"I have them this week. Gone from *here*."

Gone like Forester, Lark thinks. He pictures Lily and Bea Haverchuck, nine and seven, flung into some distant pine, broken, bent, dangling...

He banishes the image. "Did you call 911?" For one of their own, the first responders should be all hands, code red.

"I don't know if I got through."

"You don't know?"

"Dispatch was there, I think, but..." She pulls her sweatshirt off and tosses it away. "It's so *hot*."

Lark recalls Krupp's feverish, prone body in the aftermath of his manic cycles of rage. He glances into his truck. The temperature display on the dashboard says forty-three degrees.

Jamie-Lynn stands there in a white tank top, her hand in front of her eyes. A deep shadow drips across her face. Lark takes a step toward her and she shrinks away into the darkness.

"Will you help me look for them?"

"Wait."

"Please, Lark." She retreats fully into the night.

"Jamie-Lynn!" he calls out. His voice echoes across the dark fields, boomerangs around, and comes back to him as airy distortion. *You did this.* Mentally, he traces what he knows of the landscape up here. It's been some time since he's walked these fields, but he remembers the cows being in a pasture just over the rise, penned in by a massive square of cattle fence.

He runs down a cold and calculating order of events. Get the loaded rifle and the circular saw from the truck bed. Find a cow. Kill it. Cut it up into manageable sections like in the illustration on the wall at Smokin' Dave's Barbecue—rump, flank, leg. Load the pieces onto the truck. Get to the Backbone. Complete this phase of the sculpture according to Asha's interpretation of *The Worm & the Dogsbody*. Move on to *The God of the Noose* before Gumley decides to hurt Betsy in a way she can't come back from.

He scans the darkness. Jamie-Lynn's lithe marathon runner's body folds itself into the night, following the echo of his voice on a newfound jet stream. When he turns back to the truck he comes face-to-face with Krupp, blinking, magnificently confused. Krupp rubs the back of his head and winces.

"Hey buddy," Lark says cautiously. "Welcome back."

"We chucked the jar thing into the woods," Asha says.

"Was I reformatting?" Krupp's voice comes out dry as a desert.

"You sure were," Lark says. "Out cold."

Krupp turns to look out at the fields. He stares at the windows of the farmhouse. There's a subtle disturbance in the light, like a heat shimmer from a hot grill. "Is this *Haverchuck's*?"

Before Lark can explain, Jamie-Lynn slides into the headlights' beam from the other direction, an echo of Lark's dopplering voice, as if she's somehow circumnavigated the farm.

"Jamie-Lynn?" Krupp says.

"Oh my God," Asha says.

Jamie-Lynn's hands are at her sides and Lark can see her fully for the first time. A thick, dark stain rims her mouth, like she's been kissing a plate of cranberry sauce. She stands there, casting a thirty-foot shadow across the front lawn. Her eyes burn into the truck. "Help me find my girls."

Krupp turns to Lark, who moves behind the illusory safety of the open door like a cop in a gunfight.

"What happened to Lily and Bea?" Krupp says.

Lark can't stop looking at the stain on her face, a sloppy mess the color of velvet cake.

"We should get out of here," Asha says.

"Help me," Jamie-Lynn pleads with them.

"Why don't you go back inside the house," Lark suggests. "We'll go find help."

"I don't want to go in there," Jamie-Lynn says. "Ever again."

You did this you did this you did this.

He tells himself they just have to hurry—finish the sculpture and get Betsy back safe and then he can dismantle it, put things right. They'll all be back hoisting cold ones at the Shade before they know it! Ian at the dartboard, Jamie-Lynn making a face as she sips the shitty house white.

Even in his own mind, it seems like feeble reassurance. But what else can he do except forge ahead?

Asha hugs her knees to her chest, making herself into a tight ball in the passenger seat. She keeps her door closed and her eyes on Jamie-Lynn, who's started to sway very slightly. Her long shadow trembles. She drags her right hand along her lips and smears the stain up the side of her face. Then she looks at her hand in wonder.

Krupp slides out of the truck, groans, and leans on Lark for support.

"Easy," Lark says. He wonders how long it will be before Krupp figures out that he hasn't been reformatting, that Asha clocked him on the back of the head.

"Did she do something to her kids?" Krupp whispers.

"No clue," Lark whispers back. "But we can't get involved." He cringes at how craven it sounds. How self-serving.

Krupp shakes his head in disgust, winces at the pain. Then he calls out to Jamie-Lynn. "Why don't you come over here and talk to us."

"Let it go," Lark hisses.

"What is wrong with you?" Krupp says. "We're talking about little kids, man. Lily and Bea. When did you stop giving a shit?"

Lark regards his friend, thinking *Not this again*, half wishing Asha would crack him over the head for a second time.

He calls to Jamie-Lynn. "Go back inside and keep trying 911."

"But you're here *now*," Jamie-Lynn says. "We can spread out in the fields. They've gotta be out there somewhere." She wipes at her mouth with her palm, regards the dark-red stain on her hand. Then she looks straight at them, through the glare of the lights. "What is this?" She holds up her hand. "What's this on me?"

Lark remembers what a difficult pregnancy Bea had been, how after weeks in the NICU half of Wofford Falls had gathered at the farmhouse to welcome mother and daughter home. Krupp got drunk on cider and tried to race Dennis, the Haverchucks' cattle dog, to the edge of the woods and back.

That dog's a territorial little monster, Lark recalls. It ought to be nipping at them now, trying to herd them, barking its head off. Then he thinks of the horse Willa. Jamie-Lynn's prized Arabian.

Old Forester mangled up in that pine.

And the girls?

"Blood," Asha says from inside the truck. "Fucking blood, it's obviously blood!" She comes alive then, shaking off any residual fear. It's almost militaristic, the way she slides confidently into the driver's seat.

"Asha," Lark says.

"I'm doing what we came here to do," she says. Then she juts her chin at Jamie-Lynn. "I don't know this person. I'm not going to sit here all night."

The engine revs as her foot comes down hard on the gas while she gets situated. "I'm going to get this done." She puts the truck into drive and reaches for the door.

Krupp glances from Lark to Asha in disbelief. "I'm gonna look for Lily and Bea." He says this like it's something any reasonable person would do. The obvious, human thing.

Asha drills him with her eyes. "Those girls are dead, Wayne."

"You don't know that."

Asha nods toward Jamie-Lynn, who's still studying her hands, bathed in the brights. "*Look* at her."

"That's Jamie-Lynn," Krupp says. "She's an EMT. She *volunteers*."

"I don't give a shit who she is," Asha says. "I didn't go to high school with her. She's just a psycho with blood on her face to me, and I'm going to do what we came here to do before she decides to go psycho on *us*, too. So *move*."

She slams the door, Krupp and Lark just barely moving out of the way.

"Come on!" Lark says, scrambling up into the bed of the F-150, pulling Krupp up the side just as Asha cranks the wheel to the right. The headlights sweep across the farmhouse garage. Jamie-Lynn disappears behind them.

"Wait!" she calls after them. Lark, his limbs tangled with Krupp's, peers over the rim of the truck bed. Jamie-Lynn's white shirt is a streak in the darkness, closing in.

"She's coming after us," Lark says. "She's *fast*."

He remembers the way her knees lifted as she danced through the dirty slush packed against the curb on Main Street. How many days ago? Two? Three? When his world had been status quo. Before Gumley, Wrecker's place, the Backbone, the waterfall, the drone.

His father.

Jamie Lynn with a face full of blood.

The dislocation.

Bouncing across the rolling hills in the back of his truck, Lark feels a strange and horrible exhilaration. Something clicks in his mind and he vows to represent this shift in perception in the sculpture as he assembles *The Worm & the Dogsbody*. He always tries not to let the material dictate its positioning before he gets to the studio, but now it unfolds in his mind with great clarity.

Leg. Rump. Flank.

Organic extensions of *The Insomniack*.

A child's coffin smeared with gore and offal. A cow's head with sightless eyes perched on the radiator. Yes. *Yes.* This is the key to Betsy's release. And, perhaps, his own. Asha is right—he can feel it. She understands something. She's received the bright shining instruction buried in the psalter. Jamie-Lynn and her missing kids slough off him as the truck crests a low hill, then bounces through a gully. Lark grips the side of the truck bed while Krupp, tossed, cries out. Bracing himself on the bag of his sculpting tools, a hundred pounds of metal in a massive black duffel, he opens the slider glass of the cab's back window. Asha's hunched over the wheel, leaning forward, peering down into empty fields carved out by headlights.

"Hey!" he yells at Asha. "Go left." He points in the direction he knows to be west, or at least it used to be. "That's where the cattle graze."

She cranks the wheel. The headlights sweep across a picturesque silo that Jamie-Lynn built for visitors' social media backdrops. Beyond the silo sits a long, low barn with milking stalls for the cows.

"*Shit*," Lark says. There's no sign of any farm animals. The stark emptiness of the fields, that *Christina's World* forlorn desolation, persists across the rolling hills. They pass a corral and a broken fence, dismantled piecemeal, that rings the stables like broken teeth in a ruined mouth. The animals are most definitely all gone. He glances back— Jamie-Lynn's also nowhere to be seen. Across the fields, the main house is a pile of shadows. Windows, haphazardly placed yet warm with light, remind Lark of a child's drawing of a house. He wonders what it felt like, being on the fault line of a sudden dislocation. If the shunting itself broke old Forester's body, or if the disorientation broke his brain. If the shifting was internal for Jamie-Lynn, something that messed up her head so badly in the blink of an eye that she did the unthinkable…

He chases away the thoughts of that stain around her mouth.

"Hey! Asshole!" Krupp yells to him across the truck bed as Asha hits another bone-rattling bump. "I remember how it all went down now after we left your pop's place!"

Any exhilaration Lark felt burns away, leaving the despair in its wake. Too much is out of his control. The dictates of what he's come to think of as his brand of narcissism require routine, discipline, order, things done on *his* terms. Even his care for Betsy is organized this way. And Krupp is like that wild-eyed horse, loosed suddenly with a great and terrible energy to redraw the boundaries of his increasingly chaotic world.

"You reformatted," Lark calls back to him.

"Bullshit, you fucking donkeylicker!" Krupp says. "That *birthday gift* was going haywire and I was the only one doing anything about it. And you know what?" He pauses, head tilted, like a dog finding a scent. "It's still here. You didn't chuck it in the woods, did you."

Lark tries to catch the wavelength Krupp is on. He sniffs the air, waits for the confirmation that the turning-jar is reaching out. Words and feelings, phonetic and figurative, flooding his brain.

"Guys!" Asha calls back from inside the truck. She's slowing down.

"I know it's here somewhere," Krupp says. "I can feel it, it's like nipple clamps with weights on them."

"Just let it be, Krupp."

"Don't tell me what to do!" That nasty, sneering edge roaring back. Lark notes the position of the rifle, wedged against the duffel full of tools. The NY Giants bag, with its towel-clad turning-jar, is down at the other end of the truck bed.

"*Guys!*" Asha comes to a stop. Lark figures she doesn't know what it's like to ride in the back of an F-150, or she would have eased down on that brake pedal instead of stomping on it. Krupp ends up sprawled against the duffel and Lark's rib cage slams into the back of the cab.

A noise joins in dissonant tandem with the idling engine. Lark thinks of Shostakovich, dueling themes, playful and ponderous, mechanical and organic, sounds of disparate origins that shouldn't work but somehow produce glorious harmonies.

Asha speaks slowly and carefully. "You might want to grab that rifle."

Lark stands up in the truck bed to look over the top of the cab. First he's relieved—they found a cow out roaming. The round-bellied animal saunters into view and stops. The noise in the air becomes a keening whine sent out like a messenger pigeon over the fields. Krupp stands up next to him. The animal is speckled, a classic black-and-white milk-carton cow. It stares off into the middle distance with stupid, uncomprehending eyes. Its spine is crooked, humped like a sea monster on an old nautical map. The cow turns its head to stare blankly at the truck. Lark has always considered the ears of a cow to be hilarious—wide things that stick out too far, accentuating the tiny head on a massive bulbous body that make them resemble a dopey British improv comic.

"What's wrong with its eyes?" Krupp says.

"I don't know." Lark peers into them now, remembering the cow eye he dissected in tenth-grade biology class, which Krupp ditched on the grounds of ethical opposition so he could leave school to eat a Big Mac. Cow eyes are dark and milky, with big round pupils. The ones he's looking at now, over the top of the truck and across ten feet of grass, are small, almond-shaped, hazel. *Pretty*, even. They sparkle in the high beams.

Lark crouches down and comes up with the rifle that Krupp loaded earlier on the porch of his father's house. He sets an elbow atop the truck's cab and sights down the barrel. The cow's belly presents a massive target. He's pretty confident he could drill it from here. But would that be a definite kill shot? Being shot in the stomach is one of the worst and most painful ways to go. And cows have *four* stomachs! He doesn't want to inflict that on this poor animal, he just wants to snuff out its life. So that probably requires a head shot. The real issue is that he's never shot a living thing before. And so here he is, flexing his finger against the trigger guard, wondering if Damien Hirst ever killed anything personally.

Okay.

Lark steadies himself. Sights down the barrel. *For Betsy.*

The noise, that keening whine, intensifies, like a mosquito swooping too close to his ear while he's trying to sleep. It's localized around the cow but the cow's mouth is closed. The sound radiates. Little rivers of it break off and flow into his ears. The cow's beautiful eyes blink once, its long lashes coming together briefly, then separating.

Asha begins to scream. Krupp staggers back, turns away. Only Lark is left staring, poised, as the cow turns fully and reveals what had been hidden. The errant lumps aren't growths, cancerous masses, some bovine deformity. They aren't that at all.

"Kill it!" Asha screams.

"Oh no," Krupp says.

A small, delicate elbow rises from the cow's flank. Spotted cow-flesh trails out along its pale, smooth skin—spots elongated and stretched. (The beautiful eyes blink.) What could have been a forearm reenters the cowhide, then emerges as a little hand. The nails, Lark can see in the light, are painted sunflower yellow. The disruptions sweep back along the cow's flank, to its rump. Knobs of flesh. Here and there an errant digit jutting out. A finger curls as if waiting for a coat to be hung. The smoothness of a forehead, the abrasions of a skinned knee.

You did this.

The noise keens, moving in and out of Lark's ears. Near the animal's back leg is a slit that might be a mouth.

"Lark," Krupp says. Lark doesn't know what kind of entreaty it's supposed to be. Shoot it. Don't you dare shoot it.

It's an abomination.

It's Lily and Bea.

It's not them. Not anymore.

We can save them. They might be in pain.

They're gone.

Lark swallows. Steels himself. Sights down the barrel. (The beautiful eyes blink.) His resolve builds. He comes down firmly on the side of *abomination*. This is what they came here to do. And if they can put this *thing* (these girls) out of its misery, then all the better.

He moves his finger from the guard to rest it on the trigger.

There's a blur of speed off to his left. It almost startles him into shooting but he holds back. Jamie-Lynn comes bounding into the cone of light. Undeterred by the impossibility of the animal's corruption, she rushes up to its meaty, distended belly and begins to attempt an embrace of sorts. She's making a keening noise of her own as she struggles to wrap her arms in any meaningful way around the animal. She runs her hands with frantic despair along the skinned knee, the jutting elbow, the stray painted fingernails. The cow stands perfectly still. Lark gets the impression it's locked in some internal struggle to stay

alive and upright with foreign bodies displacing its organs. Surely it
has very little time left.

"Lark," Krupp says again.

"Get out—" Lark attempts but it comes out a hoarse croak. He
swallows, tries again. "Get out of the way, Jamie-Lynn!"

She throws herself against the animal as if trying to bash herself
inside to join Bea and Lily. Or whatever is left of them. Lark can't be
sure, of course, if they're alive in some way he can't comprehend. If
their consciousness has been rerouted and rewired to join the cow's,
like those beautiful eyes. Jamie-Lynn grips the elbow and pulls but it
does not budge. The cow shudders. Lark expects the animal to collapse
but it remains upright, somehow. Whatever survival instinct is at its
core is intact.

"Help me!" Jamie-Lynn screams, tugging at what might be a wrist.

Lark's finger trembles on the trigger. He remembers that party
after Jamie-Lynn finally took Bea home from the hospital. He brought
potato salad.

"I can't." He turns to Krupp, helpless. "I can't do it." He removes
the rifle from its sniper position atop the cab and lets it drop.

He can't read the expression on Krupp's face and braces himself for
anything at all.

"Kill it!" Asha screams. "What are you waiting for?" Then she
slaps her palm against the windshield. "Hey, lady!" she yells. "Those
aren't your girls anymore! Get out of the way!"

Jamie-Lynn falls to her knees and scrambles in front of the cow. She
thrusts her arms out to her sides, using her body like a hockey goalie,
blocking as much of the animal as her small frame allows. Her face is
scrunched and shiny with tears. She says something Lark can't make
out over the truck's idling engine.

"Get the fuck out of the way!" Asha gives the windshield another
smack.

Jamie-Lynn stares back, blank-faced and tear-streaked. Then she
shrieks in reply. She claws at her head and bunches hair in her fists
and rips it from her scalp. The red filth around her mouth is smeared

across her face. Her cries pierce the truck noise. Lark jams his fingers into his ears but Jamie-Lynn's hysteria slithers in, impossibly loud, with terrible precision. The vibrations of his eardrums flutter against his fingertips. A sharp pain like a seam of bright light opens in his skull and her voice is there, in his head, booming and ageless.

First the waterfall

Her mad screams coalesce into words that hammer on the inside of his head. Lark is aware of Asha, in the truck, clamping her hands over her ears.

Then the horse

Jamie-Lynn rises to her feet but her arms remain thrust straight out. She advances slowly toward the truck. Her face is twisted into a shrieking, crying mask. It's the spikes in Krupp's rage, the peaks of his personality's corruption, taking hold of Jamie-Lynn. She is fully inhabiting that zone that Krupp has only slipped in and out of.

Then the life of the world to come.

Lark glances down to the truck bed, eyes roving madly, searching for the rifle. He wonders distantly if he could shoot Jamie-Lynn, and decides that he can, that he's capable of anything in this moment to silence the shrieking in his head. But the rifle is so far away, it would require movements beyond his ability. Bent knees and outstretched arms.

First the waterfall

Lark thinks he might be screaming in return, great phlegmy strands of utter nonsense to drown out Jamie-Lynn's voice, which is no voice at all but a predatory invader in his mind. His eyes blur with tears and he closes them.

Then the horse

Her words are amplified in the darkness.

Then the life of the world—

Lark feels the truck shift into drive. Asha guns the engine and the tires spin in the grass and bite down. The vehicle leaps forward with a roar. Lark and Krupp are tossed back into the truck bed. For a brief moment there's no feeling at all, as if the wheels have left the earth entirely. He thinks he's still screaming. There is pure cacophony as the keening—all of it crashing against Jamie-Lynn's cries—reaches a new height. Then there's a massive thud and Lark's thrown against the back of the cab. Amid this new hurt, there's a sudden merciful silence: Both Jamie-Lynn and the keening animal she protects go quiet. There is only Asha now, screaming as the truck grinds down whatever's caught beneath its front wheels. The old Giants duffel slides down the truck bed and slams against Lark's body. The turning-jar inside absorbs the impact and steals Lark's breath. It's like a bag of meat. There's a squelch that resolves to a diamond-hard coldness and fades. The truck's wheels drive into one last slick grind before torque bites and kicks the vehicle up over the top of what feels like a wet berm. Asha hits the brakes. The truck stops completely. Foul steam drifts up from the tires, a mist of fine particles that disappear into the night. Slowly, Krupp picks himself up, straightens his limbs, tests his mobility. Lark does the same. Jamie-Lynn's voice is gone from inside his mind. He glances through the slider glass into the cab. Asha's sitting in the driver's seat, ramrod-straight, hands at ten and two, gripping the wheel with white knuckles, eyes focused straight ahead. Putting off as long as she can any kind of engagement with what awaits them now.

Lark does the same, following Asha's gaze into the void. He opens and closes a fist. There's a pop somewhere in his forearm. The pain is distant and dull. He turns to Krupp, who's hugging his knobby knees to his chest.

"You okay?" he croaks.

If Krupp hears him, he doesn't show it. Lark closes his eyes for a moment. Phosphenes riot behind his eyelids and he thinks of Big Tom. Then he opens his eyes to find Krupp scrambling to the back of the truck to peer out at what lies just beyond the taillights.

"Oh Jesus," he mutters. "This is so bad." His voice rises. "This is so fucking bad, Lark."

Lark catches sight of the massive lump of cowflesh marred by what appear to be the grill-marks of a madman. Charred streaks where hard rubber peeled flesh from bone and flung it like shredded cabbage in its wake. Deeply indented sacks of meat and bone where the wheels bore down and the truck came over the top. He keeps it in his periphery. He can't bear it head-on because of what else he knows must be there. What's left of her. *Them.* All of them. There are moments that rise up from the Lost Year fugue with stunning clarity that make him freeze in place and wonder—*Did that really happen?*

Climbing into a water tower, running naked from high tea at the Plaza, kicking in a man's face outside McSorley's...

Now the paralysis grips him. *Is this really happening? How can it be?*

"No, no, no, no, no." Krupp bashes a fist into the side of the truck bed, each *no* accompanied by a metallic thud. "Look at it, man," he moans.

"No," Lark says. *This isn't happening.*

"Fucking *look at it*. Look what she did."

"It's not her fault," Lark says.

"You *bitch!*" Krupp screams at the rear slider glass.

Lark vacates his body. He floats backward over the dark fields of Haverchuck's Farm while far below, time runs in reverse. The truck backs over the lump of cowflesh and the animal rises, totters, stands. The fence repairs itself. Forester springs back into bed. Lark passes over Wofford Falls, a benevolent spirit reversing the wayward course of the past two days. The sculpture on the Backbone disassembles itself. The waterfall flows up and returns to nothing. His father paints silently. Wrecker eats and sleeps. Lark drifts up into the mountains, traces Route 212 back to the stone house. He drops through the architectural shingles and slides into his body, seated in the sumptuous leather chair among the fumes of expensive single malt. He breathes life into his impotent fantasy of that afternoon, and Another Lark leaps from his chair, smashes his glass, drives the shard into Gumley's neck. The man bleeds out. Some signal or another isn't given. Betsy dies. But Jamie-Lynn lives. Forester lives. Lily and Bea go off to school. Sally makes it home with the cough medicine. Krupp stays Krupp-like as ever, while his father paints silently. The roads of Wofford Falls go where they're supposed to go. Asha stays downstate where she belongs.

His phone buzzes in his pocket, yanking his spirit back down from the mountains and into his body. Into the present. Into what, yes, is really happening.

The screen is cracked, but the phone still works. He pulls up the latest text.

Krupp pounds on the windshield, screaming obscenities at Asha, who still does not turn or take her hands from the wheel.

In the photo he's just received, Betsy's face is scored with tiny nicks, no larger than the shaving cuts he sometimes inflicts upon himself. Little red slits that sting for a moment and then are forgotten. Her eyes are wide and wet. That knife held to her eye in the last photo must have an impossibly sharp tip. He thinks of Leng Tch'e, death by a thousand cuts.

Then he thinks of Asha's impressions of the last photo sent— a put-on, a fake. Photoshopped, manipulated. But how can he be expected to take the chance, to call their bluff, to play with Betsy's life like a poker chip?

He texts back, with trembling hands: *STOP. NO MORE. ON MY WAY WITH MORE MATERIAL. WORKING AS FAST AS I CAN.*

He pockets the phone. While Krupp hammers at the glass, Lark unzips the massive canvas bag of tools and equipment and retrieves his cordless circular saw. He clicks the plastic flap of the safety off and presses the trigger, testing the charge. The motor whirrs and the blade spins cleanly. Even in the dark there must have been some faint gleam because it's enough to command Krupp's attention. He turns from his attack on the windshield.

"What are you doing?"

"What we came for," Lark says. He's shocked at how confident he sounds, when his roiling guts match the storm in his head. *For Betsy.*

"No," Krupp says, more of a plea than a command. But he doesn't move to stop him as Lark hops down from the truck bed. At the mountain of cowflesh, tinted red by the taillights, he fires up the saw and gets to work. It takes him thirty minutes to dismember the mountainous mass, to slice it into chunks he can transfer to the truck bed. Nobody helps. Nobody stops him. He works around anything human as best he can, dragging Jamie-Lynn's broken remains away from the animal. The first time he comes across a delicate hand with yellow fingernails he tosses it away, casually, as if it's simply offal, gets back to work, and then vomits a moment later. He takes the head last. The soulful eyes stay closed.

18

Dawn breaks with violence and strange intention across the Back-bone. It took them at least an hour to get here. Maybe two. A function of time's elasticity, in sympathy with the knotted roads. They looped back through a downtown Wofford Falls riddled with arson. Krupp & Sons was unscathed, but the glass was smashed in the former bagel shop's window. Lark, at the wheel, spattered in blood, was struck by the peculiar motion of the flames plastered in the window of Hud-son Valley Vape HQ. An artificial distance between the fire and the items inside on which it was supposedly feeding. Residents milled about, lost on streets they'd walked for decades. The horse from Jamie-Lynn's farm cantered across Market, headed for the baseball fields or the foothills beyond. Children gazed into mirrored glass. Someone took lamps from the antiques store and set them up along the side-walk. Asha stared silently out the window at the chaos while Krupp reformatted.

Now, up on the Backbone, *The Insomniack* rises with a magnificence that stirs an imposter syndrome he hasn't felt since before *Citadel* sold. He parks the truck at the edge of the pines and regards the sculpture. He tries to remember what it looked like the last time he came up here. How long ago was that? He doesn't know. He studies the way he's joined the material. Bricks, wax, radiator, nails, typewriter keys. The pieces of a child's coffin. He recalls the thematic binding: afflictions and remedies. A bed for the weary. The sky lightens, sending bright flares to wriggle like minnows in the waterfall. This light glints off *The Insomniack* too, a refraction that only adds to the notion that he himself had little to do with the sculpture's present state. He's not Betsy. His work isn't laced with the impossible. The gift is hers alone. And yet, the sculpture has certainly evolved.

"Well," Asha says, "it certainly insists upon itself, doesn't it."

He eyes the sword, the disarticulated bed frame. It's all grown, shot toward the sky like a weed left to its own devices. In the same way the turning-jar has been infected by an organic blossoming, a sense of malleability courses through the sculpture's DNA. *The Insomniack* has taken root in the Backbone.

"I'm not the one doing the insisting," he says. Jamie-Lynn's disembodied voice still echoes in his head. *First the waterfall. Then the horse. Then the life of the world to come.* He glances over the top of Krupp's slumped head. "Are you okay?"

"Absolutely not." She pauses, gripping the door handle. "I killed that woman."

Lark swallows. "Jamie-Lynn." Her name on his lips once again calls up the party at the farm after Bea's fraught birth, both of them heading for the potato salad at the same time, racing to grab the big plastic spoon, Jamie-Lynn boxing him out like she'd been going for a rebound in the paint. Laughing like they were kids again.

"I'm sorry, Lark."

"It wasn't your fault. We all saw her." *Heard her.* "It was over before we got there."

Somebody needs to tell Terry, he thinks. *Your daughters are dead. So's Jamie-Lynn.*

"This whole thing's on me," he says. The weight of it all. The lives, the fires, the children staring at themselves in mirrored glass on Main Street. Sally's journey to nowhere. Out the window, the sculpture seems to tremble in acknowledgment. At once a monstrous, imposing presence and a fragile thing.

"I hit the gas," Asha says. "I ran her over."

"I would have shot her, but I could barely move."

"I couldn't think straight." She tightens her grip on the handle without opening the door. "That—*thing*. So awful. I wish I could say I did it out of mercy, even if that would have been horribly misguided. At least it would have been something beyond just blind animal fear. Totally reactive. I've never felt like that before in my life. Like I had no choice. Like I couldn't stop myself." Her eyes burn into Lark's, imploring. "What kind of person am I?"

"A good one." Lark, remembering the hot blood spurting into his face as he lowered the saw blade. "You're a good person," he says again. "You came up here to help me, and you didn't have to do that."

"I had a fight with Justine." Asha opens the door. Cold morning air rushes into the truck along with the churning sounds of foam and velocity. "What I said about wanting to see you was true, but it was also true that the apartment was feeling pretty tense. It was a good excuse to get out." She pauses. "I don't know what was the stronger motivation for heading upstate. Sometimes I just do things. I'm not a good person, Lark."

"You cleaned up my messes for a whole lost year once, when I was nothing but an asshole to everyone."

"Everything you did back then was easy enough to come back from. People are self-obsessed, they barely remember anything they didn't do themselves, and anyway everyone was so fucked up in those days."

"I kicked a guy's face in outside McSorley's. Did you know that?"

"Of course I knew that. I paid his hospital bill. He ended up being fine, if I recall. Besides, it didn't exactly hurt your career that you were perceived as a bit unpredictable, for a while there, at least." Sitting next to the open door, Asha stares out at the sculpture. "Just now I did something there's no coming back from."

"It was self-defense."

"If you say so." She grabs the psalter from the glove compartment. "Let's get out there."

Lark falls in beside her as they trudge up the short trail to the naked rocks of the Backbone.

"There was somebody, once," he says. "About seven years ago." He didn't really mean to say anything at all, but his brain feels overcooked, threadbare. He's been up for too long, ridden too many adrenaline rushes. And now he's in that same openhearted zone of the painfully hungover and those on the Sunday-morning comedown. Blurting secrets, throwing admissions out into the morning air.

Asha brushes aside a branch. Dry pine needles fall away. "What are you talking about? Somebody who?"

"A woman I almost married."

They emerge onto the bald outcrop. Up above, clouds are backlit by a sun that feels much too close yet gives off no discernible heat. Lark shields his eyes.

"Why didn't you?"

Just ahead, *The Insomniack* rises. Beyond it, across the chasm, the waterfall cascades down into the gorge. The sound of its plunge seems to doppler away, quieter now, noise traveling in some vast loop.

"Celeste," he says. "That was her name. We'd been dating for two years and the plan was to find a new place, start our life together, and let Betsy stay in the house. I was totally on board, in theory, until we started to actually look at houses. Then I realized I couldn't do it. I couldn't leave her again."

"Did you talk to Betsy about it?"

"She told me to go, said she'd be fine."

"But you didn't."

"Nope. Stayed put. Celeste moved on."

"Huh," Asha says. As they cross the rocks, Lark feels like he's brushing up against the margins of whatever *The Insomniack* radiates. The air is thicker here, and one more step will take them both inside the sculpture's airspace.

He thrusts out an arm to stop Asha in her tracks and listens carefully. He has the impression the sound of the water, distinct and detached, is soaring out over the old-growth preserve that spreads for a thousand acres across the chasm. Less a loop than a sweeping vector, like a line on a radar display describing a circle. The waterfall is completely silent for a moment as the radar needle hits the point exactly opposite the Backbone, far across the embankment. Then it gathers itself up again as it completes its journey. The churn grows louder. There's an impending, kinetic buildup, as if they're about to take a roller-coaster plunge or be swamped by a massing tidal wave. Lark and Asha look at each other. She holds her breath. When the noise hits them it's deafening, and

it throws everything into a sort of

crystalline delineation, a world chopped into neat bits like the shark in Hirst's glass cases. Even prepared for this cognitive lurch

Lark finds it difficult to hold

a thought

in his head for very long. He

waits in this blank bubble of time while an equalization occurs between everything he's lost and everything he's gained

in his life.   All of it divided into shards of meaning and scattered to the winds. Lost to time.

The sound dies away as the needle begins another cycle. Linear perception snaps back into place.

"Oh God," Asha says. She looks at him for a moment, then bends at the waist, heaving. He rushes over to her, queasy and off balance. She breathes in through her nose and stands upright. Then she exhales slowly. "It's quite possible that I'm growing to hate art."

"Come on," he says, turning back to the path. "I'd guess we've only got a few minutes till that comes back around again."

"You go," Asha says. She opens the book. "I'll art-direct. It'll be faster." She glances up from the book to regard the sculpture, then turns a page. "Get something from the midsection to start with. Hurry!"

Lark heads back through the pines. He wishes she hadn't said *midsection*. So clinical, so cold. If only his butchery was as clean as her word implies—neatly sliced portions, cut with precision and the proper dissection tools. But what awaits him in the truck bed is a crime scene courtesy of the most sadistic killer, one who will never be romanticized in an irreverent true-crime podcast.

Lark recoils at the sight of what he's done. What he's taken from Jamie-Lynn's farm. (And now, in the cold gray morning, he knows he's taken more than cow parts.) In the dark it was a horrifying dream. Now he's awake, and there are already flies.

Midsection.

He thinks about searching the truck bed for a pair of gloves. He thinks about waking Krupp for help. Then he dismisses both notions and plunges his hands into a pile of lumpy, matted flesh, sticky with half-dried blood.

He retches, turns away, then refocuses himself. It has to be done.

He can't distinguish *midsection* from anything else, though he's certain this particular lump isn't a head or a leg-part, at least. He tells himself it's just raw meat, which is technically true, but it's so much heavier and *warmer* than any chicken cutlet he's ever marinated. His middle finger penetrates a blood-slick channel, some interior curvature where the meat once gave way to accommodate a snug little organ— one of those four stomachs, perhaps. He pulls the lump from the truck and it trails a long white rope of sinew. He retches again. The smell is overpowering—rust-blood and bad meat. Gripping the mound with two hands, holding it as far out in front of him as possible, he trudges back to the outcrop.

There had been a flow state to *The Insomniack*. For *The Worm & the Dogsbody*, he's submitted to Asha's will. She watches him as he comes forward bearing the cowflesh. She does not appear to be disgusted. The sculpture rises before them and seems to bend toward the distant sound of the waterfall, way out like low tide, but circling around and coming ever closer.

He looks at Asha while she studies the psalter. His fingers dig into the mound of flesh. Blood trickles down his forearms. It's completely unfamiliar, this deference to another, this lack of agency in his work. Beyond his disgust at the awful logistics of this assemblage, Lark's discomfort is a prickly, nagging thing. Yes, his studio is open to Betsy, but it's not like she stands there and dictates process to him. She's an observer. But now, he's nothing more than an intern, one of Hirst's busy little bees—except this silent hymn taking shape on the Backbone isn't played for shock value, or headlines, or manufactured outrage.

Asha is abruptly imperious, as if she's shaken off all vestiges of despair. She extends an arm and points.

"There," she says, dictating exactly where Lark should add the lump to *The Insomniack*.

The second he does so, he supposes, the sculpture ceases to be *The Insomniack* at all and becomes something more. The next movement in the grand symphony begins.

He approaches *The*
           Insomniack as the falling water begins to
rush
       through his skull, whipping back around like a fierce
   wind on a desert planet. He follows Asha's gesture to a corner of the bed frame welded to the radiator. He selects a pointed, jutting
    piece of metal and fixes
                    the cowflesh atop it. The
         mound
   slides and settles, leaving a slug's trail of crimson ooze on the rusted metal of the frame. Then, as the
   waterfall rushes away, out across the gorge to complete another cycle sweeping across the old-growth
       forest, this first foray into *The Worm & the Dogsbody* comes to rest upon this jutting portion of *The Insomniack*.

"Hindquarters," Asha commands. There's a coldness emanating from her now. Lark sees her as a black-robed figure high on a hill, issuing commands while her hair whips back. An album cover from 1983, a fantasy vixen, a priestess. She's slipped into some new persona that ratchets up with each sweep of the rushing waterfall. Imperiousness is just the surface.

He turns and obeys. He finds that he's glad to cede all decisions to Asha. While creating *The Insomniack* he'd been ashamed of his zeal for the work with Betsy's life hanging in the balance. Now he's a willing automaton. While Krupp sleeps, Lark selects a rumplike mass

from the truck bed. As he lifts it he finds that it's still attached to a
rib. Twined around the rib is a clump of auburn hair. Tangled in the
clump, fused by dried blood, is a plastic bow-shaped hairclip. He pulls
the strands of hair from the rib. They stick to his fingers. The bow
dangles. He kneels, wipes his hand in the dirt, then brings the portion
of meat to Asha. She inspects it quickly, glances at the psalter, then
points to the disassembled typewriter.

"Integrate it."

Lark goes to work, threading stray keys into the pinkish-gray mass.
He works while the waterfall dopplers back around to rush

over and through him,

the uniformity of its cascading violence shimmering across his
bloodied hands as he

inserts typewriter keys like candles into a birthday cake until
the cowflesh is a pincushion of vowels.

It isn't until his sixth trip back from the truck that Lark begins
to see the pattern in Asha's art direction. The cloud cover wanes, the
morning sun breaks through to pour down the various metals of *The
Insomniack* and the vivid pinks of *The Worm & the Dogsbody*. Cloven hooves
decorate the child's coffin. Meat from each section of the animal is in
balance around the sculpture. It's more like trimming a Christmas tree
than sculpting, although it's really neither as the act of creation has
been entirely taken from him. He's been reduced to a mindless cog in
the machinery of these silent hymns. Even Asha, who's taken charge of
this whole operation, is merely interpreting the psalter.

He's holding a thighbone. Torn flesh hangs like a tattered battle
flag. Asha eyes him with disdain. The waterfall noise is a distant mur-
mur. Atop the Backbone there's a silence, a sucked-out vacuum of quiet
that hangs like dead air.

The Insomniack, festooned with offal, crowned in chunks of raw meat,
painted in blood. There is subservience here, not so much in the result
but in the *act*. If *The Insomniack* was a true sculpture then *The Worm & the
Dogsbody* is a process, an installation in search of a rationale. And that
rationale is a hierarchy that is becoming clear to him. By reducing him

to an errand boy, Asha has transformed her own despair into a brief triumph—despite being nothing more than a human worm, in thrall to a centuries-old psalter that has twisted her life beyond recognition, she is still one rung above Lark—a man who does the bidding of a worm.

A lowly dogsbody.

Both of them dark instruments to the psalter's strange and terrible instructions.

Asha points, no longer even speaking to him. He places the thigh-bone with its tattered flesh upright, held in place by a juncture of fire extinguisher and bed frame, and marvels at her genius. He would have been too prescriptive, he knows. Even playing fast and loose with material, like in the making of *The Insomniack*, he never would have conceived of her overarching schema, her meta-engagement with this particular silent hymn. He never had much use for performance art. But Asha's well versed in the conceptual, and—more important—that invisible tipping point, identified by precious few even in her cohort, where the purely conceptual becomes highly monetizable. A magic trick, really. Turning pretension into seven figures.

Which makes her perfect for the job.

He pulls the thread even further, thinking that Krupp is a genius for contacting her in the first place. He releases the thighbone and it juts upright in the center of the sculpture, ringed by a ragged circle of flesh. He catches a delicate knee joint out of the corner of his eye, skinned from some afternoon's outdoor playtime, and wonders dully if it's Bea's or Lily's. As if any of that matters now. There is nothing left for him to throw up, and his muscles are sore from retching.

"Get the head," she tells him scornfully. Across the chasm the sun dapples the waterfall. He turns to walk back to the truck as the sound flies in from the west to smack him in the brain.

Prismatic, he thinks of Betsy's

     face scored with tiny

          cuts and tells himself he's almost there, the end of all this is in sight. But when he gets to the truck he glances into the cab and—

shit

it's empty.

There's no sign of Krupp. While Lark was out placing the thigh-bone, Krupp must have woken and run off somewhere.

He turns in a circle and scans the woods. Nothing. Filing that away to deal with in a moment, he climbs up into the truck bed, careful not to slip on the slurry of blood and torn flesh. Lying next to the Giants duffel, the head awaits with gorgeous, wide-open eyes.

Lark pauses. He's never noticed the weight of his heart before. Now, broken, it's a thousand pounds of lead in the middle of his chest. Fatigue catches up with him like the sound of the waterfall, a spring-loaded state of being set to slam him to the ground. *Just get it done*, he tells himself. He takes up the head in two hands and tries not to look into its eyes, but they draw his gaze like sirens. Pale-blue irises, long delicate lashes. A radiance at odds with the lolling tongue, the matted fur, the jagged, protruding spinal cord, raggedly severed with his circular saw in a geyser of bone. It's as heavy as his heart.

Asha's looking up at the sky. The drone is hanging there, hovering above the chasm. Something about the dispassionate, almost bored way it hovers ignites a fury in Lark. He has to stop himself from flinging the head at the little machine.

Asha's gaze levels on him. "Focus," she says. "You know where this goes."

"Tell me."

She snaps the psalter shut. "You know."

He takes a step back and regards the work as a whole. Not two silent hymns but one sculpture. He blanks his mind, imposes the walk from side yard to studio on himself. In giving him agency for the final step of *The Worm & the Dogsbody*, Asha's bringing him back to himself. He feels lost, having inhabited his role for—how long has it been?

His entire life?

The sculpture seems to tilt toward the waterfall. Even the ruined cow parts are elongated now, reaching for the empty space of the chasm.

The drone descends for a better look.

Lost Year rage flares. Lark holds the head aloft.

"Is this what you want to see?" he calls to the drone. Covered in blood and gore, he presents the head to Gumley, his employers, anyone else watching in that vast subterranean viewing room of his imagination. "Look at it!" he screams.

You did this.

"Lark..." Asha says.

Red clouds his vision. He takes one last look at the drone, imagines he can see through its lens into the eye at the other end. Then he climbs up on the base of the sculpture and flings the head down into the center. It hits the frying pan with a meaty thunk and splatters a greenish substance, like what you might dig out of a lobster's abdomen. "You like that?" he screams at the drone. "You get a good look?"

The drone swoops down to regard the sculpture. It's so close that Lark could swat it out of the sky. Instead, he glares into its lens. "Eat my shit, Gumley."

The cow's head stares up with

gorgeous eyes.

    The waterfall unleashes more of

itself, cascading down from what had begun with a trickle from some hidden place

while Lark, hurling obscenities at the drone, is drowned out by

its magnificent, deafening rush—

    and Lark, catching sight of something new behind the curtain of falling water, goes quiet, shields his eyes

against the sun to get a better look at an emergence he can't define. The drone buzzes about the sculpture, peering into its crevices. Asha holds the closed psalter against her hip and follows Lark's gaze across the chasm to the waterfall. The doppler effect stops. The noise from the falling water hangs over the Backbone, in its right place. Mist rises from the chasm.

At first the emergence is pure shadow—a trick of the light, the negative of a sunspot. A photographic glitch near the top of the cliff, where the waterfall was turned on like a spigot as *The Insomniack* neared completion. Lark glances at his bloodied hands, astonished at the correlation—even after all he's been through, it's still amazing to him that the psalter's instructions actually *work*. A bit of yesterday's shame creeps back in—his awe at what he's accomplished feels improper, a slap in the face to Betsy. To the entire town.

"What is that?" Asha shouts, pointing across the chasm.

The drone, alerted by Asha's movement, ascends straight up, as if being yanked into the clouds.

Lark watches the shadow in the falls *unfurl* itself upward, climbing the water as if it were capable of gripping the foam and hoisting itself through the churn.

Asha bends once again to the psalter. Lark, entranced by what he's wrought, barely notices when she comes to stand beside him. "Look at this," she says. He doesn't take his eyes off the falls. The shadow continues to raise itself up, haltingly, like ascending a down escalator.

"Look!" She shoves the psalter in his face. The book is open to the last third, the final silent hymn—*The God of the Noose.*

> Upon completion of the firft and fecond hymns, the harbingers of the third shall be releafed. The fcale tilts. An unbalancing cometh. Affliction and remedy as a foundation for naked subservience.
> The feast begins. The harbingers prepare the way.

"What the fuck," Lark says. He watches as the shadow—the harbinger—makes its fluid climb. "You didn't catch that part earlier?"

"I was focused on *The Worm & the Dogsbody.*"

"You didn't read ahead? Everyone reads ahead."

"Did you?"

They both watch the shadow bifurcate, then scatter like a school of fish. Slippery and quick, the shadow-bits jet to the top of the falls. A form converges, crests the rock face, and lingers, leaning out brazenly over the chasm. Lark can just make out the shape of a head, possible appendages

(*too long*)

and a stooped, wilted demeanor.

Suddenly, a rifle shot rings out. The sharp *crack* echoes across the chasm and bounces back to meet a second shot.

Lark and Asha swivel their heads. Krupp steps out from the tree line, eye pressed against the scope, black rifle trained on the figure atop the falls.

Lark's first instinct is to intervene, get Krupp to stop shooting, based on the assumption that Krupp is fucking up, somehow. But is he, really? How can Lark say that taking shots at a shadow—a *harbinger of the God of the Noose*—is the wrong thing to do, in this moment?

As always, his moral compass spins out from Betsy at its center. Whatever Krupp's doing is visible to the drone. The people at the other end of the drone might hurt Betsy, if Krupp keeps shooting.

"I finally got to see the waterfall," Krupp calls out. "I hate it. It sucks."

"They're watching," Lark says, pointing up at the drone.

Krupp raises the rifle. As Lark recalls, Krupp was the worst shot of the three of them out in Ian's backyard that long-ago afternoon. His first shot goes wide as the drone retreats.

The machine is whirling across the chasm when the second shot miraculously finds its mark and the—

Museum Interlude

—screen goes black.

"Brandt!" Helena calls to the back of the war room, where the KPM's leader resides, King Douche himself, that formidably lame jerkoff, a man I always have the urge to call "Haircut." Brandt Gumley steps out of the shadows, brandishing his drone controller. Hey, Haircut.

"I'm sorry," he says, "but there's nothing I can do. Wayne Krupp shot the drone."

"Was that our *only* drone?" Griffin inquires.

"It seems like we should have a fleet," Helena says, her voice honeyed with microbial drink. Some kind of upper-downer herbal combo, an artisanal speedball that just sort of makes her more of herself.

"We do," Gumley assures her. "You own a drone factory outside Rochester."

"So dispatch another."

"It's been done."

"And who's this woman with Peter Larkin? Another pal?"

"Asha Benedict, his art agent," Gumley says.

"As much as I appreciate her adding a bit of style to these proceedings, I have to say—come on, Brandt, seriously, your lack of attention to detail has engendered a fairly alarming ripple effect."

"Were we supposed to say to you during the planning phase," Griffin jumps in, "Brandt, please specify *no police*, and also specify no townies and no art agents? Where does it end, Brandt?"

I revel in Haircut being dressed down. I lap up his discomfort, his stiffness. "I apologize."

"You know what?" Griffin says. "Don't worry about it. Just get this screen back online."

He's in a good mood because you, Betsy, have been painting like you're possessed by the ghost of, I don't know, some super-prolific old painter. What Griffin doesn't know is that you've also been giving me shout-outs. Little messages in your mural that you paint over before anybody notices.

Hello was just the beginning.

So, how does it feel to be acknowledged after eight years of floating alone in the void?

Like my existence has a shape. Like invisibility won't lead, eventually, to madness after all.

I still can't do anything *tangible*, in terms of helping you out of this. And for that I'm sorry. But the fact that, for the first time, someone *knows I'm here*, puts me so far beyond anything I've experienced before. The next level—actually doing something to help you, to fuck over Gumley and the KPM and the Belmonts—actually feels within reach now. I'm no longer just a silent scream in an elevator anymore.

Gumley, for his part, takes in the Belmonts' criticism, absorbs it, then snaps back to his unruffled private-security self. It's irritating how professional he can be. Water, duck's back. I wonder if he's screaming internally, if there's a hollow in him that's just full of the pent-up frustration that he holds inside. It's a horrible thought, that kind of repressed torment. Like when you're watching a server at a restaurant take shit from some asshole who compensates for his tiny dick by bossing wait staff around in front of his mouth-breathing family. Except Gumley deserves it, unlike the waiters and waitresses of this world.

I also wonder, for the millionth time, if this is all about money for Brandt Gumley. If he's such a mercenary that he'd leave the Griffins tomorrow and take his whole team with him if he somehow magically received a more lucrative offer. Gumley's one of those people who come across as so painfully straightforward that they actually spark more curiosity about their lives than someone who presents as a complete weirdo. What makes him tick? I imagine him going home to an empty spotless house with one single chair and just sitting there with his eyes closed till it's time to go back to work. Like a robot in shutdown mode, preserving its energy. But presumably he has an inner life like every other human being who's ever existed. So what does it consist of?

Imagining Brandt Gumley kicking back and enjoying a movie is an interesting thought experiment. What's he watching? Some Criterion shit? *Chungking Express*? *In the Mood for Love*? Texting his pals, BRO you gotta check out Wong Kar-wai, his movies really give me all the feels!

Does he have a girlfriend? (Shudder.) A wife? (Double shudder.) *KIDS?* (I can't even.)

What kind of music does he like? Maybe he owns a copy of my album. Statistically unlikely!

Still, the idea that every member of the khaki pants mafia has a distinct personality, complete with thoughts and hopes and dreams that are no more or less "real" than anyone else's, is very depressing. I *want* them to be like the random townspeople in Zelda who move on their prescribed paths and dip into a shallow well of pre-determined phrases when they speak. I want them to be clones, pulled from dripping goo-molds from some underground clone farm the Belmonts own. (Note that clone farms, as far as I know, don't exist, because I assume if they did the Belmonts would be all over it.)

My grandmother used to tell me to be kind to everyone, *especially* when they're being difficult, or ornery, or downright unkind to you, because you never know what kind of day they're having outside of your brief moment together. Or what kind of life. All you can see is that little tip of the iceberg, when they happened to be rude to you. The million frustrations and challenges and hardships that fed that moment were invisible. It's a good life lesson for small interactions (of the kind I haven't had in eight years now), but a shitty lesson for the bigger picture. It's like trying to have sympathy for Hitler because he never got to fulfill his dream of becoming a painter (because, incidentally,

he sucked). Anyway, Mee-maw wasn't thinking about Hitler, she was
thinking about the guy at the dry cleaner, and that people are decent
by default and deserve your best effort at kindness. Mee-maw was a
good person and I miss her dearly. I assume she's passed on by now,
but that's another aspect of this raw-deal ghost bullshit. I'm not tapped
into any afterlife network. I have no clue who else is out there.

Helena mixes another drink. Brandt messes with his controller. (It
does occur to me in this moment, in a fun bit of synergy with my
racing thoughts, that he could be playing Zelda right now, while his
colleagues, the Non-Player Characters in the KPM, move along their
pathways through the galleries.)

Suddenly the huge screen comes back to life. The POV is bird's-eye,
much higher than before. I can see straight down into the gorge, where
the freshly sprung-from-nowhere falls are churning up a fine white
mist. The sound in the room is a deafening white noise—the speakers in here, embedded in the walls, are just as good as the ones in the
screening room, which are so high-fidelity it's almost maddening—
that sense that something is too good, too crisp, that reality goes all
the way around and ends up on something uncanny.

"There!" Helena says. "I told you I saw something come out of the
falls. Right before we cut away."

She's right. I can barely make it out from such a great height, but
there's something out of place at the top of the falls. A shadow bending
the wrong way.

"Brandt," she says, "take us down a bit, will you?"

"I think it's best if I keep it up here where it'll be harder to hit with
that rifle."

"Zoom," Griffin says. "Enhance. Whatever."

The lens on the drone magnifies the rocky cliffs. Gumley zooms in
so quickly that he loses track of what he's supposed to be zooming in
on, and for a moment the video feed zips around a mega-large, pixelated
view of the three figures on the cliff opposite the falls: your brother
Peter Larkin, his buddy Wayne Krupp with the gun, and this Asha
woman.

"Not on *them*," Helena says. Gumley course-corrects, zipping across the gorge to the top of the falls. "There!"

The drone lens pauses on the bent shadow. Seeing it close up, it's hardly a shadow at all. It's not even all that dark. It leans out over the falls like a tall man catching himself on the cusp of a great plunge. But it's not flailing, it's leaning with a stillness that should be impossible. There is no flesh, only what it's stolen from the scene around it—dark water running through its vaguely human form, the churn of the falls transposed into a different key to give it shape and depth. My mother made me study transposition as part of my theory courses while I learned piano, which was a weird sort of putting-the-face-to-the-name situation for me. I'd always known instinctively what a key change sounded like, and then after a while I could do it myself, at least vocally, purely by feel. But the act of transposition was like reverse engineering something I already knew lived inside me from the jump. The shadow—for lack of a better word—coming from the falls is like this. It resonates, pings like sonar off the things I already recognize—water, rocks, trees—but seems to be puffing out its chest and displaying proudly a new way of seeing them.

"The second harbinger," Griffin says. "I can't fucking believe it."

"*Emergents birthed from resurrected falls,*" Helena says, clearly quoting. My non-body gets chills.

The plural—emergent*s*—makes sense a moment later, when a few more of the things swell up from the top of the falls.

The Belmonts' eyes are glued to the screen, both of them in silent mind-blown contemplation that lasts nearly a full minute.

"I didn't picture them this way," Griffin says at last. "Father's sketches are much more . . ." He trails off, lost in thought.

"Preliminary," Helena says.

"Well," Griffin says, always defending the (very) old man, "it's not like he'd ever seen them before. All he could do was extrapolate."

Even from an on-high zoom, the emergents are arrestingly beautiful. There are at least a dozen of them now, rippling forms leaning out in one harmonious motion over the dizzying chasm. At first it looked as if they were the ones being transposed, but now that I've lost myself in their weird depths, it's as if the rest of the world has undergone the key change and the emergents have remained as-is. Each one's a little twist on the natural surroundings that somehow feels more natural than the surroundings themselves. There's the first one, with its imitation of the water it sprang from coursing through its form. One of them steals from the trees, a little cutout of pine twisted into things that can possibly still be called "trees" but bear little resemblance to the evergreens just beyond the cliffs. There's something ageless in the way they absorb scenery and repurpose it—as if they've been around so long, the way things appear to us—our entire fucking reality—is something way more slippery than we realize.

I see teeth in there too. Bright shining razors. Some kind of mouth, curled inward on itself. A pucker of stolen color and light.

"Dear God," Helena says.

"Decidedly not," Griffin says.

He rests squarely on awestruck wonder. Her version of it is beginning to curdle as she studies those razor-teeth. The emergents' puckered maws glisten and churn. There are razors upon razors, sharklike rows of them. And, I see now, a horrible asymmetry to their facial areas. One half, one hemisphere, droops and shifts like oil poured into water, while the other hemisphere remains rounded and human-like. This asymmetry persists down their entire "bodies," so that my thoughts grind against themselves in wonder at the impossibility—how could a thing like that be mobile? It looks so off balance, poorly designed—and yet, somehow, its movements are elegant.

Helena sips her drink. Her hand trembles. She looks away from the screen for a moment and her face undergoes a complex series of minute shifts. I try to follow her thoughts. I think she's trying to cleanse her mind, to wrench her attention away from the sight of the emergents. A moment later, her body stiffens. She drains her glass and gazes up at the screen once again. Losing the battle.

She mutters quiet words.

"What's that?" Griffin says. His attention hasn't wavered.

"They're not right," she says.

Griffin laughs. "I thought that concoction you're guzzling was supposed to be mind-expanding. Open your third eye, Helena. Hold it open with toothpicks."

She blinks. Opens her mouth. Closes it again. I scan eight years of memories and—nope, I can't remember Helena Belmont ever being tongue-tied.

"Did we do this?" she asks, as far as I can tell, seriously.

Griffin makes an incredulous, smirky noise. "The Larkins did, if you want to split hairs. But yes, Helena, *we* more or less did this. You seem to be having issues, do you want to talk?"

"*Birthed from the resurrected falls.*" Her voice has gone soft and lovely, its edges sanded away. She leans in closer to the big screen, lifting her head at an awkward angle, to peer at the emergents.

"Are you having buyer's remorse? This is what we've been working toward for *centuries*. The falls, the emergents, the horse, and then the God of the Noose. This can't possibly be a surprise to you."

"What else do they want?" she says dreamily.

"What do you mean, what else? How the hell should I know? They serve a single purposes in all this."

"And then what?"

Griffin's exasperated. "There is no *and then what*. There's only this." He gestures at the screen. "What's wrong with you? Put down that drink. Make some coffee."

Helena shakes her head. "Do you hear that?"

Griffin pauses. "Isolate that noise, Brandt."

Gumley fiddles with his controller. The rushing sound of the falls is stripped away, a little at a time. When it's dialed down to about half its volume, a hidden undercurrent begins to rise up.

Weeping. A chorus of sadness. A human sound, yet alien as fuck coming, as it does, in a dissonant, low-register harmony. The emergents' heads don't move—this is no heaving sob—but their mouths spew this horrible despondent wail.

Gumley dials down the noise from the falls to zero.

I shrink back away from the speakers, compressing myself along the curved back wall of the war room. In the way it imitates human sadness, it's so spot-on that it raises the little hairs on my nonexistent arms. And it's ceaseless—no break in the droning rhythm to take in a breath. Just a constant set of overlapping notes spilling from those puckers. I'm thankful for all the buffers between me and the chorus— the digital route through the drone's microphones and the speakers, the less tangible passage between the world of sight and sound and my world of invisible stasis. I can't imagine what it would be like to be up close and personal with such weird, unbroken dissonance.

Gumley seems unperturbed. (Again, a flash of wonder at his personal life—maybe he goes home and flagellates like the albino guy in *The Da Vinci Code*, or whacks his shins with a stick like Ben Affleck in *The Accountant*, and yes I watch the Belmonts watch a lot of movies.) Helena, on the other hand, is getting agitated.

"Brandt, *enough*," she says.

Instead of dialing the waterfall sound back up, he messes with the controller until the weeping chorus dies away.

It takes me a moment to recognize the isolated sound that plays in its absence. Human. Shouting. Angry.

"Pan over the gorge," Griffin says. "I want to see what's got Larkin's panties in a twist."

As the view on the screen sweeps across the chasm, Helena comes out of her reverie. She makes a disgusted throaty noise. "Don't ever say that again."

"Panties," Griffin says. "*In a twist*," he whispers.

The drone lens zeroes in on the three figures and the sculpture— which is covered in a vomit-inducing mess of blood, guts, and what appears to be a cow's head. The pedestal shape has grown into something more, almost as if the gore has been arranged into a sort of scaffolding. A half-built structure, a framework of meat.

Crack.

This Wayne Krupp fellow is down on one knee like a continental soldier and firing a rifle across the chasm at the emergents. He reloads with a creepy, methodical energy and fires again. Peter Larkin and the Asha woman scream at him to *come on*.

"We have to get out of here!" Larkin says. He's on the other side of the sculpture, backing away toward the trees. I can just see the front of a pickup truck parked fifty feet or so down a trail. An F-150, just like the one my cousins Sheena and Allie used to borrow from Uncle Henry.

"Go, then!" Krupp yells back. "I'm not letting these things get off this rock."

"We can't stay here!" Lark yells.

Krupp aims, pauses, fires. "I think I hit one!"

Lark turns. Gumley, ever the vigilant cameraman, pans back across the gorge. If functionally alcoholic Wayne Krupp, hardware scion, actually did manage to shoot one of the emergents, you could have fooled me.

They lean out in their physics-defying way, perched on the water, then plunge into a breathtaking synchronized swan dive. Falling against the backdrop of the falls, from this high drone-cam angle, they look like shimmering jellyfish. Something you'd find way down in the depths like those nightmare-teethed fish with the headlamp.

Gumley pans back across the gorge. Krupp stands up from his minuteman crouch. He looks at Larkin. Then back across to the falls. Then he lets out a bloodcurdling whoop, some kind of townie celebration noise. He raises the rifle in the air.

Peter Larkin doesn't share in whatever jubilation ritual his friend is trying to kick off. "Come on, Krupp."

"Did you see that?" There's manic energy pouring off this Krupp guy now. He's like a coiled spring, boinging everywhere. He yells across the chasm. "Fuck yoooouuuu…"

Then, in one assured motion, Krupp wheels around to aim his gun at the sculpture. "Fuck you too!"

"Krupp!" Larkin's pointing to the edge of the cliff, where the rocks spill over into the gorge like frozen lava—as if once, long ago, they tried to ooze over the edge and got stuck that way.

The first emergent is up and over in the time it takes Krupp to turn.

"Ha!" Griffin says, a note of triumph in his voice. Anticipating bloodshed. Helena leans forward.

"Come on!" Peter Larkin screams at his friend one last time, then turns and sprints for the truck.

Krupp stands there for a moment, frozen in place, as the other emergents seem to *tilt* upward from the side of the cliff.

It took them less than a minute to plunge into the foam at the base of the gorge, climb out of the depths, and scale the sheer face of the cliff on the other side.

I wonder if Krupp is thinking the same thing, calculating their speed as they gather fifty feet away from him.

Their throaty sadness must have hit a new frequency because this time Gumley's filters fail to silence it. Now they're massed in a line at the top of the cliff, weeping without pause, as they sway slightly in unison, their forms pulling hues from the rocks and the sky.

Their sadness is getting to me. It's beyond melancholy. Not like stare-out-the-window-on-a-rainy-Tuesday-afternoon-while-you-chain-smoke-and-listen-to-Joni-Mitchell. That's, like, fun sadness. This is some kind of twisted despondency.

"No more," Helena says. "Brandt, *no more*."

"Working on it," Gumley says. The keening wail begins to slip away.

Krupp's finally had enough of this shit. He follows Larkin in a dead sprint, nearly overtaking him, as they join Asha in the truck. It backs down the dirt path, kicking up a cloud. Gumley pans back to the cliff. The emergents sway.

Griffin turns to Helena and cuts in before she can say anything.

"They're here to serve a purpose, okay? You don't have to make friends with them."

"I feel different now than I did before I saw them."

"That statement can be applied to anything in the entire world."

"Like there's less of me than there was."

Griffin sighs. "Cut the feed." Brandt fiddles with his controller and the massive screen goes black. Griffin and Helena are mirrored darkly in the void. "Come on," he says, putting his hands on Helena's shoulders. "I know what'll cheer you up."

"I'm not *sad*, Griffin, I'm..." After a while, she shrugs.

"Come on," he says, taking her hand and leading her away from the screen.

Up from the war room, through the residence, into the Belmonts' inner sanctum, and there's the plain old door that spikes my anxiety. Helena takes a deep breath but doesn't say anything. She folds her arms and studies the floor while her brother performs his tongue-tracing ritual, drawing glyphs in saliva. The door pops open.

Griffin and Helena pause at the threshold. There's something different about the air in the room. Griffin gives his sister a nod. "This is what it's all for," he says. "It's good to remind ourselves, when the doubts creep in."

Together, they step inside.

It's like entering an aquarium. Dust floats like plankton, dreamy and slow, in the light from the false window. There's a murky quality to the air—a real, swampy weight. The Belmonts move through the room like deep-sea divers in those old-timey metal suits. If I had a heart it would be pounding with the wrongness of all this. The new atmosphere in the room has been expelled from somewhere inside the drab and desiccated husk of a man that is sitting on the edge of the bed, emaciated limbs clothed in tatters. His rotted feet, mottled with dark bruising as if by frostbite, are flat against the floorboards. He has pulled the thin, dusty sheet around his shoulders like a cloak. His black wide-brimmed hat sits askew on his skull. Wispy strands of hair jut from beneath the fabric. Flaps of leathery skin dangle from the ruin of his face. He leans over the carved stump and with the delicate bones of his hand moves a twist of charcoal across a piece of parchment.

"Father," Griffin says. His voice hangs in the room, stilled by the thick, soupy air. The word floats like another mote of dust. Suspended in the murk.

Slowly, Marius Van Leeman's hand comes to a halt. The parchment has been blackened from top to bottom. He has sketched a void. He purses his dead dry lips and blows a raspy puff from deep within his sunken chest. A foul wind stirs the page. Charcoal dust joins the motes in the air. With a creak that draws itself out and hangs alongside Griffin's *Father*, which has yet to fully die away, Van Leeman turns his head to regard his children. The brim of his hat rotates on its plane without moving up or down.

Helena steps back. It's difficult to tell how much of Van Leeman is rotting away and how much is healing. He opens a hand and the charcoal falls out. With a movement that's at once halting and jerky, like amateur stop-motion, he lifts his arm to his face. Two dry fingertips pinch a dangling piece of cheek and press it against bone the color of a filth-rimed bath. They affix it to the cheekbone and the dehydrated flesh sticks in place like the flap of a sealed envelope. He moves his mouth, shifts his face into a grimace, and the action of engaging tiny muscles seems to seal the flesh into place, almost as if it's been cauterized. I hate to put it this way because nothing about this is remotely healthy, but a certain vitality is restored as the skin flap's seams disappear.

With that, Marius Van Leeman opens his mouth. Helena grips her brother's arm while Griffin steadies himself. The space between Van Leeman's lips is as dark as the blackened parchment. His roach-brown teeth are nubs.

Dust leaks from the widening mouth. Words form and hang in the air, raspy and hollow. "My horse," Van Leeman says.

No *Hey, kids, nice to see you after all this time.* No *Thanks for dedicating your lives to my resurrection.* Three hundred years apart and the man just wants to talk about his fucking horse. Though, if I were reunited with my mother after three centuries, she'd find a way to tell me I looked like I'd been "eating good."

Helena, teeth gritted, eyes fixed on the wall behind her father, begins to tug her brother back toward the door. He resists and they begin an awkward underwater dance while Griffin struggles to find the right words.

"The waterfall is back," he says, words flowing into the air on a time delay, like his mouth is slightly out of sync with his audio, "and the emergents have just appeared up on the cliffs." He injects a note of earnest Boy Scout pride into his voice. "Two out of the three harbingers. I have no doubt that the horse will be here shortly, as both the sculpture and the painting approach completion."

This is a real heartstring-tugger, this reunion. Some authentic Hallmark Channel shit. (By the way, Griffin watches *Mrs. Miracle* starring James Van Der Beek every Christmas after Helena goes to sleep, and I have a quasi-crackpot theory that he connects on an emotional level with James Van Der Beek because of the actor's Dutch heritage and that conspicuous *Van* in his name.)

Van Leeman sighs. His dusty breath stirs the languid air. Slowly, he turns back to the parchment on the carved stump. Griffin and Helena watch him contemplate it for what feels like an hour. Time is gloopy in this room. Then Van Leeman begins to drag a finger along the page, drawing an angular symbol. After a while he lifts his finger and examines its blackened tip. He brings the finger to his mouth and his gums work drily as he tastes the charcoal. He inserts his entire finger. A dry suckling sound comes from his throat. Helena turns away.

"Right," Griffin says. "Almost there."

Helena quits trying to pull her brother along and leaves the room. Griffin lingers. Waiting for some kind of acknowledgment. A pat on the head. *Good boy, you did it!*

"We have so much to talk about," Griffin says. Van Leeman removes the finger from his mouth—it's completely dry—and works on adhering the flap of his other cheek to the bones beneath. Griffin hesitates a second or two longer, then joins his sister in the chamber outside. He shuts the door behind him. Both Belmonts take in fresh air.

Helena appears stricken. She stares wide-eyed at her brother. He holds up a finger and puts his phone to his ear.

"Brandt," he says, "we need to get the Larkins over the finish line. Have Leif prepare another photo shoot with Betsy. That's been a fabulous motivational tool so far." He pauses. "No. Stage it, like before.

Unless she stops working. Then Leif can cut her. But don't overdo it. We need her fully capable for a little while longer." He hangs up the phone and meets his sister's eyes. "*What?*"

Helena, tightly wound, uncoils. "Did we not just have the exact same experience in there? Did you pass into some alternate dimension where Father was the kind, loving man we used to know and not that *abomination?*"

Griffin takes her by the arms. "*Shhh!*"

Helena twists out of his grip. "Don't act so blasé. I hate it when you pretend you don't need to think critically."

Griffin's mouth does that little downturned sneer he reserves for when he's operating from a place of what he thinks is total righteousness. "*I'm* the one not thinking critically? What did you expect, Father to spring out of bed, bright-eyed and bushy-tailed, with glowing skin and coiffed hair, ready to give us a big old huggeroo and tell us he missed us so much, his beloved children?"

"Griffin, can you honestly take one look at those emergents, and at Father's state, and tell me that we've done the right thing, here? Not to mention all that shit that's happening to Wofford Falls."

Griffin's eyes are so wide, his body so weirdly contorted and pitched at such a forward lean, I'm convinced he's about to expel an *Alien* chestburster. His incredulousness is radioactive. "*Fuck* Wofford Falls! Not *once*, Helena, think about this—not *once* over the past three centuries did you express a single reservation, much less a crisis of conscience, about what we're doing. Kalina Godfrey, for fuck's sake. Every other has-been and never-was and also-ran artist we sucked dry to stay alive. Not a peep from Miss Helena. I don't know why this is a sudden season-finale revelation for you, but Father hasn't looked like that sketch we found since 1751. This process might be unpleasant, it might be slow, it might be disgusting to you, but it's Father, Helena. It's him in there, same as ever. And now that we're *this close*, you're suddenly interested in the right thing. Well, here's one for your third eye—was it the right thing when that mob of Wofford Fallsians came and dragged him off to the gallows? Put that in your Bon-Cadeau pipe and smoke it."

He strides across the sumptuous chamber to the bar and mixes himself a drink. Helena eyes the door to their father's room. "*The God of the Noose*," she says. "The psalter doesn't say Marius Van Leeman's coming back. It says the God of the Noose is."

"Same thing," Griffin says, dropping an ice cube into a smoky chartreuse drink. "And anyway, sister, I really hate to belabor the point, but you've had three lifetimes to prepare for this moment. I didn't know you were one for self-sabotage. We should get to the bottom of that particular insecurity sometime."

She joins him at the bar and reaches for a tincture. "It's not insecurity."

"*The right thing*." He shakes his head. "What moral framework are you even trying to apply here? Remember that dinner with Schopenhauer where—"

"It's those things on the cliff. When I said I felt like there was less of me now—what I meant was, they took something. Didn't you feel that?"

He shrugs and sips his drink.

"You're not going to tell me. You don't care."

"We're seeing this through. There's no stopping it now, anyway."

She pauses, lost in thought. Glances back at the door to their father's room. "I know."

I've been doing my puppy-dog thing again, following the Belmonts around, hanging on her words. I wonder if Gumley's relayed the order to Leif, if they're prepping you for another little photo shoot. Maybe I can get there before it starts. Maybe you'll talk to me.

I zip through the residence and the private gallery (something like a cat's tongue scrapes in the darkness) and there's that ostentatious door. I hesitate for a moment, studying the labyrinth inlaid in the wood. Then I slip inside the chamber and stretch along the ceiling, which gives off a humid moisture that would make my skin crawl if I had skin. It occurs to me now that Leif, as a fellow post-human, should have been a connection for me in here. A couple of unlikely chums, me 'n' Leif. Maybe a grotesque will-they-or-won't-they, cue the montage set to "Semi-Charmed Life," me and Leif on ice skates, sharing a hot chocolate, whipped cream on the part of him formerly known as his nose. But it was not to be, alas—whatever wavelength he's on, it isn't mine.

From up here I can see how busy you've been, Betsy. The little paint-coasters the KPM scattered around the room to kick off this mural have all been incorporated into your massive, endlessly flowing, heartbreakingly beautiful waterfall. The shades of gray from my last visit are still peeking through here and there as part of the underpainting, the wash that supports the complex layering you've been doing. A reverse Sistine Chapel, the artist in residence unveiling the grand masterpiece along the floor...

I've never seen anything like it—and I've seen my share of artwork in this place. The little bits and pieces of what must be other paintings that the KPM distributed around the room are like stars in a constellation, each one giving off that same feeling of transposition I got from the emergents on the big screen. As if I'm somehow looking at fragments of a key change that have leapt off the sheet music and into real life. It doesn't seem possible, because I know that they're just made out of paint, but they seem to pulsate with life, like they're some kind of circulatory system that, now you've connected it, animates the waterfall itself.

I wish we were in our own little bubble of time, where I could just float up here and watch you paint, because it's mesmerizing and relaxing and inspiring, all at once.

You add a sweeping curl to some spray near the base of the falls. I follow the precise movements of your wrist. Words appear: HI RAYANNE. Just as quickly, you swirl them into the image and they vanish into the foam.

I don't think you can appreciate how monumental this is, after eight years of bodiless isolation. A single greeting might be the shallowest interaction a normal living person might have all day, but shallow is relative. For me, it's like a profound, hormonal connection with somebody you vibe with at summer camp. A relationship that seems preordained, like it was always out there waiting for the right two people to step into it.

I'm looking down on you, Betsy, so all I can see is the back of your head—your messy hair, little glimpses of your bent neck. Your face is hidden from me. Your hands move quickly. There's unbridled joy in every brushstroke. Release. I think of Griffin, describing *freedom* to you. Despite all his self-interest, all his bullshit, I have to say, you certainly feel free to me.

Alive and present in the moment: That's how it feels. Like with the flick of your wrist, you've snapped time back into place.

You paint: I NEED YOUR HELP.

YES. Yes, Betsy. I'm here for you. I'll do my best. But—

In the dim, evasive margins of the hangar-size room, there's a stirring. Old Leif, receiving his marching orders.

Time's a factor now.

The words disappear. Betsy moves across the base of the falls, careful not to disturb the wet paint. She kneels before one of the coaster-size painting bits. This one, curiously, doesn't radiate the same energy as the emergents. It doesn't feel like a key change at all. The falls plummet around it, wrapping it in white foam. At first I think it's a lone creature, that anemone from my childhood encyclopedia set, a round furry pocket-watch-looking thing.

You focus your attention on its borders, swirling paint to encircle it.

I'm headed down to get a better look when Leif begins to cough out his mad whispers. He'll be venturing out of the shadows in a few more seconds. I can see his disproportionate form curl into itself and release, its mobility the kind of chore that makes you sorry, despite everything. A tragedy to witness.

Like everything else that stalks the crevices and hidey-holes of this godforsaken place—including yours truly—Leif was a human being, once. Remember I mentioned him as poetic justice for Helena and Griffin? He was some kind of *enfant terrible*—a term I learned because Griffin wouldn't stop calling him that, in this sort of mocking-admiration way I could never quite get a handle on. From what I understand, Leif was a scene-hopper out of sheer necessity because even in various under-ground art worlds in New York and LA, his antics were a little too fucked up, a little too *real*, like a relentlessly dark and depressing *Jack-ass*. No laughter, no camaraderie, no bros being bros—just vicious self-harm and off-putting shit that only Leif himself thought was funny, like peeing in syringes and injecting the urine into his eyeballs.

Anyway, he tried to crowdfund this epic new piece, his crowning achievement, which was also supposed to kill him. It was an eating challenge (art?) that would go from small to large, so he would start with a single grain of sand and work his way up to (in his megaloma-niacal words) airplanes, government buildings, and entire cities. He would consume the world and also die trying. It was like that video game Katamari Damacy, where the little ball rolls up small objects, then larger ones, until it's rolling up entire countries. People inter-preted this as either total bullshit, a death wish, or a sad bid for atten-tion from a no-talent art world dilettante, or else they didn't pay much attention at all. Leif was destined to join the bargain bin of stunt art-ist freaks when the Belmonts pumped half a million into his crowd-funding page out of nowhere. The catch: He had to perform the entire piece inside one of their personal galleries. Having absolutely no other option, Leif was here the next day, eating his first grain of sand. Helena was really into this transubstantiation thing at the time. But not the Catholic version—a kind of inverse of that, a way to make the body into substance instead of vice versa.

The problem was that Leif fucking *relished* the opportunity to be tor-mented and used. He embraced his guinea pig status with great enthu-siasm. This made Griffin lose interest even quicker than usual, but Helena kept at it, sticking Leif away in some other forsaken wing, per-forming these arcane rituals while Leif gleefully ate sand, bedbugs, coins, remote controls, a cat, some dishware, a cello, a motorcycle—at this point it was clear he should have died, so the fact that he didn't gave Helena some kind of validation that she was doing something right in terms of her latest occult kick. It was some weird shit to watch, though I admit, by that point into my captivity here at the museum,

I was pretty starved for entertainment. It sounds terrible, but he was so genuinely unpleasant and so recklessly willing to embrace whatever Helena was doing to him that my fascination didn't feel too out of line. Imagine watching a crazy asshole who didn't care if he lived or died consuming huge inanimate objects—microwaves, bags of nails, hundreds of pounds of metal—on a homemade altar while Helena cavorted naked like a faun in some hippie Shakespeare in the Park adaptation and poured hot wax in patterns she got from a brittle old scroll. THEN, just when that was starting to get old, imagine watching as Leif's entire body began to change its form to accommodate all the indigestible items that were now, apparently, living inside of him. That old joke about somebody eating a lot because they have a "hollow leg" actually coming to life before my eyes. Except it wasn't legs, it was other things, unimaginable growths, full of partially eaten objects rattling around like bags of coins. Extra appendages. And there was the day he got out and tried to eat the elevator, and his saliva damaged it in ways they're still trying to figure out. So now they give Leif little tasks to make him feel needed so he doesn't try to consume an entire gallery wing. And the task of the moment is taking these ransom photos of you, Betsy. Ah—here he is now, slipping out of the shadows. Whatever it is you're trying to tell me, I suggest you get to it.

Words appear, encircling the strange pocket watch.

SHOW MY BROTHER THE WAY.

Okay, great, I'd love to, but I'm stuck in here, same as you.

Her arm moves with fluid grace as Leif accordions one of his appendages out over the mural.

Betsy swirls the letters into a new sentence with practiced ease, as if she's been communicating this way all her life.

IN HERE.

Here where? The only thing she can possibly be referring to is the pocket watch, the little coaster-size cutout. In how? There's no way in. It's a painting.

I ungather myself from the ceiling and swoop down till I'm right on top of it. Leif's segmented, wormy limb approaches. There's a rattling of metal, an old junky car engine trying to turn over. He's coughing out his whispers from the shadows.

Betsy gives it one more go, erasing letters as new ones take shape, all of them of a piece with the waterfall, all of them circling the pocket watch—which isn't a pocket watch at all, I see now, but a toothy pod of some sort.

She paints: IT'S A WAY OUT.

A way out? Of this place? After eight years?

The fifth weirdest thing I've seen here unfolds before my eyes.

The pod opens up. Empty air inside.

Leif wraps an "arm" around Betsy's shoulders in a menacing parody of friendship.

GO, Betsy paints, before Leif drags her upright and sticks a camera in her face.

There is no floor behind what, a moment ago, was a flat painting. Inside the mouth of the pod is something distinctly in motion. There are voices. The hum of an engine. A million smells I've missed, woods and smoke and asphalt and gasoline.

Life.

I take the plunge without a second thought.

Fuck this place.

PART FOUR

THE GOD OF THE NOOSE

19

The school bus is on fire. Flames are pasted to the windows. They lick the air, gulping oxygen, acting like real flames. But there's something off about them. Lark stops the truck. The bus is blocking the road at an angle. He might be able to squeeze past on the shoulder of Route 212, but he's not sure. He's also not sure how they got to 212, bypassing downtown Wofford Falls completely. They sit for a moment, staring into the broken bus windows. There's an artificial crackle, cozy like a TV fireplace, one of those Yule log videos on a loop. A piece of laminated paper affixed to the front window says TIGERS. A moment later, it blackens, curls up, falls away.

"We were the owls," Krupp says. Next to Lark in the truck, his body radiates heat and sweat. His ripe odor fills the air.

Lark rolls down a window. "What?"

"In elementary school. That's how kids know which bus to get on. There's owls, tigers, sharks, a bunch more."

"I forgot about that."

"Yeah, not me."

They fall silent. Lark, heavily attuned to Krupp's spiritual oscillations, finds that since they left the Backbone and headed down the foothills toward town, his friend has been at a low ebb. Lark wonders if he really thought he could take those harbingers out with a hunting rifle. Nightmare things, reflecting light in troubling ways. And that noise—the weeping of a hundred despondent nuns with bowed heads, realizing all at once that God's not coming to save them.

Yeah, not me.

"Whatever that book says to do next," Krupp says quietly, "we have to do the opposite."

This seems to jolt Asha. She grips the psalter tightly in her lap, moves it subtly away from Krupp, as if he's about to snatch it. "We haven't finished," she says.

Krupp laughs bitterly. "Finished what? Those things came out of the falls after phase two, what do you think phase three looks like? You think something called *The God of the Noose* is gonna be like Santa Claus? Bringing presents for all the good little girls and boys of Wofford Falls? Maybe come out and do a little soft-shoe, a little *hello my baby* like that fucking cartoon?"

"Michigan J. Frog," Lark says.

"So," Krupp says, "when you sit here and say we haven't finished, I'm saying I'm going to make it my business to see that we never do."

"What about Betsy?" Asha says. "We're going to come this far and then just let her die?"

Krupp laughs again. "Don't act like you give a shit about Betsy. You don't know her." He turns to Lark. "We gotta put this genie back in the bottle. We gotta figure out a way to reverse course. You saw those things back there. What do you think happens when they get into town? They had *teeth*, man."

Asha pulls a capsule from her handbag and dry-swallows. "At this point we might as well see Betsy safely returned, *then* set about putting things back the way they were."

"How many people will have died by then?" Krupp says.

"But Betsy Larkin will be alive," Asha says, her eyes drilling into the side of Lark's head, pointedly appealing to him. "Otherwise all this will have been pointless. All those other lives will have been sacrificed in vain."

Lark understands Krupp's perspective. Asha, he's less sure of. She saw what they all saw back there. Harbingers, stealing light and shadow, weeping endlessly, moving across the Backbone with weird halting grace…

So what's driving her to be the devil to Krupp's angel? (Or is it the other way around?)

He looks her in the eyes for a clue and sees a wily hunger he recognizes from their earliest days together. A couple of mad strivers huddled together in the leopard-print booth at Merle & Bess. Lark in a perpetual state of goose bumps because Asha *saw something in him.* To be the guy whom someone with influence saw something in: what he'd always desired to be. The role he was born to step into. A high like no other. But now it makes him sick, because he thinks he knows what Asha wants.

Completion for art's sake.

"We can't stop," she reiterates.

He can read the calculus behind her eyes, cold and diamond-hard. Part of him reaches out in sympathy because it's exactly what he wants too.

"For Betsy," he clarifies. "We need to keep going for Betsy."

"Right," Asha says, "of course."

"For no other reason would we ever consider doing this."

"Absolutely not."

He recalls that moment on the Backbone when it all fell into place for him, how she's been one step ahead, constructing the framework for *The Worm & the Dogsbody,* the narrative he so neatly slotted into. How necessary her manipulation had been to even reach this point. And now he can choose to remain in thrall to it, to play oblivious as she steers the sculpture toward completion. Or he could side with Krupp, who certainly has the moral high ground here, and sign his sister's death warrant.

He considers this while the school bus burns, throwing those fake cardboard flames at the ashen sky. It's like the day never fully dawned.

"What is wrong with you?" Krupp says, his words hammering Lark's skull. He feels distant, hollow. When was the last time any of them had any food? Or sleep?

"We already did so much we can't take back," Lark says on autopilot, just to say something. He reaches for a decisive statement and misses by a hundred miles.

"Forward is the only way," Asha says.

"Are you not fucking *traumatized*?" Krupp says. He's breaking out of his post-harbinger husk, whatever spellbound state he's been in since the Backbone falling away like shed skin. "Jamie-Lynn." He ticks off on his fingers. "Bea and Lily."

"Stop," Lark says.

"Old Mr. Forester. The whole fucking downtown. Who knows what else."

Lark closes his eyes, thinking of those two years he spent with Celeste. The final days, agonizing over whether to leave Betsy again. The way his sister gave her blessing, so casually, as if it didn't matter to her one way or the other, if he moved on with his life in Wofford Falls or Los Angeles or Mars.

So who was he punishing by blowing up his future with Celeste to stick around?

"You know what we have to do," Krupp says.

Lark opens his eyes. "We go back up there."

"Yes." Krupp, eager, on the edge of his seat.

"And we rip that sculpture apart, piece by piece."

"Fuck yes."

"And they watch us do it on the drone," Asha says. "And then the harbingers kill us. And Betsy dies anyway."

"I don't know," Krupp says. "All I know is we have to try." The tendons in his neck are wiry and hard, as if he's straining to frown.

"What will that accomplish?" Asha says. "Those things are already out in the world, you think they're gonna, *poof*, disappear because you—"

THUNK.

Something slams against the back of the cab.

He turns. There, out the back window, is the New York Giants duffel bag, standing up, leaning over, hammering the glass, then recoiling to do it again.

THUNK.

"Motherfucker!" Krupp screams. He tries to climb over Asha to get out through the passenger door. While they're hopelessly tangled, Lark flings his door open and hops out. The air smells like burnt rubber and scorched pavement. He swings around, one foot on the running board, and grabs the duffel by its handle. Then he sets it gingerly down on the shoulder of the road. The bag is perfectly still for a moment, then moves with the furious energy of trapped cats.

Krupp and Asha spill out of the truck. Lark moves to put his body between Krupp and the bag.

"Hey!" calls a voice from the bag. Lark waits for the word to etch itself in his mind, the natural evolution of the turning-jar's communication, but nothing happens. He blinks. The voice is just a voice. A *real* voice.

"Betsy?" he calls back. The duffel trembles.

"It's Rayanne," the voice replies. It's garbled, a little inorganic and plastic—but also distinctly midwestern. "Where am I?"

The heat from the bus fire surges.

Krupp shouts something unintelligible. Lark turns in time to catch a shoulder to the side of his face as Krupp's bony body smashes into him.

"Hello?" the voice from the duffel says.

Lark manages to arm-bar Krupp's throat, flipping him onto his back. Krupp wriggles beneath him, spittle-flecked mouth gurgling obscenities. "Get hold of yourself, Krupp, I'm serious!"

Their historic tussles ran the gamut from play-wrestling in elementary school to drunken approximations of mixed martial arts in the Gold Shade parking lot, but this is different. As he fights to hold back his friend's rage, Lark remembers Krupp's prophetic words, delivered in the booth at the Shade: *Everything's different now.* In Krupp's eyes he sees fear and betrayal and confusion. He's sick of fighting. He's sick of Unhinged Krupp.

You did this.

"Holy shit," Asha says. Lark turns to find that she's managed to unzip the duffel bag. She takes a step back as the turning-jar emerges.

"Kill it," Krupp gurgles. "It's not right." Lark holds him down and regards the object in astonishment as it moves under its own power, freeing itself from the unzipped bag as if shedding a slouchy garment. The cilia have fused and twisted like the braided wires of one of his sculptures. The fusion of glass and Betsy's original turning has extended like a metaphor to its most logical endpoint. Dull, almost leaden, the glassy shell has taken on new proportions. A fresh intimacy between what the woman in the red dress once held and the jar that once held Red Vines. It's unclear to Lark if the substances are in harmony or if one has performed a hostile takeover of the other. Either way, its form is less jar than statue, with Botero-esque curves that appear shockingly human. The turning-jar approaches and Asha leaps back another two feet. The newly animate object stands about three feet high. As it propels itself forward on its hardened cilia-legs, Lark searches it for any sign of Betsy's original birthday gift. There, at its core, beating like a heart, is a tiny seedpod with little baby teeth that mewl and chomp.

"I'll be goddamned," the turning-jar says, the voice emanating from its core. Then it laughs, seemingly incredulous at its own existence.

Krupp screams. Lark, weakened by this distraction, loses his grip. Krupp squirms away. Asha, wide-eyed, films the turning-jar with her phone as it moves in a slow circle, taking in its surroundings. Then it heaves. Lark thinks it might be sniffing the air. Absorbing.

"I'm not talking to Betsy?" Lark says, getting to his feet. Out of the corner of his eye he watches Krupp, anticipating a rifle coming up any second. But Krupp just stands there, working his jaw, rubbing his elbow, staring at what's just emerged from the duffel bag.

Lark, fully aware that he's conversing with something that—in Krupp's words—is *not right*, pushes his mind to a new place. He forces himself to inhabit a world where a thing like this might appear.

"Rayanne Lane Boyd," the turning-jar says. Then it—*Rayanne*—begins to sing. Halting at first, but with the pitch of a natural, she finds her voice. Casual, straightforward, yet haunting. The lyrics are about how boyfriend jeans are the most comfortable jeans—until you find out that someone else has been wearing them.

He recognizes the song from the Gold Shade. Beth Two's daughter's playlist.

Lark, Asha, and Krupp stand there, staring, while Rayanne's voice devolves into joyful, openhearted sobbing. The seedpod's teeth gnash at her translucent core. Seeing it throb and cavort, suspended in its network of ingrown cilia and glass filaments, Lark's own empty stomach gnaws at him. Asha lowers her phone. Krupp mutters angrily to himself, folds his arms, finds new ways to fidget. The school bus burns in a loop without end. Up above, afternoon wears on too quickly, and masses of clouds cross and recross the sky.

"Peter Larkin," Rayanne says at last. She turns to address each of them. "Wayne Krupp. Asha the art agent."

"How do you know all that?" Lark says.

"I've seen you on a screen." The seedpod's teeth grind. The bulbous former jar trembles slightly. "You were being filmed by a drone, up on a cliff."

All those moments when Lark conjured up this imaginary place— the subterranean bunker—turn out to be not so far from the truth.

Rayanne motions with an appendage toward the burning bus. "Looks like a bona fide shit show out here, but it's all beautiful to me." She performs an act Lark interprets as *sniffing the air.* "Eight years stuck in there," she says. "Goddamn."

"I don't understand," Lark says. "You weren't born—I mean, you didn't evolve into—*that?*"

"I kind of just arrived here." She pauses. "Why, what do I look like?"

Lark realizes that she hasn't given the actual vessel that hosts her presence a moment's thought. She's been caught up in the ecstasy of just *being.*

She holds out an "arm" of twined cilia and regards it from some unseen sight mechanism—there are no eyes that Lark can make out.

He expects her to scream. Instead, she's dead silent. After a moment, she says, "May I see the rest of me?"

Asha steps forward and holds out her phone, camera flipped to selfie mode. Lark braces himself for a shriek, for Rayanne to become a babbling fool, pushed over the edge into madness by a self she can't possibly comprehend.

Instead, she simply says, "Huh. All right. Here I am, I guess. Thank you." She seems to nod. Asha lowers the phone and steps back. Then Rayanne turns to Lark. "This is only, like, the fourth weirdest thing I've ever seen," she says by way of explanation. "I bet you were expecting a total meltdown, though. Like the Joker when they take the bandages off for the first time in *Batman*. The Michael Keaton one. Iconic moment, right?"

"Um," Lark says.

"I watched them watch a lot of movies. You figure three or four a week for eight years, that's a ton. Can't do the math off the top of my head."

"*Them?*"

"The Belmonts. Helena and Griffin."

Lark shivers. He knows without having to ask that he's just heard the names of Gumley's employers for the first time.

Helena and Griffin Belmont. They sound like assholes.

"You know Brandt Gumley?" Lark asks.

"You mean Haircut? King Douche? Commander of the Khaki Pants Mafia?"

"I think we're talking about the same guy."

"Not a fan."

"How do we know you're not fucking with us?" Krupp says. His voice is even, but Lark notes the edge to his words. Brittle and exhausted. "How do we know you're not working with them. Gumley. The Belmonts."

At that moment, Lark's phone buzzes. He takes it out of his pocket at the same time that Krupp and Asha check their devices, and his heart sinks. Here we go again.

"Ah, shit," Rayanne says. "Betsy?"

"Yeah," Lark says, forcing himself to examine the photo closely. Something's curled around Betsy's neck, propping her up. A pudgy arm? It's dimly lit and Lark can't really tell. There's something between resignation and defiance in her eyes. The vast inscrutable spectrum his sister perpetually inhabits, making it maddeningly difficult to parse her state of mind. He loves her for this strange and unknowable diffidence. He always has.

"What's that around her neck?" Asha says, bringing her phone close to her face. Krupp brushes a cloud of fallen ash out of his scraggly hair.

"That's Leif," Rayanne says. "Long story. I'll tell you what's up on the way. Lemme know if I'm rambling, it's been a while since I've said anything out loud."

Krupp laughs. He turns to Lark. "I'm not going anywhere with this thing. Nothing's changed as far as I'm concerned." He gestures at the burning school bus. "If we don't try to set things right, starting now, then we're complete pieces of shit. This is our home that's fucked up, Lark. Our friends who are dying."

"Where are we supposed to be going?" Lark asks Rayanne.

"To tear down that sculpture," Krupp says. "Throw it piece by piece into the gorge until there's nothing left on the Backbone."

"You want to set things right," Rayanne says, "then you follow me to Betsy. And time's a factor."

"Are they going to kill her?" Lark says.

"Her, you, everybody. If Wofford Falls ends up some uninhabitable radiation zone, it's all the same to them. You have to understand—you, Lark, and your sister, and everybody else who lives here—they're not real people to the Belmonts. At best they're like actors on a stage for the Belmonts to direct. I don't know what will happen when Betsy's finished. But she's almost done. And she can't stop herself."

"Finished with what?"

"Her painting. She's been going nonstop since they brought her there."

"Shit," Lark says. "Do you know if it's a forgery?"

"I think it's just *hers*," Rayanne says. "I mean, there's a book with some guidelines, but Griffin said she was free. That was the whole point—that you weren't there, that she was finally free."

"Okay." A dizziness settles over him. For a moment he's back in his loft, listening to a frantic message from hungover Krupp. "And you know where they've got her?"

"I was stuck there for the past eight years," Rayanne says. "I know all the passageways and forgotten rooms. I've got a map in my mind."

"Can you get us in?"

"Lark," Asha says.

"We can't trust it," Krupp says.

"Betsy sent me," Rayanne says. "She told me to show you the way. I can take you to her. I swear."

Lark turns to Krupp and Asha. "Do whatever you want, but I'm going with Rayanne."

They stare back at him and he wonders what a good person would do in this situation. Bust out a rousing speech, a pep talk to reinforce their camaraderie, this team with various skill sets that Krupp's always wanted to be a part of. He doesn't say anything at all. He waits for them to make up their minds. Rayanne tests the mobility of her new form while the school bus burns.

20

Drinks are on the house at the Gold Shade. Beth Two's been slinging freebies to the regulars for what feels like days. All the blinds are down but there's been a gradual lightening through the slats, which is now tilting once again toward darkness. Dazed stragglers show up from time to time, seeking shelter. Lifelong Wofford Falls residents gawping at the booths, the dartboard, the jukebox, like they've just stepped onto a movie set.

"Nothing," she announces, flipping channels from static to static on the bar's single television, mounted up in the corner above the video poker machine with 1990s bowling-alley graphics.

"Try the local stations," Jerry suggests.

Constance slams a hand down on the bar. Beth Two's anxiety spikes. It's a very un-Constance thing to do. She's picked up on these personalities shifting out of joint. An undercurrent of random aggression. As if she needed something else to freak out about.

"She said *nothing*, Jerry," Constance says. "I'm sure Beth knows how the TV works. For a small-minded man you're a real know-it-all."

Jerry's mouth drops open. Then he closes it, shakes his head, and studies his drink.

Beth Two hands Constance the portable. "Try the landline again for me, will you, Constance?"

Cell service is long gone. She doesn't expect anything from the landline either—she's tried 911 a million times—but at least it'll keep Constance busy for half a minute.

Beth Two's not sure if the Shade is technically open or closed. Either way, the door's unlocked for anybody who needs a place to lie low for a while and escape the madness in the streets. Her daughter, Taylor, is in the back office. Safer here than at home, now that home is the walkup on the corner of Main and Market, the epicenter of downtown Wofford Falls. The Shade's nestled on the western edge, the last bastion of walkable commerce and historical markers.

Beth Two knows it's nothing more than a mental Band-Aid, a sleight of hand for the brain—this notion that playing business as usual at the Shade is any "safer" than doing anything else right now. She presses a pint glass down on the rinser and water spritzes up. Then she pulls a Labatt and plunks it down for Angelo.

"You're a saint," he says.

"Tell it to the pope."

She doesn't mention to any of the grateful patrons that the second the fires started she threw Taylor in the Hyundai and tried to get the fuck outta Dodge. Made it as far as the Haverchucks' farm when she realized she wasn't headed in that direction at all. The whole town's coiled in on itself like a maze on a crumpled diner place mat. And Assface Hank's nowhere to be found, as usual.

Speaking of Haverchuck's: As if on cue, Terry bursts through the door, a wrecking ball of nerves Beth Two can sense from behind the bar.

"Oh shit," Terry says, when he sees that there are actually people in here drinking. "You're open."

Beth Two shrugs. "Why the hell not. Usual, Terry?"

He shakes his head and makes his way to the bar with a strange gait, as if he's shaking off the damp, though as far as Beth knows it's perfectly dry outside. He smells of sweat and smoke. His shiny bald head is smeared with soot.

"I can't get hold of Jamie-Lynn or the girls," he says.

Beth makes herself pointlessly busy with a bar rag. She can't stop moving. If she stops moving she'll have to think about what's happening. "You been out to the farm?"

"I tried," Terry says. By now it's understood by all what this means. How absurd and terrible. *I tried but I couldn't find it.* The place I lived for twenty-three years. I drove to the creek instead, or Smokin' Dave's Barbecue, or the filling station out on 78. And on the way I saw things I shouldn't have seen. "She been in here at all? Jamie-Lynn?"

"Nah," Beth Two says. "Haven't seen her since the birthday party for Lark."

"He had a birthday party?"

"Impromptu. Anyway, she hasn't been in."

"The girls," Terry says. He glances off into the middle distance, at the dartboard, where Ian's last cricket score lives on in chalk. He shakes his head. "Fuck, I don't know. Everybody's going through the same thing, I guess. I just wish I could talk to 'em, confirm they're all right."

"I'm sure they're fine." Beth Two plunks down Terry's unasked-for usual, a double Maker's on the rocks.

The door flies open. Eddie the Can Man's there, bleeding from a lacerated forehead. It looks like he tried to carve his own homemade wrinkles into his brow.

"The prodigal son!" Angelo exclaims.

Jerry turns on him. "*Shut the fuck up!*"

"Hey!" Beth Two points at the jukebox. "Calm down. Go play a song." She turns back to the door. "C'mere, Eddie." She sticks a fresh bar rag under warm water. "Let's wash out that cut."

"It's burning," he says.

"What is?"

"All of it."

"You're safe in here," she says.

He shakes his head. Then he begins to laugh. He doubles over, losing his shit. The funniest thing ever. The ultimate joke. He spits blood on the floor.

"Come sit down," Beth says. Without another word, Eddie staggers back through the door. Gone.

Roy Orbison's "Only the Lonely" booms from the jukebox.

"Jesus, Jerry," Beth Two says. "You depress us any further we're gonna all be in the ground."

The lights go out. The music stops. Angelo laughs. "God provides."

"Motherfuck," Beth Two says, tossing the rag in the bus bin.

"Language!" Constance says. "Stupid whore."

Beth Two ignores the old woman. "Hey, T!" she calls back to her daughter. "There's candles in the file cabinet, can you bring 'em out, please?"

No answer. Angelo laughs again. Taylor silently flinging teen disaffection out the office door.

Jerry fills in where Roy Orbison left off, in a quavering, heartbreaking croon.

"Taylor!" Beth Two tries again. She gives her daughter twenty more seconds, then heads into the back office herself.

Taylor's tilting way back in a wooden chair not meant for tilting. Knees tucked into her chest, her sneaker-clad feet are on the edge of the desk, which is *verboten* at home, but this desk is the owner of the Gold Shade's, and Beth Two doesn't give a fuck if Taylor leaves muddy shoe prints on it. What's Kevin going to do, fire her? Good luck finding a Beth Three to put up with everybody's shit.

"Hey!" Beth Two leans on the doorjamb and addresses her daughter. In the silence that follows, Beth Two can hear the tinny bleed of some hyper-pitch-shifted pop music that sounds like a video game soundtrack played at triple the speed. Taylor's got her new noise-canceling headphones on underneath her hoodie. Her eyes are closed. She's totally motionless, vibing to the music, oblivious to her mother's presence or the power outage or anything else. Beth Two wonders if her daughter's friends have introduced her to marijuana already. Then she amends the *already*. Hell, Beth herself was toking daily by the time she was Taylor's age. It only seems out of line because she's old now and Taylor is a goddamn baby in comparison. Plus she still has braces.

"Taylor," she tries again, halfheartedly. Then she shakes her head and goes to the dented filing cabinet in the corner. The top drawer is crammed with Kevin's precious "documents" in folders the color of tree bark. Beth Two roots behind the sideways stack of yellowed papers and comes up with three half-burned votives and a box of tall red candles you might use for a Thanksgiving centerpiece.

"Thanks for your help," she says. Taylor takes a Sharpie to the knee of her jeans. Beth Two watches for a few seconds, remembering the day she bought her kid those damn jeans—at the good mall!—which are now in the process of sporting a brand-new pentagram.

Standing in the office doorway, she listens as Constance sinks into a crying jag. The woman's either fierce or maudlin with no in-between. Just what they need right now. Beth Two closes her eyes, thinking about the inexplicable route that brought her across town and then hopelessly back into it. Nausea grips her. The impossibility of it. Constance's woe-is-me act cuts right through, embedding itself deep in her bones. Beth Two shudders. The old lady's really going for it. Well, whatever. Let it all out, Constance. The Shade is your safe space. Lord knows you don't have anybody else to cry to.

One of the other regulars joins the chorus with despondent murmurings of his own, these weird measured sobs that hum along at a low frequency. Beth Two opens her eyes, puzzled. Who the hell is that? Jerry?

Candles in hand, she heads out of the office without another look at Taylor. She rounds the corner and takes a deep breath to ready herself for the gloom of an outage on top of an old woman's despair on top of every goddamn other thing that's happening in this town.

She finds that the bar is rippling with a strange new energy. A pair of figures, trembling and unreal, travel across the floor. They are each listing hard to one side like sinking ships. Both weep from puckered mouths that gleam with colors Beth Two has never seen. Parodies of shades she's always known, hues that don't exist yet still seem pulled from the booths, the crooked posters on the wall, the old aluminum ceiling tiles.

She grips the candles tightly and finds that she cannot move. Nor can she tell if she desires to move. Fear is a cold yet distant presence. Constance, Jerry, and Angelo sit hunched over their drinks, eyes trained on the intruders. Wary but not overly terrified. Constance's mouth hangs open.

The two intruders lean at such an angle that forward motion should be impossible, yet they glide up to Terry with a smoothness that belies their strange appendages. From where Beth Two is standing, she can see, with a certain distant and dull fascination, Terry's lip begin to tremble. Tears stream down his face. One of the intruders shifts to move upright, so that Terry is looking right into its puckered mouth. Beth Two watches as the mouth picks up bits of Terry's checked flannel. The pattern becomes the teeth of the pucker. Terry stares into what's been stolen from him. Then he stands very straight as if a rod has suddenly been inserted along his vertebrae. He opens his mouth and whimpers like a lost puppy. Beth Two, holding the candles, hears herself join the growing chorus.

The first weeper stands before Terry, inches from his face, and they seem to stare deeply at each other, though Beth can't make out any eyes on it.

She wonders, distantly, if they all ought to be running. But the sadness is such a great weight, and she's so tired. Besides, how fast could the ancient regulars possibly move? Better to just sit and finish their drinks.

The second weeper takes hold of Terry's right arm and appears to scrutinize it closely. Then it takes hold of his left and repeats the inspection. Beth Two thinks it must be difficult to stand so perfectly straight. The second weeper moves an appendage at great speed. A blur corrupts the air. Terry's hand, neatly and bloodlessly severed at the wrist, falls to the floor. He cries but does not scream. The weeper must have—what's the word?—*cauterized* the wound at nearly the same time it made the cut. There's another blur and the weeper removes Terry's left arm at the shoulder. Once again, there is no blood. It's very peaceful. Beth Two's mind wanders a bit as the weepers take part of his midsection. When they vivisect his right thigh from groin to knee, Terry stands up straight on one leg. Snot leaks from his nose as he cries.

The first weeper collects hand, arm, abdomen, and thigh into a neat pile on the floor. Then the pair move on down the bar. One by one, the regulars drop out of the chorus as the weepers perform their ministrations. The pile grows.

By the time they approach Beth Two, the sad sounds have become a single droning note. The weepers have brought quiet contemplation to the bar, and she's vaguely grateful for them. It's okay to be sad, because without sadness, happiness can't exist. Beth's denim top shows up in the weeper's puckered maw, which spins like the rim on a fancy tire. Her eyes blur with tears and her spine convulses, then straightens with a series of cracks. There's a mild tugging sensation at her hip, then her ear, then her knee. Then nothing.

21

Urgency becomes extra problematic, Lark thinks, when time's stretched and bent. As they wind ever upward into the mountains, the clouds race through an afternoon that bleeds into evening with alarming quickness. The issue is, the truck's passage up the winding roads Lark's traveled his entire life doesn't run parallel to the movement in the sky, the gradient of light becoming shadow.

"Why are they doing this?" Asha says. She's holding Rayanne in her lap so Rayanne can see out the window to alert Lark to the turnoff that will apparently lead to a forgotten sluice gate beyond the mansion proper and the bunkers embedded in the mountain.

"This is really gonna tweak your melons," Rayanne says.

"Lay it on us, talking jar," Lark says.

"Helena and Griffin Belmont are the children of Marius Van Leeman."

"So that makes them..." Lark's tired mind creaks through a calculation.

"Almost three hundred years old," Rayanne says. "You know the legend of their father?"

"Founded an artists' colony up here in the mountains. Freaked out the townsfolk. The mob came for him."

"It's all true," Rayanne says. "The book you and your sister are working from, that's Van Leeman's artistic legacy, passed along to his children. From what I gather, his intention was that they'd be the ones to create the sculpture and the painting, as his artistic heirs, but it didn't happen that way. They never had the talent. What they did have was a knack for getting rich, and when you live that one percent of the one percent life, it unlocks access to a lot of hidden treasures. Occult shit from all over the world. And most of it's bullshit. But you throw enough spaghetti at the wall, some of it's bound to stick."

"Spaghetti?"

"My mee-maw used to say that. Terrible cook. So Helena and Griffin learned how to tap into other artists' creative genius and suck it dry to suit their purposes. That purpose being to prolong their lives while they found the ones who *could* execute their father's crazy-ass vision. Enter you and your sister."

"*Fuck* these assholes," Krupp says with venom. He hammers a fist into his thigh, again and again. The other reason Asha's holding Rayanne is because Lark doesn't trust Krupp not to smash her to bits in a fit of rage. Krupp's trapped-animal sweat, a musk of anger and fear, fills the truck. He can hear his friend breathing as if there's a baseball card in the bicycle spokes of his throat.

"Hey, Krupp," Lark says. Off to their left, beyond the guardrail, the creek flows high and swift. "You all right?"

"I'm ready to kill these motherfuckers."

Silently, Lark parses Krupp's emotional arc. Back at the burning school bus, he'd argued that he wasn't ready to trust an abomination calling itself Rayanne. Now he seems to have refocused that hesitation into a forward-thinking viciousness. But this is a situation that might require restraint, tact, negotiation. Betsy's life is probably in even *more* danger with them charging headlong into the compound like this.

Lark would give anything to have regular old Krupp back. The guy who cried when he discovered the very jar that's now been integrated into Rayanne. The guy who earnestly proposed that he and Lark split custody of the jar, who relishes Saturdays at the Shade and makes a pickle-and-cheese sandwich called the Krupp Special and never remembers where he left his lighter.

The guy who doesn't set his jaw and clench his fists and vow to kill people. Even if those people deserve it.

Well, Lark thinks, the only way out is through.

"Their methods don't always work," Rayanne continues. "In fact they rarely do because they're not systematic. Like I said, spaghetti, wall. So mostly it fizzles out and people die, or these artists they kidnap get transformed into something awful. I've seen it fail a million times." She pauses. "I'm one of their failures."

Lark registers the hand-lettered sign for a long-ago yard sale. They'd passed that same sign twenty minutes ago. "What did they do to you?"

"Helena cut off my face and had my vocal cords removed."

"*Fuck!*" Krupp rocks back and forth in the seat. He can barely get the words out through the froth coating his lips. His body gives off a feverish heat. "Those motherfuckers."

"Easy," Lark says.

"My God," Asha says, "that's awful."

"So they got Betsy and me to execute their father's vision—for what?"

"The God of the Noose," Rayanne says, "is Marius Van Leeman himself."

Krupp lets out a scream and brings his fist down onto the dash.

"Jesus!" Lark says. "Would you try to chill out?"

"Yeah," Krupp says blankly. He squeezes one hand with the other.

"Turn right," Rayanne says.

They just passed that yard sale sign again—how could they be close to the Belmonts' compound? But he turns off 212 all the same. Full-on dusk has settled over the mountains. There's a low-grade snowfall. He wonders how long it's been since he's slept. Rayanne's movements on Asha's lap are hesitant but gaining confidence and fluidity as she acclimates to her form.

"If you knew this sluice gate was here," Lark says, "how come you didn't use it to escape?"

"There was no escape. Because the one ghost cliché that actually applied was that I couldn't leave the museum. For two years I thought it was one of those unfinished-business-type things, where if I could only set things right I'd be released from my eternal limbo. That's actually what kicked off my futile quest to help the Belmonts' other victims. A selfish wish. Anyway, like I said, the place is mapped out pretty extensively in my head."

The road is so overgrown that the vehicle plows through the underbrush with a series of alarming scrapes and thuds. Focused on keeping the truck from veering into some uncharted gulley, Lark can't look to the side to catch Krupp's grotesque expressions as he spins through his emotional cyclone. Lark can only *sense* them, the way you might get wise to a dog who's got it in for you, for whatever dog-brained reason.

"So how'd you get out this time?" Asha asks.

"Betsy did me a solid," Rayanne says. "Stop here."

Here seems to be *nowhere in particular*, but Lark does what she says and kills the engine. When the headlights go out, dusk wraps around the truck like a gray glove. *In the gloaming*, his wired and frightened mind tells him. This is how it is now: Thoughts just open the door and make themselves at home without being invited in.

He notices for the first time, now that the light is faint, that Rayanne's core—what's left of what the woman in the red dress used to hold—gives off a soft glow the color of lemon meringue. When Rayanne speaks, the light stutters through a strobe effect.

"A few things to know before we head in," Rayanne says. "One: The whole place is wired up for some pretty heavy surveillance. As soon as we hit any of the gallery wings, they'll know we're here. If they don't already know. I'm not sure if they have eyes on the perimeter."

"Or if that drone's been following us," Asha says.

"We've got a gun," Krupp interrupts. "Some ammo. I don't know how much." He vibrates with an eagerness Lark hasn't seen since they first learned to drive, sophomore year of high school. That precious interval after you tell Wayne Krupp Sr. goodbye and run out to the driveway, get in the car, crank up the stereo. The first time the world's truly opened up to you, when just last month you were relegated to your ten-speed…

Lark puts a hand on Krupp's knee. He feels his friend's leg bounce with revved-up quickness. "If Brandt Gumley and the Belmonts can see us coming, what's to stop them from killing Betsy?"

"They need her to finish the painting."

Lark thinks of the time she told him to go, start a life with Celeste, and he did not. Did the opposite, in fact. Another intrusive thought, delivered with polite formality: *You've always been the caretaker.*

"Fuck it." He opens the door. They all pile out after him. Krupp goes immediately to the truck bed, comes back with the rifle. Asha sets Rayanne on the ground. She flexes her twined-cilia limbs and sets about leading them down the dirt path. As Lark follows Rayanne's dim yet cheery glow through the woods, he clocks an uptick in her evolution. The jar-shape has all but disappeared. It's as if Rayanne's presence—what he now can't help but think of as the *soul* of the turning-jar—has helped it come into its own.

Lark slows down so he's walking nearly side by side with Krupp—or would be if the brush weren't so thick.

"Why don't you give me the gun?" he says.

"No. You can't pull the trigger."

There's an icy undercurrent in Krupp's voice. Whatever topographic shift that's bleeding into his friend's brain, he hopes to God that getting Betsy out of here is the first step in setting things right. Yes: He can *feel* the good energy of that notion. The warm cozy comfort of the right course of action. Their separation is at the heart of what's been going on. Reunited, they can set things right. The roads, the falls, the town itself. The harbingers. His father. Krupp.

Lark picks up the pace to join Rayanne. "King Douche," Lark says. "I like that."

"Yeah, I mean, it's serviceable, you know? I had eight years to come up with better names for that asshole, but I figured he didn't deserve an ounce of creativity."

Lark keeps an eye on Rayanne's curious mobility as she goes from walking to stopping. It's like the inertia of a half-full orange juice container shoved across a table. There's a quick halt followed by a little hiccup of a forward hop. The lemony light stutters. Rayanne illuminates a corroded iron grate.

"Dear Lord," Asha says, her voice going nasal as she plugs her nose. "It smells like human waste."

Lark stares at her. "Is *human waste* what you instinctively call shit, or is that an affectation?"

Krupp takes a big whiff. "That reeks."

"Sorry about that," Rayanne says. "I figured it'd be best to let you find out it was the sewer system for yourselves, rather than me telling you in advance. Was that not the right move?"

"Eh," Lark says.

"Now I'm self-conscious," Rayanne says. "Did I totally fuck that up? Eight years is a long time not to talk to anybody."

"You're doing great," Asha assures her. "So how do we get in?"

Krupp answers by smashing the butt of his rifle directly through the center of the corroded metal grate. The bars flake away. Then he rips the remainder of the grate away with his bare hands.

"Okay," Lark says.

They stoop to enter the Hobbit-size entrance in the mountainside. The stench is immediately overpowering. Lark's shoes squelch in the fetid muck. Asha scoops Rayanne into her arms, saving her cilia-limbs from getting shit-smeared. She holds her out in front with two hands like an extremely heavy lantern. The weak light emanating from her core is enough to illuminate the tunnel in front of them. Beyond that, all is dark.

"I guess I should warn you about where we're going," Rayanne whispers. Something scurries past Lark's feet. He tries not to think about what kind of creature lives in a river of shit. Nobody responds to Rayanne. Lark refuses to open his mouth, even to breathe, lest he let in stench particles that will invade his body. He's never been a germophobe but all he can think with each step through the slurry is *disease, disease, disease.* He wonders if he has any open cuts anywhere.

"This place is a giant bunker dug into the mountain. It's huge. After eight years there were still places I was just discovering. It could shelter the population of a medium-size city. The Belmonts use it as their private museum, where they stash away pieces from the artists they obsess over till they get bored, and also whatever's left of the artists themselves."

Whatever's left? Lark thinks.

"So between Gumley and his team hunting us and the things prowling the galleries of this place, you're gonna want to stay frosty."

Stay frosty?

"Through here," Rayanne says, leading them—via Asha—through an archway. Wilted, unhealthy growths of mossy flora dangle and caress Lark's face as he follows. The floor becomes slippery cobbles, the walls so cave-like they look fake, like a theme-park attraction— this way to the Tunnel of Love!

Treason, Lark thinks, the word implanting itself in his mind like the earlier incarnation of turning-jar, that pre-Rayanne edition. It cycles through formulations as they emerge from the archway into a small, poorly lit chamber. *Treasonous. High Treason.*

The chamber is styled like a courtroom. Everything appears slightly shrunken, three-quarter-size. Lark recalls Krupp's discomfort in the booth at the Gold Shade—*Were people smaller back then?*

"What the hell is this?" He turns in a full circle, scanning the faded paintings on all four walls—spectators in strange hats sitting grim-faced, arms folded, regarding a trial that does not exist. The judge, bewigged, curlered, and stern, presides over the courtroom from a bench hung with torn and tattered crimson vestments. On the floor in the center of the room is a tiny, mouse-size guillotine ringed by a neat pool of dried blood.

"You don't want to know," Rayanne says. Asha sets her down and she leads them through another archway. The word *treason* tickles the back of his mind once more and vanishes. The light in here is better, the chamber much larger, the ceiling impossibly high. An indoor sculpture garden of sorts. Fungal tents sprout from the concrete, huge wet-looking masses boiling up from a floor that looks teleported here from a Costco. They pass the bulbous growths and Lark realizes that they're made of fabric, hardened and shiny. The effect is like some vast festival encampment doused in shellac. Krupp mutters to himself. An earthy smell emanates from the tent-growths. Asha reaches out to touch one, hesitantly, with a single fingertip.

"I wouldn't," Rayanne says. Asha lowers her arm.

A sight stops Lark in his tracks. There, placed in the center of a ring of fungal tents, is the eight-foot conglomerate of wire and wood he sold to the Belmonts a few days ago.

"They moved it," Rayanne says, "or else it moved."

Lark finds that its placement both excites and annoys him. What does it mean, to have a sculpture inserted into this landscape of some other long-gone artist's work? His piece is like the curly fry that sneaks into the basket of tater tots. And yet this was no accident. Someone clearly took the time to art-direct its placement. But why? In a gallery that receives no visitors, whose whim does this satisfy?

He is struck by the thought that his works have been placed in rooms and gardens and galleries all over the world, and whether the placement is intentional—a little to the left, an inch to the right—or totally random, it's still the result of some human's thought process. To have what amounts to a glorified *object* he created in his yard subject to a series of decisions, out of his hands, regarding where and how it will be displayed. And for what purpose. What a strange occupation.

To Lark's surprise, Krupp walks reverently up to the sculpture. He regards it for a moment, then turns to Lark, his eyes shiny with tears.

"You really are good," he says. "I've always loved your work. I don't know if I ever told you that before."

Lark finds that despite the circumstances, he's truly touched. "No," he says, "you haven't. But thanks."

Krupp smiles. His lip trembles and the left side of his face stretches back. The tendons in his neck tighten. He closes his eyes, struggling mightily to control an onrushing episode. He turns back to the sculpture. Then a shot rings out, Krupp's body jerks to the side, and his black rifle clatters to the floor.

Asha and Rayanne act quickly, ducking down behind a fungal tent. Lark, frozen in place, watches as Brandt Gumley steps out into the open. His silver handgun is trained on Krupp—who is still standing upright. Then Gumley swivels with practiced ease to train the weapon on Lark.

"Don't," he says calmly. Lark does a quick mental calculation. The odds of diving for the rifle and getting a shot off before Gumley puts one in his brain with casual precision are not in his favor. Gumley frowns, and seems to regard him with genuine curiosity. "How far did you think you would get?"

Lark's eyes go to Krupp. His friend places a hand over the wound on his shoulder, then pulls it away and studies the blood smeared on his palm. Without taking his eyes off Lark, Gumley's arm swivels back to aim the gun at Krupp. "The next one blows your head off, Wayne." His mouth hints at a smile. "Finish the sculpture, Mr. Larkin. It's the only way. Turn around right now, leave this place, and *finish the job*. That way, no one else needs to get hurt."

Krupp laughs. It's too loud, too strange. It makes Lark nervous. Gumley's eyes narrow as Krupp's laughter spirals up to the ceiling, capers around the fungal tents.

"Krupp," Lark says, "easy."

Krupp looks back at him from the shadow of Lark's latest piece, his eyes still wet. The sculpture looms over him. Lark silently begs for whatever dark energies swirl in this place to breathe life into his sculpture like a golem, take Krupp in its arms and bear him away. Instead, the sculpture remains motionless, and Krupp smiles.

"Take care of the store for me," he says. The old Krupp, the real Krupp, shining through.

With astonishing speed he charges Gumley.

Gumley, flustered for a split second, gets off two shots. Krupp's left ear is sheared from his face. Blood spatters Lark's sculpture. The second shot punches him in the chest but it barely seems to slow him down.

Krupp's feet leave the floor and he launches himself at Gumley. A third shot removes the side of his jaw. Krupp and Gumley go down in a tangle. Another shot, squeezed off from between their bodies, slightly muffled, makes Krupp bounce and come back down on Gumley.

Lark makes his way toward them like you might approach dogs in a fight—slowly at first, then quickly, as it dawns on you that you'll have to pull your dog out yourself because there's no other way to stop it.

He's halfway there when Krupp's newfound rage breaks through its last tepid filter and unleashes fully. He brings the bare-toothed remnant of his jaw down on Gumley's eyes and begins to hammer at them with his exposed incisors. Gumley screams and bashes the side of Krupp's head with his silver pistol.

Krupp, undaunted, squeezes Gumley's thick neck while he draws blood from the man's face, again and again. He is screaming too as his mouth comes up between savage attacks on Gumley.

"RUN."

At the same time, Asha grabs Lark's arm and tries to pull him the other way. "Come on!"

Krupp uses a protruding piece of his jawbone like a knife to saw at Gumley's neck. Flailing, he gurgles as he drowns in his blood. Lark shakes Asha off. Krupp turns his head and the look in his eyes pins Lark in place.

"RUN," he growls.

Beneath him, Gumley twitches and goes limp. His neck leaks dark blood. His fingers uncurl from the grip of the gun.

Krupp looks down at the body, then back to Lark. He approximates a slow, dazed grin from his ruined face. Then Gumley's arm comes up and sinks a switchblade into the base of Krupp's neck, just behind his collarbone. Krupp collapses face-first onto Gumley, driving the jagged bone deep into the man's neck. They both lie still. A fine red mist settles about them. Lark and his sculpture look on. The word *TREA-SON* drifts in from the other chamber, where a painted judge regards a small execution device like a seventeenth-century scold.

"Lark, we have to move," Asha says.

Lark always figured it's bullshit that your life flashes before your eyes at the moment of death. But now Wayne Krupp Jr.'s life sparks and pops behind his eyes, from the fourth-grade photograph of the two of them examining the flower like kid scientists to all those Saturdays at the Shade, lost to time.

Asha and Rayanne are exhorting him from someplace far away. The next thing he knows he's at Krupp's side, kneeling in blood, trying to turn his friend's body over. But it's stuck fast to Gumley, fused by that jagged bone. Asha pulls Lark away from the corpses, both of them sliding in blood. Some lizard-brained part of Lark reminds him to pick up the discarded rifle. Rayanne is urging them to follow, quickly, past one fungal tent, then another, and another. This chamber seems endless. Footsteps approach.

Lark can feel grief massing like a thunderhead, ready to soak him to the bone. But for now, there's only this confounding room and its sprouting, shiny growths and the relentless pounding of boots on concrete. Rayanne says something and they move in a different direction. But the men come storming in from every angle. Guns bristle like pins in a pincushion. Lost Year rage makes him grip the rifle tighter. He wonders two things simultaneously: what it feels like to be shot and who in his stead will take Krupp's body to be buried in the Krupp family plot in the cemetery west of downtown.

Asha raises her hands. The men move in and take her. Lark can smell their cologne. He glances up in search of a sign, and finds only a blank and empty ceiling. He drops his weapon and allows the men to take him. As he's marched roughly away he looks over his shoulder, but his line of sight is blocked and he can't see Krupp's body. The last thing Krupp ever said to him was *RUN*, but he didn't do it fast enough, and now here they are.

Sorry, buddy.

I'm so sorry.

22

Ian Friedrich reverse-pinches the blinds and peers through the opening in the slats. Then he takes his hand away, sits down on the stool behind the register, and raises his vape to his lips with a trembling hand. He draws in twice as much smoke as he normally would and waits for the mango cloud to seep into his brain. What he wouldn't give for a genuine, machine-rolled, mass-produced, lung-ruining, tar-laced American cigarette. The harshest one in existence. Marlboro Reds, unfiltered Lucky Strikes.

To finally have reached that moment where he's supposed to sit and smoke like a condemned man, and to be without a real cigarette to savor. What a joke. He sucks in the mango cloud and lets it out slowly, watching it dissipate in the darkness of Clementine's Yarn & Tea.

The shop's namesake, his peanut-butter-swirl-colored tabby, arches her back to rub her fur against his feet perched on the bar of the stool.

"You want a snack, Clemmy?" Ian upends a bag of pricey artisanal cat treats and scatters them across the shop floor. Clementine gives him a long mewl of astonishment at the bounty that's just rained down. Then she gets to work. "Scarf 'em up, baby."

He empties the vape's cartridge and loads another one: mint chocolate chip. Shakes his head. Who wants to smoke ice cream? Nevertheless he pulls in a prodigious cloud, lets it out, and watches his exhalation cling thickly to the ceiling. Shakes his head again. Playing the doomed badass gearing up for his last stand with flavored vape smoke is just flat-out ridiculous. The kind of movie-trope-in-real-life event that would absolutely slay Krupp down at the Shade. Maybe elicit a wry grin from Lark, too.

He takes a puff and smiles into the darkness. He can hear Krupp now: *Sucking on a USB drive is no way to face down imminent death!*

Lark and Krupp. He wonders how they've fared in all this. Maybe they managed to get out of town. He likes to apply that thought to anyone who's disappeared. Maybe they're sitting pretty down at the Phoenicia Diner, talking about the crazy shit that's going down in Wofford Falls, trading theories like the batty old regulars at the Shade.

But he knows it's far more likely that they've ended up like the guy who owns Hudson Valley Vape HQ.

A pile of neatly segmented body parts, minus various pieces taken for unknown purposes. He turns on his stool and glances out at Main Street once again. There it is: a neat pyramid, as if pushed by the street cleaner into the slush on the curb. Atop the pile of limbs sits the guy's red Supreme cap.

Across the street, the Hudson Bread Company and Early Bird Chocolates have become one. The red schoolhouse bricks of the bakery and the fudge-colored vinyl siding of the candy shop joined as if by some giant's hand. An overgrown baby who reached down into his playset and crashed two Wofford Falls institutions together. Except there is no violence, no ruin in the structures' reimagining. It's as if they've simply gotten together and decided to occupy the same space for a while. Looking at the new building makes Ian feel sick to his stomach. The second-floor apartments above the shops burn with two-dimensional fire. A window air-conditioning unit belches dark smoke. There are figures in the windows that have been weeping for hours. At irregular intervals they lean out nearly horizontally, parallel with the street, and commune with the world around them. They process the once solid elements of downtown Wofford Falls through their unstable systems. Ian finds himself mesmerized by the sight of them. The dread only comes rushing in when he forces himself to lower the blinds and shut them out.

It's then that he remembers what they did to the Vape HQ guy.

Right there in front of the window. Three of them, moving their long limbs in a ritualistic dance. The Vape HQ guy didn't scream. He just stood there, straight as a signpost, in some kind of peaceful trance while these *things* bloodlessly vivisected him.

"What do you think, Clemmy?" he says. "Should we make a run for it?" The cat snarfles up treats. "No? Fine by me. Let's just sit tight."

He runs his fingers along the contours of his vintage cash register and remembers stumbling across it at Wrecker's when he was first out-fitting the shop.

"You were a tiny kitten then," he tells Clementine. He hits the vape and closes his eyes. When he was a kid sent to live with the isolationist wing of the extended Friedrich clan, thanks to a rebellious ninth-grade year, he used to lie in his bed in the loft above the barn and fantasize about a cosmic disaster hitting the Greater Wofford Falls area. The kind of catastrophic event that would render his problems suddenly and irrevocably meaningless. To his fourteen-year-old mind, living through some epic disaster seemed like a saving grace. It was aspira-tional. He longed for it like other kids longed for the latest PlayStation upgrade. He scribbled increasingly elaborate scenarios in his compo-sition books. Rising floodwaters infested by great whites. A plague of serial killers. Razor-blade tornadoes.

Well, here you go, Ian. You moron. It's here, and it totally sucks.

Outside, that awful weeping amplifies. It's infectious. He begins to tear up in solidarity. Or maybe because it's fucking sad, the choice he's faced with. For the tenth time, he checks the drawer beneath the register. His uncle Burl's old Magnum revolver, as vintage as the register itself, is right there where it always is. He doesn't want to use it. He'd rather just sit here, vaping, and take the end as it comes—even if his fate is the same as the Vape HQ guy. But Clementine, she's the wildcard. What would these things do to a cat? Would they both be better off with a bullet to the brain, one-two, see you on the rainbow bridge, Clemmy?

He sighs, blowing smoke from his nostrils. Then he sets down the vape and picks up the gun. At his feet, Clementine collapses onto her side and rolls around like a maniac.

Clementine's a stoop cat. She prowls the entrance to the store, greeting passersby. He's long since quit worrying that she's going to take off. Now he wishes she could unlearn that habit in an instant so that he could crack the door and send her packing. But he knows she'll just slink around the doorway, and then eventually he'll have to watch those things come for her.

Maybe they'd ignore her completely.

Maybe they'd sever her little paws.

It could go either way.

He hefts the gun. Speaking of movie tropes, Uncle Burl used to set bottles on the fence for Ian and his friends to aim at. Krupp and Lark, missing every goddamn shot. Burl shaking his head, spitting brown jets of tobacco juice into the dirt.

The chorus of crying and sobbing is getting louder. Sometimes they join in perfect unison and become one, until the sounds separate out into dissonance once again. Holding the gun in one hand, he parts the blinds with the other—and finds himself staring into a puckered, swirling maw, crammed with teeth.

He screams and moves away from the window in a backward stagger that upsets the stool. Clementine darts away as it hits the ground. Ian trains the gun on the window. The minty aftertaste sours instantly. His mouth goes dry. He should have made a run for it an hour ago. Except that's what the Vape HQ guy was trying to do, and once Ian witnessed his fate, he was stuck.

"Okay, Clemmy," he says, glancing over the counter into the darkened shop for any sign of the cat. "You just stay out of sight."

In true cat fashion, Clementine does the opposite. He catches a slinky blur moving through the shadows of a shelf piled with wicker baskets full of yarn balls.

"Stay put!" he stage-whispers. But Clementine keeps moving, quickly and oddly. Ian rubs his eyes. Something's not right. There, just above the Darjeelings on the highest shelf, Clementine blurs past. How did she get up there so quickly?

Slowly, carefully, he backs away from the window, still aiming the gun at the glass. He glances over his shoulder. There's Clementine by the accessories—knitting needles, stitch markers, crochet hooks. A second later, she pops up by the tea diffusers on a shelf with assorted knickknacks—fridge magnets, handmade candles, notebooks. Something glitches in his mind. He's queasy, his center of gravity knocked loose.

Ian does a 180 to aim the gun into the darkened shop. It's too late, of course. Now that he knows the motion he's catching out of the corner of his eye isn't Clementine at all.

His heart pounds as the thing emerges and stands before him. Then it slows again. He begins to relax. He wonders how long the creature's been inside the shop, if it was watching him sit and vape and look out the window this whole time. Its weeping joins the chorus of its fellows standing just outside the window. He wonders if Clementine managed to hide. Either way, he supposes, it would be all right.

He has experienced moments like this before, where he realizes something has been happening for much longer than his awareness would suggest. The yarn-faced thing glides toward him. His entire life has been like this, he understands at last—realizing only in retrospect that he's missed out on what was really happening. Ah, well. That doesn't matter anymore, does it?

There's a blur of movement, a slight tug at his wrist. The gun clatters to the floor. Ian's back cracks as he stands up straight to greet his visitor with a calm and settled mind.

23

You're a curious little nugget, aren't you."

Griffin Belmont kneels down to examine Rayanne. His sister, Helena, hangs back and mixes a drink. The glasses are rimmed in gold, the liquid an autumnal spectrum. Her movements are languid and narcotized. Lark watches in a daze. Imposed upon his vision is a two-second clip of Krupp on a loop, gurgling *RUN* from the wreckage of his face, over and over...

They've been shepherded through a warren of unearthly delights, a Boschian zone of bad energy, marched into an elevator, and presented to the Belmonts inside a vast subterranean room. The Gumley acolytes hold them at gunpoint, fanned out at their backs. The wall in front of them is a single monstrous flatscreen.

Lark can't tell if it's that thunderhead of grief beginning to open up, or the terrible vapors loose in the galleries—he shudders at the thought of those wilted monoliths, the evocations of some nightmare castration out in the barren desert—but he finds himself drawn into a near trance by the proceedings on the screen. A drone's-eye view of his sculpture on the Backbone.

"Fuck off," Rayanne says. Lark is vaguely aware of a broad smile creasing Griffin's face.

"Such a hateful little thing! We'll have plenty of time for you here."

Rayanne seems to sag. Lark feels the hope jet out of her. Eight years trapped, a brief lunge at freedom, and now she's back inside.

A disruption comes across the screen, a wave of distorted pixels. The drone lens wavers, then steadies itself. Lark takes in a sharp breath. There, on the outcrop, are three of the creatures that appeared when he completed *The Worm & the Dogsbody*. The asymmetry is more palpable now. Appendages on one side shorter than the other. A sagging hemisphere bolstered by a ramrod-straight humanoid posture. One angular shoulder blade, one soft. They move with ease and confidence. Without his knowing why, exactly, they evoke for Lark the busy interns at Hirst's compound, tending to vivisected farm animals.

Helena downs half her drink and turns her attention to Lark. "Hi, Peter," she says. Her voice ripples across his skin. "It's wonderful to meet you at last. My brother and I have been huge advocates for your work for some time now." She pauses to drain her glass. "If I can be frank, though, I don't think you ever topped your *Citadel* series. We're in talks to acquire it now, actually."

"*Art Forum* agrees with you," Asha says. "I think it's a bullshit opinion, personally. His work has matured in fits and starts. Not the graceful aging you see from less exciting artists, but a kind of jagged road to a new sensibility. So, like Rayanne said, fuck off."

Griffin rises.

"*Rayanne*," Helena says, raising her head, staring out at the back of the room. "Rayanne."

Griffin whispers in her ear. Her eyes narrow. Then she nods. "How did you come to be?"

"I've waited eight years to tell you this," Rayanne says. "You're both giant pieces of shit."

Griffin laughs. "You had eight years to come up with something and you went with *pieces of shit*?"

"Giant ones," Helena says.

"Why was my life worth less than yours?" Rayanne says.

"Is that a serious question?" Griffin says. "You were a middling pop-country artist. 'Boyfriend Jeans,' if I remember correctly." He shudders.

"Krupp loved that song," Lark says. His thoughts veer back to

Krupp's decline and abrupt end and he teeters on the brink of letting Lost Year rage propel him straight into the Belmonts in a whirlwind of fists and teeth. He wonders if one of the acolytes has informed his bosses of the loss of Gumley. He assumes they know, perhaps even watched it on closed-circuit TV. But they give no indication that it has impacted them in any way.

"You cut off my face," Rayanne says. "Do you know what that feels like?"

"God, no," Griffin says.

"I am sorry about that," Helena says, voice huskier than before, coated in velvet. "Truly. But the ritual called for it." She turns back to her goblets and droppers and mixers.

"All this misery"—Rayanne teeters on her spindly limbs— "because the two of you weren't ever good enough to do what Daddy expected of you."

Griffin laughs. "Do you think we've never been haunted before? Do you think you're capable of cutting to the quick, of making us reassess, at this late stage? I squint at your distant notions of conscience from the vantage point of centuries, you child."

Movement on the screen draws Lark's attention. Hypnotic, synchronized, the three creatures approach the sculpture and begin to fuss with its margins.

"Zoom in, please," Griffin calls out to the room. The drone lens snaps into a close-up on the sculpture. He claps his hands once in delight. "Fascinating! Credit to you, Peter, for taking it as far as you did, but the emergents have got it from here."

Lark watches with a cold knot in his gut.

With assured grace the emergents place neatly severed limbs upon the fly-specked lumps of cow. One of the creatures balances the lower half of a leg, cleanly sliced below the knee, atop the cow's upturned eye. With the methodical persistence of an assembly line, the emergents build a scaffold. An assemblage of freshly gathered pieces of the citizens of Wofford Falls, lashed into struts and support beams with entrails stretched taut.

Next to him, Asha heaves. Her vomit spatters the floor.

An acolyte comes out of the shadows with a bucket and mop—the same man who scrubbed Lark's puke off the horseshoe driveway outside the stone mansion.

Helena downs radiant white liquid from a long-stemmed glass. Then she sits on the floor, directly across from Rayanne, and stares at her. Rayanne's cilia quiver.

"I *am* sorry," Helena says. "It's not something that comes easily to me, so my first instinct is that I'm not sorry at all. Like I try to access the concept and it's just a blank void." Her speech is slow and deliberate. "But, when I really step back and see it from a different angle— what I've done to people, I mean. What I've done to you, and Leif, and everybody else. There's something there." She looks away, deep in thought. "I'm not *sad* about it. But I understand that if someone did it to me, or someone I loved, I'd be upset. I'm not a sociopath. I was, for a while. But I'm not now."

"For fuck's sake, sister, please shut up." Griffin extends a hand and helps her to her feet. "Why don't you go take a nap."

"Why don't *you* go take a nap."

"Because someone has to finish what we started." He looks from Asha to Lark. "To that end, why don't we all repair to the work in progress."

Lark feels the cold steel of an acolyte's gun at his back. His eyes flick to the screen as he's escorted from the room. The emergents' scaffold of severed limbs has doubled the height of the sculpture. Thighs, forearms, feet, hands—interwoven with precision and purpose. And there's something else, now, too—movement at the edge of the frame.

Jamie-Lynn's Arabian. Her prized horse, poised with unnatural stillness at the cliff's edge. The wind lifts its mane in gauzy wisps. It watches the sculpture grow.

24

What lies beyond despair?

Big Tom Larkin paints a swooping acrylic accent line and steps back to test its balance. His daughter's face is taking shape, absent definition in the eye sockets, the hint of cheekbones. The eyes themselves are finished. He always begins with the eyes. That's the way Betsy wants it. So she can watch him paint.

But what lies beyond despair?

Big Tom shrugs and flicks his brush to feather the dangling ends of her stringy hair. *Hope*, perhaps—if you could throw a rock so hard that it could circumnavigate the globe and then strike you in the back of the head, that's how far you have to go beyond despair to find hope. Down down down till down becomes up.

His arm moves mechanically back and forth from palette to canvas. Despair. Hope. Everything in between. It's all the same to him.

When the noises come from downstairs, he remembers the visit from his son. It could have been days ago, it could have been months. Or was it a dream? He remembers that they spoke of the past, but it's a past he can't recall. Yes: a dream. There were other people with his son. All of them, speaking of things come and gone. It must have been a dream. He and his son don't speak. Certainly not of the past. With a fine brush he blends the shadow on his daughter's neck into the wall behind her head. It's good to have a little unnatural bleed of light and dark. It's not realistic but it feels sophisticated. Big Tom is still learning, still trying to be what Betsy wants him to be.

The noises are coming from the doorway behind him now. Weeping. Slow and steady crying, like how someone might cry in an old-time play. Big Tom works and reworks the arc of Betsy's forehead. Eventually, he puts down his brush and turns around.

"Hi, Betsy," he says. His daughter is here. Her face is radiant and bursting with color pulled from all the paintings on the walls of his studio, which used to be her bedroom. All his experiments, his progressions, are represented before him: cubist eyes, impressionist mouth, abstract hair, pointillist brow. She moves toward him, weeping, and he loses himself in her approach. He feels the same as he always does.

25

Griffin Belmont opens the massive, ornate door. A blast of cold air escapes. *Mountain air*, Lark thinks. Carrying with it hints of pine, dirt, water. Sense-memories of the Backbone. An acolyte's gun jabs into his back, urging him inside. Asha cradles Rayanne against her chest. Streaks of mottled light play upon the glass of her vessel.

The chamber he's only ever seen in photos is muddled like smudged pastels at its margins. He walks through a room insecure about its own solidity, giving a false impression of itself. Built according to some World's Fair conception of scale. High above throbs the dim suggestion of a ceiling.

"So much gray," Asha says, scanning the floor. There are visible gradients, phase-shifting layers of slate and graphite and lead. She lifts a foot and drags up strands of watery hues, flecks of blue glinting dully among the gray.

"Oh," she says. Surface tension stretches to thin filigrees and breaks away. Her shoe splashes back down onto the floor. Or, more properly, *into* the floor. An oily sheen ripples outward.

Prodded by his captor, Lark shuffles ahead. His feet skim a shallow puddle with inborn eddies and whirlpools. He comes to realize that the mural soaks the entire floor of the chamber. It takes a moment to register the mural's subject—a waterfall that has no beginning and no end, no top and no bottom, as if gravity has been run through a prism. Foam churns at every edge. Pools gather and swirl around tiny pops of color, scattered all over the floor, and he knows without having to look very hard that these are the turnings stolen from Betsy's paintings. He can feel the familiar nudge of their sickly energy, giving life to the fleeting reactions that simply come and go when he looks at other paintings, regular paintings, paintings that hold no sway over him.

"Cadbury eggs," he says softly as they approach the turning stolen from *The Wounded Deer*: a sprouting nine-pointed antler, one for each arrow in the Kahlo-deer, the hybrid self-portrait. Redolent of a shared childhood moment, the submerged turning wavers. The antlers bring up that memory of hiding in the spare room closet, sharing a treat stolen from the corner store.

A yawning vastness overtakes him that has nothing to do with the chamber. The infinite mystery of his sister, that enigmatic soul in an oversize windbreaker, the kind with the hood hidden in the collar.

"For me it's Good & Plenty," Asha says, staring transfixed at the cutout just beneath the surface. At first Lark is startled by her reaction. But of course the turnings don't just work on him alone. "Justine's favorite," Asha continues as they move along. "I always make fun of her because what is she, eighty-six years old? Whenever we share a box of them I'm the good and she's the plenty. It's a whole thing."

"Jalapeño poppers," Rayanne says. "That's what I got from it. Me and my cousins at the diner. The best thing ever."

Their feet slosh through the endless pool. Lark thinks an arena could fit into this place, one of those South American soccer stadiums built to hold half the country.

"This is a weird thing to say about a forger," Asha says, "but your sister is truly an original." There's no attempt at an appraisal, none of Asha's trademark professional eye-fucking. Just the awe anyone would feel in the presence of the inexplicable.

"I wish I brought her to the city," Lark says. "So you could have met both of us back then instead of just me. I wish—"

He shuts his mouth as soon as he spots her, appearing out of the haze and the shadow. Far away, a hunched figure in the rough center of the room.

"Betsy!" Heedless of the gun at his back, Lark runs to her.

Krupp, dead, behind him.

Betsy, alive, just ahead.

His feet skim the water, never quite touching down, like that Cartier-Bresson photograph of the kid hovering forever above a puddle.

He bounds across turning after shimmery turning, splashing mercury-slick shades of blue-gray paint. The photorealistic knot from *The Lovers*. Slenderwoman from the Cassatt. That envious slice of de Chirico's towers. A jokey O'Keeffe.

Eventually he comes upon her kneeling down, dragging a paintbrush through the water. She glances up when he's a few steps away. The look on her face breaks his heart—helpless, hopeless concentration. Her hand doesn't stop moving. Water seems to blossom, somehow, in the brush's wake, as she sluices through the infinite rush of the falls.

"Oh my God," he says, leaning down to kiss her forehead. "Oh my God, Betsy."

"I missed you," she says.

"I missed you too. So much."

She turns back to her painting. "I can't stop. I feel like I've been here forever. I'm sorry."

For a moment, everything else falls away: the Belmonts, the acolytes, this terrible place. There's only Lark and Betsy, together again. Even in here, now, he feels light and infinite. It's as if he's run to the edge of the Backbone and taken a flying leap to find that he's not falling. He's just hanging in the air, suspended, forever. "I'm sorry too."

"For what?" She drags her brush through the falls, turning her hand, rotating her wrist, so that the entire architecture of her hand goes slippery and boneless. She manages to look up at him again. "It feels so good."

The thunderhead bursts open. "Oh, Bets."

All at once he nearly chokes on the stench of rot and mold. He turns in time to see a pair of acolytes come through the door. Griffin and an unsteady Helena wait to greet them. The acolytes carry a simple wooden chair upon which sits a thin figure bundled in a coarse woolen blanket. It wears a black wide-brimmed hat that hides its face in shadow. They set the chair down directly over one of the little whirlpools and step back in reverent formation to stand with bowed heads and folded hands. Lark wonders which of Betsy's turnings is at the center of the maelstrom under the chair.

The chamber constricts. A claustrophobic panic he's never felt before licks at his skin. He glances around to reassure himself that the walls aren't trash-compacting inward. The edges of the room swim in sheets of fog. He raises his eyes to a ceiling still shrouded in shifting atmosphere and imagines it coming down on them with pulverizing force.

"My God," Asha says, fumbling for his hand. "Do you feel that?"

"I do," he says, taking her hand in his.

Rayanne quivers. "I think we might be fucked."

Practically folded into the mural, Betsy paints with methodical urgency, bent to her task like some fierce and dedicated monk over a manuscript.

Griffin positions himself behind the figure in the chair and very carefully removes the blanket and the hat. The stench grows more potent as the coverings are disturbed like sour old sheets on a stained bed. Lark's struck by the baked-in rot of centuries spent immobile, the trapped air of a world he can scarcely imagine. A stale sadness, like opening a time capsule to find only emptiness and the lingering odor of something long rotted.

At his side, Asha heaves. There's nothing more inside her to expel. Lark's entire body goes weak with nausea. The back of his neck is clammy and cold.

Griffin carefully unwinds a decaying scarf wrapped like a bandage around the figure's neck and head. Dust settles into the mural, tiny glinting motes swirling in strange currents.

Lark fights the urge to look away as the man beneath the blanket is revealed.

"Marius Van Leeman," Asha says.

"It can't be," Lark says. But it is—there's no doubt.

Marius Van Leeman, hanged on the Backbone in 1751, rises slowly from his chair. The acolytes look on, expressionless. Lark wonders what horrors they've become accustomed to in this place.

Van Leeman sighs with great pleasure, like a man sinking into a hot bath after a long day. His bare flesh has the graying pallor of meat on the cusp of going rancid. Yet he does not look decayed or leprous. Whatever binds him together does so seamlessly. His sunken eyes meet Betsy's as she looks up from her painting.

"Marvelous work." His voice is dry wings rubbing a chitinous shell. His eyes shift pointedly between Betsy and Lark, animated by a fiery lust. "My children."

Griffin's mouth works in mute fury at the snub. Helena turns away and folds her arms low across her stomach, clutching herself.

A moment later, Van Leeman's breath follows his voice, bringing its own strange weather. Lark finds himself cocooned in centuries of halitosis, a striking potency to the stench that carries with it, like so many turnings, impressions of Van Leeman's festering thirst. A sharp vinegar tang scorches his nostrils, worms its way into his sinuses.

He bites down, hard, against a new ache in his head, like a knot being untied between his eyes. He cries out as it intensifies, some horrible writhing insect that's crawled into his head and laid its eggs. What hatches is a terrible understanding of Van Leeman's ruined and bitter soul.

Lark doubles over and stares with wet eyes into the mural at his feet. He has lived so long in the presence of the inexplicable, but nothing has prepared him for this. His frame of reference has always at least centered on the human. This is like being caught in a toxic spew of unclean wounds and open sores and maggots and horrible eighteenth-century medical practices, released like sickness in an epic sweat and flung heedlessly into the atmosphere of the chamber. The bones of his face feel like they're made of glass. He dribbles saliva into the puddle at his feet. He tries to get hold of himself, clutching Asha's hand, fighting to stay upright in the onslaught of a long-dead man brought forth as something else entirely.

"Spoiled," Betsy says, painting gorgeous whitecapped waves.

Rayanne, clutched hard to Asha's belly, begins to cobble together some kind of prayer.

Asha begins to weep. Lark hears her say Justine's name over and over again.

He manages to look up in time to see Van Leeman sink to his knobby knees. Water rushes over his lower legs. Only the sad gray balls of his heels can be seen.

"Father!" Griffin rushes to Van Leeman's side. Helena stays put, swaying languidly, averting her eyes. With surprising force, Van Leeman thrusts out an arm. A low hiss escapes his mouth. Griffin halts.

Van Leeman bends at the waist and splashes face-first into the mural. He begins to drink, lapping greedily at Betsy's creation. It's a moment of pure rapture. Moans float up through the lingering stench. The muffled cries of the truly ecstatic.

Lark watches in despair as Van Leeman gorges himself on Betsy's masterpiece, the sum of her life's work. The resurrected body stutters and heaves like a cat in the throes of vomiting. With each slurp the air in the chamber grows more polluted. Then Betsy groans and lets her paintbrush sink into the mural as she crumples. Lark goes to his sister. A sharp wave of nausea sends him reeling. He can barely keep his hand pressed against his sister's bent, bony spine. She begins to wail in distress.

With his hand on her back, he can feel her body begin to shrivel as Van Leeman draws strength from her work. Her skin grows taut against her bones.

Without leaving her side, Lark turns his head. The chamber clicks into place a split second behind his vision. He zeroes in on Griffin, who is watching Van Leeman with a mixture of impotence and revulsion.

"Take me!" Lark screams. "Take me instead, you fuck!"

Griffin gives him a passing glance. "You've done your part."

Van Leeman draws his head slowly up out of the mural. Liquid cascades from his mouth, dribbling onto his scrawny chest. His skin has lost its rancid sheen. He is more fleshy than desiccated now. His eyes are penetrating. A cloying sweetness infects the miasma of his horrible breath.

Lark watches as something hidden in thin air yanks Van Leeman straight up to his feet—and then up and out of the water. His legs dangle and kick a foot above the surface, as if he's being hung by some invisible cord.

Helena chokes and sputters. Griffin begins to turn away, pauses, then turns back slowly, as if under great duress. He watches, pale and drawn, as Marius Van Leeman's head leans violently to one side. His neck snaps. He hangs limp and suspended above the turning's whirlpool.

As his body sways at the end of an unseen rope, Marius Van Leeman's wrinkled mouth opens. His teeth are like jagged nubs of dry old wood. His sharp yellow eyes settle on Lark and Betsy.

His cracked lips stretch into a grin.

26

Helena gets herself together first. She seems to sober up as she sloshes over to Griffin. She detours around the hanged man, giving the swaying, grinning figure a wide berth. Again and again Lark traces what should be a rope from Van Leeman's neck up to some crossbeam hidden high above. Yet there is nothing. Lark's mind teeters on the edge. Van Leeman keeps Lark and Betsy in his wolf-eyed sight, looking positively ecstatic as he hangs somewhere beyond life and death, baring his rancid teeth.

Helena comes at her brother with furious, uncorked anger. "I told you this was fucked up, but you wouldn't listen!"

Griffin stands very straight and motionless. The mural laps at his feet. He swallows. "Helena," he says without taking his eyes off the hanged man, "now is not the time."

Helena follows his gaze, takes in Van Leeman, then whips her head back around. "Oh, not in front of *it*, right? We wouldn't want that *thing* to be offended."

"Fuck you," he says quietly.

"What?" Helena puts a cupped hand to her ear.

He takes a step toward her, forcing her back. Her foot slips in the mural and paint sloshes up her leg. "I said *fuck you*, Helena. This is a great way to welcome Father. Real classy."

Helena laughs joylessly. "You poor bastard, you really do think that thing is Father, don't you."

Griffin clenches his fists. "Of course it's Father. Who else could it possibly be? You think by some great coincidence we've brought someone *else* back?"

"Yes!" Helena shouts as if this is obvious. "The God of the Noose!"

"That's *him*, you stupid bitch!"

"*Look at him!*" Helena shrieks. She thrusts a finger out toward the hanged man, dangling gleefully. "Does this look like the man who left us little drawings by our beds while we slept?"

"Of course not! That was two hundred and fifty years ago! What did you expect?"

"Something to make everything we've done worth it. Not a *monster*."

Lark keeps both hands on his sister, propping her up while she mutters weakly to herself. Her arms hang as limp as Van Leeman's malodorous flesh.

Griffin takes Helena by the shoulders and stares into her eyes. "Don't pretend like you didn't enjoy the ride, sister."

"Hey, Asha," Rayanne says softly as Helena wrenches herself out of her brother's grip. "I'm gonna need you to put me down."

Asha kneels and sets Rayanne gently into the mural, like a child launching their toy boat at the edge of the pond.

Griffin lifts his knees with great purpose and splashes toward Van Leeman. "Tell her, Father!" he calls out. "Tell her who you are. Helena requires *affirmation* at this late stage."

"Griffin," Helena says, "be careful."

Griffin shoots her a disgusted look and plows ahead. Lark is conscious of the movements in the room, the groupings of the Belmonts and the Larkins, with the trio of acolytes orbiting the perimeter.

He turns his attention to Rayanne as her cilia flail and churn to keep her afloat in the mural. "What are you doing?"

"Getting you out of here so you can tear that sculpture to pieces and burn it down and salt the earth and make sure they build some stupid bullshit in its place. Like Chipotle." She pauses. "I haven't had Chipotle in a long fucking time."

"Wait," Lark says, but it's too late—she's off. He marvels at

Rayanne as she turns toward the Belmonts with an ungraceful, hectic wriggling.

"When you get out of here," she says, "make it count, okay?" She propels herself across the mural, kicking up spray.

Asha kneels down beside Lark and supports the back of Betsy's lolling head. The skin of Betsy's face cracks open along her cheekbones. Thin lacerations widen as her flesh sucks itself down like shrink wrap. Her eyes, wild and unseeing, search out Lark's.

"Stay with me," Lark says. He tries to pinch her skin shut to keep the wounds from spreading like fissures. Betsy slips deeper into the feverish state that used to drive his father away for days. Her glasses are fogged and speckled with pointillist bits of gray. Out of the corner of his eye Lark watches Rayanne churn a path through the painted falls. One of the acolytes keeps his gun trained on her as she moves along.

"Griffin!" Helena is yelling at her brother now as he reaches the hanged man. "Stop trying to prove a point and *get away from it*."

"Show her, Father, please!" Griffin pleads with Van Leeman. "Helena's always been a visual learner. Show her that it was all worth it."

The hanged man jerks as if some puppeteer high above has pulled on the unseen rope. The stench kicks up again, searing Lark's sinuses, and he begins to cough.

Van Leeman's bent neck abruptly straightens. Without taking his eyes from Betsy and Lark, his previously limp arm flings itself up and out. The elbow cracks as the arm straightens and the fingers close, rigid and clawlike, around Griffin's neck.

Helena screams, "Do something!" The acolytes glance at each other, hesitating.

Van Leeman sighs with pleasure. The vinegar stink floats through the chamber. Griffin slaps uselessly at the pale grublike fingers clamping his windpipe shut. Van Leeman's other arm raises itself with a series of crackles. His hand moves to one side of Griffin's face as if to caress his cheek. Griffin tries to get words out but can only gasp a strangled plea. Even through his hatred and fear, Lark sees in Griffin's eyes the betrayal, the utter incomprehensibility of a father's actions. He does not care in any sympathetic way, but he can tell there was love between them once, and he wonders what that might have been like. The thumb of the caressing hand moves to Griffin's eye. Lark, holding his sister in his arms, can't look away.

Van Leeman keeps his gaze fixed on Lark and Betsy. His grin does not waver.

Lark braces himself for the thumb's intrusion upon the soft bulb of Griffin's wide and disbelieving eye. It doesn't happen that way. The pale-grub thumb, hanging useless a moment ago, traces a line down from Griffin's eye until it rests just below his cheekbone.

Then it begins to push inward. Effortlessly, as if it's molding a block of clay, the thumb enters Griffin's flesh. Like a tent busted inward, the skin collapses easily and the bones beneath it shatter. The thumb drives itself deeper into Griffin's face. Lark watches the first knuckle disappear, then the second. Helena screams and kicks at the mural, splashing paint up Van Leeman's pasty torso. Griffin's agonized shriek escapes his ruined windpipe in a squall of wheezing, an overdriven woodwind squawking out desperate nonsense.

The thumb vanishes inside Griffin's newly concave and lopsided head. His jaw protrudes to one side. Then Van Leeman's other fingers make divots of their own from Griffin's temple to his ear.

"No no no no." Helena scrambles back and falls into the mural. "Help him!" she screams at the acolytes. For the first time, Lark sees two of them acknowledge the proceedings with something like fear. The third keeps his weapon aimed squarely at Rayanne as she proceeds on her gradual course away from Lark, Betsy, and Asha.

At the same time, Van Leeman's hand closes around the pulped flesh and bone that had been the side of Griffin's head. Griffin's body slides from Van Leeman's closed fist to the floor with a soft sploosh. Van Leeman opens his hand and a slurry of blood and bone fragments dribble atop the corpse.

Two of the acolytes wordlessly agree that now's a good time to get the fuck out. They run across the chamber toward the door.

"What are you?" Helena shrieks at Van Leeman. She tries to push herself to her feet and slips and falls again.

Van Leeman's grin subsides. "The life of the world to come."

Despite being hanged, he speaks with the utmost clarity. Then he vanishes. Blinks out of existence completely. The stench subsides, whisked from the chamber along with Van Leeman. Lark gazes beyond the place where the man had hung from nothing a moment ago. He scans the edges of the chamber, an everlasting gloom that thwarts any true sense of space. The waterfall churns, its living, breathing, stage-set flatness reminiscent of the fires in downtown Wofford Falls and in the windows of the abandoned school bus. Paintings intruding upon the real. Everything a desolate Edward Hopper street. Nothing what it seems.

Betsy's head thrashes from side to side.

He lays a hand on her forehead. "Shh. It's okay."

How many times has he said this to her as she endured some fever beyond his comprehension? He remembers heating up soup in the silent kitchen, his father gone without so much as a note.

"What do you want me to do?" the remaining acolyte calls out to Helena. Discipline. Chain of command. Loyal to the end.

Helena sits up in the mural, spattered in paint. Dazed, she looks from Rayanne bobbing in the water to Lark and Asha.

"I don't know," she says wearily. "How about you kill them."

The acolyte swivels his gun so it's pointing straight at Lark.

"We can all walk out of here," Lark tells the man. He puts up a hand to shield Betsy from the shot, as if that will do anything at all.

"Shut up," the acolyte replies.

"Everything's gone to shit," he points out. "Gumley's dead. Griffin's dead. You can just leave."

"You have no reason to kill us," Asha says.

"Who needs a reason?" He walks toward Lark. The gun never wavers.

"Hey, Leif!" Rayanne calls out.

"Quiet," the acolyte says.

"There's nobody keeping us here anymore except these assholes!" Rayanne continues. "Let's go eat Chipotle, you remember Chipotle?"

The acolyte turns back to aim his weapon at Rayanne. "I said shut the fuck up!"

"Shoot them!" Helena cries.

"Chicken burrito bowls!" Rayanne calls out to the chamber at large. "You and me, Leif, chowing down! Chips and guac! Unlimited sodas! Fuck these assholes!"

"Shoot her right now!"

The gunshot shatters Rayanne into pieces. The toothy pod at her core sinks into the water and reverts to what the woman in the red dress holds. Asha screams.

There's a great displacement of air and atmosphere from somewhere behind him.

A defiantly inhuman limb, perhaps once an arm, wraps constrictor-like around the acolyte. It stretches into the shadows at the wavering edges of the chamber. *Leif*, Lark thinks. The man jerks in its grip. His gun falls into the water. The segmented limb squeezes until rifts open up beneath the man's neatly pressed khakis and button-down. His insides, forced out through blooming wounds like toothpaste, stain his clothes darkly. Lark holds his breath as the smell of shit bursts from his extruded bowels. The man's eyes bulge, then his head lolls and his body goes limp.

The shards of Rayanne bob gently in the mural and drift away.

The limb withdraws into the shadows.

Lark cups his hand and dips it into the mural and dribbles the liquid over the wounds on Betsy's face. "I'm going to get you out of here."

Her eyelids flutter. Her mouth forms words.

"What?" Lark leans in.

"She said *Rayanne is free*," Asha says.

Lark smooths her sweaty hair. "How do you know?"

"I can't hear her anymore."

As gently as he can, Lark pulls his sister to her feet. She leans against him. Asha lifts one of Betsy's arms and slings it across her shoulders.

Lark takes the other and they carry her as best they can. Her feet drag in the agitated mural. They move past the whirlpool, through the place where Van Leeman had been a moment ago.

"What about her?" Asha nods at Helena, who gets to her feet and turns around, scanning the shadows for Leif.

Lark catches movement, the massive lurch of some hidden thing.

"Wait!" Helena calls out to them as they head for the door. "I've always been a huge fan of your work! You've got spatial awareness. And a way of seeing. A freshness."

"Shallow," Asha says.

"I can show you how to stop all this!" she cries. "I never wanted it to happen this way! It was all my brother! He's a psychopath! I just wanted our lives to be worth something! Please, take me with you, I can—"

The limb unfurls like a whip and cracks her across the jaw, sending her spinning down into the floor. On her back in the water, she puts up an arm to shield her face. "Leif, wait! Please!" Her words burble out in a froth of blood and saliva.

Lark thinks of Krupp. His best friend would go for the parting shot right here, something to regale the Shade crowd with.

"Hey, Helena!" he calls out as the limb drags her into darkness. There's a keening wail, and then a loud squelch comes across the chamber. It brings to mind the time he and Krupp took a baseball bat to an overripe melon. "Thanks for the whiskey!"

Asha frowns at him. His eyes fill with tears.

Sorry, Krupp. Best I could do.

PART FIVE

THE LAST TURNING

27

Lark steers the truck through the outskirts of Wofford Falls. He's sure it has taken them years to get here, that he's crested the midpoint of his life and is plummeting toward the end. There's nothing on the radio but static.

"Talk," he tells Asha, over and over again, for distraction to chase away the visions of Krupp's last moments. His best friend weaponizing his own ruined face, driving his jawbone down into Gumley. "Please." He clears snot from his nose and wipes it on his shirt.

"About what?" Asha says.

"Anything." He's practically begging. His mind banishes visions of Krupp, only to load a new slide into the player. What used to be a man named Marius Van Leeman, caught in some between-place for centuries. Hanging by his neck and grinning. *The life of the world to come.*

Suddenly the chamber's reek invades the truck, rotten teeth and vinegar and sour rags. Lark's eyelids feel peeled back, his mind pulled taut, threatening to snap.

"Watch out!" Asha says. Lark cranks the wheel to avoid the lamppost he's just nearly drifted into. A flock of dark birds scatters up from a leafless tree. Even with this reality check, the visions refuse to leave him alone.

"Sorry," he says. "I keep seeing Krupp. And everything else."

The depths of the museum, lingering sourly in his mind like hard-liquor fumes in the throes of a bad hangover.

"Pull over," she says. "I'll drive."

"No. I can't just sit and stare right now."

"Can you get us to the sculpture?"

Make it count. He grips the wheel as hard as he can. "I'll get us there."

And now here comes the slow-motion replay of Rayanne exploding into shards.

Make it count make it count make it count make it—

In the middle seat, Betsy stirs. Her eyes are closed, and Lark can feel the heat coming off her body, feral in its animal intensity.

"How's she doing?" Lark takes a left onto Market, which is more or less where it should be. There's the EMT station with its LED sign, red pixelated gibberish.

"The farther we get from that place," Asha says, placing the back of her hand against Betsy's forehead, "the better she gets."

Betsy has ceased her thrashing, at least. "She seems like she's just sleeping now."

Something gnaws at him from the inside. Not bad images but the sick loathing that plagues the guilty.

He turns onto Main Street and beholds the fires. Krupp & Sons Hardware, the old bagel place, Vape HQ, Clementine's Yarn & Tea— the whole block perpetually alight with flames sprung from a painting. Plumes of black smoke are plastered to the sky. Backlit shadows stretch long-limbed across the street.

Betsy opens her eyes. He catches the moment in the rearview. She sucks in a sharp breath like she's just been rocketed up from a nightmare.

"It's okay!" Lark says as she gasps for air. "You're safe." This is such a stupid thing to tell her it makes him want to bash his head into the steering wheel. A flash of Krupp's last moment on earth surges hard, and he fights to keep the truck from jumping onto the sidewalk and plowing into a mailbox.

"She needs water," Asha says, mopping Betsy's damp forehead with a dusty yellow rag from the floor of the truck.

"Okay," Lark says, but he's not stopping now.

Make it count.

"Oh, fuck!" Asha says, pitched with sudden hysteria. Her hand goes to the door handle like she's going to jump out, but at the same time she leans away from the window. "Oh my fucking God no."

Lark sees them a moment later. Sculptures, after a fashion. Neat piles of vivisected citizens on the sidewalks of Main, rising up out of the dirty slush. Torsos of friends and neighbors stacked like firewood. The inexplicable cleanliness of them—bloodless, surgical—making it all so much worse, somehow. And the question they beg, which he can't even articulate because his mind has quit on him, his thoughts made up entirely of misfires and bad connections.

Where are all the limbs?

28

We did this," Betsy says, leaning forward, looking from side to side. Main Street stretches on. They should be well across town by now. Lark is pretty sure he's passed the exact same arrangement of torsos twice. A loop of discarded midsections, flabby and distended, packets of flesh that serve no purpose, connected to nothing but other packets through some infernal methodology.

"Not on purpose," he says. He doesn't recognize his own voice. It hangs thick as syrup in the truck's dead air. Asha is curled up in the front seat, hiding her eyes, trembling. "They forced us."

Didn't they?

"I should have killed myself," Betsy says.

Dread rises inside him. What would any of it—his very life—be for with Betsy dead? He looks over at his sister. The wounds on her cheeks are nothing more than tiny slits, no thicker than paper cuts. Her skin has recovered its vitality. "I'm glad you didn't."

"I mean years ago. After I painted the church."

"No." He winces at a burst of cold pressure behind his eyes. "Listen to me. You did nothing wrong. You couldn't help it."

"After what I did to those people. I should have known, then, that it would never be okay."

"You're worth more than any of them."

"Why?"

Instead of an answer, Lark gets a painful flash of Krupp's last word, biting into his skull. *RUN.*

Growled like an animal from the bloody wreckage of his mouth.

"It felt so good to paint like that," she says, "Completely free. I'm barely conscious while I'm doing it. I'm just floating." She gestures at the scene outside the window. "But nothing's worth this. Our lives aren't worth this."

Lark recalls his exhilaration upon completing *The Insomniack*, the rush of the working and the joining. The deep narcotic satisfaction he feels whenever a piece comes together. Shame burns him from within.

He finally happens upon the road up to the Backbone and hopes it doesn't just deliver them back into town. He knows he can't survive another run through the gauntlet of perfectly flat stumps sheared down flush with shoulders and rib cage and pelvis, a sushi-like semi-glaze to the portions that makes them perpetually glisten.

"Careful!" Betsy grabs the wheel and yanks the truck back from its drift onto the shoulder. Lark rubs his eyes. He takes a breath. He tells himself, *I'm sitting here with my sister, and that's worth something.* Betsy, who once urged him to go live his life. Betsy, whom he never should have left in the first place.

"Hey, Betsy," he says. His frayed mind lands on a broken, dangling thread. "Were you forcing Dad to make all those paintings?"

"No," she says. "I mean, I didn't intend it to be anything like that." She turns her head. Her eyes are red-rimmed. "It was just supposed to be a gift. I thought it might help him."

"Help him how?"

"I thought maybe if he understood where we were coming from... I don't know."

In the front seat, Asha begins to weep. Lark keeps his eyes on the road.

After a while, he realizes she's not crying. She's laughing. A full-body hysteria that rocks her back and forth in the seat as she curls up even tighter and buries her face in her knees. Each lilting peal grates on Lark's nerves, sending shock waves into his skull that advance the slideshow. Flashes of the hanged man's dangling legs, Griffin's collapsed face, Krupp's manic unpredictable energy in his final hours.

"*What*, Asha?" he says.

"I was just thinking—you know you're right, Betsy, you *should* have killed yourself. But then I thought, you're both so goddamn codependent, Lark would have killed himself too, as soon as he found your body. And *then* I thought, if you had both died years ago, none of this would have happened, and everybody would be going about their lives, including me—but you know what? Griffin and Helena would have just kept at it until they found people who could do what you just did. A hundred more years, two hundred, what do they care? And so, since you didn't kill yourselves, it actually gives us the chance to save those future people. Which means, if you do the math, even with those *things* coming out of the waterfall and doing what they did to the town, maybe we still come out ahead on the tally of people whose lives we're potentially saving, versus people you're sort of indirectly responsible for massacring." She stops moving completely, and Lark can sense her exhaustion. "Maybe you're part of the reset for all this, so you're better off alive, even with all the death that stems from you being alive in the first place."

"Yes," Lark says, struggling to keep the truck on the road. "Yes." Every time he blinks the guardrail seems to come at him from a different angle, the half-frozen creek beyond sparkling bright and beckoning. Krupp turned the wreckage of his own body into a weapon. Lark arms himself with Asha's words.

He hits the gas. The road winds ever upward.

29

The white Arabian stamps and snorts. Jamie-Lynn's prized horse stands astride the path to the Backbone, watching them as the truck pulls up. Lark recalls seeing it on the monitor in Griffin and Helena's war room. A pang of great loss jolts the base of his spine. He blinks away the pain, focuses on what's ahead of them.

He stops the truck, kills the engine, and opens the door. "Let's take this thing apart."

The horse doesn't move as they approach, except for a little bob of her head. Acknowledgment? Lark wonders. Either way he is grateful for it. He focuses on the horse to buy him time. He doesn't want to look at the sculpture. He doesn't want to see it. He wants to snap his fingers and unmake it down to the last bit of wax and skip the part that actually requires him to dismantle what he's wrought.

The horse has a presence unlike any animal he's ever known. An intelligence that seems tied, somehow, to the weight of her body. Lark remembers the hooves coming down on the hood of the truck, the steam issuing from her nostrils. Lark finds himself unable to meet her eyes.

Betsy places a hand atop the horse's head and whispers in her ear. Motionless, the animal listens intently.

Lark watches, befuddled. He is sure that his sister has never before interacted with a horse. Yet she has come to this one like an old friend. Lark and Asha move past without a word, while Betsy stays behind, talking to the animal.

Something queasy and off-kilter blooms in his chest. A feeling that takes him back to Betsy's forged Max Ernst, the first time he recognized a turning for what it was.

"Do you feel that?" he asks Asha.

"It's like the antlers," she says.

"Yeah," Lark says, troubled. "Like when you get too close to one of her turnings. But she's not painting anything at the moment."

He throws a glance over his shoulder. Betsy is deep in conversation with the horse. He feels like he's going to be sick. His thoughts are murky and jet-lagged. Just beyond the tree line, the waterfall sounds like it has settled into its existence at last.

Suddenly, the pressure in his head nearly brings him to his knees. He reaches out for Asha. There's a flash of Main Street's carnage. *Click.* The slide show advances and Krupp's face comes back to him. Not how it was at the end, but how it always looked when he was half in the bag at the Shade, psyched for the evening ahead.

This memory is worse, somehow.

Just ahead, the sculpture rises majestic in the sunlight.

30

Lark and Asha stand together in the shadow of the symphony of silent hymns. All the labor and toil, everything he gave for *The Insomniack* and *The Worm & the Dogsbody*, forever rising. The sculpture's brightness is in constant motion. A dance around the perimeter.

Emergents.

Soaking up the sun, refracting light as they work to finish what he started. He spots a tattooed forearm that once belonged to Ian. It has been placed vertically upon three stacked ankles and a thigh. There are dozens of limbs and precise bodily cutouts. Jawbones attached to forearms, slotted into calves. Bloodless elbow joints fitted together like Lincoln Logs. The remains of the town's inhabitants.

Black spots crackle as if he's viewing the sculpture through a burning lens. He tries to cling onto Asha's words of hope, a thin thread to preserve his sanity. It might not be in a way he's ever imagined, but he's going to give his life its worth.

The emergents don't register Lark and Asha's presence. They are single-minded in their rote construction. And what they are building upon the framework of Lark's awful creation is a gallows of flesh.

Lark feels his mind slipping away. It's remarkable how conscious you can be of this. A marvel, really: to be fully aware of the moment when you pass through the shadowlands on the border of insanity. Like coming over a hill on an afternoon stroll to find that the old spruce tree you used to climb as a kid is a charred heap of bones.

Eventually the emergents finish their work and retreat to the edge of the cliff. Their swan dives arc high and there is a moment at the apex of their staggered leaps that they hang in the air with remarkable stillness. They plummet soundlessly into the gorge. The potency of the completed sculpture remains: a sturdy and immobile scaffold. A structure with platform, drop, and crossbeam from which hangs a noose of entrails. The clinical smell in the air, the fresh, almost antiseptic odor of clean vivisections, is joined by this fecund ripeness.

One by one the remaining emergents file away toward the chasm. As the last creature leaves the sculpture, a hanged man is exposed. Wrapped tightly around his neck, corded and pulled tight, is the other end of the tough, stringy entrails.

Big Tom Larkin, a heavy pendulum, swings back and forth. He is naked and glistening with sweat. A black tongue lolls from his mouth. His head tilts unnaturally, his neck broken.

Lark's mind goes dark like a cloud passing over the sun. For a moment there is nothing at all. Then the cloud moves on and he hears someone screaming and realizes it's him. He rushes the sculpture without thinking—there is no more thought—and grabs a forearm and casts it aside with a tormented cry. He pulls a thigh from the scaffold, squishy as an old sausage barely contained by its casing, and flings it out toward the edge of the cliff.

"I'm coming, Dad," Lark hears himself say.

"Wait!" Betsy says from behind him. He turns to look over his shoulder. She has led the horse across the Backbone to the base of the sculpture. The horse regards him with passing interest, that grand intelligence muted and wry. Betsy's hand rests on its flank. "Stay back," she warns.

"We have to tear it down."

"It's too late. Look."

Asha takes his arm and drags him back down to earth. At the same time, seams appear in his father's face. They open into wounds like blooming petals. Raw slices of flesh, as if his body is being sectioned by an unseen wire.

Big Tom splits open to match the human figure rendered in great anatomical detail in the psalter.

Lark loses track of time. He finds himself up on the radiator, pawing at limbs, crying out as he unmakes a wall of flesh. Frantic, animalistic swipes. Asha lunges for him and he fights her off.

With a shred of awareness, Lark notes Betsy's continued fascination with the horse. They appear to be engaged in a serious conversation as he breaks through a tightly woven braid of bent legs. A toenail cuts his palm. Big Tom Larkin is a patchy cloak of desecrated skin, the taut cord of guts still tight around his neck. He begins to tremble and jerk. Lark's mind is twisted and bent as much by Betsy's engagement with the horse as with the awful sight before him. He rips at the sculpture, clawing at flesh, tearing blindly. Big Tom Larkin steps out of himself. Or, rather, his corpse births a living being. With pieces of Big Tom clinging to him, the God of the Noose emerges fully into the light.

31

My son." The God of the Noose greets Lark with great affection. His voice is hearty and resounding. Whatever remained of the foul, broken wraith has been fully reborn into this new vessel, hatched from Big Tom's husk.

The God of the Noose is breathtaking. Chiseled marble given life. A Renaissance specimen sprung from a master's canvas. When he smiles at Lark, his teeth shine with radiance stolen from the sun. He smells very slightly milky, like a newborn, but not at all unpleasant. His eyes are full of love.

Lark falls to his knees. He does not mean to genuflect, but his body fails him in this moment. Blood thunders in his ears. The waterfall roars.

Asha sits down and gazes up with awe.

The God of the Noose sheds bits of Lark's father as he walks, haltingly at first, toward Betsy and the horse. Gobbets of Big Tom Larkin's stretched and broken corpse litter the Backbone. His steps find their rhythm. He picks an errant flap of skin from the nape of his neck, pops it into his mouth, and swallows.

"My daughter," he says, giving Betsy a respectful nod. He lays a powerful hand on the horse's crest. She lowers her head in submission. The God of the Noose climbs onto the horse's back. He smiles down at Betsy and extends his hand. "Join me." She reaches out and he helps her up. She sits behind him and wraps her arms around his waist. He tilts his head back and takes in great draughts of mountain air. Then his piercing gaze turns to the gallows of flesh.

"We will need more of these, children. An apparatus for every township, fed by its population. There is much work to be done."

Lark flashes forward to a countryside littered with infernal contraptions, piles of discarded torsos, artfully balanced limbs. It is such a vast and incomprehensible terror that his mind balks at understanding. He is witless and blank at the prospect.

The God of the Noose turns to Asha. "You have nothing to fear," he says. "You are part of my ministry now." He selects another scrap of flesh from his kneecap and holds it aloft in a cupped hand. Then he offers it to Asha. "Take this, and eat."

Betsy meets Lark's eyes. There is a sudden intrusion in his weary, blank resignation—the sickening wave that marks his proximity to one of his sister's turnings. She gives him that crooked smile that speaks of sleepless nights spent at her easel, of birthday pranks and all the inside jokes they've shared over their long years together. There's a twist to her face, a smear like a careless brushstroke that blends her features into the backdrop of rock and pine. A sudden wrongness in the composition of the world.

"No," Lark says.

The God of the Noose frowns. He seems to sense something amiss. Betsy's heels dig into the horse's flanks. The God of the Noose clutches his shoulder as the growing smear pulls his muscles out of joint.

"Wait!" Lark leaps to his feet and reaches out, but it's too late.

The horse breaks into a gallop and leaps off the edge of the Backbone into empty space. They hang there for a moment: the horse, Betsy Larkin, and the God of the Noose, pasted to a flat sky.

Then they fall.

Lark's mind, ripped from its moorings, pulls him to the edge of the cliff. He peers down into the chasm. A river fed by the frothing waterfall snakes through the ancient gorge. The horse is a white blot tossed by rapids. There's a wrongness to her motion now that has nothing to do with the deadly plunge. The same unfettered spiral of creative energy that birthed every one of Betsy's turnings animates the horse as she's washed away. Lark forces himself to watch. In the horse's wake come two figures, intertwined, smeared with indelicate, patchy colors, writhing in and out of view as if diving and surfacing in impossibly quick rotation. Like this, Betsy's last great turning is washed away, out of sight, as the canyon curls.

Lark screams and his ragged cry echoes back to him across the expanse. Asha pulls him in, and they hold each other. When he stops screaming his jaw clenches and he bites down hard and buries his head in the soft curve where Asha's shoulder meets her neck. One of his elbows hooks around her other shoulder. He lets his body hang from her and she holds him up like she always does. A desperate craving for solace comes and goes, and hot on its heels a lust for a second god to rise and grant him salvation. Eventually the sun goes down and the waterfall dries up. Lark and Asha don't look back.

ACKNOWLEDGMENTS

I'm grateful to the wonderful team at Orbit/Redhook: Angela Man, Lauren Panepinto, Lisa Maria Pompilio, Rachel Goldstein, Xian Lee, Bryn A. McDonald, Laura Jorstad, Roland Ottewell, Janine Barlow, and everyone else who designed, marketed, brainstormed, routed, emailed, scheduled, copyedited, proofed, and met to discuss aspects of this book's publication. Special thanks to my editor, Bradley Englert, for his astute suggestions, insights, and knack for drawing out the humanity in the strangest of fictional circumstances.

Another big thank you to my brilliant and hilarious agent, Cameron McClure, for her guidance both on and off the page.

Profound thanks to Anne Heltzel for her love and partnership in all things, including her detailed close reading of this book when it was just a few mewling baby chapters and again when it had grown significantly.

In addition to the artists mentioned in this book, I want to pay tribute to a few others who inspired elements of the story: Leonora Carrington, Zdzisław Beksiński, Remedios Varo, George Bellows, and Chris Baily.

Finally, thanks to Marius Van Leeman for leaving behind such detailed instructions for this novel's completion. See you soon.

MEET THE AUTHOR

Stan Horaczek

ANDY MARINO is the author of *The Seven Visitations of Sydney Burgess*. He was born in upstate New York, spent half his life in New York City, and now lives with his partner in the Hudson Valley.

if you enjoyed
IT RIDES A PALE HORSE
look out for

THE SEVEN VISITATIONS OF SYDNEY BURGESS

by

Andy Marino

Possession is an addiction.

Sydney's spent years burying her past and building a better life for herself and her young son. A respectable marketing job, a house with sustainable furniture, and a boyfriend who loves her son and accepts her, flaws and all.

But when she opens her front door and a masked intruder knocks her unconscious, everything begins to unravel.

She wakes in the hospital and tells a harrowing story of escape. Of dashing out a broken window. Of running into her neighbors' yard and calling the police.

The cops tell her a different story. Because the intruder is now lying dead in her guest room—murdered in a way that looks intimately personal.

Sydney can't remember killing the man. No one believes her.

Back home, as horrific memories surface, an unnatural darkness begins whispering in her ear. Urging her back to old addictions and destructive habits.

As Sydney searches for truth amid the wreckage of a past that won't stay buried for long, the unquiet darkness begins to grow. To change into something unimaginable.

To reveal terrible cravings of its own.

1

The man in my house is wearing a mask. Even so, I can tell he's as surprised to see me as I am to see him. It's in the way his shoulders jump and erase his neck when I open the door with a triumphant shove, driven by the promise of a rare night alone. With my boyfriend and son camping upstate, I'll be picking the movie I want to watch, ordering Thai food with the spice level cranked, starfishing out in the middle of the bed, dozing off with the windows open to let in the breeze off the Hudson—

"What are you doing?" I blurt out as if I know him. As if I've caught the neighbor kid prowling around the side yard again. He's wearing gloves and a black tracksuit. The drawers of the front hall credenza are pulled out. He steps toward me.

It happened so fast, say people who have lived through sudden bursts of violence—but for me, time's a slow drip and I can see everything at once. Black sneakers on our reclaimed tiles, old appliance manuals in the junk drawer, the RSVP to the wedding of my boyfriend's cousin, a small lace-trimmed envelope waiting to be mailed. The man's eyes are framed by the slit in his balaclava, a word I know from the tattered paperbacks I tore through in the rehab center's shabby library.

I take one step back, jam my hand into my shoulder bag, and rummage wildly for the pepper spray. But I've never used it before, and it's buried under travel Kleenex packs and lip balm and generic ibuprofen and noise-canceling headphones and laptop and charger and Moleskine notebook and tampons.

His hand closes around the Jesus candle my boyfriend bought from the bodega by the train station. Señor de los Milagros de Buga, $3.99 plus tax. It's the size of a relay runner's baton, glass as thick as a casserole dish and filled to the brim with solid wax.

My fingers brush the pepper spray canister. There's a little rim of plastic that acts as a safety—I just have to flick it to the side. *Too slow, Sydney.* The candle comes at me in a fluid sideways arc.

Half ducking, half flinching, I twist away. His sidearm swing smashes the candle into my left ear. There's an unbelievable volcanic *thud* inside my head, a searing, blinding flash, and time's not a slow drip anymore, it's a film reel with missing frames.

I am holding myself up, clinging to the door.

I will stay on my feet.

There's an electric current buzzing through my teeth. The front hall is full of bad angles, a nonsense corridor in a dream. The coats are swaying on their hooks. I raise the pepper spray, but my arm can only aim it in the direction of the baseboard, the off-white trim that doesn't quite touch the tile, a haven for crumbs and lost earrings. In the gilt-framed mirror next to the closet door, I see a gloved hand holding the candle up in the air. The man is very tall, and the tip of the candle hits the ceiling before it comes down.

The walls are tinted red and the whole house roars like the ocean. There's a hot-penny tang I can taste in the back of my throat, a cocaine drip that fills my mouth and overflows. Tissue packs and hair clips are scattered across the tiles, coming up fast.

I shouldn't be here. These words can't really form because the darkness is thick enough to stifle thought. It's more like a sharp sense of injustice wrapped in the fear that throbs somewhere in the void. An impression that I have been cheated by circumstance.

I shouldn't be here.

2

You're a lucky woman," says Dutchess County Sheriff Mike Butler.

I ride a wave of displacement. Lucky? I don't feel lucky. I feel like I want to unzip my skin and wriggle out of my body and into another. By what metric is he measuring my luck? I suppose he means that I'm luckier than a woman whose attack has resulted in her murder. I want to tell him: *lucky* is what you are when you win the lottery.

I calculate how much time has elapsed since the attack. Ten, eleven hours at most. Now I understand all those survivors' stories on *Dateline* and *20/20*. It happened so fast. It's amazing what can be compressed into mere seconds of a human life.

Butler takes off his hat and rocks on his heels. I know his face and name from a campaign billboard near my town's highway off-ramp. On the billboard, his face is somehow both jowly and chiseled, as if the features of a hardass drill sergeant were superimposed onto a mall Santa. In person, Butler's the kind of guy whose middle-aged weight gain makes him look even more powerfully built, his barrel chest and gut filling out his uniform without seeming flabby.

Behind his shaved head is the classic hospital corner-mounted television. Wan light comes through vertical slats in the blinds and paints staccato lines on the wall. *Saturday morning*, I think—words that conjure up Pilates for me, a long run for my boyfriend, Matt, and an extended gaming session for my son, Danny. And then, like a ravenous, plundering army, we take our reward: brunch. When my boys and I brunch, we brunch hard. Pulpy juice straight from the gleaming contraption, huevos rancheros, black beans, avocado, crispy bacon, home fries, strawberries from the little roadside stand...

Butler clears his throat. "Okay," he says. Then he puts his hat back on and studies the cup of water on the bedside table like it holds the key to cracking this case wide open. I think, perhaps unfairly, that he has no idea how to talk to a woman wrapped in bandages lying in a hospital bed. I am his mother, his sister, his wife. My victimhood disturbs him. It's not what he signed up for.

He takes a step closer to my bed. "You took quite a shot," he says. From this angle, I can see the landscape of razor burn under his chin. "Lucky lady."

It's almost funny, in an existential nightmare kind of way: trapped in a hospital bed while a man reminds me how lucky I am, over and over again.

He glances at my freshly bandaged wrists, and his eyes travel across my older scars, exposed by my short-sleeved hospital gown. Then he looks me in the face. "I was just at your house. That's quite a thing you did."

For the first time, it dawns on me that my house is a crime scene. It's probably crawling with cops and forensic techs. I think CSI is called something different in real life, but I picture a team in HAZMAT suits, spraying luminol. In reality it's probably two local cops in rubber gloves poking around our dressers and desks, combing through the front hall, the guest room. Suddenly I'm laser focused. I can feel a manic surge begin in my toes and course through my body. The jagged mosaic of sights and sounds from last night comes together in the man's cold eyes framed in a tight oval of black fabric.

I manage to hold on to it for a second, but then the mosaic goes out of focus. Cobbled-together images of things I didn't actually see run through my mind. A man in a tracksuit and balaclava walking down the sidewalk in broad daylight. His arms are long, too long, and his shadow pours like oil down the street, up my driveway, through my front door...

"I can come back later," Butler says. He sounds far away. I realize

that my eyes are half-lidded. It's not just my thoughts that are drifting. I refused the Vicodin regimen the doctor wanted to put me on,
three hundred milligrams every four hours for the pain. Opioids were
never my thing—I was a fiend for the rush, not the nod—but I've seen
addicts with decades of sober living fall off because of back pain, griz-
zled old alkies who figure what's the harm in a few pain pills if they're
prescribed by a doctor? Or at least, they pretend to think like that. I'd
wager most of them know exactly what the harm is, they're just falling
back on the oldest addict trick in the book: self-delusion.

And so, all I'm on is ibuprofen. Four gelcaps. It's barely enough for a
stress headache. I might as well be taking vitamins.

"The doctor wasn't too keen on me talking to you now," Butler says.
"But I'd really like to take your statement sooner rather than later, if
you're up for it."

"It's okay," I say, gathering my strength. "I'm good. I want to help."

"Anything you can remember, then."

"I wasn't supposed to be there," I say. "Home, I mean. I was supposed to be camping with my boyfriend and my son, up at Cedar Valley. Taking a long weekend. But I got called in for a last-minute pitch
at the agency I work for. In the city. Matt and Danny"—my heart
quickens as I try, and fail, to sit up—"the park's a total dead zone,
there's no way to call them, they won't know—"

Butler holds up a hand. "We've got state police out of Poidras Falls
tracking your family down."

Your family. There's a deep, sweet hurt behind those words.

"Tell me about the man in your house."

"He was tall," I say, flashing to the candle hitting the ceiling before
it came down and the house roared and the walls turned red. "Taller
than Matt, and he's six-one." I pause. "Taller than Trevor, too."

"Who's Trevor?"

"My ex. Danny's father."

"Okay," Butler says, flipping open his notebook and jotting something down. He's not using one of those standard-issue cop notepads,
but a green Moleskine.

"I have one of those," I say.

"My daughter works in a coffee shop in Poughkeepsie," he says. "They sell these things by the register." He shakes his head. "Kid drops out of SVA, down in the city, after her freshman year, says school is sucking the life out of her painting. So now, you know what she does? Brings home a bag of the day's used-up coffee grounds, smears them on canvases. Not my thing, art-wise, but she's saving me forty grand a year, so I can't complain."

I don't know what to say to that. In the moment of silence, I can feel myself drifting again. "Gray eyes," I say.

"Gray?"

"They were cold. Like the winter sky."

"Winter sky," he says.

I suddenly recall hurried questions from a different cop in the more immediate aftermath. A woman. Severe ponytail, wine-dark lipstick. My neighbor, the pediatrician, who found me on his lawn, hovering awkwardly in the background, holding a mug in two cupped hands. I am disturbed by how the memory comes on: from nothing to something, a bucket of paint splattering a blank wall.

"I remember," I say, "I told all this to somebody at my neighbors' house."

"You were in shock," Butler says. "This isn't going to be like it is on TV, where you give your statement and you're on your way. It'll be a process. You'll remember new things days, weeks from now. But this is a good time for us to talk. Most people..." He trails off with a frown and lowers the notebook. "Most people would be doped to the gills after what you just went through, but the doctor said you refused the heavy-duty painkillers."

I hesitate. I don't hide the fact that I'm an addict in recovery from anyone, but I don't ordinarily talk to county sheriffs. It feels like I'm planting an asterisk in our conversation, something for Butler to come back to later, casting a pall over everything I tell him.

"I've got nine years clean," I say. I know that this is admirable, that I have nothing to be ashamed of. But talking to cops twists my thoughts.

It's like putting my bags through the scanner in airport security. Of course I know there's nothing in there, and yet still, after all these years, anxiety engulfs me and my heart pounds and I think, *what if*—what if they find something?

"Good for you," Butler says. He sounds different now—guarded, maybe. I wonder about his daughter, behind the counter of that coffee shop. Is she an Oxy fiend? Is Butler's father an alcoholic, dying of cirrhosis? Addicts orbit everyone's life, and a person's reaction to addiction in general—whether they believe it's truly a disease or just an excuse to stay high all the time—tends to be reflected through the lens of their own experience.

Is Butler himself a clandestine pill-popper, a raider of confiscated evidence?

His eyes flit once again to my scars. I don't volunteer any information about them.

"So, I'm sticking with ibuprofen," I say, trying to end this conversational tack. But I can see something in his hooded eyes, and a knot forms in my stomach. I know what Butler is thinking. He might not even know it yet, but the kernel of an idea is forming.

Nobody's as clean as they say they are. We're dealing with a drug thing. Some dealer who didn't get paid, some old city debt getting settled up the river, darkening our quiet suburban doorsteps.

I keep my mouth shut. I don't want to protest too much, before he's even brought it up. But the way my mind is working now—telling me I have to manipulate, steer the conversation—makes me feel like I'm a suspect being grilled in a stuffy, windowless interview room.

There's a sharp pain in my head, a cold needle piercing the dull, pounding ache. The edges of the room are fuzzy, lenses smeared with grease.

Butler glances over his shoulder at the door. When he looks back at me, his gaze is unclouded. "The doctor also said you refused a rape kit." His tone is as matter-of-fact as ever.

"I wasn't raped."

"No sexual assault."

"No. I told you guys what happened."

"You told Deputy Carlson, back there at your neighbors' house."

"Right. I remember. Sort of."

He consults his Moleskine. "Approximately seven forty-five p.m., you open your front door and interrupt a robbery in progress. The perp bashes you in the head with a"—he flicks his glance to me—"Jesus candle. The next thing you know…"